I LOVE THIS BAR

CAROLYN BROWN

sourcebooks
casablanca

Published by Sourcebooks Casablanca, an imprint of Sourcebooks, Inc.
P.O. Box 4410, Naperville, Illinois 60567-4410
(630) 961-3900
FAX: (630) 961-2168
www.sourcebooks.com

Printed and bound in the United States of America
RRD 10 9 8 7 6

To my fabulous editor,
Deb Werksman

Chapter 1

ALL THE AIR ESCAPED DAISY'S LUNGS IN A WHOOSH WHEN THE cowboy collapsed on top of her body. She sucked in air and pushed at the weight, but her arms were pinned. She opened her eyes to see a head full of dark hair and felt the sharp bone of his nose pressing into her left breast.

He raised his head and looked over at her, his face only inches from hers, his eyes zeroing in on her lips.

Hot damn! That's one sexy face, they both thought at the same time.

She shut her eyes and started to lean in for the kiss, then reality hit. She had fallen flat on her back on the floor of the Honky Tonk beer joint and taken the nearest cowboy down with her. She popped her eyes wide open and wriggled back away from the sexiest gray eyes she'd ever seen.

Oh, shit, who saw us? Daisy looked up to find everyone staring down at them, the cowboy's body still touching her from breast to toe, even though he had rolled to one side. The blush that filled her cheeks had nothing to do with afterglow.

The joint was as quiet as a tomb. It was a hell of a time for the jukebox to go silent.

"You all right?" Tinker, the bouncer, asked. He was hovering over the two of them, worry etched in his face as he bent to touch her shoulder.

"I'm fine. Make sure he is too," she panted.

Tinker held out a hand and in one swift movement the cowboy was on his feet.

Tinker picked up Daisy carefully and set her on a barstool. "You sure you're all right?"

"My dignity is in tatters and I might have a bruise or two, but I'll live," she said.

"I'd better get back to the door. Motion if you need me," Tinker said.

She nodded and raised her voice to the customers, who were still watching the whole scenario as if it were an X-rated movie. "I'm fine, everyone. I promise. Get on back to having a good time."

Someone plugged coins into the jukebox and George Strait's song "River of Love" filled the place. Several people started a line dance and by the time the song ended everything was back to normal.

All except Daisy's heart. It still raced.

She looked at the cowboy. He was just as sexy sitting on the barstool as he'd been lying on top of her. "Sorry about that. I hope you don't have anything broken."

The cowboy barely nodded. "Just a little stunned. Stupid things like that happen so fast it's like it happened to someone else. Might have a bruise—but you broke *my* fall."

Daisy forced a smile.

"Guess we stepped in that beer at the same time. Where's the bartender? We both ought to sue the hell out of him." Jarod was amazed that he could utter a single word the way his pulse was racing. That was one dazzling lady he'd taken a fall with. One minute he'd been walking toward the bar; the next he was grabbing for anything to break the fall. Then as if in slow motion he'd seen the girl slip in the same slick puddle of spilled beer and grab for him.

Daisy knew every rancher, cattle rustler, and hot-blooded male and female in five counties, but she'd never seen that damn fine looking cowboy before. Snug fitting jeans covered one sexy tight butt hitched up on the stool. Bulging biceps underneath his snowy white T-shirt stretched the knit. His black hair and high cheekbones said that he had some Native American blood somewhere, but his eyes were the color of heavy fog. He could have played the resident bad boy in an old movie: maybe James Dean in *Rebel Without a Cause*. She remembered watching the movie with her grandmother back before Granny died. From that day forward, Daisy O'Dell had been attracted to bad boys, and that had been her downfall.

For the first time she seriously considered breaking the rules and taking a man through the door into her apartment at the back of the Honky Tonk. She shook her head to remove the crazy notion. The man could be a serial killer or a drug pusher. Hell, he could be worse than either of those two things—he could be married.

She blushed scarlet. She'd been ogling the stranger rudely.

His straw hat had somehow found its way to the bar in front of him and she wished she could pick it up to fan her scorching face. Not that it would have helped a whole hell of a lot. The way her hormones were overreacting, she could have melted ice on the North Pole in December.

Why did that dark-haired, broad-chested cowboy give her hot flashes? Maybe it was because when she felt him collapse on her for a microsecond she'd felt as if they'd just finished a hot bout of sex. She reached up and rubbed the back of her head to see if there were bumps or indentations. Something had to have knocked every bit of sense out of her brain. She couldn't find a bump or a sore spot, so maybe he'd rattled her hormones instead of her brain cells.

"Is this a help-yourself bar or is there a bartender somewhere out there?" He motioned toward the dance floor. He thought about asking her for a dance, maybe as an apology for knocking her down. Anything to touch her again and see if the jolt that shot through him was something other than a free fall to the dance floor.

She hopped off the barstool. "Guess that would be me. I was on my way back to the bar when we collided." Her heart kept up a steady beat in her ears like the drums in Garth Brooks's band.

Jarod drew his heavy dark brows down in disbelief. Surely she was teasing. That exquisite woman couldn't be the bartender. She looked as though she might be the newest up-and-coming country singer taking a break from the stage. He glanced around the room and saw only two jukeboxes—no stage in sight.

As she made her way behind the bar located the whole length of the back wall of the Honky Tonk, she shook her head hard enough to send her dark brown ponytail swinging. It didn't work. She was still picturing him naked except for scuffed up cowboy boots and maybe the hat.

Good grief, she had to get control of her thoughts. She had a bar to run and he was most likely one of those rare strangers who was just passing by and stopped for a cold beer on a scalding hot night.

The jukebox rattled the walls with Toby Keith's booming voice singing "I Love This Bar." It was Daisy's theme song. She had loved the Honky Tonk since the day she'd walked into the joint. Twenty-one years old, broken-down car in the parking lot of the Smokestack restaurant, not even a mile from the Honky Tonk and barely enough gas money to get back to Mena, Arkansas, she'd been looking for a phone and some help. What she found was Ruby Lee, a salty old girl full of spit and vinegar who'd given her a job and a place to live and taken her under her wing. Since then not a single one of the drinkers, smokers, lookers, or even hustlers had taken her eye until that cowboy collided with her and drove her mind straight into the gutter.

He's married and has six kids and a chain smoking mother who lives with him in a double-wide trailer.

Chigger, the Honky Tonk's equivalent of a hooker, caught her eye and winked. Daisy picked up her step and barely beat Chigger to the tall cowboy.

"What'll it be?" Daisy asked.

Chigger leaned forward on the bar, shoving four inches of cleavage and a big smile so close to his face that his eyes crossed. "Name it, darlin', and I'll provide it."

"Coors," he said. He didn't want the hooker to provide anything. Now, if that bartender offered? Well, his heart skipped a beat just thinking about what he'd name in that case.

"Tap or bottle?" Daisy asked.

"Tap is fine. Is it good and cold?"

Daisy nodded. His voice was so deep it gave her shivers. As if that wasn't enough, he had a dimple in his chin that begged her to lean forward and brush a kiss across. She felt like shutting the place down for a week and spending every moment of it in bed with him. Maybe she'd been standing too damn close to Chigger and her loose-legged morality had rubbed off on her. The woman's heels were so round that all a fellow had to do was push her and she fell backwards, dragging him down on top of her as she fell. Daisy wondered if "slut" was contagious.

He raised his voice and said, "Hey, none of that light stuff either. Real beer with all the calories and taste."

Chigger inched a little closer and laid her hand on his knee. "Now, what else would you be needin' this night? I betcha I can provide it and, honey, it won't be none of that light stuff. I've got a full menu with whatever you want."

"Reckon beer is all I'll need for right now," he said. A hooker coming on to him and a barmaid throwing his heart into double-time. What in the hell was going on?

Most of the time Daisy didn't mind Chigger hustling a good time, but that night it annoyed her like a pesky fly buzzing around her ears. Chigger was one of those women who had no morals. If she saw something wearing jeans and boots and wanted it, she set about getting it. These days she went home with Jim Bob Walker on Friday and Saturday nights, but Daisy remembered times when it was a different cowboy every weekend. And the way she was flirting with the new cowboy, Jim Bob might be sleeping alone that night.

Chiggers in the real sense are little red bugs that burrow down into the skin and itch terribly. Chigger got her nickname because she said she was just like one of those little bugs. She could make a man itch so bad he had to let her scratch the itch for him. Most men fell all over themselves when Chigger took notice of them. Evidently the newcomer had put on bug repellent because she wasn't having much effect on him.

Daisy filled a Mason jar, the standard beer glass at the Honky Tonk, from the tap and carried it to the cowboy. "That one's on the house if you don't sue me. I'm the bartender that should have seen that puddle of beer."

"Deal," he said curtly. What he'd like to make a deal for didn't have a damn thing to do with a puddle of beer and a lot to do with finding himself back on top of the bartender. And without an audience. He touched his head—must've hit it harder than he realized to be entertaining such crazy notions.

Jarod McElroy hadn't come into the bar for conversation and he'd have run a country mile if he'd known his first walk across the dance floor was going to net him a fall on top of the bartender. God knew he listened to plenty of talk from his eighty-six-year-old uncle, Emmett McElroy, who provided enough words in a day to make Jarod's ears hurt. And most of his words would fry the hair off a billy goat's ass.

The family had known that Uncle Emmett was failing the past year, but a couple of months ago Jarod's mother had made a trip from Oklahoma to Texas to see him. When she found out that he'd been diagnosed with Alzheimer's in addition to a multitude of other ailments, she'd come home with the suggestion that Jarod move down there and help him run his ranch. He'd been more than willing, since he remembered Uncle Emmett and Aunt Mavis fondly and figured living on the ranch would be just as great as when he was a kid.

He'd been wrong.

Uncle Emmett had gone plumb crazy since his wife died the year before and refused to listen to a word or idea that Jarod had to say. After that day, Jarod was seriously considering throwing in the towel and going home to Oklahoma. Right now he was almost glad he didn't.

He looked down the length of the shiny bar at the bartender who'd taken his order. When he'd raised his head up and seen exactly who'd broken his fall, he'd had the urge to kiss her. Looking at her, he wished he had. He could have blamed it on the moment. Now he'd never know what those full lips tasted like.

"She's a barmaid." Aunt Mavis' voice perched on his shoulder and whispered in his ear. *"Remember your second fiancée?"*

Jarod's jaw muscles worked like he was chewing peanuts.

"Man don't get a good woman in a bar, Jarod. You done proved that," she taunted in that gravelly voice of a fifty-year smoker.

"I hear you," he mumbled aloud.

Sure, the barmaid at the Honky Tonk was a looker and there was something about those long legs and that tiny waist that made his mouth go dry, but a vow was a vow and Aunt Mavis would claw her way up from the grave and haunt him if he looked at a barmaid twice. Well, maybe he'd better make that three times because he'd already had a very long second look at her.

Daisy felt his stare. A sideways glance told her that he liked what he saw. The set of his jaw said he wouldn't act on it. Owning a bar or tending a bar didn't make her a slut or an immoral person, and it was her damn business. Not his. She wouldn't let him buy her a dime paper cup of lemonade from a school kid's stand if he asked. Not after that condescending, sidling look he'd shot her way.

Billy Bob Walker slapped the cowboy on the shoulder. "Hey, Jarod, where's Emmett? Just heard this week that you were over there helping him. You should have called us. Why didn't Emmett come with you tonight?"

Daisy moved a few steps closer. With lots of effort she tuned out the noise of the jukebox and forty people talking at once and zeroed in their conversation.

Jarod took a long pull from the Mason jar and said, "I don't think a stick of dynamite could blow his sorry ass off that ranch. Won't do a thing with it, but he's not about to let me do what needs to be done. And he sure won't leave it for five minutes for fear I'll move the damn salt shakers. I've been here six weeks and I'm thinkin' about committing myself to the nearest asylum."

"Since Mavis died he's got worse. I reckon it's that Alzheimer's stuff settin' in," Billy Bob said.

"That's what the doctor says and there's no getting any better. Some days he's barely tolerable. Today is not one of them. He got a burr up his butt this mornin' and the day went from bad to worse. I had to get away or else I was going to give myself a concussion banging my head against the barn door," Jarod said.

"I hear you, man. Got a grampa just like that over at Morgan Mill. Him and Emmett were sawed out of the same old bull hide leather and they ain't neither one ever goin' to change. They used to have coffee over there at the café a couple of times a week and bitch about the young people and their high-powered ideas."

"God save us from anything new. Where's your brothers?" Jarod asked.

Years before, when Aunt Mavis was still living, he'd spent a couple of weeks each summer on the ranch. She'd always invited the Walker triplets over for him to have kids his own age around in those days. Jarod was convinced that if you looked up *redneck* in the dictionary you'd find the Walker triplets' picture. They were identical with their red hair, freckled faces, and green eyes. He'd loved it when they came to the Double M, but he hadn't had time to give them a call since he'd been back in the area. His uncle had demanded every waking moment and lots that should have been sleeping ones as well.

Billy Bob pointed across the room. "That'd be Jim Bob hugged up to Chigger. He's in love with that woman. One of these days he's goin' to talk her into marryin' him and he'll be one happy fool."

"I took her for a hooker," Jarod said.

"Naw, man. A hooker charges. Chigger ain't never charged a dime. She just likes a good roll in the hay and so does Jim Bob. They'll make a good pair if either one of them ever gets their wild oats sowed and settled down."

"And Joe Bob?" Jarod asked.

"He's shootin' a little pool. Lost twenty dollars last night, but he's already won it back in the couple of hours we been here. Merle stayed home tonight."

Jarod raised a heavy black eyebrow. "Who?"

"Merle Avery. She was one of Ruby's friends, that'd be the woman who built the Honky Tonk and ran it 'til last year when she got killed in a motorcycle wreck. She was seventy and still ridin' a Harley. Anyway, Merle still comes around a couple of times a week to take all Joe Bob's money. She might be past seventy, but she's pure magic with that cue stick. Joe Bob would probably marry her just to learn her tricks," Billy Bob laughed.

Jarod's nostrils twitched at the idea. "She's almost old enough to be his grandmother."

"Ah, age is just numbers on paper. How old you think Daisy is?" Billy Bob asked.

Jarod raised an eyebrow. "Who?"

"Daisy, the barmaid who owns the Honky Tonk. Ruby, the woman who built the place, left it to her when she died last year," Billy Bob said.

So her name was Daisy. That sounded just like a redneck barmaid's name. Jarod took another long look down the bar at her. He had never been so attracted to a woman in the first few minutes of meeting her. The word thunderstruck came to mind, but he didn't believe in such folderol.

Daisy tried so hard to hear the answer that her head pounded. She blamed it on the fall and could have strangled Joe Bob for choosing that minute to yell at her to draw up a beer.

Jarod didn't even try to mask the calculating stare. Aunt Mavis would just have to understand, and after all, it was just looking. The woman had the body of a kickboxer, no spare fat cells anywhere, and could be anywhere from sixteen to twenty-nine. When her gaze met his, sparks lit up the room between them. Her steely-blue eyes dared him to answer the question. The physical attraction was so strong that his first knee-jerk reaction was to flirt; his second was to run. His third was to trip her, catch her when she fell, and kiss her just to see if those lips were as soft as they looked.

No way had she seen thirty yet; there wasn't even a tiny little crow's foot wrinkle around those beautiful eyes. Her dark hair was pulled back into a ponytail that swished when she moved from one end of the bar to the other wiping up spills and filling orders. She wore a white tank top with sparkling jewels sewn into the front along the neckline and tight jeans hugging her hind end. Her eyes looked like they could cut a man apart like a laser gun, but those lips were definitely made for kissing. Nice full lips that could have been on a commercial for lipstick.

"So?" Billy Bob asked.

It took a minute before Jarod could remember the question. His hands were clammy and his voice husky when he asked, "Why are you askin'?"

"Because Jim Bob is happy as a piglet in a fresh mud hole when he can talk Chigger into going home with him on Friday and Saturday nights. Joe Bob would be Merle's slave if she'd teach him all she knows about shootin' pool. Daisy O'Dell is my dream gal. I'd probably rob banks or kill for her," Billy Bob said.

"What's that got to do with how old she is?" Jarod asked.

"I was just bringin' the conversation around to her, man, so I could tell you how I feel about her. She's a looker and she owns a bar. Now that's a combination that could make a man's heart just plumb ache. Just don't go gettin' no ideas that you might waltz in here and do some serious flirtin'. When the time comes for her to get all serious, it's goin' to be with Billy Bob Walker."

"So you didn't care a whit about my Uncle Emmett. You came over here to piss on the bar and stake a claim?" Jarod asked.

Billy Bob chuckled. "Guess I did."

Daisy pretended to come in at the tail end of the conversation. "You got to piss, you do it in the bathroom."

"Ah, honey, you know I love you," Billy Bob said.

"You'd marry Lucifer's sister to get a bar of your own, Billy Bob Walker. Love ain't got a blessed thing to do with anything. Hell's bells, the money you and your brothers spend in here could buy a bar of your own in a year's time. Go on up the road to the Trio or The Boar's Nest and buy one of them if you want a bar," she smarted off. "You need a refill on that beer?" she asked Jarod.

"No, I reckon one is enough if I'm going to drive back home," he said. He wished she'd argue with Billy Bob some more. Her voice was like maple syrup with a touch of Wild Turkey—fiery and sweet. He wondered if she'd be like that in bed. Good God, he had to get control of his thoughts and stop letting them romp all over the bar.

"Which is where?" Daisy asked.

"North of Huckabay, west of Morgan Mill. Right next to the Walker ranch," Jarod said. *Want to go with me?* He touched his forehead. Did he have a slight concussion that caused all of his thoughts to wallow in a gutter?

Billy Bob waved a hand between their gazes. "I'd build a bar but Chigger and Merle are regulars at the Honky Tonk. You promise me and the boys that they'll change over to the Walker Roadhouse and I'll build one across the road and buy out the Trio and The Boar's Nest to eliminate the competition."

Daisy cocked her head to one side. "Walker Roadhouse?"

"Yeah, that's kind of what I had a mind to change the name to once I talk you into marryin' me," he teased.

"Better not hold your breath on either issue. You look like hell in that shade of blue. I'm runnin' this bar until they carry my cold dead body through the doors and I'll have my fingers wrapped around a longneck bottle of Coors when they do. And honey, this is the Honky Tonk and always will be. Ruby left that in her will. No name changes, so you just scoot your boots on down the road and put in some competition," she said.

Billy Bob chuckled again and picked up his beer. "Never know what the future might bring. I'm going to find a sweet little thing and dance away part of the beer I've done drunk. Jarod, you tell Uncle Emmett we'll be over and see him someday soon," he said as he headed toward the jukebox.

Maybe that would make Daisy jealous and she'd see that he was quite a catch. After all, Billy Bob and his brothers owned the Bar W, the most prosperous ranch in Erath County. Jarod might be a shade better looking, but not by much, and neither his bank account nor his pickup truck was as big as the Walker boys.

Besides all that, Emmett's ranch wasn't going to be worth a damn in a couple of years. Mesquite was taking over and his stock was worthless. By the time Emmett croaked, the Walker men could probably pick up the whole ranch for next to nothing. One thing for sure—if they did, they'd turn it around right quick. That ranch had been the cream of two counties back when Mavis was alive. It would take time and hard work, but it would double the size of what the Walkers already had. Yes, sir, Daisy would wake up someday and see the wisdom in tying the knot with Billy Bob. He wasn't in any hurry. He'd waited seven years. He'd wait a few more.

Back at the bar Jarod downed the last of the beer, picked up his hat, and slid off the stool. He scanned the floor in case someone else had sloshed beer out of their Mason jar. He wasn't letting a blast of physical attraction overrule his better sense. Like the song playing on the jukebox said, they all got prettier at closing time when a man was drunk off his butt. Some were pretty; some looked like hell. But a barmaid was a barmaid, pretty or not.

What in the hell can I be thinking anyway? he asked himself. *I've got Emmett to take care of and a ranch that's falling apart at the seams. I wouldn't have time to date even if she wasn't a barmaid.*

"Don't be a stranger, and tell Emmett we miss him," Daisy said, breaking into his thoughts.

Jarod looked over his shoulder. "You know my uncle?"

Damn it! Those are some sexy eyes. I wonder what they'd look like right after… she stopped herself from even thinking the next words.

She cleared her throat and said, "I overheard Billy Bob mention Emmett. He and Mavis used to come in here every Saturday night. He had a draft Miller and she had a longneck Coors. They were almost as good at pool as Merle Avery. Truth is, I was a little surprised that Emmett didn't take up with Merle after Mavis died," she said.

"Probably because she's too damn smart for that," Jarod said.

"Ah, he's just old and cantankerous. God only knows how we'll be when we get that old and can't do what we once did. We might be hard to live with too."

"Hard to live with would be all right. Downright mean is another thing."

"Well, tell him hello from Daisy."

Jarod nodded and headed for the door.

Chigger blew him a kiss.

Jim Bob shot him a dirty look.

Billy Bob waved from the dance floor where he was hugged up tight to a lady in a knit shirt that accentuated thirty extra pounds around her midriff. She reminded Jarod of his first fiancée, Sasha, who'd gained fifteen pounds after they were engaged. She went to a fancy spa to lose the weight before the wedding and wound up eloping with her trainer. He wondered as he made his way through the vehicles in the parking lot if she ever lost those extra pounds.

The night air was blazing hot, but he drove slowly with the window down. The beer and the day's hard work had made him sleepy. Even if it was hot enough to fry the brains out of a lizard, he didn't dare turn on the air conditioning. If he got that comfortable he'd fall asleep and run off the road. That would give Emmett enough griping fuel to last two lifetimes. The only thing worse would be if Jarod went back to the ranch and started talking about a bartender.

"That'd stroke him out for sure," Jarod said aloud.

In an attempt to keep his mind off Daisy, he thought about his third fiancée. Emily had a business degree and was the head she-coon in the admissions office at Oklahoma State University. He'd figured the third was the charm and Emily would be with him right up to "death do us part." Two months before the wedding she got a job offer to go to New York City and expected him to leave the ranching business and go with her. After the argument, she went, he stayed, and a third engagement ring was tossed into a dresser drawer with the first two.

Not a one of the three had caused the physical reaction that Daisy had those few minutes when he was tangled up in her arms on the floor or when their gazes locked up across that bar. How old was she, anyway? Billy Bob never had told him. If he'd met her anywhere other than a bar he would have definitely flirted. But Billy Bob had done everything but tell him to back off and the Walker triplets were his only friends in the whole state.

Besides, Jarod had sworn off women until he was forty. Hopefully at that age he'd have enough sense to pick one that would last. Until then he'd be content with an occasional romp in the hay.

"Wonder if Daisy would be interested in a one-night stand?" he asked aloud as he parked the truck in front of Emmett's two-story house. He doubted it. That look she gave him when he was studying her up and down to figure out her age said that she wouldn't abide any kind of nonsense like getting hay in that long dark hair.

He opened the door to the truck and shut it as quietly as possible. Easing the front door open to the loud snores of his uncle coming from the twin-sized bed that had been set up in the corner of the living room since he had trouble navigating the stairs, he tiptoed into the house. Jarod froze when the noise stopped. When the loud snores continued, he removed his boots and padded upstairs in his socks, heaving a sigh of relief when he was safely in his bedroom. Thirty-five years old and he felt like a teenager sneaking back into the house after a night of skinny-dipping with his girlfriend.

What would it be like to skinny-dip with Daisy? Would she look as good out of those tight fittin' jeans as she did in them?

The house had been built back in the fifties when Mavis and Emmett first married. Four bedrooms and a bathroom were off a landing upstairs. Living room, dining room, and a kitchen were downstairs. At least four children were supposed to fill the house with laughter and arguments, but they'd never come along in the marriage.

He yanked his boots off and set them beside the bed and turned on the computer and checked his emails. If only he could convince Emmett the value of getting his business out of his hip pocket and entered into a reasonable program on the computer, he'd feel like he was getting somewhere.

What was it Daisy told Billy Bob? "Don't hold your breath."

Jarod felt her words rather than just heard them. Emmett would let him make changes the day that nuns danced on the bar in the Honky Tonk. He took a quick shower and crossed the hallway naked to stretch out on his bed. His fingers laced behind his head and he stared at the shadows on the ceiling. Daisy had put Billy Bob in his place with the bare minimum of words. Jarod didn't figure she'd take sass from anyone, but then she was a barmaid and no doubt she'd had lots of experience dealing with drunks.

Is that all the experience she has? Surely she has a boyfriend or a fiancé with those looks.

The words to Toby's song began to rattle around in his head. Like Toby said, Jarod had seen it all in the bar that night. He'd seen smokers. A fine fog of smoke hung about two feet from the ceiling. If secondhand smoke was as detrimental to health as folks said, then the Honky Tonk was cancer central. He'd seen boozers sitting at the bar and gathered around the five or six tables in the corners. A hooker if he counted Chigger. What on earth Jim Bob saw in that rough old gal was a mystery. She'd been rode hard and put away wet far too many days. She looked fifty at least. Toby mentioned cowboys. Well, Jarod had seen more boots, silver belt buckles, and hats that evening than he'd seen since the last barn dance at his folks' place up in Payne County, Oklahoma. Toby had sang about brokenhearted fools and suckers. If he'd taken time to talk to anyone other than Billy Bob and Daisy, he'd have found some of those too. He fell asleep to the melody playing and words about drinking his beer from a Mason jar running through his head.

At two a.m. Daisy shoved the Walker triplets and Chigger out the front door. The Honky Tonk was their home away from home on the weekends. They were good-natured fellows for the most part, except when Billy Bob started that nonsense about marrying her. She picked up a longneck Coors from the ice chest, wiped it off, and pulled out a chair at the nearest table like she did every night at closing. She propped her long legs up on the table and crossed them at the ankles. After a lengthy draw on the beer she looked around at the damages. Not bad for a Friday night. Few beer bottles left on the tables but Tinker had racked the pool balls and left them ready for the next night. There was one cue stick still on the nearest pool table that he'd forgotten to put back in the cabinet. Floor needed sweeping and she noticed a circle on the wood where she and Jarod collided.

She'd clean it all up the next day. That was one thing Ruby taught her from the beginning. Shut the doors and go to bed. Clean up the next morning when she wasn't dead tired from running up and down the bar refilling Mason jars or mixing drinks.

Daisy finished off her beer and put some coins into the jukebox. She pushed the right buttons and Toby's voice filled the room as he sang, "I Love This Bar." To sing that song with conviction like he did, he had to have spent some time in a bar in his lifetime, just like Daisy had.

"Some time, hell," she muttered.

She'd spent her whole life in and around bars. Her mother had gotten married at sixteen and had given birth to Daisy when she was barely seventeen. Widowed before Daisy was even born, she'd lied about her age and got a job as a bartender in a dive south of Mena, Arkansas. Daisy stayed with her grandmother most of the time until she was nine and then Granny died suddenly. After that she went to work with her mother every evening and spent her time during the school year doing homework in the stockroom. She had a sleeping bag, books to read, and a television that picked up no stations but had a VHS player attached so she could watch movies. At two o'clock her mother awoke her and they went home to a trailer on the outskirts of town. At seven the alarm went off and Daisy got herself ready for school, packed a lunch, and boarded the school bus at the entrance to the trailer court. She always left her mother sleeping and always hoped she was alone in the bedroom. Sometimes she got her wish; more often it was wasted.

She set the beer on the table and danced alone in the middle of the floor as Toby sang about liking his truck and his girlfriend, liking to take her out to dinner and a movie now and then. Daisy pretended she was dancing with Jarod McElroy on the banks of a river after a steak dinner at a fancy restaurant and giggled at her own silliness.

How had he gotten into the bar without her seeing him in the first place?

She made her way around the pool tables and the bar to the door leading back into her living quarters in the dark.

Ruby had built the Honky Tonk back in the early sixties and it looked like an old-time saloon with weathered wood on the outside. It had a wide wraparound porch around three sides. Rocking chairs for those who'd gotten too hot dancing or needed a breath of fresh air were scattered on the porch. A big neon sign on the roof flashed HONKY TONK.

Double doors led from the porch into a large room with a bar across the backside, pool tables to the right, and half a dozen wooden tables with chairs on the left. Two jukeboxes provided music. The antique one was Ruby's favorite and had only the old country music artists on it like George Jones, Lefty Frizzell, Waylon Jennings, Willy Nelson, and Merle Haggard. The other was modern and offered the newer artists like Toby Keith, Brad Paisley, Josh Turner, Jim Currington, Sara Evans, and Sugarland.

Through the locked door at the back lay a modern one-bedroom apartment that had been Daisy's home for more than seven years. She headed across the living room floor to the galley kitchen and made a ham and cheese sandwich. She carried it to the table in the corner of the tiny living room and pulled out a chair.

Was Jarod McElroy married? How long did he intend to stay with Emmett? Why in the hell had he come to Texas anyway?

"Damn," she swore. "This is ridiculous."

The biggest question was why in the devil was she interested? Every kind and shape of testosterone had come through the doors of her bar and not a one of them had made her think about breaking rule number one in Ruby's agenda: Men were not allowed into the apartment.

She showered, dried off, and headed for her bedroom where she crawled naked between the sheets. Her cell phone rang just as she shut her eyes. She checked the caller ID before she answered it.

"Hello, Merle," she said.

"It's Rack. He's got a terrible cough and he's hacking like he's about to die. Can I bring him over?"

"Sure you can. I'll get the hair ball medicine out and be ready for you," Daisy said.

In ten minutes Merle carried her enormous orange and white cat through the doors of the Honky Tonk. She had him wrapped in a blanket and he had another hacking attack when she laid him on the bar.

"It's not his heart, is it?" Merle asked nervously.

Daisy pulled a stethoscope from her black bag and listened to the cat's heart. "No, his heart sounds pretty good for a cat that's three times the size he ought to be. You really should stop giving him scraps."

"But I can't stand it when he looks at me if I'm eating steak or cheese. He loves his food. So it's just a hair ball?"

"That'd be my guess," Daisy said as she squeezed toothpaste looking substance from a tube onto a tongue depressor.

"He'd scratch my eyeballs out if I put that in his mouth," Merle said.

"Rack has got your number. He knows I've got the stuff in that bag to fix it so he'd never have another chunk of your rib eye steak, don't you, boy? Open your fat little jaws and there we go." Daisy rubbed his neck and the medicine went down in a couple of swallows.

"Now it's back home so he can puke it up on my carpet," Merle said.

"Or your bed," Daisy laughed.

"You are a doll to get out of bed and help me at this hour." Merle laid a bill on the bar. "The day Ruby found you was the best day this county ever saw."

"Merle, I'm not a real vet."

"Shhhh, don't tell Rack. He thinks you are a high-dollar specialist. Vet. Vet tech. Ain't no difference in my books. See you tonight." Merle picked up her cat and carried him out the doors into the hot night.

Daisy turned out the lights for the second time and went back to bed.

Chapter 2

Daisy was semi-awake when a hard knocking on the back door startled her into a sitting position. She grabbed a kimono-style robe and stumbled barefoot across the bedroom and living room and peeked around the curtain.

"Well, shit," she mumbled and checked to see if Chigger was holding a dog or cat or goat—nothing but Chigger leaning against the porch post and smoking a cigarette. When she saw Daisy looking out the window, she stabbed out the butt on the heel of her boot.

Daisy slid the chain lock back and opened the door. "Mornin', Chigger. What brings you out this early? You got a cow or a horse needin' help?"

"Darlin', this ain't early. It's almost dinner time. And the only thing I got needin' help is Jim Bob Walker. I 'bout wore him out last night, but I guess a bartender or a vet neither one would have anything for that unless you keep them little blue pills in your black bag."

"Good God, Chigger."

Chigger giggled. "Got any coffee?"

Daisy motioned her inside. "I can make a pot. Come on in."

Chigger held up the cigarette butt. "Thanks. Where's the trash so I can get rid of this?"

Daisy pointed.

Chigger opened the pantry door and disposed of it before she pulled one of the two chairs away from the table and slid into it.

"You couldn't get Jim Bob to make you a pot of coffee this morning?" Daisy asked as she measured grounds into the coffee machine.

"He brought me breakfast in bed. Bacon, biscuits and gravy, coffee, juice, pancakes. Whole buffet on a tray and then I gave him breakfast in bed, if you know what I mean."

Chigger was taller than Daisy by at least four inches, making her about five feet ten inches. Slim built except for a set of enormous breasts that she swore were all hers and without a drop of silicone implanted in them. She wore skintight knit tops that accentuated her *God given assets* as well as her small waist. That morning she'd borrowed one of Jim Bob's chambray work shirts and it hung outside her jeans. Her blond hair had a bedroom tousled look to it and her face was clear of any makeup. She looked more like a soccer mom than a beer joint hustler.

Daisy toasted a couple of blueberry pastries in the microwave and served them with the coffee. "It's hot. Give it time to cool a bit or it'll burn the hell out of your mouth."

Chigger dipped a pastry into the coffee, blew on it, and popped a bite into her mouth. "Take more than that to burn the hell out of me, girl. You got a nice place back here."

"Thank you," Daisy said.

Chigger looked around at the sparsely decorated apartment. "You are definitely not a clutter person.

A woman's house says a lot about the kind of person they are. You are straightforward and speak your mind. Me, I am a clutter person. I collect angels and they're everywhere, even on the ends of my ceiling fan cords. I'm one of those women who wants everything she sees. I wish I had a setup like this. Make it a lot easier to have a good time if I didn't have to wait to get Jim Bob home."

"Ruby said I could go to the motel or get laid in a hay loft, but no men were allowed in the apartment. It made sense. By the time I get a man to a motel, I usually change my mind about sleeping with him and save myself some heartache."

Chigger shot her a dirty look. "Are you digging at me?"

"No, just statin' facts," Daisy said. She picked up her pastry and took a bite.

"My hair appointments don't start until three o'clock today. Got four and won't be done until six and then I'll be right back at the Honky Tonk for the evening." Chigger sipped coffee between words.

"How'd you get off so easy on Saturday? I figured folks would be clamoring to get their hair done for church on Sunday," Daisy said.

"More like for partyin' on Saturday night. Actually most of my older folks get beautified on Friday. It's my busiest day. Only thing that keeps me going is knowing that when it's all done I go to the Honky Tonk."

"Nothin' any closer than this place?" Daisy asked.

Chigger had been coming to the beer joint for years and suddenly the day after Jarod McElroy showed up, she paid a home visit? It didn't make much sense unless she was there to stake a claim. Poor old Jim Bob Walker was about to get his heart broken.

Chigger winked. "You tryin' to run me off, girlfriend? Damn, girl, I'm your best customer and just think of all the good lookin' men I drag in for you."

"Seriously? Why do you drive all this distance?" Daisy asked.

"Seriously? I live in Stephenville, darlin'. Cats don't potty in their beds. And besides, Erath County is dry. This is the closest place I can find with dancin' and hunky horny ranchers wantin' a good time."

"What's that supposed to mean? Cats don't potty in their own beds? "

Chigger talked with her hands and waved them around in circles before she answered. "Think about it. Cat has to find a place to potty but it ain't goin' to be in their bed or their own backyard. They'll jump the fence to go dig a hole in the neighbor's yard. In Stephenville, I'm Willa Mae Jones. I live next door to my momma and fix hair for a living in a beauty shop out behind my house. Momma thinks I've got a friend named Daisy O'Dell up here in Palo Pinto County that I spent a lot of Friday and Saturday nights with. I wouldn't cause Momma no grief for nothin'. She was forty when she had me and she's seventy-five now and getting old."

Daisy did the math and had to swallow hard to keep from spitting coffee across the table all over Jim Bob's shirt. "You're thirty-five?"

"I know, darlin'. Most folks wouldn't believe I'm that old. Don't you tell on me, now. It's this deal I have with Revlon. Wasn't for hair dye and good makeup I'd look every bit of my age," Chigger said with another of her famous winks.

Daisy nodded and hoped Lucifer didn't jump up from hell and drag her into the fiery pits for agreeing with such a blatant lie. She'd figured Chigger was at least ten years older than Jim Bob's thirty-five years and maybe even kissing fifty firmly on the lips. Thirty-five! Still young enough to start a family. Now that was a scary thought. The offspring of Jim Bob and Chigger! Hell-raisers for sure. She'd have to hire more than bouncers when they were legal-aged drinkers.

"Want to know why I came to visit this morning?" Chigger said.

"Oh, yes, I do," Daisy said.

"You don't have to answer like that. It damn sure ain't to ask you for a job."

"O… ka…y." Daisy dragged out the word.

Chigger bit her lower lip. "Truth is I saw the way that cowboy made you all hot and horny last night after he fell on top of you. Can't say as I blame you one bit either. Must have been a second there when you thought he was finishin' up a good rousting bout of sex before you come to your senses and saw that you'd both fell down together. Your eyes were flashing around like Christmas tree lights. Never saw you look like that before."

Crimson flushed Daisy's cheeks.

Chigger laughed and clapped her hands. "Why Daisy O'Dell, you are red as Rudolph's nose. Let's go clean up the bar and have some lunch."

"What?" Daisy asked.

"I know that you clean up the beer joint the next mornin'. I'll help you and then I'll buy you lunch at the Smokestack. I'm partial to their chicken fried steaks and fries. Then *you* have to go meet Momma. She sees a sweet lookin' little thing like you, she'll think I'm up here in Mingus paintin' my toenails on Friday and Saturday nights. That's what I told her and you are going to help me make her believe it."

Daisy looked at Chigger as if she were seeing an alien straight from a little flat spaceship. Any minute now and Chigger's eyes were going to roll up in her head and antennas were going to sprout from all that thick, dyed-blond hair.

"Okay, here's the deal. I'll even spell it out real slow so you'll understand," Chigger said each word like she was a first grader with a brand new reader. "I will leave the cowboy alone. I won't seduce him. I'll help you clean up and take you to lunch. For all that you got to meet Momma. She's been after me for more than a year to bring you around to meet her. Ruby went once and it is your turn."

"Good God!" Daisy said.

"Momma says He is. I reckon I'd have to change my ways to find out." Chigger resumed talking like normal. "And please call me Willa Mae when you're around Momma. She don't have any idea about my nickname."

—⁓—

Jarod popped open a can of biscuits, fried bacon, and eggs and made a small skillet of gravy. *I'd like to take Daisy breakfast in bed this morning. Damn, I've got to stop thinking about that woman. The Honky Tonk was full of good lookin' women last night, so why do I keep thinking about her? I swear, I must've jarred something loose in my brain. I bet it looks like scrambled eggs in there.*

Using a walker, Emmett shuffled to the table, complained that the biscuits were store bought, the bacon was too crisp, the eggs were overdone, and the gravy needed more salt.

"Boy, you got to learn how things is done here if you ever want to be a rancher," Emmett said.

It's not Daisy who's scrambled my brains. It's a result of beating my head against the wall because of Emmett.

"Uncle Emmett, I know how to be a rancher. I've owned my own place in Oklahoma for more than ten years. It's paid for and making a good profit. Let me get this ranch back into top-notch running order. Your stock is barely more than culls, and the mesquite is about to take over. We could put up one of those new windmills and save a bundle in bills. We need to get the finances into the computer."

Emmett fired up angry. "Don't you tell me how to ranch. I was doin' a fine job of it when you wasn't even a gleam in your old man's eye. And you can take those fancy ugly windmills and your computer and go to hell with both."

Jarod bit back the words on the tip of his tongue. "I'm going to work on clearing some land today. You want to ride out and sit in the truck?"

"Hell, no. It's hot out there. I'm stayin' in the house and watchin' television."

"I'll be back in time to make you lunch then," Jarod said.

"It's dinner, not lunch, and I'm not an invalid. Who the hell do you think fixed my meals before you got here?"

"You *asked* for my help," Jarod reminded him.

"Didn't realize you'd grown up to be a pain in the ass."

When Jarod didn't answer, Emmett went on. "It wasn't my idea that you come down here and disrupt my life this summer. It was your dad's. Mavis always did like you, but I figured you was too big for your britches. You and your big ideas about improving the place. Hell, boy, it supported me and Mavis all those years. Find a good woman and settle down and it'll support you too."

"If you don't like the arrangement I can be gone in an hour and you can leave the place to whoever you damn well please," Jarod said through clenched teeth.

Emmett snorted. "Mavis will rest easier in her grave knowin' your family is running the place when I'm dead and gone. But you ain't goin' to take over before I'm dead. It's mine until I'm six foot under the ground and then you can plow it under and spread monkey shit on it for all I care."

"That might be all it's good for by then," Jarod grumbled.

Emmett glared at him. "Mavis said you was cut off the same log I was. I don't see it."

"Me either. I think the tree they cut your sorry ass out of was the meanest one in the forest."

"And the one they got your sorry ass from was the know-it-all tree. Get on out of here and fight the mesquite. When you are eighty years old you'll find out you don't know jack shit, boy."

Jarod changed the subject. "You think you're strong enough to wash these dishes?"

"I could out work you if I had a mind to. Get on out of here and pull up some of those mesquite trees you think are such a nuisance. I'll do the damn dishes and make my own dinner. Probably do both better than you can," Emmett growled.

"How about taking a shower?"

"Don't need one. Had one three days ago and I ain't done enough work to sweat," Emmett said. "Where'd you go last night?"

"For a ride."

"I'm thinkin' I might want to go for one tonight so don't be makin' any plans to go by yourself. There's a beer joint about fifteen miles up north of here me and Mavis used to go to once in a while. We liked to shoot a little pool and have a beer. You can drive me up there tonight," Emmett said.

Jarod did not want to see Daisy again. Didn't want to think about her or the sexy dream he'd had concerning her just before he awoke that morning. If he was going to stop thinking about her, he had to stay away from her.

Emmett raised his voice. "You hear me?"

"I heard you. I'll stop in plenty of time to take a shower and drive you up to the Honky Tonk, but I'm not taking you smelling like an old boar hog. You want to go out tonight, you'd best be cleanin' up and shavin' today."

"Never said where we were goin'. Means that's where you were last night. How'd you like Miz Daisy? She's a fine lady, ain't she? Like her just as well as I did Miz Ruby, only Ruby was a wilder sort."

Jarod could scarcely believe his ears. Emmett McElroy had just said five sentences without cussing or ranting about something. He'd actually paid Daisy a compliment. But then if Emmett said Daisy was a fine lady then it meant the Alzheimer's was getting worse. Daisy was a barmaid. Period. End of story.

He put a package of cheese crackers and an apple in a brown bag, made himself a gallon-sized cooler of iced sweet tea, and headed out the back door without another word. His mother had warned him that he'd have his hands full with Uncle Emmett. Jarod hadn't known that "hands full" was the understatement of time since the first day of creation.

He slapped the steering wheel of his truck when he was inside. Damn it all, anyway, how was he supposed to get that woman out of his mind if he had to see her again? To admit that he didn't want to go would just cause Emmett to set his mind even more. The only thing to do was go and sit in the back corner until the old fellow was ready to go home, and pretend he had a wonderful time. If Emmett ever thought for one second that he was miserable, he'd insist on Jarod taking him to the Honky Tonk every single night.

"Shoot me graveyard dead if I ever get Alzheimer's," Jarod said aloud as he started the engine of his truck.

––––⁓⁓⁓––––

Daisy backed her car—a vintage 1976 completely remodeled baby blue Ford Maverick with seats upholstered as close to the original fabric as she could find—out of the garage behind the Honky Tonk and followed Chigger south toward the Smokestack.

She pulled in the parking lot beside Chigger's truck.

"I'm starvin' to death. You'd think all that breakfast Jim Bob brought me would be enough to last a week instead of just a few hours. But then last night was a busy night," Chigger said as they walked side-by-side into the restaurant. "I found out how much I liked sex when I was fifteen. How about you?"

"I don't kiss and tell," Daisy said.

"Well, bless your little southern heart. How's a girl supposed to know without tastin' the goods if her friends don't tell her whether or not it's a good place to eat?" Chigger asked.

"Guess she has to pay the price for the buffet and try out the food for herself," Daisy said as the cool air hit them inside the restaurant.

The restaurant had started more than thirty years before in Thurber's old drugstore, but it burned in the early nineties. The owners then rebuilt it in the north end of the old Texas & Pacific Mercantile building. The place was made with original Thurber bricks in the late 1800s and had sold everything from cribs to coffins to the company miners back when Thurber was a flourishing town. The restaurant got its name from the 128-foot tall power plant smokestack that once provided Thurber with electricity. Memorabilia of the days when Thurber was a booming town decorated the walls. An old upright piano graced one corner. An oak freezer that required ice blocks sat beside the doors into the kitchen. T-shirts in every color were stacked up in a glass case with the Smokehouse logo on them.

Daisy had been intrigued with the place the first time she ate there, but nowadays she was more interested in the food than the memorabilia. Besides, the day was a bittersweet one. The last time she'd eaten at the Smokestack was with Ruby the day before she was killed on that damned motorcycle of hers. Daisy had told her that she was too old to be out riding a motorcycle. Ruby had declared that the best way to die was to run the cycle all day and drop dead of a heart attack when she parked it.

"What are you thinkin' about? That cowboy I've promised to keep my hands off of?" Chigger asked.

"Ruby Lee," Daisy said.

Chigger nodded seriously. "Miss her, do you?"

"She was like a mother to me. Took me in when I was down and out," Daisy said.

"You were the daughter she never had. It was a two-way street. You was good for her," Chigger said seriously.

"Thanks," Daisy murmured.

The waitress appeared with a notepad and waited. Chigger handed her the menu and said, "I'll have the chicken fried steak, the big portion, with a baked potato, sour cream, butter, cheese, and bacon, and honey mustard dressing on my salad. Sweet tea and save us a couple of pieces of coconut pie."

Daisy shut the menu and handed it to the waitress. "Same for me, only ranch dressing."

"Now let's talk about that cowboy, Jarod," Chigger said.

"Let's don't," Daisy said.

Chigger eyed her carefully. "Woman don't talk about a man, something is the matter. Either he's butt ugly, son-of-a-bitch mean, or else they got a thing for him. I been watchin' you for a helluva long time. Either you are damn careful about your men or you dance to a different drummer. I never seen you leave with one or flirt."

Daisy threw up her hands defensively. "Hey, I'm straight! I like men," Daisy said.

"Well, I'm damn glad to hear it. I was worried about you. Now what's so different about this Jarod McElroy? You don't light up over Billy Bob."

"Why do you go home all the time with Jim Bob?" She didn't know why Billy Bob didn't set her hormones to singing or why that dark-haired cowboy sent her into a gushy mess of hot flashes.

"Jim Bob is a sweetheart and he's in love with me. I'm going to marry that lonesome old red-haired cowboy one of these days. I just want to get all my wild oats sowed first. Once I say 'I do' I'll have to be good and only sleep with him. I'm not ready to do that just yet."

"Why?" Daisy asked.

"Way I figure it is this. I started having sex when I was fifteen. If I have it twenty-one years before I get married, it's kind of like growing up and coming of age. That's next year. I won't be so old, not really. I reckon that'll give me five or six years to have a bunch of little mean red-haired boys for Jim Bob and make him real happy."

Daisy shook her head. "That's a cockamamie way to rationalize something as important as marriage."

"How'd you rationalize it then?" Chigger asked.

"Become friends. Fall in love. Marry. Have kids. Traditional, I suppose." First it was friends, so that nipped the whole process in the bud. Jarod would never be friends with a barmaid, so the fall in love part was a moot point.

The waitress brought their tea and salads. Daisy didn't realize how hungry she was until she started to eat. The salad and toasted garlic bread tasted wonderful.

"I reckon each person has to find their own way around the L and M words. You do it your way and I'll do it mine. If you find out you don't want that cowboy, honey, you will be upfront and honest with me. I'd like to have a taste of that tall drink of water before I settle down with Jim Bob, but only if you decide you don't want him. I won't get in your way," Chigger said.

"Who says I want him?" Daisy asked.

"Your eyes say it all. I'd like to strip him down and have him for supper and maybe again for breakfast, but I'll be good. At least until after you meet Momma."

"Chigger, you are thirty-five years old. I wasn't that afraid of my mother or Ruby Lee either and I was only twenty-one when Ruby Lee hired me. I had you figured you'd take on a rattlesnake bare-handed," Daisy said.

"Rattlesnakes ain't nearly as mean as Momma. Don't use your southern manners when it's time to leave. Don't you dare say something like come on up and see me sometime. She'll bug the hell out of me to go with me on Friday night."

"What about if she asks me what kind of work I do?"

Chigger got serious. "Here's the story I told her. I met you one day when you came to town to get your hair done. You are married to a rancher and you got two of the cutest little girls. You introduced me to Jim Bob who is a good, God fearin' man and sometimes he comes over to your house and we play Monopoly. We don't play cards because that's a sin right next to covetin' your neighbor's ass. Which I never understood anyway. I mean, if your neighbor ain't married and he's got a fine ass, why can't you covet it?"

Daisy giggled.

"And your husband's name is Jarod."

"Good God Almighty," Daisy sputtered.

"I just thought of that this morning. Pretty good touch, ain't it? Far as she knows, I spent the night at your ranch last night like I do lots of Fridays, and since you need to come to town to buy some vet supplies today I suggested you run in and meet Momma. I told her that you couldn't stay long. Runnin' a dairy farm takes a lot of time," Chigger said.

Daisy's Irish temper flared. "You planned this whole thing?"

"Been plannin' it for months. Good story, ain't it? And if you don't play along with it, I'm going to have wild passionate sex with your cowboy tonight."

"That's blackmail and he's not my cowboy," Daisy said.

"Call it whatever you want. You'll have plenty on me to do some blackmailin' after today, believe me."

Daisy raised a perfectly arched eyebrow. "Oh?"

"Oh, yes. And I'll even sweep up the floor again if you play nicely."

"This is worth more than sweeping up the bar and a chicken-fried steak," Daisy grumbled.

Chigger shrugged. "I'm sure it is, but then what are friends for?"

"We're not friends. We are business partners," Daisy said.

"Honey, that's the best kind of friends," Chigger said.

By the time they finished lunch and Daisy drove twenty miles to Stephenville and pulled her car into the driveway of the white frame house where Chigger's mother lived, she was ready to strangle the woman.

Chigger twisted her hands nervously as they walked up on the porch. "You remember the whole story?"

"I got it and I'll improvise if I don't," Daisy said.

Mrs. Jones met them at the door. "Y'all get yourselves on in here. I made a pecan pie and sweet tea. Come on in the kitchen and sit up to the table. I just been dying to meet you, Daisy. Willa Mae talks so much about you and your ranch and two sweet little girls. I pictured you a little taller. Guess that's because you are a vet. How does a little old thing like you vaccinate cows? Well, I been tellin' her to bring you around for months. It was a shame the way her other friend got killed. That Ruby was a saint if I ever knowed one. But at least she didn't have children like you do. I'm glad to see my girl take up with someone nearer to her own age, but Willa Mae always has had a soft spot for the elderly. Now tell me about yourself, Daisy. How long have you been a rancher's wife?"

Daisy shot Chigger a drop-dead look.

Mrs. Jones didn't wait for an answer but kept right on talking. "Set down, now. We've got so much to talk about. I should've invited her brother's wives over to meet you, but they talk too much. Lawsy me, but I wouldn't get a word in edgewise if they was here. Women just go on and on. Guess it's their age. Willa Mae's brothers was twenty and twenty-one when I had her so they're most awful protective. Their wives are probably going though the change and that makes them get all flustered and talk too much. Willa Mae says that she's met a man. Jim Bob Walker. Is he a good man? I won't have her takin' up with a man who's a rabble rouser. No sir. He's got to be a God-fearin' man with upright morals. So you tell me the truth, now Daisy. Is this Jim Bob a good man?"

Daisy shoved a fork full of pie in her mouth. She held up a hand and mumbled around the pie, "Wonderful pie."

Mrs. Jones took off on another tangent. "My mother's recipe. Grind the pecans. When you leave them in halves it makes a nice lookin' pie but it's tough as leather. We was talkin' about Willa Mae's friend. Does he like pecan pie?"

Daisy swallowed hard. "I think Jim Bob would love your pie. He's kind of shy but I bet maybe in a year or so we'll talk him into coming around to meet you."

Chigger rolled her eyes.

"A year! Lawsy me, girl, it better be before a year. You tell that boy that my Willa Mae is a good girl and she's awful shy too. Why, she ain't never even been out on a date if you don't count that boy that picked her up for the senior prom. He was just her friend and not a real date but he did bring her a corsage. I dried it upside down and put it away so she'd have it for her memory box. Woman needs those things when she gets old."

"Yes, ma'am," Daisy said.

"Did you go to the prom in Palo Pinto or over at Mineral Wells?" Mrs. Jones pried.

"I grew up in Mena, Arkansas," Daisy said.

"Well, imagine that. I reckon you met your husband, Jarod, up there?"

"Actually I met him in Mingus," Daisy answered.

"You'll have to tell me all about that next time you come visitin'. And bring him with you. What's his favorite pie? I'll have it ready. Maybe you could bring Jim Bob with you and we'll all have a game of Monopoly. Now wouldn't that be a fun evening?"

"Momma, I've got to get to my appointments and Daisy has to buy groceries and get home. Jarod can only watch the girls so long and then he has to get the cows milked," Willa Mae said.

"Well, I understand ranchin' and dairy work is time takin'. But you come on back around, Daisy. Any old time. I'm always here and I'm glad Willa Mae has struck up a friendship with a good woman like you." She talked all the way to the door and followed Daisy out onto the porch.

Chigger walked her to the car. "Thank you. I owe you big time," she whispered.

"Yep, you do. And you'd best never cross me or I'll stand up on the bar and tell this story right out loud."

"That would be bitchy."

"Yep, it would," Daisy said.

"Honey, I done told you I won't seduce your man."

"He's not my man. He's not my husband. And if you can seduce him, I wouldn't want him anyway," Daisy said.

"Whew! You don't share worth a damn, do you?"

Daisy started the engine. "No, I do not!"

Chapter 3

"Hey, hey, finally you open the doors and let us old cowboys in the joint. We been sittin' on the porch for half an hour," Jim Bob said when Daisy unlocked the front door of the Honky Tonk.

"You probably spent the night there," she said.

"Didn't think of that. I'll bring my tent next time and just camp out in the parking lot. Jim Bob, you bring the grill and we'll fix hamburgers. Hell, we might make enough to pay for Joe Bob's pool losses by selling your famous whiskey burgers," Billy Bob suggested as they trooped inside.

Daisy vowed she'd never smart off again.

They hadn't been there ten minutes when a dozen of Ruby's old biker friends arrived. Daisy filled beer orders as the place went from quiet to the walls rattling when someone put coins into the jukebox. "Sweet Home Alabama" had folks on the dance floor and others wiggling their shoulders as they chalked up the cue sticks.

Does Jarod shoot pool? Lord, I hope not. I'm lousy at it. I wouldn't give him a bit of competition. Damn it, I've got to stop thinking about him.

"Hey, Daisy, fix us up two pitchers of hurricanes," Wilma yelled.

"Soon as I finish drawing this beer," she yelled back.

By the time she had that order filled and the money in the register, five young women came through the doors.

They stopped when they saw Tinker and produced identification, then settled at a table in a corner. They were all dressed in cute little sundresses and sandals. They giggled for a few seconds before one of the brides-maids came to the bar and ordered three pitchers of piña coladas and five empty glasses.

"We serve everything in Mason jars. You want pints or quarts?" Daisy asked.

"Better be pints. We don't want to get the bride drunk too fast," she laughed.

"Bachelorette party?" Daisy asked.

She nodded and took several bills from her tiny purse to pay for the order.

Chigger arrived at nine in her tight skinny-legged jeans and bright pink stretch top that hugged every curve. Her blond hair was freshly done and her finger-nails matched her pink shirt. She made her way to Jim Bob's table and pulled him out onto the dance floor.

The bride and her ladies were finishing up their third pitcher an hour later when the front door opened and one hunky, handsome policeman strutted over to their table.

"Hey," he raised his voice above the din of the jukebox playing "Hell Yeah" by Montgomery Gentry. "I hear there's a pretty woman in here who's going to be a bride come tomorrow afternoon at two o'clock."

They all giggled and pointed at the petite little blonde who was definitely going to have a headache the next day when she walked down the aisle if she didn't slow down.

Chigger claimed a barstool and watched the circus. "Hope she ain't got a big old fancy hairdo and a veil in mind for the weddin'. The way she's tossin' back those drinks she's going to have one hellacious headache tomorrow."

"Maybe she needs them to marry the sorry sucker," Daisy said.

"If that's the case I hope she takes off like Julia Roberts did in *Runaway Bride*. Ain't no man worth that and she's so damn young."

"That's the truth," Daisy agreed.

The policeman snapped velvet cuffs on her hands and led her to the door saying loudly that he was charging her with being too beautiful to be out in public. About the time he reached Tinker's chair he announced that he couldn't arrest a pretty little thing like her. He removed the cuffs and she ran back to her pack of giggling friends while he meandered over to the jukebox and plugged in "Redneck Woman" by Gretchen Wilson. By the time the words were out about never being the Barbie doll type, the policeman had jumped up on the girls' table and snapped off his uniform. He did a bump and grind in a skintight zebra print Speedo that had all the girls giggling and putting dollar bills in the waistband when he crawled across the table toward them.

"Well, that's a first for the Honky Tonk," Daisy said.

Chigger didn't answer. Her eyes were glazed over. Daisy could imagine Chigger's momma grabbing her chest and dropping dead with a heart attack if she ever saw that wanton look in her daughter's eyes.

"Shy, my ass," Daisy muttered.

"What about your ass?" Billy Bob asked when the show was over and the policeman grabbed up his clothing and disappeared out the door.

"Nothing you'd be interested in." Daisy filled another Mason jar with Coors Light and carried it to the far end.

"Honey, I'm interested in everything about you," Billy Bob said in his most seductive low country drawl.

Daisy pretended she didn't hear him and kept working.

"He could have done it twice. Hell, I'd a paid him double the rate to come over here and do it on the bar in front of me," Chigger all but panted.

Daisy leaned over the bar. "I don't think you'll be ready to marry your cowboy in one year. The way you were salivating at the sight of that stripper you'll have a tough time straightening up your act in a single year. You might need to give it two years before you're ready to settle down with Jim Bob and play Monopoly on Saturday nights."

"Whew! After that, I might ought to marry him tomorrow. That made me horny as hell. Wonder where I could buy him one of them uniforms and a zebra print bikini thing like that," Chigger whispered back.

Daisy giggled.

Chigger crossed the floor in a few long easy strides and pulled Jim Bob out on the dance floor where she hugged up to him so tight that the shadow they cast looked like one person instead of two.

One minute Daisy was wiping a beer spill from the counter and the next she was looking into Jarod's gray eyes across the space of a two-foot bar. In that instant the bones dissolved in her legs and her insides melted into a gushy pile.

It made her mad as hell that he'd snuck up on her, but by damn she would get over it instantly. It would never be said that Daisy O'Dell didn't learn her lessons and learn them well. Once upon a time she'd been in love, and happy-ever-after lasted until the first time her fiancé,

Chris, got stinking drunk and mean as a grizzly with a toothache. Trust was something she guarded closely and she never gave it away carelessly. Other than Ruby Lee, she hadn't fully trusted anyone in years and didn't intend to start now. She inhaled deeply and stubbornly willed her legs to support her.

"What can I get you, cowboy?" she asked in an even tone.

"Two beers. Coors. From the tap." Jarod had hoped he had remembered her all wrong from the night when they'd slipped and fallen. But he hadn't. Her skin was like silk that begged to be caressed and those eyes belonged in a dimly lit bedroom, half open and begging.

"Want them on a tray?" Daisy looked around for his date.

"That would be nice." He cleared his throat. He'd been right. Seeing her again would make forgetting all about her impossible. "And make it five beers. I'll treat the Walkers to a drink while I'm at it. They deserve it since they're over there entertaining Uncle Emmett."

Daisy tried not to look in that direction but she didn't have that much willpower. No wife. No girlfriend. Just a table full of men surrounding Emmett McElroy.

"Will do." She hoped he couldn't hear the breathlessness in her voice. She drew up five beers and put them on a tray.

He handed her two bills and their hands brushed in the transfer. The heat between them was like a fireplace blaze on a cold winter night. It wasn't fair to be attracted to a man who was most likely married or already branded. His wife or girlfriend must be waiting at home or had slipped into the ladies' room when no one was looking.

She put his change on the tray with his beers and turned to the next customer to find Amos waiting. He wore his black leather biker duds that night.

"Amos, where did you come from? I didn't see you come in. Thought you'd let the gang ride without you tonight." Daisy leaned across the bar as far as she could and hugged him.

"I was talkin' to Mac on the front porch. Gang ain't goin' to ride without their leader. Put three longneck Coors on a tray and I'll carry them over to the pool table. Merle's got a bet goin' with Mac. One of these days he's goin' to learn she could whip him with crossed eyes and a hand tied behind her back. That feller who just got the beers, the one sitting back there in the corner with Emmett McElroy, who is he?" Amos asked while she took the lids off the beers.

Amos Lambert had been Ruby's friend since they were kids in grade school. They'd been wild together, ridden in the Wild Breed motorcycle gang since they were in their twenties, and probably had more secrets than Daisy could listen to in her lifetime. When Ruby took Daisy under her wing, Amos did the same. If Ruby had been a surrogate mother, then Amos was the same as a father.

"I can take care of myself," she said as she made change for him.

"Don't doubt it for a minute. Taught you well, me and Ruby did. I'm just askin' who is that feller?"

Daisy sighed. "His name is Jarod. He's kin to Emmett and helping him out from what I hear. Why are you asking?"

"Just hadn't seen him around. Ruby said for me to keep an eye on you. He keeps stealing glances over this way. I might be old but I damn sure ain't blind and I know what he's got on his mind. He ain't respectful, you just motion and me and the boys will put him out of here on his ass."

Daisy patted him on the arm. "He's just a harmless rancher, and puttin' people out on their asses is Tinker's job." She nodded toward the door.

Ruby had always said that Tinker could toss a drunk out the door quieter than any bouncer this side of the Mississippi. Daisy believed it to be the pure unadulterated gospel. Tinker said very little but he had arms of steel and took his job seriously.

Ruby had told her that he'd been wounded in Vietnam and lived in a trailer way up in the woods. He'd been working at the Honky Tonk since the day Ruby opened the doors and nobody messed with Tinker, Ruby, or now Daisy. And no one finished a fight in the Honky Tonk. They might have the balls to start one, but Daisy had never seen anyone brave enough to stand up to him.

"You just mind what I say," Amos said.

"Don't go shootin' a payin' customer, Amos. But if you want to shoot Billy Bob Walker, I wouldn't raise much fuss. He's been lookin' at me a lot lately too, and he's sittin' right over there." Daisy pointed.

"Ah, honey, Billy Bob is playin' a game. That Jarod, when he looks at you it's different. He's serious," Amos said.

"You better not have any more to drink. You're getting slap silly. This is only the second time Jarod has even been in the Honky Tonk. He doesn't even know me and I damn sure ain't interested in him." Daisy had heard the same thing from Amos about every man other than Billy Bob for the past seven years. If there was a serious look in Jarod's eye, it was the same kind that a jackrabbit had when it saw a Catahoula hound nipping at its ass.

"I just call 'em the way I see 'em. I'll take these beers on over to the pool tables and watch Merle whip Mac's ass again," Amos said.

Daisy did her best to ignore the McElroy party in the back corner, but when Chigger drew up a chair and sat down between Emmett and Jarod, a green jab of jealousy shot through Daisy's heart.

You had better stop this nonsense right now. He's one hunky, hot cowboy but he's not for you.

How do you know? That annoying little inner voice asked.

She was quick to shoot off a silent answer. *Because any man who'd have that kind of control over me could hurt me and it ain't happenin' again.*

A few minutes later Chigger opened the swinging doors at one end of the bar and stepped into the area. "I'll bartend for a few minutes. Emmett wants to see you."

"Tell him to come up to the bar. This is my job, not yours."

Chigger picked up a white bar rag and wiped up a puddle of foam. "He's using a walker, for God's sake. Don't be hardheaded. I can do this job for five minutes and besides, I still owe you. Momma put you through the wringer even worse than I figured she would."

Daisy finished the draw she was working on, took the customer's money, and nodded at Chigger. She was reminded of an old song that had been one of Ruby's favorites by Ray Price and was still on the antique jukebox. It had a line in it that said the longest walk he'd ever take would be across the floor. If it hadn't been Saturday night she would have unplugged the fancy new jukebox and plugged in the old one. But the young crowd came to hear the upbeat newer country music on Friday and Saturday nights.

Ruby had always said that folks didn't give a damn if music came from a jukebox or a band. They just wanted a good time, plenty of beer, and room to wiggle around with their dancing or shoot a little eight ball. She'd been right. The Honky Tonk drew more business and had lasted longer than any other joint within fifty miles.

"Miz Daisy!" Emmett exclaimed when he looked up and saw her at his elbow. "You still runnin' the Honky Tonk with a steel hand, I see."

"That's right. Got my bluff in on them early and they're all afraid to test me. Besides, Tinker puts the fear of God into most of the rabble rousers." She laid a hand on Emmett's shoulder.

"You keep it that way, darlin'. Want you to meet my nephew, Jarod. He's moved down here to wait for me to die so his family can inherit my place."

"Good God, Uncle Emmett!" Jarod exclaimed.

"Well, it's the gospel truth," Emmett said.

Jarod's face lit up like a neon sign. "I'm not a gold-digging bastard. You're making me sound like one."

"Ah, we all know he's just joshin'," Billy Bob said. "He's goin' to leave his spread to me, ain't you, Emmett?"

Emmett grinned. "Naw, Mavis said Jarod's dad was to have it and I wouldn't want that woman on my bad side for eternity. Miz Daisy, set a spell. Talk to me. I hear

Jarod came visitin' last night. Did he behave himself or flirt with Chigger?"

Daisy didn't sit down. "He was a good boy."

"Something the matter with him, you reckon? Don't know of many men who'd come in the Honky Tonk and not flirt with Chigger. He didn't even flirt with her when she leaned down and give us all a peek of those big old honkers while ago. Tell me," Emmett lowered his voice, "did he flirt with Jim Bob?"

Jim Bob slid his chair back so fast that he almost spilled himself out onto the floor. "Hell, no, he didn't flirt with me and I was with Chigger, so that's why he didn't get next to her."

"I'd say you don't have a lot to worry about, Emmett. I think he's straight as a judge," Daisy said.

"Well, halle-damn-lu-yah for that. Way he argues with everything I say, I'd begun to wonder if there was a bitchy little girl hidin' in him," Emmett said.

"I'm sittin' right here," Jarod said through clenched teeth.

"We can see you and we're just teasing so don't get your dander up, cowboy. So you are here to help Emmett?" Daisy asked.

He wore his jeans just right, bunched up at the bottoms on top of cowboy boots that had been dusted off after a hard day's work. His blue knit shirt fit snugly over a broad expanse of chest and was tucked into the waistband of his jeans behind a silver belt buckle with a bull rider on the front. It was engraved but she didn't let her eyes linger long in that area.

"That's the general idea."

"Good. He shouldn't be out there alone," she said.

"Why not?" Jarod asked. "He's too tough for anything to hurt him."

Emmett nodded. "First thing he's said that I can agree with. Jarod's dad thought I needed help so he talked me into letting Jarod come on down here. God Almighty, ever since he got here he's been talking idiot notions about windmills and computers and the craziest thing is that he wants to bring a jackass on the property."

"Settle down, Emmett," Daisy said sternly. "Don't be workin' yourself up into a frenzy that'll cause a stroke. Ain't never had a death in the Honky Tonk and I ain't plannin' on one now."

Everyone went silent until Emmett chuckled. "She's a sassy little thing, ain't she? She's like my Mavis. Reminds me, Daisy. I looked on the calendar. You need to make a visit to the ranch. It's time. You can eat supper with us. Not tomorrow but the week after that. I'm going to hold you to your word."

"You been promising me for years you'd hire someone else. Sunday is my day to get things done around here," she said.

"Woman is only good as her word and you said that you'd be glad to help us until I could find someone. Ain't no one else I trust. You tellin' me your word ain't worth shit?" Emmett asked.

Daisy had been cornered and the only way out was straight ahead. "My word is good as gold, you cantankerous old goat. I'll eat if you make steaks and baked potatoes and corn on the cob. I'll bring dessert."

"Cherry cheesecake?" Emmett asked.

"You got it. The one from the freezer section at the grocery store. It'll have time to thaw out on the way.

I've got to get back to work now. You be good and don't be startin' any brawls. I run a decent place," she said.

"I could whip anyone in this joint," Emmett said.

"Don't doubt it one bit but if you feel the need to fight you get outside or I'll throw your sorry ass out myself. I won't even let Tinker do it. I don't abide brawls and you know it," Daisy reminded him as she headed toward the bar.

Jarod watched her go from the corner of his eye. Damn it all to hell on a silver platter. He'd never get her out of his mind with that visual firmly implanted there.

She heard Emmett telling the guys that Ruby didn't allow fightin' in the Honky Tonk either. She couldn't make out what Jarod said in response. They all laughed loudly and Emmett went on with another story. She wondered if it had anything to do with Ruby and would have loved to listen in but there was entirely too much noise.

"Well?" Chigger said.

"Well what?"

"Your cowboy make any moves?"

"He's not my cowboy and no he did not."

"You sure he's straight? Me or you, neither one affected him? Is he blind or just dumb?" Chigger said.

"He's straight and he's not blind or dumb. Emmett has sure gotten cantankerous in the past year. I'm figurin' Jarod has a woman stashed somewhere. Maybe a fiancée that he doesn't want to bring down here to meet Emmett for fear the old coot will run her off."

Chigger handed off the bar rag she'd been using to Daisy. "That Emmett always was a pistol. Mavis kept him in line. Now that she's gone, he's runnin' wild, so to speak. I wouldn't take Jarod's job for all the dirt in

Texas. Way I figure it is that when a person gets old they just become a bigger whatever they were when they were young. If they were sweet and kind then they become that kind of old folks that can't do enough for others. If they were an asshole like Emmett then it intensifies and they're unbearable as old people."

"How'd you get to be so smart?" Daisy asked.

"Fixin' hair. I can fix a girl's hair for the prom and tell you what she's going to be like when she's eighty," Chigger said.

"So what's Jarod going to be like when he's eighty?" Daisy asked.

Chigger giggled. "I knew you were interested. I shouldn't tell you but you got me on Momma's good side, so here goes. Jarod's got tunnel vision. When he sets his eyes on a woman, that's the only one he'll see the rest of his life. But he's got Emmett's genes in him too, which means there's a hell of a lot of fire and temper."

"And Jim Bob?"

"Like a big old cuddly teddy bear." Chigger winked.

"Then you aren't going to seduce him?" Daisy asked.

"Who we talkin' about? Jim Bob? I don't have to seduce him. He's ready all the time."

"You know who I'm talkin' about," Daisy said.

"Jarod? I gave you my word," Chigger said.

"You know what I think?"

Chigger smiled. "That I flirt with lots of men but I go home with Jim Bob and have for the past year?"

"You are a clairvoyant witch," Daisy said.

"Maybe so, but when Jim Bob finally catches me, he'll think he's won the lottery," Chigger said.

Daisy slowly shook her head from side to side. "Were you ever as wild as you claim?"

"Oh, yes, ma'am. Every bit, but that red-haired cowboy tamed me pretty quick and, honey, he's been just as wild as I have been so he can't ever play goody-two-shoes with me. I just don't want him to think I'm a pushover. If he has to work for the goods, they'll be a lot more valuable."

Daisy narrowed her blue eyes. "You never did intend to seduce Jarod, did you? It was just a story to get me to go meet your momma."

Chigger shrugged. "Guilty as charged. Got to go protect my cowboy now from the other women. Don't get mad. We're friends now. We wouldn't have been if you hadn't met Momma."

"How in the hell do you tell them apart? You could be going to bed with a different Walker triplet every night and not know the difference. That might be why you think he's so good in bed. You got three of them keeping you happy."

Chigger threw back her head and laughed. "Jim Bob is the best lookin' one of the three. Billy Bob has bigger ears and Joe Bob has a bigger nose. I know my man, girl, and he's the biggest Walker where it counts."

Daisy blushed. "Jesus, Mary, and Joseph!"

Chigger shook her finger at Daisy. "Momma will have to pray for your sorry ass if you keep talkin' like that. And here she thought you were such a sweet little lady."

"I don't think your momma's prayers make it past the ceiling. She's got to be getting calluses on her knees prayin' for you and look what the results are."

"Hell, honey, just think how bad I'd be if she wasn't prayin'," Chigger said.

"You got a point there. You ever figure out why they all got Bob for a middle name? Is their father's name Bob?"

"Naw, his name is Harlin and he's a sweetheart. Love his momma to death, too. They both think I'm just the ticket for their son. Jim Bob says they all got the middle name of Bob because his momma was so bumfuzzled at havin' three at one time she didn't know what to name them so she thought up first names and then put Bob on all of them. Actually, she told me one time that her maiden name was Roberts and the boys have real fine names. It's just that they got shortened down. Billy Bob is William Robert. Jim Bob is James Robert and Joe Bob is—"

"Joseph Robert," Daisy finished for her.

Chigger nodded. "The whole family is wealthy ranchers and oil men. You could do worse than Billy Bob, Daisy."

"Probably, but he don't make my little heart dance. I'm not ever settlin' for less than passion," Daisy admitted.

"That's right, sister. Have it all or take nothing," Chigger threw over her shoulder as she headed back toward the table where Jim Bob waited.

Daisy filled two jars with Miller beer and watched Chigger sashay across the floor. She said something to Emmett before she turned her attention to Jim Bob who popped up like a windup toy and led her to the dance floor. Daisy wished she had life by the horns as well as Chigger did.

At midnight she turned around to find Jarod leaning on the bar at the far end. She made her way to him, filling a couple of orders as she went. "What can I get for you?"

"Nothing. I'm taking Uncle Emmett home. He's tuckered out. I just wanted to tell you that you don't have to come to dinner that Sunday. He'll forget all about it by tomorrow. The Alzheimer's gets worse every day. He'd argue with a stop sign. I swear he would."

Daisy could have listened to him talk for hours. His deep voice mesmerized her. Her eyes were half closed and a smile tickled the edges of her full mouth as her imagination ran rampant. Would his voice go even deeper if he was in bed with her and whispering sweet things in her ear as he nibbled his way to her lips?

"Did you hear me?" he asked.

"Sorry. My mind was somewhere else." She blushed. "I gave my word and I'll be there. I was joking about the beef steak. I will definitely bring the cheesecake in case he remembers. It's no trouble. I'll just pick one up at the grocery store."

"I'd rather you didn't. What did he mean it was time for you to come out there?" he asked.

"It isn't your ranch and what goes on is between me and Emmett. You don't want to be there for dinner, that's fine. Go somewhere else. Why are you staying anyway if you don't want to be there?"

Jarod shook his head. "Don't call it dinner. It's supper. He'll really go off the deep end if you call it dinner. That's the noon meal. And I'm there because he needs help. My dad will probably sell the place or else give it to one of the grandsons when Emmett is gone."

"It's the old way of thinkin'. He's just holdin' on to what he knows. Why aren't you going to keep the ranch?"

"I don't want it. I refuse to let it dry up and blow away, but I damn sure don't want to live in this godforsaken country. And you got that right about him holdin' on to what he knows. He won't let go of a damn thing. Guess I'll see you a week from tomorrow."

"That's your choice. I'll be there. You decide where you'll be," she said.

"Sassy piece of baggage, aren't you?"

"I am what you see."

He let her have the last word and made his way through the dwindling crowd for the door where Emmett was shuffling along with his walkers, in the plural sense of the word. He had his aluminum walker surrounding him. Jim Bob Walker was on one side, Joe Bob on the other, and Billy Bob held the door open for him. Jarod wondered if it wouldn't solve a whole hell of a lot of problems if he went back to Oklahoma and let Emmett bequeath his ranch to the Walker brothers.

Daisy shut the doors at two o'clock. She popped the top off a bottle of beer, propped her legs up on a table, and went back over the night's events. Every single thought either began with a vision of Jarod or something he said.

"Damn it," she swore and attempted to turn her thoughts away from him by thinking about the Honky Tonk. The beer joint had been good to her, had given her a job and a family of sorts. What was a family anyway? A bunch of people connected by a bloodline? Well, the Honky Tonk was home to a bunch of people connected by friendship. That could make a family, couldn't it?

She raised her bottle up in a toast. "Ruby, I don't know what in the hell you saw in me that day, but I'm glad for everything you did. Thank you. You changed my life. Now could you erase that sexy man out of my heart and mind?" Daisy asked.

She started across the floor when a hard pounding on the front door caused her to change course in the middle of the room. Before she took two steps, they hit the door again, this time harder and longer. She swung it open, expecting to see a Mingus citizen with a cat that had been hit on the road and needed to either be sewn up, bones set, or put to sleep. She hoped it wasn't the latter; she still got misty-eyed when she had to put an animal down.

"You didn't even ask who was here. You got a death wish or something?" Jarod asked.

"What do you want? And it's none of your business what I do."

"Uncle Emmett left his wallet on the table back there. I told him you'd find it and I'd come back tomorrow but he can't sleep until it's safe in his hands. I asked him what was in it and he said Aunt Mavis' picture when she was a young woman."

"Well, come on in and find it," she said.

Jarod went straight for the table. The wallet had been kicked back against the wall. He held it up for Daisy to see. He damned sure didn't want her to think he'd invented an excuse to come back to see her that late. He'd tried every argument in the world to keep from driving fifteen miles back to the Honky Tonk at two thirty in the morning. He'd been sound asleep when he heard Uncle Emmett yelling at him from the bottom of the stairs. He'd thought the old guy was sick or had fallen. Adrenaline had shot through his veins like lightning and he didn't even remember how he'd gotten to the living room, but he could have strangled Uncle Emmett when he heard what the commotion was all about.

"Can't sleep so I wanted to talk to Mavis and when I do I look at that picture. It's at the Honky Tonk. You go get it right now," Emmett had said.

"I can't go back there now. The place closes at two o'clock. Besides, that bartender will find it and put it up for you," Jarod had argued.

"Daisy isn't just a bartender, boy. She's a fine woman. Why, one time your Aunt Mavis even said that she'd make you a wonderful wife. You could do a hell of a lot worse in this world than Daisy O'Dell."

"I wasn't being snide or condescending."

"That ain't what I heard. I heard you say 'bartender' like it was dirty."

When he'd exhausted every excuse in the world, he'd dressed and gone to retrieve the wallet. Now he felt pretty stupid standing there with it in his hands.

"Lock the door and ask who's there before you answer it," he said.

"Don't tell me what to do."

"You aren't big enough to stop someone from hurting you."

"Good night, Mr. McElroy."

She'd no more locked the door and started back across the dance floor when he knocked hard again. She slung the door open. "This is not funny."

"You need to ask."

"You need to mind your own business."

"What if I'd been drunk and rushed inside to hurt you?"

"Try it," she said.

He took two steps forward only to find a sawed off shotgun pressed firmly in his ribs. He held up his hands in surrender, his left one still holding Emmett's wallet.

"How'd you do that?"

"I told you not to worry. I can take care of myself. Just remember that it's loaded at all times. Permit to have it is posted right beside my license behind the bar. And I'm not one bit afraid to use it."

"Did you ever have to?" he asked.

Not only was Daisy full of sass, she was brassy as hell.

"Not at the Honky Tonk. Now go on home and take Emmett his picture. Bar is closed at two o'clock and I'm too tired to play these games with you," she said.

"What'd you mean, not at the Honky Tonk?" he asked.

"That's my business. Good night, Jarod." She shoved him out the door and locked it behind him.

She went back into the apartment and poured a bowl of Lucky Charms cereal.

Lucky.

Charms.

Two words she didn't really believe in. A person made their own destiny. Their choices brought their consequences. Luck was a figment of someone's imagination. Charm? Well, some folks had it. She, like Emmett, did not.

She'd always figured that she'd used up her share of luck when she landed at the Honky Tonk. And she'd never been accused of having much charm. That was her mother's claim to fame. So charming that she had three husbands and too many boyfriends to count before she died in a car wreck at the age of thirty-seven.

She filled her mouth with the cereal and looked at the leprechaun on the front of the box as she chewed. Suddenly the critter had Jarod's face. She moaned. She had to get him out of her mind or else he was going to drive her crazy as an outhouse rat.

Chapter 4

THE WIND BLOWS CONSTANTLY IN TEXAS. COLD WIND in the winter months, warm breezes in the spring, and then June comes and it feels like it's coming straight out of a bake oven with the temperature going from hot to hotter to hottest as July passes a day at a time.

Daisy slathered sunblock all over her pale skin, donned as few clothes as possible, and fired up the lawn mower. The backyard wasn't very big, but by the time she finished mowing the temperature had raised in direct proportion to how sweaty she'd gotten. She put the mower back into the garage, wiping at her forehead with a bandana she'd tucked into the back pocket of a pair of cutoff jeans. She sat down on the small back porch shaded by one lonesome old scrub oak tree and fanned herself with the damp bandana. A tall glass of sweet tea sounded wonderful but she'd have to make a pitcher.

The cell phone in her pocket began to vibrate and she fished it out.

"Hello."

"Miz Daisy, Runt is down and havin' trouble gettin' the baby out. Momma said to call you."

Daisy recognized the voice immediately. It was Tommy Joe Horton and Runt was his show goat for the 4-H club.

"You reckon I need to come out there and help?" she asked.

"Yes, ma'am. Wait a minute. Momma is hollerin'. She says that Runt has got the baby out now and it's breathin'. Thanks, Miz Daisy. I knew things would be all right if I talked to you."

"You are very welcome, Tommy Joe. Take care of the new baby."

"I will."

She shoved the phone into her pocket and leaned her head back against the porch post. A coyote howled out in the woods beyond the area she mowed. Hounds bayed to the north. Before she could figure out if the hounds were actually chasing the coyote, another noise obliterated everything.

It sounded like a thresher coming up the road but it was too early for wheat harvest. When the thing turned off the highway and into the Honky Tonk parking lot, she stood up and peeked around the end of the building. She shaded her eyes with the back of her hand and watched an old Ford pickup rumble right up to the back porch.

She was already headed for the door to get her black bag when Chigger crawled out of the passenger seat and yelled, "Hey, Daisy!"

"Good grief!" She stopped and looked again. Surely there weren't two identical trucks in Palo Pinto County running on rust, dirt, and prayers.

Chigger crawled out of the passenger side of the truck. "What're you doin'?"

"You buy that truck from Henry Green?" Daisy asked.

"Yep, I did," Jim Bob yelled from the driver's window. The truck had been white at one time but now it was covered with rust spots. The front bumper had long since fallen off and the tailgate was gone. "It's my new fishin' wagon."

Chigger winked. "Cute, ain't it? We come to take you fishin' with us. We got beer and pop and bologna sandwiches."

Chigger wore jean shorts cut off so short the pockets hung below the denim, a pink tank top, and her signature pink cowboy boots.

"It's too damn hot to fish. And why'd Henry sell his truck?"

"Cause he bought a newer one," Jim Bob said.

"It's not too hot where we're goin'." Chigger stuck a cigarette in her mouth and cupped one hand around the lighter to keep the wind from blowing out the flame.

"You goin' to be fishin' under air conditioning?" Daisy asked.

Chigger took a deep drag. "No, but there's shade trees all around the pond and Jim Bob says if we catch anything he'll cook them for supper and catfish is my favorite meal. Besides, I told Momma the reason I wasn't comin' home for church is because I was going with you over to the Mingus church this mornin' and we were goin' fishin' afterwards. You goin' to make a liar out of me?"

"I don't have to. You do a fine job of that yourself," Daisy said.

"Way I see it is you got two choices. Either get your ass up off that porch and in the truck with us, or else Jim Bob will come throw you over his shoulder and put you in the truck. All you do is bartend and run around the whole country fixin' folks' ailin' animals. You need a day of fun. What's it goin' to be?"

"You already lied. You didn't go to church with me. What's one more matter?"

"God overlooks one little white lie. He don't abide two, especially on Sunday. You got to pee, you better go before we leave because it's about fifteen miles to the pond and I'm guaran-damn-teein' you, that truck will give your bladder a workin' out. If you got to go out there you'll be squattin' behind a mesquite tree and usin' a McDonald's napkin for toilet paper," Chigger said.

"I don't own a fishin' pole," Daisy said.

"We got a dozen in the back of the truck and we dug worms for bait before we left Jim Bob's place. You mean enough to bait your own hook?"

"I can put a worm on a hook."

"Then let's go," Chigger said.

Jim Bob leaned out of the driver's open window and yelled, "Do I need to come on over there and help persuade her?"

Chigger shook her head. "Naw, I think I've got her talked into it."

"Okay, okay, I'll go fishin'," Daisy said. "But I've got to go inside and get my purse and my bag. I better take my car."

Chigger eyed her suspiciously. "Promise you won't lock the door and stay in there."

"You got my word on it. I'll go fishin' with you. I just need to get things."

"You ain't goin' in your car. Whole reason to have a fishin' truck is to go fishin' in it or maybe use the bed for lookin' at the stars at night." Chigger giggled softly.

"If I have to make an animal run, you going to drive me?"

"Yep, I am. I can drive a stick shift good as Jim Bob. If you have to go sew up a dog's leg or take care of a horse, I'll take you."

"Okay, I'm holdin' you to it." Daisy went inside to get her emergency bag and purse. She thought about cleaning up but figured she didn't look a bit worse than Chigger or that rattle trap truck.

"I wasn't sure you'd keep your word," Chigger said from inside the door when she reached the living room.

"I always keep my word. Didn't I go meet your momma?"

Chigger smiled. "Yep, you did. Why don't you leave that cell phone and bag at home today? How long's it been since you just had an afternoon with no calls?"

"What if someone needs me?"

"They can call the vet out of Stephenville and pay for a weekend emergency call. Come on, Daisy. One day with no phone or bag."

"Can't do it. I'll compromise. I'll go fishin' but I'll take my bag and my phone. Couldn't live with myself if something happened and I could have helped."

"That's not a compromise."

Daisy picked up the bag. "It's the best I'm going to do."

Chigger led the way to the truck and scooted across the seat to sit in the middle. "Then I'll be satisfied with that much. Grab a beer out of the red cooler. You look hot as hell and I don't mean in the take-me-to-bed hot, but weather-hot."

Daisy followed behind her and set her vet bag behind two tackle boxes.

"Y'all want one?" She brought an icy cold can of beer from a cooler.

"No thanks," Chigger said.

Daisy pulled the tab and gulped a couple of times before she hopped up into the seat beside Chigger. "You sure this thing will go fifteen miles? I'm going to be one pissed off woman if I have to walk home in this heat."

Jim Bob grinned. "Trust me, she's a lot sturdier than she looks. Sounds like a thrasher and looks like hell but it's a fine fishin' wagon."

South of Thurber, Jim Bob took a dirt road and dust boiled up around them as thick as cigarette smoke in the Honky Tonk on a busy night. It rolled behind the truck then chased after them, scattering all over the cow tongue cactus lining the sides of the road and drifting into the cab of the truck. It stuck to the sweat on Daisy's face and neck and smeared when she wiped at it.

Chigger left a dirt smudge when she swatted a mosquito on her neck. "If someone could figure out a casserole dish to make from cow tongue cactus, they could make a fortune. You got any bright ideas about how to cook up cactus, Daisy?"

"Not me. How about you?"

"Well, if we can't cook the sumbitches maybe we could figure out a way to boil them down and use them to run car and truck engines. Save a hell of a lot on gas. Or if we could figure out a way to make mosquito repellent out of it, we could make a fortune." Chigger smashed another bug on her bare arm, leaving a dime-sized blood stain.

Jim Bob slung his right arm around her shoulders and drove with his left hand. "That's my girl. Ain't she the smartest thing you've ever seen?"

"I don't know. If it killed mosquitoes it might kill Chiggers and then she'd be in big trouble. What are we doing here?" Daisy finished the last sip of beer and looked up at Emmett McElroy's house.

"Fishin'," Chigger said innocently.

Jim Bob took a cell phone from the bib pocket of his overalls and poked numbers. "Hey, we're here. We're goin' on down to the pond. Got enough fishin' poles and worms for all of us so don't go tryin' to hunt up any of Uncle Emmett's. Bring him along. Seeing Chigger might sweeten him up the rest of the day."

Daisy poked Chigger in the arm. "Who is he talking to?"

"Shhh, he can't hear on that phone if there's noise around him," Chigger said.

"Well, then let the old codger sleep if he's too stubborn to leave the air conditioning." Jim Bob flipped the phone shut.

Chigger looked at Daisy. "He was talkin' to Jarod. He lets us fish in his pond and Jim Bob is askin' him if he wants to go with us."

"You did this on purpose. You are a bitch from hell," Daisy said.

Chigger winked. "You are one fickle friend. You just agreed with Jim Bob that I'm the smartest thing either of you ever saw."

"I did not agree with him. I didn't answer at all."

"That's agreeing. You didn't disagree."

Daisy looked down at her scuffed up cowboy boots, the worst pair in her closet. Her jean shorts were like Chigger's—cut off so short the pockets hung below the denim, only Daisy's had paint splotches on them as well as dirt and sweat. Her red cotton halter top was faded and speckled with paint too.

Chigger grinned. "If you don't like that cowboy then why does it matter that you look like shit?"

"Thank you so much," Daisy grumbled.

Jim Bob stomped the clutch and put the car in first gear. "Well, I think both of you are sexy as hell in them getups. Fish will come up to the top just to cop a look at the two prettiest women in the whole state."

Chigger kissed him on the cheek and whispered something in his ear that caused him to chuckle.

Daisy looked out the window and wished she'd shot them both with her sawed off shotgun. All that sweet talk and love cooped up in the cab of a truck when she couldn't shake a vision of Jarod from her mind was downright sinful.

Jim Bob parked the truck under a big oak tree, opened the door, and Chigger slid across the seat and under the steering wheel into his waiting arms. He kissed her so hard that Daisy blushed.

Chigger grinned at Daisy when the kiss ended. "Might as well stop poutin' and get out. Who knows, maybe you'll get a kiss today."

"You are really a bitch from hell," Daisy seethed as she got out and helped carry a couple of quilts and fishing gear to the enormous pond not a hundred feet away from the truck. A gentle breeze teased the tall grasses in the pasture and the white clouds dotted the broad expanse of blue sky above her head.

Chigger shook a quilt out and it floated down to the earth, wrinkle free. Jim Bob brought the coolers, one at a time, and set them on the quilt. Then he brought a

CD player and a small black case and handed them to Chigger. She flipped through the case and found the CD she wanted, put it in the player, and cranked up music from Toby Keith. She had her hands above her head and was moving in time to the music by the time Jim Bob had a worm threaded on his hook.

Chigger motioned toward the extra rods. "Might as well bait a hook. We ain't goin' home until we catch supper or dark, whichever one comes first."

Daisy grabbed the extra quilt that Chigger had tossed to one side, threw it over her shoulder, picked up a rod and reel with one hand and a hand full of wiggling earth worms with the other, and circled the pond to the other side. She was at their mercy when it came to transportation, but she'd be damned if she'd be nice about it.

She laid the earth worms on the ground and they all immediately began to wiggle their way into the earth. She hurriedly tossed out her quilt, not giving a damn if it was wrinkle free or not, grabbed the worms, and shoved them into the zippered pocket on the outside of her purse, baited the hook, pressed the release button on the reel, and threw the line out into the pond.

"You goin' to pout all afternoon?" Chigger yelled when the music stopped.

Daisy nodded.

Chigger laughed.

She heard a truck in the distance and grimaced as Jarod parked his shiny white truck next to the old one.

"Hey, everyone. Looks like you're already set up," he called out. He wore bibbed overalls over a white gauze undershirt. The overalls were faded and worn, but that didn't make her feel a bit better about the way she looked.

He gathered up fishing equipment from the other side of the pond and slowly made his way to her quilt. In that getup she looked like Daisy from the old *Dukes of Hazzard* television show. The reaction his fickle body had to the sight of her standing there with one hip cocked out, sweat glistening on her body, and those long shapely legs made him damn glad he was wearing baggy overalls.

"Why are you pouting?" he asked.

"Who said I'm pouting?"

"Chigger did and said I was to come over here and make you laugh."

Daisy glared across the pond.

"Where's the bait?"

"In the zippered part of my purse," she said.

Jarod threw back his head and laughed. "What in the devil are they doing in your purse?"

It wasn't funny but his deep laughter was infectious. At first it was just a schoolgirl giggle and then it was a full-fledged laughter blending with his and floating on the wind across the pond.

"You did good," Chigger yelled.

Jarod gave her a thumb's up sign. "She's got worms in her purse," he shouted.

Chigger and Jim Bob both got tickled.

"I couldn't toss out the quilt and hold them both. When I put them down they started to wiggle back into the earth so I put them in my purse. You got a problem with that?" Daisy asked.

"No, ma'am," Jarod chuckled.

Music floated on the wind across the pond. Toby sang about getting on down to the main attraction with a little less talk and a lot more action. It was the hot wind heating up Daisy's body, or so she kept telling herself. But honesty prevailed after a few seconds and she admitted it was really Jarod's presence that had her sweating even more than normal. Damn, but he was sexy even in overalls and scuffed up boots.

He fished a worm from her purse, wound it around a hook, and flipped the line out into the pond. He stole long glances at her from behind his sunglasses. No makeup. Hair escaping her ponytail and sticking to her sweaty, dirt-smudged face. Shorts with paint speckles, and the bare minimum of a top that looked like Aunt Mavis' mop rag. And still she was beautiful.

"Didn't know you and Chigger were fishin' buddies?" he asked.

"She's my worst enemy," Daisy said.

"Then why are you spending your Sunday afternoon with her?"

"That's the six-million dollar question. How's Emmett?"

"I wanted to bring him along but he said Sunday was a day for resting and I was crazy to go out in the heat when we had good cold air in the house and fish in the freezer. Back when I was a kid he'd spend the whole day out in the heat. Didn't even have an air conditioned cab on his tractor. Come in covered in dirt and singing Hank Williams songs, grab Aunt Mavis around the waist and dance all over the kitchen with her. Old age isn't for sissies. It's tough," Jarod said.

Daisy nodded. "He went down fast when Mavis died."

"You got older relatives like him?"

Daisy shook her head. "Nope. Momma died in a car wreck at the age of thirty-seven. Granny died when she was forty-five. My folks didn't live long enough to see if they'd be sissies or not."

"Your dad?" Jarod asked.

"Army. Died before I was born."

"I'm sorry. You all that's left?"

"You're lookin' at it except for one cousin up in Mena, Arkansas."

"I've got this big family up in Payne County, Oklahoma. Two brothers. Mom. Dad. Nieces. Nephews. Even two great nephews. All ranchin' folks," he said.

"So why are you here?"

"As in here today or here permanently?"

"Both."

"Aunt Mavis took a shine to me when I was a kid. She and Uncle Emmett didn't have children so they kind of adopted me. She wanted my dad to have this sorry excuse for a ranch and Uncle Emmett finally agreed to let me move in and help. I'm the only one of Dad's three sons without a wife and kids so it was easier for me to move in with him and help out," Jarod said.

"What makes it a sorry excuse for a ranch?" Daisy asked.

"I guess Aunt Mavis got too tired to make Uncle Emmett work at it a few years ago. It needs updating to be productive. The land is good for running cattle and making hay, but not if we don't control the mesquite. Good ranchin' requires a lot of hard work."

"What would you do different?"

"Windmills for one thing. Save a bunch of money if we harness the wind that blows down here all the time and use it for electricity to run the pumps for water and irrigation and that would raise the value of the ranch. We've been using them for a couple of years now. A donkey for another," he said.

She turned her head quickly. "A donkey?"

"Sure. They hate coyotes and mountain lions. They're nature's best damn protection for new calves in the world. Let something come into the pasture threatening the calves and the donkey will take care of it faster than you would with that sawed off shotgun."

"I know that but I figured you'd be one of those all-business types who wouldn't think about natural protection. Why wouldn't Emmett want to get one? They don't require much upkeep."

"It's not his idea and God forbid doing anything that wasn't his idea first," Jarod said.

"Hey, y'all want a beer?" Chigger called from the other side of the pond.

"Love one," Jarod said.

"Daisy?" she asked.

"I'm not talkin' to you but I'd like a beer," she said.

"Then come and get it. If you ain't talkin' to me then I'll be damned if I carry a beer over to you," she said.

"I'll go get a couple if you'll watch my rod," Jarod said.

Daisy blushed at the comment about watching his rod. She'd like to watch any part of him in any stage of dress or undress at any time of day or night. Rod, as some romance writers called it in her sexy romance books, thighs, butt, biceps, broad chest; she'd watch any or all of it.

Jarod had a beer in each hand and was halfway around the pond when Jim Bob started yelling, "I got a big one. I ain't peelin' potatoes tonight."

Before Daisy could ask what peeling potatoes had to do with catching a fish, Jarod's bobble went under.

Daisy grabbed his pole and yelled, "We got one over here too."

Jarod hollered as he picked up his speed. "Not we. That's my equipment."

"Well, get over here and pull it in or I'm claimin' it," Daisy said.

"Bet it's not as big as mine. If it was, Daisy would be out in the water by now," Jim Bob challenged.

Jarod set the beers on the pallet and reached for the rod and reel.

Their fingers brushed and Daisy forced herself not to jerk her hand back from the heat between them. Her blue eyes locked with his gray ones and he started forward, almost tasting the sweetness of the kiss, when the rod jumped in his hand. Right then he didn't give a damn if the biggest blasted catfish in all of Erath County was on the end of his line. He would have given it up for one of Daisy's kisses.

He fought the line but it was a chore to keep his mind on the fish when Daisy was so close. Beating Jim Bob wasn't the big issue anymore. Like those Norman Rockwell pictures of little boys trying to win little girls' favors, Jarod wanted to win the contest to show off for Daisy. If he couldn't feel her lips on his, then by damn he ought to catch the biggest fish. It was a poor second place and it confused him as to why he wanted to kiss her so much, but he damn sure did.

"Hey, look at this!" Jim Bob held up a catfish that easily weighed five pounds. "I'd say we're havin' a fish fry tonight. Jarod, you're on for the potatoes."

"Not if my fish is bigger than yours," Jarod yelled.

The line grew so taut that Daisy thought it would break. The rod bent into an arc. Jarod gave the fish some line and let it run.

"Mercy, I feel like I'm deep sea fishing. This thing must be the moaf," he said.

"What is a moaf? Be careful, it's going to shake that hook out. You've got to reel him in," Daisy squealed.

"A moaf is the mother of all fish." Jarod reeled fast and the fish flopped five feet from the bank. The line went slack and the adrenaline rush left Daisy. It returned in a flash when the rod arced again and Jarod began reeling. She wrapped her hand over his on the rod without thinking. Jarod had to win just so she'd have one-up on Chigger for tricking her that day.

"Pull," Jarod said.

They jerked the rod back at the same time and a catfish flopped up on the bank. It flipped around desperately trying to find its way back into the water and to dislodge the hook, but Jarod grabbed it and held it up for the rivals across the pond to see.

"Ours is bigger," Daisy chanted.

Jarod grinned. She'd said "our" fish was bigger, not Jarod's, not mine, but *ours*. He liked the sound of that.

"Not until we measure it," Chigger yelled. "I'm not trusting you."

"You trusting me. That's the pot calling the kettle black, sister."

Jarod carried the fish around the pond and he and Jim Bob laid them out for measurements. Jarod's was six inches longer and about a pound heavier.

"Don't look so smug," Chigger said.

Daisy shrugged. "Payback."

"I'll teach you payback," Chigger said. "You're fightin' with the big girls now, honey."

"You girls stop spittin' at each other. Let's take 'em home and clean 'em up," Jim Bob said.

"Girls or fish?" Jarod asked, his eyes twinkling, making Daisy smile in spite of herself.

Daisy slapped his shoulder. "That was mean."

"I told you that you look like shit," Chigger said.

Jarod ogled Daisy. He looked long and hard at her from boot tips to the top of her dark hair. He wanted her, plain and simple. He couldn't have her, just as plain and simple.

"What are you lookin' at?" she snapped.

"Prettiest pile of shit I've ever seen." He grinned.

She folded her arms across her chest. "That's the most underhanded compliment I've ever heard."

"It ain't a compliment. It's a fact," Jarod said and turned to Jim Bob. "I'll check on Uncle Emmett then drive on over to your house. Be there before you get the first filleted and I'm talking about the fish," Jarod said.

"You bring Daisy with you. She's got to get her things gathered up," Chigger said to Jarod and then tapped Daisy on the shoulder. "Remember paybacks are hell."

Daisy took off in a fast jog around the pond, threw everything including her purse into the middle of the quilt, and gathered it up into a hobo type bag… but not fast enough. Jim Bob and Chigger were driving away by the time she jogged back to the other side. They had her bag in the back of his old work truck. Damn it all, anyway. If she did get a call she'd have to go to Jim Bob's place before she could go anywhere.

Jarod leaned against his truck. "Guess you are going with me."

Daisy was tongue-tied. Words simply would not go from her brain to her mouth. What she wanted to do was kick something, preferably Chigger, and cuss a blue streak, but she was totally speechless. One thing for absolute sure, Chigger was going to fry the next time she came into the Honky Tonk.

Jarod held the door for her. "Crawl on in here. At least I've got air conditioning. Can't imagine why Jim Bob brought that old work truck out today. His new club cab has all the bells and whistles." If he'd been the one picking Daisy up for a day of fishing, he'd damn sure have shown up in something nice. He imagined her sitting close to him, her hand on his thigh as he drove.

Damn, damn, and double damn, he swore silently. *I've got to get this shit out of my head.*

Daisy hopped into the seat. Jarod didn't snarl his nose at the smell of her so she guessed her deodorant was still working. He shut the door, circled behind the truck, and got inside.

"I really do need to check on Uncle Emmett. That all right with you?" he said.

"Would it make any difference if it wasn't?"

"Not a bit. I'm just being polite. Why are you so prickly anyway?"

"I'm not," she lied.

"Yes you are. I'm just giving you a ride. That's all." She didn't answer.

Emmett was sitting on the porch when Jarod parked. He waved and yelled, "Come on in."

She got out of the truck, crossed the yard, and propped her elbows on the porch rail. "Hot today, ain't it?"

"You need to wear more clothes. You ain't decent," Emmett said.

"That's my business, isn't it?"

"Woman oughtn't to go around naked. It'll cause talk."

"Still my business."

"I'm tellin' you, my boy in there, he ain't blind. You dress like that you're askin' for stuff."

"What stuff?" Daisy asked.

Emmett's face turned splotchy red. "You are a vet, girl. Don't you play dumb with me. You know what I'm talkin' about."

"I was mowing the yard and Chigger said we were going fishin'. I didn't know your boy was going to be anywhere around," she said quickly. "Don't be havin' a heart attack because I'm not covered from head to toe."

Emmett pointed at her. "Is he takin' you home? If he is, you put on a robe."

"We're going to Jim Bob's place to fry fish. You come with us and you can make sure *your boy* don't get the wrong ideas about me."

"You tell Jim Bob to give you a robe or a sheet and you wrap up in it," Emmett said. "You ain't decent. I'm not going anywhere. If there's leftovers you make Jarod bring me some for dinner tomorrow. You put on something other than your underwear when you come and vaccinate my herd."

"I'll wear my jeans and shirt. That make you happy?"

"I don't care if you wear long handles, long as your skin is covered. And bring the cheesecake?"

"I'll do it."

Emmett leaned forward and whispered, "Is my nephew courtin' you? If he is, he'll think you are a loose woman in them duds."

"Hell, no. We just wound up at the same fishin' pond together. Chigger invited me and Jim Bob invited him."

Emmett leaned back and rubbed his chin. "Better watch them two. They'll hoodwink you."

"I don't doubt it a minute."

"Still runnin' all over hell and half this part of Texas fixin' broke animals?"

"Pretty much," Daisy said. Damn, she hadn't even thought to check her phone for missed calls, and it was tangled up in the quilt with all the fishing gear and her purse full of worms. She'd have to dig it out at Jim Bob's place and see if anyone had an emergency.

Emmett shook a finger at her. "You ain't getting' no younger, Daisy. It's time you gave up that damned old beer joint and that vet stuff and settled down. You could do worse than my nephew."

"Not interested," Daisy said.

"You better listen to me."

"Why?"

"Because I said so."

Jarod carried a ten-pound bag of potatoes out the door. He'd taken time to change clothes and water droplets hung to his dark hair testifying that he'd even showered. His jeans were worn and soft. All three of his shirt buttons were undone, giving a peek at enough chest hair to make Daisy's breath catch in her chest.

She felt even more frumpy.

"You want to go with us over to Jim Bob's for a fish supper?" Jarod asked Emmett.

"Hell no. I already told Daisy, I'm not going anywhere."

Jarod stopped at the edge of Emmett's chair. "Let me help you back inside where it's cool then."

"I got myself out here and I'll damn sure get myself back inside. Get out of here before Daisy changes her mind and stays here with me," he snapped.

"I'll see you later then." Jarod didn't want to fight or joke with Emmett. The day had been the best he'd had since he'd arrived in Texas. He damn sure didn't want to spoil it.

"Don't make a lot of noise when you come in tonight. You wake me up and I'm going to gripe about it," Emmett said.

Jarod let him have the last word and followed Daisy back out to the truck. She opened the door and was in the passenger's side with her seat belt on by the time he got there.

"So you're bringing potatoes after all?" she asked.

"Sure, but I'm not peeling them."

"Why not? You're going to help clean the fish. What's the difference?"

"Matter of honor. I caught the biggest fish. Peeling potatoes is grunt work," he told her.

"Since when?"

"It's a contest from when we were kids. I fished a lot with the Walkers. Aunt Mavis had a rule. Whoever brought in the smallest catch peeled the potatoes."

"I didn't catch anything so I'll peel the potatoes," she said.

"Honey, a fish fry is a man thing. You ladies will not lift a finger. We'll do the cooking tonight. All you and

Chigger have to do is tell us how wonderful it tastes and look pretty."

Her heart caught in her chest when he used an endearment whether he meant it as such or not. Why couldn't she have such a reaction when Billy Bob called her the same thing? Why couldn't she look into *his* eyes and have the desire to drag him off to bed? Not one blasted thing was right in her world anymore.

Chapter 5

JIM BOB LIVED IN A TRAILER SET BACK IN A COPSE OF pecan trees, surrounded by a wide porch across the front scattered with rocking chairs of every color and description. The back side sported a deck twice as big as the trailer overlooking a pond as big as a small lake. Angus cattle watered at the pond; two Catahoula dogs lazed on the deck and kept watch on the cattle; five cats, all variations of black and white, slept on the patio furniture.

It wasn't Daisy's first time at Jim Bob's place. She'd been there often when he had the need for a vet, but she'd never been inside the trailer. She quickly let herself out of the truck, reached into the bed, and dragged the quilt close enough to retrieve her purse. She unzipped the side pocket and turned all the worms loose up next to the porch where Chigger sat in a rocker with two cats in her lap.

Jarod stood by and watched. "Anything else you need before I go help Jim Bob?"

Like maybe a hug or a nice long kiss?

"No."

Why didn't you ask me that before we had an audience of a dozen animals and Chigger and Jim Bob?

Jarod headed toward a shed south of the trailer where Jim Bob was busy cleaning and filleting the two fish.

"You two fightin'?" Chigger asked.

"Nope." Daisy melted into a rocking chair with wide arms. One cat jumped into her lap and purred as she rubbed its head and ears. "It's about time for your shots, old girl."

"I'm not takin' any shots." Chigger shivered. "Why'd you say something like that?"

"If there was a shot for deviousness and loosc-leggedness, I'd hold you down and give it to you. But I was talking to the cat," Daisy said.

Chigger giggled. "Afraid it might be contagious?"

Daisy frowned. "What?"

"Loose-legged. Have you been thinkin' naughty things when you see Jarod lookin' like sex on a stick? Hot damn! And you're afraid it might be contagious, ain't you? Well, it is. I drank out of your water jar you keep behind the bar last week. The very next night you attacked Jarod and made him fall on top of you to see how it felt. Got to hand it to you, it was a wonderful idea. I'll have to try it sometime."

"You are horrible." Daisy forced herself not to grin.

"Be careful what you call me. Horrible might be as contagious as loose-legged. Still pouting?"

Daisy kicked off her boots and drew her feet up under her. "I might pout for a week. Why on earth did you do this?"

"Wanted to see if I was contagious for real. The fall on the floor might have been an accident so I decided to put you two together outside the bar. It worked and I was right. I can infect any woman I want to with my sexiness. I'll have to be very careful not to drink out of the water fountain in Momma's church. But hey, I can always sell my gift to homely girls. They can give me a sip of their beer or daiquiri and I'll spread sexy all over the place. Besides, you never know if oil and vinegar will mix until you put them together."

Daisy wondered if maybe Chigger was right. Jarod did look like sex on a stick and the thoughts dancing through her mind sure enough weren't Sunday-school clean. "Oil and vinegar never mix unless you shake them up and then it's only for a little while," she said.

"Guess today is the shaking process then. Would you stop pouting if I said you could take a shower?"

"What good would that do? I didn't bring extra clothes."

Daisy would have promised to never pout again for a change of clothes and a shower, but she didn't want to give Chigger that much satisfaction.

"I keep clothes here. I got a sundress back there with a stretchy top on it. There's a brand new pack of bikini underwear in the drawer so you can have a pair of them," Chigger said.

"Are you going to clean up?"

Chigger nodded. "Hell, yeah. I plan to get all pretty and seduce Jim Bob one more time before I go home tonight. I damn sure don't want him to remember me smelling like pond water and sweat. There's two bedrooms in this place. You want the second one to shake up the oil and vinegar real good?"

"Hell, no!"

"It's your call. Now about that pouting?"

Daisy moaned. "You win. I'll stop pouting for a shower and new underpants and the use of your sundress."

Chigger stood up and stretched like a wild lioness. The woman had more complex sides than a soap opera heroine. Hollywood was missing a dang good mini-series idea by not coming to Erath County, Texas, and paying her big bucks for her life's story.

Daisy followed Chigger into the trailer and down a short hallway where she opened the door into a bathroom. "Towels and washcloths are under the sink. I keep a basket on the back of the potty with all my oils and soaps. Use whatever you like. While you shower I'll hang the dress on the hook on the back of the door and put the panties on the countertop. And if you pout again all night, I'll make you give them back right where you stand."

Daisy's eyes glittered. "You and whose army?"

Chigger laughed. "You might be mean, but darlin', I'm a helluva lot bigger than you. Push comes to shove, I'll jerk the dress and panties off you and Jarod can take you home naked."

"Jarod is not taking me home," Daisy said.

Chigger giggled as she shut the door.

Daisy adjusted the water in the shower, left her clothing on the floor, and stepped under the cool water. She washed her shoulder-length dark brown hair and conditioned it. Using one of the disposable razors in Chigger's basket, she shaved her legs. When she finished, she wrapped a towel around her head and another around her body. Sure enough, there was a package of new bikini underwear on the counter and what passed for a sundress on the back of the door. As tall as Chigger was, if she'd worn that thing for a dress it would have shown her underpants.

"Or lack of them," Daisy muttered as she picked up Chigger's hair dryer and worked on her hair. She noticed mascara and blush lying on the countertop and used it too; stopping pouting came at a great price. She dropped the towel and found that the underwear fit fine.

The dress was a Hawaiian looking affair with bright yellow flowers on a background of hot pink.

When she stepped out of the bathroom, Chigger handed her a plastic grocery bag and raised both eyebrows. "That's for your dirty clothes and, honey, in that getup oil and vinegar would mix up just fine for about fifty years and then you'd have to shake it again."

"Chigger, you've got cow chips for brains."

"My brain is workin' fine. Why are you fightin' the heat between you and Jarod?"

Daisy crammed her dirty clothing down into the bag. "Because it's not right."

"Save that thought. We'll discuss it when I get out. Wait for me on the porch. There's cold sweet tea in the fridge and beer. Help yourself."

Chigger shut the door.

It didn't take Daisy long to figure out that Jim Bob was really in love with Chigger. One trip down the hallway and through the living room and kitchen was proof enough. His whole place was a picture gallery of her. She lazed on the deck in a bikini. She wore jeans and a shirt tied up under her big boobs and leaned on a fence. She sat tall in a saddle and was decked out in shorts and a halter top. Then there were the glamour shots. She photographed better than she looked. Another good reason to bring on the Hollywood moguls and not only let her tell her story but star in the television series as well.

The living room had a flat screen television in one corner, a worn leather recliner facing it, and matching leather sofa with pop out recliners on both ends. Western lamps in the shape of leather saddles sat on heavy end tables. A bar separated the living room from the kitchen where a table for four was shoved under a window overlooking the front porch. Everything was spotless. Either Jim Bob was a neat freak or else Chigger had cleaned before she kidnapped Daisy that afternoon.

There was a big pitcher of iced tea in the refrigerator and a six-pack of cold Coors in longneck bottles. Daisy took out the tea and scrounged around in the cabinets until she found glasses. She filled a glass with ice and tea and carried it to the front porch where she sat down in the rocker.

She could hear Jarod and Jim Bob's easy banter out in the shed but couldn't understand the words they exchanged. Was Jarod telling Jim Bob that oil and vinegar didn't mix? Or did men folks even think about things like that?

"So tell me, what you think about Daisy? Chigger is dyin' to get you two together," Jim Bob said.

"She's a pretty woman but not for me," Jarod said.

"Why?"

"She's a barmaid and she's not one bit attracted to me. Matter of fact, I think she hates me. Ain't no use wastin' time and besides, I've got all I can handle with Emmett and trying to get that ranch back in working order. I just plain haven't got the time or energy for her."

"Yep, she'd be a handful, all right. It'll take a strong man to tame that one. I see the way you look at her. You've got bit, old man, by the lust bug. But you probably couldn't keep up with her anyway. She's out of your league," Jim Bob taunted.

"It won't work, Jim Bob. Give it up. And besides, since when is a bartender out of my league?"

"I can tell Chigger I tried and believe me, Daisy is a hell of a lot more than a barmaid."

Jarod chuckled. "Tell Chigger you gave it your best shot and leave it at that."

Jarod listened to Jim Bob sing Chigger's praises but his eyes kept straying to the porch. Daisy had disappeared inside with Chigger then reappeared a while later wearing a dress and her hair down. He couldn't wait to get the fish cleaned so he could get a better look at her all dolled up.

Chigger joined Daisy in a few minutes. Her blond hair had been blow dried and floated on her shoulders. She wore a sundress, not unlike the one she'd loaned Daisy, only it was made of a demure pink and white gingham check and came to her ankles. Like Daisy, she was barefoot and her shoulders were bare. Daisy was ready to argue that no way were her big breasts that perky without silicone and then she noticed the clear bra straps across Chigger's shoulders.

"Where'd you find a bra with clear straps in your size?"

"Victoria's Secret. You should shop there. They've got the cutest things. Not that you'd ever need a bra with clear straps with those perky girls you've got, but you could get a little lace teddy and seduce Jarod."

"Shhh." Daisy nodded toward the two men taking long strides toward the house.

Jarod's mouth went as dry as desert sand when he saw Daisy sitting there in a dress with her bare feet drawn up in the rocking chair. If only he'd met her at a friend's house and not in a bar. If only she was a teacher or a lawyer or even a waitress, and not a barmaid.

Jim Bob bent to give Chigger a lingering kiss on the mouth. "Well, lookee here. You two sure do clean up nice."

Chigger pointed toward the door. "And we're hungry, so go cook."

"Want some help?" Daisy asked. The electricity between her and Jarod was almost visible and the tension it created was thicker than the walls of a nuclear fallout bunker.

"Naw, we'll take care of supper. Chigger's too pretty to be comin' in the kitchen. Besides, she can't cook worth shit. Only thing she makes that's fit for human consumption is sweet tea." Jim Bob carried the bowl of fish fillets inside the house.

Jarod followed. He felt a need to say something, anything. But not a single word came to mind. Daisy looked good enough to eat, but it was more than that. He knew she was smart, hard-working, and feisty. Cleaned up and dressed up she looked beautiful, but with the intelligence in her eyes and her capable hands, she also looked like a woman who could dance all night, get up at dawn, and work until dusk, and then do it all again. She looked vulnerable and strong at the same time and Jarod had gotten shot with a bolt of lust, and something else, like had never happened to him before.

Whatever it was, it's killing me, he almost groaned.

"I think he liked what he saw," Chigger whispered.

"You really can't cook?" Daisy tried to change the subject. Anything to get her mind off the way Jarod's eyes swept over her, creating a demanding desire that she had trouble controlling.

"Let's get on the same page. Some things is not contagious. Momma tried right hard to infect me with the cooking bug. It didn't take. I was immune to it. But the first time I looked at a *Cosmopolitan* with a big headline on the front about pleasing a man, I was hooked on sex."

"I'm avoiding *Cosmo* today. So does that mean you don't cook?"

"Throw that damned cookbook into the fire. I really do not cook. I clean like a maniac and I can make a man moan in the bedroom, but I do not make him do the same in the kitchen. I'd rather be reading a good erotic romance as a recipe. You ever read anything by Jasmine Haynes? Lord, after reading one of her books, it's all I can do to get to the Honky Tonk and find Jim Bob. Saw a hitchhiker last week on the way and almost stopped and picked him up just to take the edge off."

"Damn, Chigger!" Daisy exclaimed.

"Well, I did. I'll bring you a few of her books, but don't you drool on the pages. Bet by damn when you read one of them you'll be peelin' Jarod's clothes off every chance you get. And that stupid rule Ruby had won't even enter your mind. Do you really like to cook?"

"Love it when I have time and people. It's been a long time since I had either," she said.

Chigger shrugged. "How are you in the bedroom?"

"What's that got to do with anything?"

"Woman that's hot in the bedroom and a cook too? Why in the hell ain't you married?"

"I almost was at one time. My cooking or my bedroom skills couldn't keep him tied to one woman.

We fought. He hit me and I hit him back. But I only got one hit in and he kept hitting me hard until I figured out he was the meanest one of us. When he finally stopped, I pulled out my sawed off shotgun from the corner and had the hammer jacked back before he took off out the front door. Never heard from him again."

"What'd you do?"

"Shot the glass out of the back window of his pickup truck. Wished the whole time I'd blown the back of his head off but I missed. Only time I ever did."

"What would you have done if you had killed him?"

"I'd have gone to the hardware store, bought a shovel, and buried his sorry ass out in the mesquite. Instead, I packed my clothes and what I wanted out of the apartment we were sharing and started driving. Got to Thurber before my car died. How do you ever know who to trust?" Daisy asked seriously.

"I reckon it's a learned thing. We ain't born with it for sure. I think you can trust Jarod."

"Think ain't good enough for me anymore. It has to be know."

"Then I expect you'd best get to knowin', girl, or else the heat between y'all is going to fry both of you," Chigger said. "Let's go in there and do some supervising since you know how to cook."

"Hey, I didn't say I knew how to cook fish. I can fry chicken and mash potatoes, even make lasagna that's presentable and cook up a roast to die for, but—" Daisy protested.

Chigger cut her off mid-sentence. "That's more'n I can do. We're going inside so you can figure out that oil and water thing, and besides, it does a woman's heart good to see a man in the kitchen. Come on."

Chigger led the way to a couple of stools on the living room side of the bar dividing the living room and kitchen. Together they watched Jim Bob peel potatoes and Jarod mix up cornmeal, flour, and cayenne pepper to coat the fish.

Jim Bob stopped long enough to kiss Chigger on the forehead. "You think you could set the table out on the deck without causin' a disaster?"

"If we're usin' plastic."

"I'll trust you with the good stuff since we got company, darlin'," Jim Bob said.

"I'll help," Daisy offered.

She and Chigger were suddenly bumping into the men in the small area as they gathered up plates and cutlery. Daisy didn't have a single reaction when her arm brushed against Jim Bob's, but when she backed into Jarod's chest her pulse raced like it did the night they both wound up on the floor of the Honky Tonk. Could that have only been three days before? It seemed like weeks.

Damn that Chigger, anyway, talking about erotic romance books. Now every time she looked at Jarod, she pictured him lying on black satin sheets with nothing on but a big smile.

"Excuse me," she said the second time it happened.

"Small kitchen," he said hoarsely. If she touched him again he was going to have to take a cold shower before supper time.

She and Chigger carried the dinnerware out to the deck and set places on the glass-topped table surrounded by four chairs.

"Might as well have a seat. No, not there. You can't see Jarod from that angle. Pull your chair around here beside me. That way we can watch them," Chigger said.

"Chigger, for the last time. We are not compatible. He's a rancher—"

"And you are a vet who loves animals. What better combination? Hell, you could dress up as a nurse in one of them little short sexy things from Victoria's Secret and he could be your horse and—"

Daisy stuck her fingers in her ears. "Shut up or I'm leaving," she hissed. God Almighty, didn't Chigger understand she didn't need a bit of help in creating a scenario with Jarod? And she sure didn't need sexual props. One king-sized bed and candlelight was plenty.

"He sees me as a bartender and that's what I am more than a vet tech, which is not a full-fledged vet at all," Daisy said.

"You're a vet to all the folks around here. You bring that black bag of yours and do as good a job as any certified vet so don't give me that shit."

The tinny ringtone of "I Love This Bar" came from the living room loud and clear.

"Well, shit. I forgot to prowl through your purse and turn that damn thing off. Tell whoever it is that you don't have a vehicle and no one is driving you out to any ranch to pull a calf. Besides, you are wearing my sundress and you can't ruin it." Chigger kept talking the whole time Daisy rushed into the house and fished the phone from her purse.

"Hello," she said.

"Daisy, this is Cathy. I was about to hang up or leave a message."

"What's going on? Are you all right?"

"No," Cathy said.

"Talk to me," Daisy said.

"It got ugly last night. His name is Brad and he…"

"You have my permission to kill him. Want me to send the shotgun by FedEx?"

Jarod and Jim Bob stopped what they were doing and stared.

She covered the mouthpiece of the phone and whispered, "My cousin and her boyfriend. I'll explain later," Daisy explained and turned her attention back to the phone. "What are you going to do?"

"He's gone. He's not moving back in here," Cathy said.

"I can always use a damn good bartender at the Honky Tonk."

Cathy's heavy sigh came through the phone. "Thanks. I hate to leave Mena. It's home and my other job is here."

"Home is where you hang your hat, girl. Keep me posted."

She flipped her phone shut and turned to find Jarod and Jim Bob still staring.

"What?" she said.

"Someone going to get killed?" Jarod asked.

She perched on a barstool. "If I had my way about it I'd order up a backhoe for the Mena, Arkansas, cemetery today."

"And?" Jarod asked.

"Not that it's a bit of your business, but here's the story. Daddy was in the service and had an army buddy from Cherokee, North Carolina, where Momma lived. So he went home with the friend for a weekend and met Momma. Love at first sight and all that. They got married after a quick courtship and he moved her to Mena where he intended to come back to once he got out of the service. She got pregnant on their wedding night and he got killed a month later. So Granny moved from Cherokee to Mena to take care of Momma, who refused to leave the place where he was buried."

"God, that's sweet," Chigger said from the doorway.

"It was until I was about six months old and she found a new boyfriend," Daisy said. "Daddy had one brother who had a daughter, Cathy. We're only a few weeks apart in age and Mena's not a big place so we were pretty good friends. We usually meet in Dallas once a year for a couple of days and catch up on everything. That's who just called."

"I see." Jarod went back to frying fish.

"So what'd her boyfriend do?" Chigger pried.

"He got drunk and mean," Daisy said.

"Must be a family thing. Does she need your shotgun to make a believer out of him like you did that old boyfriend of yours?" Jarod asked.

He looked up at Daisy. Was that why she hated him? Was he paying for some other sorry sucker's mistake? Was the man a total nut case? Anyone who'd hit a face made for kissing and a body made for loving had to be out of his mind.

Daisy changed the subject. "How long until that fish is done? I'm starving."

"Got to fry some hush puppies and potatoes and cut up a salad and supper will be ready," Jarod said. Suddenly he wanted to know everything about Daisy, especially whatever the old boyfriend did to make her mad enough to get out the shotgun. Was that what she was talking about when he went back to the Honky Tonk for Uncle Emmett's wallet?

"You cooked both of those enormous fishes in that time?" Daisy asked.

"No, we cooked enough for our supper. The rest went into the freezer for the next time," Jim Bob answered.

The question hanging in the air between Jarod and Daisy was whether there would be a next time or not. The answer they came to at the same time was that there probably shouldn't be. Oil and water might mix on occasion. Gasoline and matches did not—ever!

Chigger dragged Daisy back out onto the deck so she could pry the whole story of her cousin and the abusive boyfriend out of her. By the time she had all the details, Jim Bob and Jarod carried supper out. Jim Bob sat down beside Chigger, which left Jarod to sit on the other side of the table so close to Daisy that his knee touched hers.

She couldn't shake the satin sheets vision from her head but kept reminding herself as they passed the food around the table that after that night she'd be a hell of a lot more careful. She would never ever put herself in a situation like that again.

"This is reach-and-get night since the table is so small," Chigger announced.

Every time Daisy reached for something she either touched Jarod's hand or pressed her knee tighter into his. She glared at Chigger. The woman hadn't been born of woman. She'd been spawned in a voodoo kitchen from the sperm of a warlock and the egg of a witch.

To keep from reaching across perfectly good fish and slapping the shit out of her, Daisy tried conversation. "This is the best catfish I've ever eaten."

"Thank you. I'm better at it than Jim Bob." Jarod grinned.

"The hell you are. You always get too much red pepper. If I hadn't grabbed the can, this would be too damn hot for anyone to eat," Jim Bob protested.

Too damn hot! Those words crept into Jarod's mind and flashed across Daisy's face every time he stole a look her way.

Too damn hot! The words snuck in Daisy's head and every time she glanced at Jarod they were branded across his forehead.

"You had a funny look on your face. Don't you eat red pepper?" Jarod nudged Daisy. His touch was damn sure hotter than the red pepper coating on the fish.

"Whatever is on it is wonderful and it's perfect. I didn't mean to have a strange expression. It's just that the last time I had a Sunday supper like this was when Ruby was alive. Sometimes the cycle gang would gather up at her house and we'd cook. I miss that," Daisy said. Hopefully they'd all believe her and not read the real thoughts in her head!

"Who was Ruby?" Jarod asked.

Chigger answered. "You missed something when you didn't have the privilege of knowing Ruby. She was a hell-raiser who was probably the first one in line when the women threw their bras on the bonfire. She was her own person and didn't give a damn what anyone thought of her." She picked up a hush puppy with her fingers and bit into it.

Jim Bob picked up where she left off, "Ruby built the Honky Tonk. She was raised in a little town over in east Texas and wound up in Fort Worth or Dallas with an aunt who died and left her a wad of insurance money. So she decided to put in a beer joint and got just as close to the county line as possible. She built one foot inside the legal limits. Then she bought that big sign out on the highway. Before long she was running the best joint in the county."

"I thought it was the only joint in two counties," Jarod said.

"Why would you think that?" Daisy asked.

"The sign I guess. I didn't see any advertisements for anything else."

"Lots of joints have come and gone in and around Mingus over the last forty years. There're empty buildings with the signs on them to prove it. And there's still the Boar's Nest and the Trio Club on up the road from the Honky Tonk. Trio has been there fifty years, just a little less than the Honky Tonk. Its claim to fame is live entertainment and unescorted ladies get in free on Sunday nights," Daisy said.

"Why don't people go there? How can there be that much trade to support three joints? It seemed to me like everyone in the area was in the Honky Tonk," Jarod said.

"People always like to have a good time and for years Mingus was the first place to find it. Used to be that there were more honky tonks and beer joints that a person could shake a stick at," Chigger said. "You ever watch *Cheers*, that old sitcom on television?"

"Uncle Emmett never misses it."

"Well, folks like me and Merle and the Walker boys have our favorite place, which is the Honky Tonk, just like Norm has his barstool in *Cheers*."

"So I'd find a different crowd if I went up the road a few miles?" Jarod asked.

"Hell, yeah," Jim Bob said. "Trio has live entertainment and I heard they even have free hot dogs on Sunday. The Honky Tonk ain't open that night so they get all the trade then."

"Why doesn't the Honky Tonk open on Sunday or have live entertainment?"

Daisy answered, "Ruby said that folks don't care if it's a human singing the blues or a jukebox. They just want to drink, dance, shoot pool, and have a good time. I live by the rule that if it ain't broke, don't fix it. And she said that even a bartender needs one night off."

"So that's why Billy Bob doesn't put in another joint. There're already three and that's all the area will support," Jarod said.

"You got it! Plus he wants the Honky Tonk because he also gets Daisy that way. You know what she says. The only way she'll ever leave the place is when they drag her cold dead body out the doors and she'll have her fingers wrapped around a longneck bottle of Coors when they do," Jim Bob said.

"So a man takes you and the Honky Tonk or nothing?"

Another shrug. "Pretty much."

"That's why old Billy Bob is just the woman for her," Jim Bob said, then jumped. "Ouch! Why'd you kick me, Chigger?"

"Because I don't think Billy Bob is the man for her."

"Why? Don't you like him? He's my brother and just like me and you like me," Jim Bob said.

"Of course I like you, darlin'. But Billy Bob isn't half the man you are and Daisy is my friend. She deserves someone as good as you are."

A wide grin split Jim Bob's face.

"Let's get the cleanup done and I'll give Daisy a ride home," Jarod said.

Daisy pushed back her chair. "I'll wash."

"Stack them by the sink. Jarod, run along and get Daisy home before midnight. She might turn into a pumpkin or a witch if you don't or maybe even a cute little—" Chigger said.

Daisy interrupted. "No, I'll just turn into a barmaid. You sure about the dishes, Chigger?"

Chigger winked broadly. "Oh, yes, I've very sure. You two run along and I'll take care of this little job while Jim Bob gets a shower."

Daisy came very close to blushing. "Okay, then, thanks so much for the day and the good supper."

"We'll do it again, I promise," Chigger said.

Not if I see you coming, Daisy thought. "See you later," she said.

Jarod had his hand out to place it on the small of her back but shoved it inside his pocket instead. Their bodies brushing against each other in the kitchen would have caused him embarrassment if his shirt tail hadn't been hanging down below his belt buckle. He couldn't take a chance like that again.

"So how'd you end up at the Honky Tonk?" Jarod asked when they were in the truck. Two feet of empty air separated them. He hated bucket seats right then.

Had he bought a car with bench seats he could have made a sharp turn and she'd have slid right over next to him. Tomorrow he was trading his truck for Jim Bob's old fishing wagon. Hell, he might throw in a couple of thousand dollars to boot.

"Car got hot and started smoking on the highway and I pulled into the next exit. Closest place to stop was the parking lot at the Smokestack in Thurber, which is spitting distance from the Honky Tonk. Ruby had come there for lunch and she asked if she could help. Ended up buying my lunch and putting me to work. Been there seven years now. She died last year and I inherited the Honky Tonk. Tinker got her house in Mingus, which he rents out. Says he can't live in town," Daisy answered with the short version.

"Where'd you live before that?"

"Mena, Arkansas, until I graduated high school. Worked a year until I saved enough for a semester of college and went to a little school down in Tishomingo, Oklahoma. Murray State College. Then I came home to Mena. From there it was to the Honky Tonk. So where did you go to school?" She turned the conversation around to him.

"Cushing for thirteen years, kindergarten through high school. College in Stillwater," he said. *I don't want to talk about school. I want to talk about how beautiful you are and how bad I want to touch you.*

"You have to go to college to be a rancher?" she asked.

"These days with the big business eating up the small farmers and ranchers, it helps. I've got a degree in agri-business. Thought in the beginning I wanted to get away from the ranch but figured out right quick how much I love it. I should stop by and see about Emmett again. That all right with you?"

"That's fine," she said.

"Want to come inside for a few minutes? Uncle Emmett would probably love to see you again," he asked when they reached the house.

"Sure. Why not?" At least the old toot could see that she'd changed clothes and maybe forget that she'd been dressed in short shorts and a halter top.

Emmett picked up the remote and muted the sound when he noticed them. "Why Miss Daisy, don't you look nice. Don't reckon I've ever seen you in a dress before. What's the special occasion?"

"Nothing special. Chigger loaned it to me."

"Don't be tryin' to josh an old man. I know you two been up to something and I bet I know what it was. You sure didn't look like that when you left here a few hours ago."

"What would you think we'd be up to? We cleaned fish and had supper at Jim Bob's. Chigger was there too."

"Just remember, you can't fool me. I know what y'all been out doin' and it wasn't eatin' fish," he said. Before either of them could answer he turned the sound back on the television and ignored them.

"I'm takin' Daisy home," Jarod said. *But I'd rather be taking her upstairs.* He reached up to slap his forehead to knock the silly notion out of his head but shoved his hand in his pocket instead.

Emmett waved a hand at them without taking his eyes from the television. "Get on out of here. You done lied to me. I told you to bring me some fish for my dinner tomorrow, so you didn't go over there at all. Go on and don't be thinkin' I'm so old I can't smell a lie."

"I'm sorry. He's getting more belligerent every day. Any idea that didn't come from him is wrong." Jarod whispered as they crossed the foyer on their way back outside.

"It's all right, but what on earth does he think we are hiding?"

"Who knows? He may think we brought a donkey on the place without asking him. Who knows how his mind works? We were talking about Tinker. So why can't he live in town? I wouldn't think of Mingus as a metropolitan area," Jarod asked as he drove toward Mingus. Maybe talking about Tinker would take his mind off her bare shoulders and long neck meant for nuzzling.

Damn it. There I go again, he thought.

"Tinker was in Vietnam. Ruby knew him before he went and said he was a different man back then. Something happened and he doesn't talk about it. When he came home he spent a long time in a hospital out in California. When they let him out he came back to see Ruby and she put him to work. He's a damn good bouncer and he does very well with the crowd at the Honky Tonk. But Ruby said he couldn't live in amongst lots of people anymore."

Jarod tapped the brakes and reset the cruise control to a lower speed. "Wonder what happened?"

"Ruby didn't even know. Tinker doesn't talk about it. He don't talk about anything much, but I'd trust him with my life."

What about your heart? Jarod thought as he passed the Smokestack in Thurber and drove the short distance to the Honky Tonk.

"Thanks for the ride."

He started to get out of the truck.

"This is not a date, Jarod. You don't have to walk me to the door."

He got out anyway. "I'll have to give up my gentleman badge from the Boy Scouts if I don't. You want me to be the shame of every McElroy male in the family? We've had our chivalry badge for more than a thousand years. I can't be the reason the grand hoorah came all the way from Ireland to take it back."

"I'm sure that would be an unforgivable sin." She smiled.

"You cause all that trouble, they'll burn you at the stake. Only a witch could make a McElroy give up his chivalry badge."

He slowed his long stride to keep up with her. When she reached the porch she dug her keys out from the bottom of her purse and opened the door. She turned to thank him again to find herself in a snug enclosure made by one arm braced on the door jamb. Instinctively she threw up her hands to his chest.

He brushed the tips of his fingers down her cheek and leaned in. She tiptoed and their lips met in a clash of passion. Every burning nerve in her body screamed for more than one kiss, yelled for her to drag him through the door and begged her to ignore that troublesome inner voice telling her to put a stop to his kisses.

He broke the kiss but kept her in his arms. His heart ached at the idea of stepping away from her.

Desire was so thick in his veins he had no room for blood.

"It wasn't supposed to be a date." She rolled up on her tiptoes and he bent slightly. Their lips and tongues met in another fierce battle of blazing heat.

"Daisy?" he said hoarsely.

"Mmmm," she mumbled.

Before he could answer she reached up and pulled his mouth to hers again. He moaned, picked her up like a bride, and kicked the door the rest of the way open with his foot. Without breaking the kisses he carried her into the living room and she stiffened in his arms.

"Does that mean no?" he whispered.

"It means not here," she whispered back.

"Why?"

She wrapped her arms tightly around his neck. "Long story. Grab that quilt and let's go out to the bed of your truck."

"You got it." Holding her with one strong arm, he grabbed the quilt with the other hand and threw it over his shoulder. He carried her to the truck, let the tailgate down, and eased her into the truck bed.

She pulled him down on top of her. Kisses continued until she was breathless. She ran her hand up under his shirt and he quivered, proving that he wanted her as much as she did him. It might be nothing more than a one night stand, but she couldn't have stopped at that point if it had meant facing a firing squad. She pulled the shirt over his head and he kissed the hollow of her neck.

She moaned.

"Like that, do you? God, you are so damn beautiful. Your skin is like fire-hot silk. When I touch you every sane thought leaves my head."

"And you, darlin', are a damn fine lookin' cowboy. Anyone ever tell you that your chest is so damn sexy that... oh, don't stop. Please, Jarod, don't stop."

"Honey, if there's any chance you want me to quit, say it now. If you slip your hands over my body again, wild mustangs couldn't stop me," he said.

"I'm not saying anything, darlin'," she whispered in his ear.

He slipped his hands under the top of her dress and pulled it down slowly, tasting every bit of her skin as he tugged it all the way to her ankles. Then he started back up from her toes to her breasts. By then she was lost. There was no tonight, no yesterday, no tomorrow: just a red-hot fire in the pit of her insides that begged to be eased.

He wanted to rush things and it was going to take a ton of willpower to restrain the excitement ripping at his heart. When she arched against him during a deep kiss, he peeled her bikinis from her hips.

She moaned and begged, "Oh, Jarod, please."

"I sure do love to hear my name on your lips, beautiful," he said.

"I'll say it over and over, Jarod, if you'll just... please." Her body melted against him again.

"Yes, sweetheart. Did you know that the moonlight on your body makes you even more beautiful?" He hurriedly shucked out of his jeans.

He managed to make it last long enough that the stars flew out of the heavens and landed all around them in the bed of his truck. She heard a loud hum in her ears that sounded like the whine of a country fiddle just before he whispered her name in a deep throaty southern drawl. She shivered and he hugged her closer to him in a crushing embrace. He rolled to one side without letting her out of his arms and buried his face in her hair.

Deep down, Daisy felt what she'd only heard about before—that sensual aura called an afterglow. She pulled the quilt over them even though the night breezes were scorching and snuggled down closer to his chest and shut her eyes. If only... but that didn't happen in real life. Happily ever after was for people like Chigger and Jim Bob and maybe occasionally in a big thick romance book.

Jarod stared at the twinkling stars in the sky and the big round full moon. His heart and pulse still raced even after she snuggled up to his side. Nothing had prepared him for the passion lying between them after the sex was over. Nothing would ever be the same and yet it couldn't change. She was a bartender who had no intentions of ever leaving the Honky Tonk. He was a rancher who wanted a wife beside him every night and morning. He wanted her to be there when he came home at noon or when a new baby calf was born. Daisy had made it very clear she would never leave the Honky Tonk. It didn't keep him from hugging her tightly that night.

So much for not having time or falling for a barmaid, he thought as he fell asleep.

An hour later she awoke. "Hey, cowboy, it's time to wake up and go home."

He opened one eye. "Why?"

"Because it's a wonder someone hasn't driven past, saw a strange truck, and stopped to see what was going on," she said.

"Who cares?"

"I'm going inside. You stay here as long as you like." She wrestled the quilt from around them and wrapped her body in it. She picked up her underwear and Chigger's dress, silently cussing both the whole time. If she hadn't been wearing something of Chigger's she wouldn't have just had sex with a man she'd only known a few days. Chigger had probably really had put some kind of "slut" curse on them before she loaned them out. In all her life, Daisy had never slept with a man she'd only known a couple of days. Chigger's morals were truly contagious. She'd guard her water jar with a shotgun from that day forward. She wondered if there was an anti-slut antidote?

She almost forgot her vet bag and grabbed it at the last minute.

"Tackle box?" he asked.

"Something like that," she said.

Jarod sat up in all his naked glory. "Why are we out here and not in your apartment?"

Daisy eased down off the tailgate and tucked the quilt firmly around her like a strapless prom gown. "Because the one rule Ruby had was that I didn't have men in the apartment."

"Ruby is dead. You own the Honky Tonk. You make the rules."

"Like I said, if it ain't broke, don't fix it. Good night, Jarod."

"Good night, Daisy. Hey, aren't you going to thank me for a good time?"

"Are you going to thank me?" She was inside the apartment before he could answer.

She heard his laughter as she slid down the wall to sit on the floor just inside the door. What in the hell was she going to do?

She touched her lips, amazed that they were cool and not still fiery hot. Ruby's rule played through her mind. "No men in the apartment to avoid hasty mistakes."

"Hasty or not, I'm not going to regret tonight."

Chapter 6

DAISY AWOKE THE NEXT MORNING AT NINE O'CLOCK to the ringtone of her cell phone. She grabbed it and answered without opening her eyes, hoping to hear Jarod's deep voice on the other end.

"Miz Daisy, this is Rayford. Some fool cut my fence and my stud bull went through it. Done tore up his side somethin' horrible. Can you come out here and stitch him up?"

"I'll be there in twenty minutes." She was out of bed and finding her jeans before she broke the connection. She threw on a T-shirt and tucked jeans down into her work boots. She had her purse in one hand and her black bag in the other when she opened the back door. The phone rang in the Honky Tonk but she didn't have time to talk to the beer distributor right then. Rayford's bull needed stitches.

She made it from Mingus to Gordon in fifteen minutes and met Rayford in the pasture beside his house. The rangy old bull was bleeding and rolling his eyes, daring anyone to come near him.

"How'd you get him corralled?" she asked.

"Led him along with a feed bucket. I ain't sure how you're goin' to handle 'im. He's not friendly when he's well."

"You just stay on this side of the fence. I'll take care of him," she said.

She crawled over the split rail fence and started talking calmly. The bull lowered his head but he didn't charge. She told him what a handsome old boy he was in a sweet voice. Before long she was so close she could touch him and in a few deft movements, she had a needle loaded with deadening medicine and shot into the wound. She cleaned it thoroughly before she tied off thirteen stitches in his hide and then gave him a healthy dose of antibiotic to keep down any infection.

"You sure got a way with animals, Miz Daisy. Don't know why you don't stop workin' at the Honky Tonk and go into it full time," Rayford said.

"I'm in it full time," she laughed.

"What do I owe you?" He laughed with her.

"I'll send out a bill first of the month. Have to figure up the medicine," she said.

"Might as well come on in and have breakfast with us. Dora has it cooked up and ready. She'll be mad if you don't."

"Thank you," Daisy said.

Dora met them at the door. "You two wash up at the sink while I put this food on the table. It might not be as good as it was when it was fresh, but that old bull had to be took care of before anybody could think about eating. I heard Emmett's great nephew, Jarod, is over there takin' care of him. Somebody needs to. Since Mavis died, that man has really gone down. You met Jarod?"

Daisy started at the name. Couldn't she go anywhere without someone bringing it up?

"Yes, he came into the Honky Tonk." Daisy related the story of the clash.

Dora and Rayford laughed so hard they almost choked on their pancakes.

—⁓—

Jarod didn't think to get Daisy's cell phone number before he left early on Monday morning and it took an hour to locate a phone book among all the clutter in Emmett's house. When he called the Honky Tonk business number, a fine bead of nervous sweat bubbled up on his upper lip. While the phone rang he went through a dozen first liners, all of which sounded lame and stupid.

Five rings later he'd decided on one. Ten rings later he'd forgotten every one. Surely she could hear the telephone ringing. Was she deliberately not answering it because she didn't want to talk to him? On the twelfth ring he slammed the phone back down on its stand and turned around to find Emmett right behind him.

"What?" he snapped.

"Ain't me with woman problems. You bring her home where she belongs and you won't have to be callin' her," he said.

—⁓—

The crowd at the Honky Tonk was slim that night. A few truckers stopped by and four older ladies who always came in for a gossip session claimed a corner table and asked for a pitcher of piña coladas. Daisy kept a watchful eye on the front door as she worked and listened to the Bellamy Brothers sing "Let Your Love Flow" and "He'll Have to Go," by Jim Reeves. The old 45 rpm records still spun around a turntable inside the rounded sixties-style jukebox and dropped down when quarters were put into the slot.

One trucker laid his head on the bar and sighed. Daisy patted his big broad shoulder. "Got troubles, Mac?"

"Wife's on her six-month kick. About twice a year she gets like this. She doesn't like for me to drive a truck and bitches about it for a solid week. We can't live without the money I make so she'll come around, but she's in a mood until she does," he said.

Merle claimed a stool next to him. "Give me a Coors. Longneck. What's the matter with you?" she asked Mac.

Merle was seventy years plus and wore her jeans tight. Her pearl snapped Western shirts were always flamboyant and the one she wore that night was turquoise with bright red appliquéd roses on the detailed yoke across the back. Her stovepipe black hair was pulled back into a ratted French twist and piled high on her head.

"Wife troubles again," Mac said.

"Stop your bellyachin' and come shoot some eight ball. That lazy Joe Bob Walker don't come around except on weekends. How in the hell he expects to keep his skills honed up is beyond me."

Mac sighed again. "I couldn't whip you so what's the use."

"Oh, stop your carryin' on and give me a little competition anyway. God Almighty, you reminded me of that jackass on Winnie the Pooh that's always dragging around in a bad mood."

"You watch cartoons?" Mac asked.

"Well, hell yeah. They're cute, all but that Eeyore jackass. He's a whining pain in my ass. Now get a stick and let's play. You know damn well that you are one of the finest pool sharks this side of the Louisiana line."

Mac perked up. "You ready to lose?"

"Tell you what. We'll play for jukebox music. I win, you keep the music going. You win, I'll put the money in the box. I'll put in the first five dollars. That'll take us through the first game. After that loser pays. How about some old George Jones? He's a good one to listen to while we play," Merle asked.

Mac nodded. "That feller knows the pain of lovin' a woman, don't he? Get your quarters out, Merle. I feel lucky tonight."

Merle winked at Daisy.

Daisy thought of Chigger's infamous winks, which brought on thoughts of Jarod and sex in the back of a pickup truck. She fanned her burning face with a dry bar rag. George Jones sang a song that had lines in it about how tomorrow night they'd meet again. Daisy glanced toward the door but Jarod didn't materialize. Surely he'd call or stop by in the next couple of days.

Merle cocked her head to one side. "What are you all dressed up for tonight?"

"I'm not," Daisy said but she felt the slow burn of a blush on her neck. Hell's bells, she hadn't blushed so much since she was sixteen.

"Yes, you are. I ain't never seen that cute little shirt. And you've got on makeup and your hair is down. That nephew of Emmett's got you all hot and bothered?"

"Good lord, Merle, go shoot eight ball and drink your beer."

"He's a good lookin' cowboy. He might have me all hot and bothered if I was thirty years younger. Hell, today I couldn't keep up with him."

Daisy pointed toward the tables. "Go."

Ray Price sang next, an old beer-drinking, snot-slinging song about how his woman didn't love him anymore. He said his new love's lips were warm and the one waiting at home was cold. Were Daisy's kisses cold?

Hell, no! My kisses set him on fire as much as his did me. It might have been a one night stand, but by damn, it was red hot.

Dolly Parton and Ricky Shelton started singing "Rockin' Years." Dolly said that her heart only had room for one and sang about rockin' chairs, rockin' babies, and rock of ages. She said that side by side they'd be together always. Was there really that kind of love left in a crazy mixed up modern world?

"What're you thinkin' about?" another trucker named Buddy asked.

"My future."

"Got old Billy Bob in it?"

She shook her head. "Probably not."

"He'll be disappointed. Since he's not in it, how about me?"

"You got six kids and a wife. Listen to the song, man. That's what you get to go home to. You ever mess that up I'll shoot you myself."

Buddy chuckled. "Honey, you wouldn't have to. Holly would blow my ass all over Georgia if she ever found out I was messin' around on her."

Daisy laughed with him.

The jukebox rattled out Ronnie Milsap singing "Only One Love in My Life."

Buddy moved his shoulders to the music as he drank a longneck beer and sang along with Ronnie. When he finished the last of the drink and the song ended, he waved at her and headed for the door. "Good night, Daisy. See you next week on the run back through here. Have a good one, Tinker."

"Drive safe," Tinker told him.

"I'll do it."

A couple more songs played and Merle lost the first game. Mac wasn't nearly so sad. She flipped him several quarters and he plugged them into the machine. She gave Daisy a thumbs-up sign while she chalked up her custom made cue stick. "Next time your money is feeding the jukebox," she yelled at Mac.

"Merle, you're on a losing streak. It's a good thing Joe Bob's not here. You'd lose your place among the pool table angels," he shouted above the music.

Merle cackled. "Me an angel? That's a sight I can't even conjure up when I'm drunk."

Daisy wished to hell it wasn't Monday night. The old slow songs were killing her.

Elvis Presley's smooth voice came through the speakers with "Are You Lonesome Tonight?" and Daisy leaned on the bar. Was Jarod as lonesome as she was?

<hr>

Tuesday morning she'd just finished cleaning up the Honky Tonk when someone pounded on the door. She threw her bar rag on the floor and ran to unlock it hoping to see Jarod. Maybe he'd had an emergency at the ranch and couldn't call the day before but surely he'd stop by that day.

"Mornin', ma'am. I'm from the telephone company. I'm Holt Bellman." He pointed to the patch on his blue uniform. "Would you check your phone please? We got a call that the lines are down. Think a squirrel is in a transformer again. Pesky little critters cause us a lot of trouble."

She picked up the receiver on the phone at the end of the bar. Sure enough it was dead. "No service here."

"Thanks. Hopefully, we'll have it back on by evening." He disappeared out the door. She locked it and was barely back to the bar when her cell phone rang.

"Daisy, it's Rose out at the Flying Z. Fancy stumbled this morning while I was exercising her. Reckon you could come out here and check it? Damn, I hope I don't have to put her down. Don't think I could do it." Rose's voice broke.

"Don't do anything foolish. I'll be there in a few minutes," Daisy said.

Daisy stopped outside Rose's yard fence half an hour later. Fancy, a fine roan horse, was holding her front leg up. Tears were streaming down Rose's face as she petted the horse's nose.

Daisy ignored the gate, hopped the fence, opened her bag, and bent down to check the leg. She carefully ran a hand down the entire leg. "It's not broken. It's sprained. I'll tape her up and you let her rest for at least a week."

Rose wiped her eyes. "Thank God."

Daisy sweet-talked the horse just like she did the bull. She taped the horse's leg, checked all four feet to make sure there were no embedded stones causing a problem, and shut her bag.

"Come on in the house. Mandy made cookies. We'll have some with a cup of coffee. Tell me, have you met that Jarod McElroy? I heard he came in the Honky Tonk the other night."

Daisy sighed. "I've met him. He's helping out over at Emmett's place."

"I heard he was a hunk," Rose said.

"I didn't look that close," Daisy lied.

—⁓—

Jarod tried calling at a different time on Tuesday. He waited until Emmett was taking his afternoon nap and dialed the numbers from memory. It went straight to a busy signal. He hung up, waited ten of the longest minutes of his life, and tried again. Straight to a busy signal.

"Damn it all to hell and back," he mumbled.

"I'm takin' a nap. Stop your cussin'," Emmett said from the recliner.

Jarod flipped the phone book open and looked up "florist" under the yellow pages. He'd send flowers. Women liked flowers. He had the first three numbers dialed before he hung up. Daisy would shoot him if he sent flowers to the Honky Tonk that evening. She'd have to explain who they were from and why. Billy Bob would have a hay day with it and she'd be teased so terribly that she would hate him forever.

He tried calling off and on all afternoon when he was in the house checking on Emmett, but it always came up with a busy signal.

Had she put the phone off the hook so she didn't have to talk to him? Was she regretting what they'd done?

Tuesday night was a little busier at the Honky Tonk. Amos and the riders hit the bar at nine o'clock. They were thirsty and itching to dance to the old tunes so Daisy unplugged the newer jukebox and turned them loose on the old one to play the songs they loved. Don Gibson started off a two-stepping song with "I Can't Stop Lovin' You."

Amos danced with a new woman in the bunch, a bottle-blonde wearing tight jeans and enough wrinkles to prove she was near Amos' age. He didn't let go of her when Hank Locklin sang "Send Me the Pillow You Dream On."

"I'm not sure I can stand this all night," Daisy said under her breath.

"What?" Merle asked. "You are all dressed up again. Whoever it was didn't come in last night, did they? I betcha my best cue stick against a bottle of your cheapest beer that it's Jarod McElroy, isn't it? One night it's Mac and now you. Is all this damn melancholy shit contagious? If it is, I'm going home." She wore a red, white, and blue plaid Western shirt that night. The red yoke was decorated with a flag waving in the wind.

"The words to the songs are getting to me. Lyrics seem like they're talkin' right at me," Daisy said.

"Honey, that's because country music talks to the heart. Ruby loved it and so do I. It's life told in song. It ain't none of that newfangled stuff with an orchestra behind it that don't say much."

Daisy nodded. "You got a point, but Gretchen Wilson's 'Redneck Woman' makes a statement too."

"Yep, that girl is going far. She's got enough pure old country to get her there. She's a modern day me and Ruby. We were redneck women a hell of a long time before that cute little thing made a record. We could have written that song for her," Merle said.

"That's the gospel truth?" Daisy asked.

"Well, it looks like Amos is about to get winded dancin' with that hot little chick. Thank God. He's promised me some competition. That man knows his way around a pool table, I'm here to tell you. We're playin' for big bucks."

"Who is she?" Daisy asked.

"That's Walter's new girlfriend, Stella. Last one got to thinkin' he would sell his bike and buy a travel trailer. He said it was like Brad Paisley singing that fishin' song. Told me that she said it was him or the bike and he was goin' to miss her. It didn't last long though. He had Wanda ridin' with him the next week," Merle said.

"You goin' to jaw all night or shoot pool?" Amos asked at her elbow.

"Show me the money. I'm not playin' for jukebox music tonight," Merle said.

Amos flipped a fifty dollar bill on the bar. "Daisy, you can be our bank."

Merle pulled a fifty from her bra and laid it on top of his money. "Two out of three? And if you get pissy when you lose and want a grudge match it'll cost you another twenty."

"Deal," Amos said. "Same goes for you. If I win two out of three and you get all het up about it, you got to pay the same for a grudge match. Now chalk up that fancy cue stick of yours and I'll rack the balls."

"I love it when you talk dirty," Merle said with a big grin. "Put that money in a safe place, Daisy. I'll be collecting it before the night's over."

"In your dreams, darlin'. That will more than pay for my gas and beer and it's mine," Amos told her.

Daisy put the money into the cash register and tried to keep her eyes away from the door. At midnight, she handed Merle both fifties and Amos danced one more time with the blonde. Did Jarod like to dance?

On Wednesday Daisy slept all the way to noon and was halfway through breakfast when the cell phone rang. It was Miss Edith from up north of Mingus. She was eighty-nine years old and her dog, George, was sick. He was throwing up all over her good rug and she didn't know what to do.

"Miss Edith, do you want me to drive over and see about George?" Daisy asked.

"Speak up, darlin'. You know I'm deaf in one ear and can't hear out of the other. You got to yell a little. George is at it again. I got to get me some paper towels. You stay right there while I clean this up."

Daisy waited.

"I'm back now. He's waggin' his tail but oh, no, he's gaggin' agin!" Edith shouted.

Daisy wanted to tell her that *she* wasn't deaf but it wouldn't do a bit of good.

"I'll be there in ten minutes," she yelled into the phone.

"No, don't come just yet, I think he might be better. I don't want to bother you none if he can puke it up on his own. I bet that rascal has eat a dead mouse. I put out poison last week. Got one that's been eatin' George's dry food and it just plumb upsets George," Edith said.

The phone in the Honky Tonk rang loudly. Evidently the transformer had been repaired but the pretzel and peanut man who always called on Wednesday would just have to wait. Daisy couldn't talk to him and Edith both at the same damn time.

"Well, now I believe he's all better. Was it chocolate I wasn't supposed to let him have, Daisy? I forget. Chocolate or lemon. I made two pies yesterday and he begged for a little piece of each one."

Daisy sighed. "He doesn't need either one," she yelled.

"Well, darlin', he's goin' to get it if he wants it. I don't cotton to starvin' an animal. I did stop givin' him that half a bottle of beer at night but I ain't goin' to make him give up his pies," Edith said.

"Is he better?" Daisy asked.

"I believe he's going to live. Thanks for talkin' me through it again, Daisy. I'll make him eat light today. I'll make him some potato soup with whippin' cream in it. That'll be right nourishin'," Edith said. "Bye, dear."

Daisy flipped the phone shut and got the giggles. Edith with her dog named George after George Jones, and Merle with her cat, Rack.

Life was never dull.

—⁓—

Jarod dialed the phone at straight up noon. He didn't even care if he interrupted her meal. He intended to talk to her that day, come hell or high water.

Emmett tapped him on the shoulder when the phone was on its twentieth ring. "I don't feel so hot. Reckon you could run me into the doc's office this afternoon? That woman of yours is a stubborn filly, ain't she? You got to put your foot down, boy. Sweet-talk her or burn that damn place down. Her place is here, not out there with all them men lookin' down her shirt."

Jarod's heart sunk down to his boots. Daisy was avoiding him. She hadn't felt the same after that fantastic night in his truck bed.

On Wednesday, Tinker had to turn a whole carload of kids away at the door when they tried to get inside with fake IDs. He told them to go on up the road and they told him they'd already been there and neither bar was open on Wednesday night.

Tinker took care of the problem but it made Daisy think about the first time she'd used a fake ID to go to a bar. She'd gotten past the doorman and actually had a beer in her hand when the police raided the joint. Her mother and the current boyfriend living in their trailer both went on a rampage, cussing at Daisy for disgracing them.

"Yeah, right. That boyfriend didn't have a damn thing to disgrace."

The night was so slow that she caught Tinker yawning several times. But that's the way it was pretty often on Wednesday when everyone went to church. Come the weekend and the joint would be hopping and her cash register full. Talking to God only lasted so long and then folks got an itch to find out about hellfire and damnation for themselves instead of listening to the preacher tell all about it. Did Jarod go to church on Wednesday nights with Emmett? Was that why he hadn't been in the Honky Tonk?

~~~

Thursday started off in a rush at nine that morning. The cell phone rang a dozen times before she located it under the sofa cushion where it had fallen out of her purse the day before.

"Hello," she said breathlessly, hoping that it was Jarod.

"Miz Daisy, please come quick. It's Herman. He's sick."

"I'm on my way," Daisy said. She grabbed her bag and took off out the door. If that damned goat died, Tommy would cry his eyes out. It was his show goat for the county fair that fall and he'd groomed him for months.

Tommy's mother, Lylah, met her at the car and took her straight to the goat pen. Herman had his head down and was staggering around like a Honky Tonk drunk on Saturday night.

"He got into the feed bin last night and I found him all bloated up," Lylah said.

Daisy opened her bag, shook up a bottle of Pepto-Bismol, and poured out fifteen cc. She held Herman's head up and stroked his throat, then shot the medicine into his mouth and stroked some more until he swallowed.

"Bet you wish you hadn't gorged right now," she said.

"Think he'll live?" Lylah asked.

"Oh, yeah. But Tommy needs to shore up the pen so he can't get into the feed bin again. Silly old goat thinks he can eat all he wants," Daisy laughed. She pulled out a syringe and loaded it with 5 cc of CD Antitoxin SQ and poked it into Herman's hip. "I'll run by tomorrow afternoon and give him another dose of this and he should be fine."

"Lord, what would we do without you?" Lylah asked. "Got time for a cup of coffee? I heard that Emmett McElroy's nephew is out on the ranch and that he's one sexy cowboy. You seen him, yet?" Lylah asked.

Daisy wanted to throw something. Perhaps a shoe at Herman, but the stupid animal would probably eat it and then she'd have to force more Pepto down his throat. "He's been in the Honky Tonk. I haven't seen you and Roger in there in a while," she said.

"Been busy with this damn goat business. I tell you, if we make it through the county fair with these things, I'm goin' to shout. Come on inside."

"I still got things to do at the Honky Tonk so I'll take a rain check. Y'all come on out some evening. And I'll run by tomorrow." Daisy made a beeline to the car. She'd heard all she wanted to hear about how sexy Jarod was. Lylah and the rest of them had only heard about him or seen him with his clothes on. She'd seen the real thing.

***

Jarod tried calling again on Thursday but no one answered. He was ready to beat down the Honky Tonk door, but Emmett was ailing. The doctor gave him a new medicine and it made him nauseous, so Jarod was stuck playing nursemaid and listening to him give advice about how to keep Daisy on the ranch. According to

Emmett, Jarod didn't know how to court a woman and even after the marriage there had to be courting.

Jarod didn't tell him that he'd love to court Daisy. He'd like to take her to dinner, to a movie, to a rodeo, to anything where he could sit beside her and talk. But Daisy didn't want to speak to him. God, he dreaded Sunday. He'd called every single day to ask her out on a real date and she was avoiding him like the plague.

—◦◦◦—

Things picked up considerably at the beer joint that night. She still checked the door every time it opened, but no Jarod. By Friday, Daisy was so glad to see Chigger that she could have hugged the woman. Then the Walker triplets appeared all together, looking exactly alike in their plaid button-up Western shirts and creased Wranglers. Jim Bob headed straight for Chigger and gave her a lingering kiss, reminding Daisy of the one she'd shared with Jarod. She fanned her scorching cheeks with the back of her hand.

Jim Bob kept his arm around Chigger's shoulders. "I missed you, darlin'."

"Ah, you just had a long week bailin' hay and now you're ready to roll around in it. Don't you be gettin' any ideas though. It's too hot and hay sticks to sweat out in the hay barn. That's for fall and winter, cuddled up under a big old fluffy blanket. Give me a big old king-sized bed anytime in the hot summertime," Chigger giggled. "Dance with me, honey. I'm so tired of fixin' hair I could cry. Go put on some Gretchen Wilson or Sugarland. Something to make the heart race instead of cryin' the blues."

Chigger's hot pink T-shirt had the outline of a bull in rhinestones stretched across her chest. Her nails and hair were freshly done. Daisy wondered how in the hell she got past her momma in that getup? She had a vision of Chigger leaving the house in a loose fitting pair of jeans and a floral baggy shirt, then stopping along the side of the road to change into her provocative clothing.

Daisy felt dowdy in comparison in her red T-shirt with the Honky Tonk logo on the front and a pair of faded jeans. She hadn't even worn her boots that night, opting instead for Nikes that had seen better days. Jarod hadn't called or come by. Hell, he might have gone back to Oklahoma after that one night stand, never to be seen again.

Jim Bob returned from the jukebox and Gretchen's voice came through the speakers announcing that she was a redneck woman. He picked up Chigger's hand and kissed the palm before leading her out to the dance floor. He moved pretty good for an old ranching fellow and his eyes never left his woman. Chigger wiggled and kept time with the music as she rubbed all over Jim Bob.

When the song ended she leaned on the bar while Jim Bob went to pick a cue stick from the wall. Joe Bob already had the balls racked and was waiting.

"Joe Bob's got to get warmed up or else he'll be broke for sure when Merle gets here. Fix me up a margarita," Chigger said.

"You drink beer," Daisy said.

"Not tonight. I've got a hankering for a margarita. Just a plain old José one. Not a fancy Patron one, and give me lots of salt on the rim. So what happened after you and Jarod left on Sunday?"

"You sly old coyote. You got me busy making a drink that you usually don't order and then ask that question. You almost had me there. What happened at the trailer?" Daisy said.

"We damn near had to call in the fire department to put out the blazes we started in the bedroom. I didn't see any smoke damage on your back door. So what happened?"

"Are we goin' fishin' on Sunday?" Daisy changed the subject.

"Hell, no. You got to go shoot cattle or whatever it is that you do when you vaccinate them. Remember, you promised to take Emmett a cheesecake and Jarod is fixin' steaks."

"Then I'll kidnap *you* and *you* have to go with me or else I'll tell your momma what you look like tonight. Those duds don't tell the world you are a shy little old maid beautician one bit. Hell, I bet you've even played a little strip poker with Jim Bob and no telling what else you let him do," Daisy said.

"You're damn right and I lose on purpose just to make him happy. If I told you what else he does to me you'd have to sink your whole body in the ice machine. Jarod kissed you, didn't he?" Chigger asked.

Daisy shot her a look.

Chigger licked the salt around the rim of the jar and then took a long drink. "Only thing that could make you so jumpy and checkin' out the door every five seconds is that you had sex with him and he hasn't called."

"Go dance with your man. There's Merle. She can take over with Joe Bob," Daisy said.

"He's a tease to do that to you and I'm going to tell him he's a low-down sumbitch next time I see him."

Daisy pointed to the dance floor. "You read too many of those magazines you keep in your beauty shop. Every one of them have an article on how to get and keep a man. Go on and dance with Jim Bob and quit analyzing me."

"I don't need to be told twice to dance with that good lookin' hunk," Chigger said and went to meet Jim Bob in the middle of the floor. She backed up to him, wrapped a hand backwards around his neck, and wiggled so much that Daisy wondered how he kept from hauling her out the door to his pickup. All that movement had to be affecting him enough to put a strain on the zipper of his jeans. She remembered the effects she'd had on Jarod and fanned herself for the hundredth time that week.

Chigger and Jim Bob danced to Sugarland singing "It Happens." The singer talked about life not going quite like you planned it and the irrefutable indisputable sh... it happens.

"Yep, shit happens." She drew up another beer, turned around to give it to a customer, and found Billy Bob sitting next to him.

"What kind of shit you talkin' about?" he asked.

"I was just singing with the song," she lied.

"So what's been goin' on in my little woman's life this week?" he asked.

"I'm not your little woman. Go flirt with someone who cares."

"You are just plumb breakin' my heart. I'm goin' to play a slow song and hug up to someone to ease my achin' soul. Will that make you jealous or at least feel a little bit bad for hurting me?"

She dug a handful of change from the pocket of her apron and handed it to him. "Neither one but I'll buy the first two songs. Hug tight."

"You're a coldhearted woman."

She smiled. "That's the God's gospel truth on a silver platter. Get on over there before someone puts in a fast song and you can't hug up to a sweet little rosy. Be a shame if you didn't get some relief for that achin' soul of yours."

He took the money and hurried to the jukebox. Travis Trett sang "Long-Haired Country Boy," and the Friday night crowd made their way to the dance floor for a line dance. Everyone in the joint was dancing except Joe Bob and Merle, who were in a heated pool game, Daisy who kept time with her feet behind the bar, Tinker who sat on a chair beside the door, and one lonesome old cowboy at the end of the bar who appeared to be waiting on someone.

Daisy studied the cowboy. He had blond hair curling up on his shirt collar and green eyes like her ex-boyfriend. Chris had been a bouncer but he wasn't a big burly man like Tinker. He wasn't much taller than Daisy. His size often made rowdy drinkers think they didn't have to listen to him, but his arms were made of steel. Daisy rubbed her cheek as she remembered how hard he could hit.

Billy Bob must have had a hankering for Travis that night because the next song was "Where Corn Don't Grow." Daisy remembered the CMT video of the song and related to Travis wanting to get out of the town where he grew up. She'd wanted the same thing too, but a couple of years later she was right back in Mena, Arkansas.

"And that's when the weeds really got out of hand," she muttered.

Daisy had loved the song the first time she heard it and figured that if corn didn't grow in the fields then weeds did. A person had a choice of what they'd cultivate. Corn or weeds.

Billy Bob cut through the crowd to the bar. "What're you talkin' about weeds for? I need some more money if you're not going to marry me and make me part owner of this beer joint."

She handed him another fistful of coins. "I'm not buyin' you off. This is the last of the free music. Besides, you have more money than I do."

"This is my payment for a broken heart, remember?"

"Sure it is. You're just a con man, Billy Bob. You don't love anyone. Don't play any more Travis, either. Choose something else," she said.

"I'll find something to make everyone want to drink more beer. By the way, I heard you were two-timin' me with Jarod on Sunday and even let him bring you home. I was hurt that you and Chigger didn't invite me to go fishin'. And you *never* let me take you home."

She pointed at the jukebox. "Go play music and dance, and I wasn't two-timin' you, Billy Bob. I'd have to be one-timin' you to do that."

"Well, that's your choice. Mine is that I am one-timin' you already."

"Then go two-time me with someone who gives a damn," she told him.

He clamped a hand over his heart and skewered up his face. "My heart is broken with your cold words."

He chose George Strait's old song, "I Cross My Heart," and Daisy wished to the devil she hadn't told him to play something other than Travis.

"Damn you, Jarod," she looked at the shut door.

~~~

Saturday morning the phone rang and Daisy had her bag in her hand before she even answered it. If Herman had gotten into the feed bin again she intended to see what barbecued goat tasted like that night.

"Hello," she said.

"Daisy, it's Edith, darlin'. George is beggin' for his beer again. He just sits in front of the refrigerator and looks at it with this forlorn thirsty look. He's just like old George Jones. I'm afraid if I don't give it to him, he'll lay down and die."

Daisy held the phone a foot from her ear until Edith stopped talking, then she shoved it as close as she could and yelled so loud that the folks at the Smokestack could hear her on a clear day. "Edith, he doesn't need beer. It will bloat him and make him sick."

"Ah, honey, I don't mind the dog farts. They smell like shit but they don't last long. If that's all that it'll do to him, I reckon half a bottle won't hurt him. Thanks, Daisy," Edith shouted and hung up.

The Honky Tonk phone set up a howl when she finished talking to Edith and Daisy made a beeline for it. Maybe Jarod had decided to call after all. She stumbled over a romance book she'd dropped on the floor the night before and went sprawling out on the carpet. By the time she reached the phone it had stopped ringing.

"Damn it all to hell on a silver poker," she swore. "Next week I'm having an answering machine put in even if everyone with a sick animal leaves so many messages it clogs up the thing."

***

Jarod replaced the phone receiver and made Emmett a milkshake. His uncle was feeling better physically. Mentally was a different matter. Every waking minute was centered around Daisy and how Jarod wasn't doing his duty by her.

Jarod didn't know what in the hell more he could do. The woman wouldn't answer her phone. She didn't have an answering machine. For all he knew she'd sprouted wings and flown off to a foreign country after that Sunday night.

Jarod was so angry that he wanted to storm into the Honky Tonk and carry her out like Richard Gere did in *An Officer and a Gentleman*. But he couldn't leave Emmett to go anywhere. Life was a total bitch. Emmett fussed at him to make Daisy come live at the ranch. He just wanted to talk to the woman. She was supposed to be at the ranch the next day and by damn then he'd have it out with her. Until then he'd just hope that he didn't have another one of those dreams that woke him up in a horrendous mood when he found she wasn't in bed with him.

***

Saturday night was even busier than Friday. Chigger and the Walker men were there and she didn't have a moment to think about songs or their hidden meanings.

She drew up more beer and popped the lids off more bottles and cans than she'd done in one night in years. By the time Tinker told her good night and went home and she picked up her customary beer and put enough coins in the jukebox to play Miranda Lambert's "Gunpowder and Lead," she barely had enough energy left in her long legs to prop them up on the table.

Daisy figured Miranda's songwriter had written the song especially for her. It was the thing that brought her to the Honky Tonk. She had loaded her shotgun, the only inheritance she'd gotten from her granny when she died, and Chris got the fight he wanted. Just like Miranda said in the song, he'd slapped her face and shook her like a rag doll but by damn when it was all said and done he was running and she was staying.

The idea of staying brought her to the issue with Jarod. He wasn't a permanent fixture. As soon as Emmett had breathed his last, he'd be gone and Daisy wasn't going anywhere. So that fixed that.

Yeah, right. I had sex with him. He didn't call or show up for a whole week. That tells me it wasn't anything but a one night stand and I need to grow up and get over it.

She'd get over the attraction.

Someway.

Somehow.

She had to or it was going to drive her stark raving crazy. Every time a man walked into the Honky Tonk all week, she'd checked him out, hoping it was Jarod, and then she'd been disappointed. She couldn't endure life walking on a tightrope with no net under her. She had a choice just like she'd had with Chris. In that case she

could stick around and let him abuse her physically. In
the one with Jarod she could hang onto a one night stand
and pine away mentally wanting more. Neither one had
a future. She'd gotten over Chris and by damn she'd get
over Jarod McElroy too.

Chapter 7

THE SUN WAS HOT ENOUGH TO RAISE A BLISTER ON A PAIR of alligator boots and Daisy was not in the mood to vaccinate cows that afternoon. She sure wasn't in the mood to face Jarod after he hadn't called her all week. She drove past the ranch and down the road to the back of the property where the corral was located, grumbling the whole way. With any luck at all, he would have lit a shuck back to Oklahoma without even looking back.

The little blue Maverick bounced along for twenty minutes at less than ten miles an hour. Someday she was going to break down and buy a small pickup truck, an old one like Jim Bob's fishin' wagon, to do her vet business.

When she reached the corral she slapped the steering wheel with her palms. "Damn it all to hell. Does luck run when it sees me coming? Where are the cattle? I'm a vet tech. Does Emmett expect me to bring them in from the four corners of this place as well as take care of them?"

She got out of the car and listened intently, hoping to hear the bawling of a few cows being herded toward the corral. Nothing. She walked to the fence and climbed all the way to the top rail, balanced on it like a gymnast, and squinted as she looked out over the land. A cow over there eating what green grass it could find. Two over there close enough together that they looked like they were gossiping. Was one telling the other about the stud bull over in Jim Bob's pasture? Maybe the old bovine had been talking to Chigger. There was at least a dozen down there belly deep in dirty pond water. They'd better not let Emmett catch them skinny-dipping or he'd have a fit.

"Damn, damn, damn," she swore as she made her way down the split rails to the ground. Using the sleeve of a chambray work shirt she wore over a faded red tank top, she wiped the sweat from her brow as she got into the sweltering hot car and started it up again. How on earth a car that had been so cool ten minutes before could heat up so fast was a mystery as strange as a man who could turn to ice after the hottest sex she'd ever had.

She was halfway back to the ranch before the air conditioner cooled the car. She parked out behind the backyard fence and carried her bag to the porch where Emmett's two old Catahoula dogs were sleeping. She would vaccinate and worm them and tell Emmett to call a certified vet or the Walker men to work his cattle that year. She wasn't wasting another day and putting her car through the torment of driving to the back of his ranch.

"I won't desert you two old boys, but the cattle business is over and that's a promise," she said as she opened her bag.

Neither dog twitched an ear when she popped the needles into their hips.

"See, that didn't hurt and it'll keep you going for another year." She made notes in a small book she carried in her bag concerning dates and times the dogs had their shots. Later she'd transfer the information to her laptop back at the Honky Tonk.

Guinea opened his blue eye.

"It's not your fault I'm in such a foul mood," she said.

Duck opened both his blue and brown eye and wagged his tail a few times.

She rounded the two-story white frame house and found Emmett sitting on the porch in a rocking chair. He wore a sweat-stained, broad-brimmed straw hat, faded bibbed overalls, and a white T-shirt.

"For someone who loves air conditioning and refuses to go anywhere, you sure spend a lot of time on the porch," she grumbled.

He narrowed his eyes and pointed at her. "Where in the hell have you been? I been waitin' on you all day and I can't see you comin' if I'm sittin' in the house. At least you got on enough clothes today. What you had on the other day wouldn't sag a clothesline if you'd been swimmin' in them and they was soppin' wet. Don't know why you have to keep runnin' that Honky Tonk. Hire you some help. Hell, if you can't afford it, I'll even pay for it."

"Don't you be tellin' me how to run my business, Emmett McElroy. And why aren't the cattle in the corral? You usually have the Walkers or someone come get them ready for me. I'll be damned if I'm going to haul those bawling critters up from the farm ponds."

He completely ignored her question and kept talking nonsense. "I want you to stay at the ranch now. Get somebody else to run that damned old beer joint. We need you here."

"What in the hell are you talking about? Why would you think I need to stay here?" Daisy asked.

"Hello, Daisy. You're early," Jarod said from doorway. One look and he forgot that he'd been ready to spit nails that morning when he awoke. His mouth went dry and his hands trembled with the urge to rush out on the porch and gather her into his arms.

"Hello, Jarod," she said, surprised that she could utter a coherent word. She felt as if an elephant was sitting on her chest, crushing her lungs, keeping her from taking the next breath; so much for ending the attraction. She hated the morning after the first night of an affair. It was even more uncomfortable when it was the week later—a whole week of not hearing a single damn word. How dare he stand there, looking all sexy, reminding her how those strong arms felt holding her under a sky filled with twinkling stars and a full moon, and say nothing but that she was early.

Jarod was amazed that he'd gotten out a simple hello. He scanned her from head to toe and back again, stopping several times along the way. She looked like she'd just come in from a hard day's work out on the ranch. Dust on her jeans and scuffed up boots in bad need of polish. Staying away from her for a whole week damn sure hadn't kept him from wanting her. If anything, it made it worse.

She opened the door and handed him the cheesecake. "Yes, I'm early. I'll be leaving in a few minutes, though."

"Why? I do believe it was grilled steaks, baked potatoes, and corn on the cob?"

Daisy shot him her meanest drop-dead look. "Yes, it was, but since you haven't even started cooking, you can forget it."

"Why would I?"

"Because evidently you don't want me here."

"Why do you think that?"

"Come on, you aren't stupid. I haven't heard a word from you all week."

"I called you every single day all week. I called first thing in the morning. I called at noon, in the middle of the afternoon, even at two o'clock one morning, hoping I'd catch you before you left the bar. So don't tell me about not calling, woman. I tried. Don't you ever answer your phone—or do you leave it off the hook so you don't have to talk?"

"Oh!" The air gushed out of her lungs. "I was out on Monday morning and Tuesday a squirrel got in the transformer and blew the lines and…" She stopped. "You could have come to the Honky Tonk any night."

"Emmett's been sick," he whispered.

Emmett hit the rocker arms with his fist. "Now you two stop that bickerin'. I know the first year you do a lot of fightin' and makin' up, but I want to see more makin' up and less fightin'. Has he made you mad, darlin'? Is that why you stayed gone all week? Come on over here and sit down beside me and we'll talk about that boy of mine. He's a lot like me. Until I got Mavis I wasn't too swift with the women folks either, but I've been givin' him advice this week and I think he'll be better today."

"He's been like this all week," Jarod whispered through the screen door.

"Stop that whisperin' behind my back. And for God's sake, Jarod, give her a kiss. I'll shut my eyes if it embarrasses you to do it in front of me. Things I see on television these days would have put my grandma's eyes out and you can't even kiss Daisy in front of me. You ain't seen her all week. Don't know why she has to run that damn Honky Tonk anymore. This place can support her and we need her to help take care of things," Emmett said.

Jarod would have loved to kiss her but not with the tension still hanging between them. She had an excuse for Monday and Tuesday, but every single day in the week? He didn't think so. She owned a Honky Tonk that didn't close until two a.m. What would she be doing out every day?

Daisy sat down beside Emmett. "He'll be out here soon as he gets his boots on. Now you tell me why those cattle aren't in the corral."

Emmett snorted. "You need to go upstairs and put on a dress. Woman shouldn't run around on Sunday lookin' like you do. You expect that boy of mine to be nice then you need to be nice to him. Dress up so he'll take you out for ice cream. Me and Mavis used to drive over to Mineral Wells on Sunday afternoon. They had this little ice cream parlor and she ate strawberry. I damn sure wouldn't take you for strawberry ice cream in that getup. Mavis always dressed up in her best dress and waved her hair all pretty for our ice cream dates."

"I was supposed to vaccinate cows today. I didn't know anything about ice cream," Daisy said.

Emmett snorted. "Don't you make excuses, Daisy. You know very well we never work cattle on Sunday. I want you to be nice to Jarod and stop this bickering with him. He's not too bright. He don't see things as well as I do. He's been busy gettin' the ranch up in crackerjack shape before I die. Me, I got time to notice things now that I'm old," Emmett said. "Why would you think we work cattle on Sunday anyway?"

Emmett's blank eyes said that he really did not remember telling her that he wanted her to come to the ranch and vaccinate the cattle that day. Talking about it would only agitate him further so she changed the subject. "There was a whole family of coyotes in the pasture. Looked like a momma with five or six half grown babies. You got a donkey out there that'll kill them if they try to harm a baby calf? There were enough of them they might try to take down a small heifer. I don't reckon they'd mess with an old rangy bull though."

Before Emmett could answer Jarod joined them. He hadn't put on his boots but rather a pair of sandals. Even his naked toes made her hormones go into overdrive.

He chose a rocking chair on the other side of Emmett rather than the one right beside Daisy. He couldn't trust himself to sit that close to her without at least reaching across the space and touching her cheek.

Emmett's blue eyes narrowed and he pursed his mouth so tight the wrinkles from the top blended with those on his chin and erased his narrow lips. He glared at Jarod. "What in the hell have you done with my donkey? I ain't seen it around in a few days. Damn thing didn't die, did it? I hope to hell not. If that bunch of coyotes take down one of my baby calves, I'm holdin' you responsible."

Jarod almost choked. "I guess he's out in the back pasture."

"Well, put him up closer to the house. Them coyotes are gettin' brazen what with the hot summer and all. We might ought to buy another one. Keep one out with the cows and one up close to the house too. I thought I heard a mountain lion the other day settin' up a squall out in the pasture. Bet that donkey killed it 'cause I ain't heard it since then."

Daisy cut her eyes around at Jarod.

He barely shook his head and quickly mouthed that he'd tell her later.

"Let's have some of that cheesecake for an afternoon snack and then I'm going to take my Sunday nap," Emmett said. "Maybe you two can talk out this fight if I'm not here. Don't know why y'all are in a tiff but I know it. Jarod shoulda kissed you when you got here even if you are dressed like shit. You can't fool me, Daisy. You ain't been home all damn week so I know you are fightin' and right here at the first that ain't a good sign. I might be old but there ain't a damn thing wrong with my brain. You make him apologize and toe the line."

"Yes, sir, I will do that," she said.

"And you'll stay here tonight and not go to the Honky Tonk since it's closed, right?"

"Of course I will. I'll go fix us all a piece of cheese-cake. Want coffee to go with it or sweet tea?"

"Coffee. Black with just a touch of milk," he said.

"I'll fix it," Jarod said. "You two go on and visit." He had to get away from her even if for only a minute and collect his thoughts. Would he believe her if she had a plausible excuse for every day?

Emmett waited until he was in the house before he started on her again. "You going to tell me what it is you're fightin' about?"

"That's our business and we'll work it out," she said.

"It's my business if I've got to live with you, by damn."

"You're a nosy old fart, aren't you? You tell your mother-in-law everything you and Mavis fought about?"

He chuckled. "Hell, no. Nosy old woman didn't know when to keep her mouth shut."

"Do you know when to keep your mouth shut? What if I told you what we're fightin' about and you told Chigger or Jim Bob?"

Emmett shook his bony finger at her. "Don't you try to hoodwink me, young lady. I'm not so old that I don't know when you're sidetrackin' me. Married folks need to be together. You get rid of that Honky Tonk and come on out here to the ranch where you belong. Jarod can use your smarts as a vet to help with these cows. I'll give you three months and then I'll burn the damn thing down if you don't get rid of it."

For a split second, Daisy couldn't have uttered a word if it had been a matter of life and death. If Jarod hadn't returned with the cheesecake and coffee on a tray she might have bolted and ran. She cleared her throat twice. She looked at Jarod who stood there with a cheesecake on a saucer in front of her. She was careful not to touch him when she reached for it.

She held it in her lap and glowered at Emmett. "What in the hell are you talking about?" She accentuated each word with a jab of her finger against the arm of his rocking chair.

Emmett narrowed his eyes and leaned right up into her face. "I mean it. I'll burn it to the ground and spend the rest of my life in jail for doing it if you don't come to your senses. From what the doctor tells me about these worms in my body, I ain't got long anyway so I don't give a damn if I spend it behind bars or sittin' in my chair. Now I'm going to eat my cheesecake and take my nap and you two are going to get this shit settled.

I ain't in the mood to listen to fightin'. It'd make that cheesecake sour on my stomach."

He didn't say another word until he was finished and his coffee cup empty. "And this will be taken care of when I get up. I ain't havin' my supper ruined because you two are acting like a couple of bratty kids."

"Yes sir," Daisy said.

"Sorry about that," Jarod whispered when Emmett slammed the screen door.

"What in the hell is going on? He thinks that we are…" She stumbled over the word.

Jarod nervously ran his fingers through his hair. "I know what he thinks. He's been like this ever since Sunday. Let's go for a walk around to the backyard. I wouldn't put it past him to be eavesdropping."

He led the way across the porch, around the south end of the house, and to the backyard to an old swing hanging from an ancient pecan tree. He sat down on one end of it and patted the other end.

"Have a seat and let me explain."

She sat down and waited.

"I took him to the doctor. He said it's typical of the Alzheimer's and he's got kidney failure on top of that. Said that when the kidneys start to go they produce too much nitrogen and it eats little holes in the brain. Depending on what portion is being destroyed, it affects whether he wants to eat everything in sight or nothing sounds good. That's the worms he says are eating him up. He's got less time than we figured," Jarod said.

"But where did he ever get the idea we were…" She still could not utter the word.

"He got the notion in his head last Sunday night. Started in on me that it wasn't right for you to stay at the Honky Tonk at night and only come out here on Sunday. I argued with him and told him we were *not* married. He got so mad I thought he'd blow a fuse and have a stroke. Said I couldn't pull the wool over his eyes and he wasn't born yesterday. He could tell by the way we looked at each other that we'd snuck off to Oklahoma on Sunday and got married. What were you two talking about? Why would you be upset because the cattle weren't up in the corral? What would you be doing with cattle on Sunday or any other day?"

"I'm a vet tech. I've been vaccinating his cattle for about four years now. I'm not a licensed vet but I can take care of what he's got left. Herd is diminishing pretty fast but then he's not able to take care of them. Usually he gets the Walkers to come over and round them up for me."

"You are vet tech and you work as a barmaid?" Jarod cocked his head to one side. His dark eyebrows knit into a line across his gray eyes.

"You got a problem with that?" she snapped.

"Why aren't you working for a vet?"

"Bartending pays better. I take care of a few animals on the side. Emmett and Mavis hired me when they got to where it was too much of a job. Most ranchers as you know take care of their own cattle unless it's an emergency. I stay busier than I want."

"But," Jarod started.

Daisy exhaled loudly. "All I ever wanted to do was work with animals, especially on a ranch. I got a job with a vet in Mena, Arkansas, and I really loved it. But one night I had a boyfriend problem, got in the car, and started driving." She sat back and looked off into the distance for a moment with a pained look in her eyes that made Jarod want to jump up, find the jerk who'd hurt her, and beat him senseless. Then, with a little shiver, she seemed to shake off the bad memory and shrugged. "The car broke down on Interstate 20 not far from Thurber. I pulled off and met Ruby. She offered me a job as a bartender and I took it. I'd been working as a bartender for years, even before I was legal. Kept at it on weekends when I finished my tech training to pay the student loans off."

She smiled, thinking about Ruby. That chance encounter with the woman who was like a mother to her had been a turning point in her life. "Anyway, when I took the job Ruby offered, I called my vet boss. He said he was glad I was getting out of Mena and away from the scumbag boyfriend who would never leave the area and to let him know if I needed a reference for a tech job. Ruby told Merle that I had vet tech training and word got out here in Texas. Merle started it when she brought her cat to the Honky Tonk for me to treat it one night. Before I knew it I was treating everything from chickens to horses. This week on Monday I had to sew up a bull that forced its fat way through a barbed wire fence. I've given a goat Pepto for bloat and talked to a sweet old lady who insists on feeding her dog, George—named for George Jones, no less. Anyway, she wants to let him drink beer. She says she can put up with dog farts."

The chuckle started down deep in his chest and erupted into a guffaw that scared the sparrows out of the pecan tree. He laughed until his sides ached and then laughed some more.

"Go on," he said finally.

"It's not really funny," Daisy said, although she was starting to grin—his laughter was contagious. "Some days I don't know if I'm comin' or goin'. Now, do you think Emmett will be over this married shit when he wakes up?"

Jarod's shook his head. "You are really something, Daisy. I was so mad at you for not taking my calls I couldn't think straight."

"Why?" she asked.

"I wanted to see you again. I thought you had another fellow…" he stammered.

"I thought you didn't call because it was just a one night stand for you," she said softly. "And I was mad enough to call for the backhoe for the local cemetery."

"Guess we both got things wrong, didn't we? Miss Daisy O'Dell, could I please have your cell phone number before you leave here so this doesn't happen again?"

She smiled. "Yes, sir, you can. Now answer my question about Emmett."

"I don't think so. He's been on the kick all week long. First thing he asks every morning is when you are coming downstairs. I finally told him you were trying to get someone to help you at the Honky Tonk and until you did you'd be here on Sunday and Monday. He's been antsy every evening like a little kid asking when you were coming home." Jarod could hardly believe his ears. Daisy, a vet tech? What other tricks did she have up her sleeves?

"What are you going to do?" she asked.

"Beg," Jarod said.

She snapped her head around to face him. "Oh, no. Huh-uh, not in a million years. Not for all the dirt in Texas. Besides, I don't owe you jack shit."

"He's been a nightmare. I couldn't leave him all week or I would have driven up to the Honky Tonk."

They were adults, not whimpering teenagers. Sitting beside him with her pulse racing and wanting to reach out and run her hand down his jawline before she kissed him passionately, she wished she was a teenager instead of an adult.

"I'm not staying. You can deal with him," she said. What she didn't say was that she didn't trust herself to stay in the same house with Jarod. Just sitting beside him on the swing put her on an emotional roller coaster.

"I'll pay you," Jarod said quickly. "He won't know when we go upstairs at night that we are sleeping in separate rooms. He's put you into Mavis' place. Whatever she said went around here and he's been lost since she's gone. You've given him a reason to live. I can't believe you got him to agree to a donkey on the property. Next thing you know he'll be puttin' up windmills if you say you think they're a good idea." *Hell, woman, I'd buy windmills, a donkey, and anything else you can think of to get you to stay here tonight.*

Daisy took a deep breath and let it out very slowly. To sleep one door down the hallway from him every night for several weeks would be pure hell. She'd spent a hell of a week trying to get him out of her mind. She'd never get it done if she slept with him again, and every minute of every night would be a temptation. And like he had just said, letting it go on would be pure foolishness.

The swing stopped and Jarod started it again with the heel of his sandal against the hard packed earth. "Please stay the afternoon and night before you say no. See what happens when he wakes up. Could be he'll get up in a whole new world but I don't think so. It's set in his mind like chiseling on a tombstone."

"The afternoon and night?" she said weakly.

"You told him you'd stay," he protested.

"I was just following your lead in appeasing the old goat."

Jarod crossed his arms over his chest, more in a gesture to keep from touching her than to exhibit an attitude. "If he doesn't forget the whole thing when he wakes up, you're the one telling him you aren't staying. I damn sure am not going to be in his bad graces the rest of the week. He's bad enough when he's looking for you to drive up any minute. If he thinks you aren't staying he'll go off in a tantrum that'll rival any two-year-old kid's fit you've ever seen."

She stood up.

"Where are you going?" he asked.

He damn sure didn't want to worry with Uncle Emmett if she left. He was damned if he got what he wanted and damned if he didn't. He'd get the blame and a ten-hour lecture on how to treat a woman properly if she left. The same one he'd listened to every day all week. However, if she stayed, the scalding heat between them could burn down the place. He'd take a chance on the latter if she'd just consent to stay.

"To get a glass of tea. I can't think when I'm sitting still," she said.

Jarod followed her back into the house. "If you stay it only has to be until he goes to bed or maybe we can even invent an excuse before that. I'll step outside and call on your cell phone and you can say something about having to go take care of one of your animal things. Just until dark tonight, please."

"Until dark and then I'll think about the rest of the time."

Good God Almighty, why did I say that? I don't want to spend my whole afternoon here and I'm damn sure not going to spend nights on end sleeping so close to Jarod that I can smell his cologne in the evenings.

"Thank you," Jarod said. He touched her shoulder and the world stood still. When it started spinning again it made him dizzy.

The heat from his hand left a burn mark on her back. She was sure of it because she could feel each joint of his finger engraved there. A single week of pretending and she'd be a drooling moron in a white straightjacket. "Don't thank me yet. I just agreed to stay until dark."

They were walking up on the porch when Emmett pushed his walker out the door. Jarod grabbed Daisy around the waist and kissed her hard and long. When she pushed him back, he whispered, "It's part of the pretending."

Pretend, hell! I'll show you pretend if you do that again. I'll pretend to haul you out to the barn and I'll pretend to have another bout of sex with you. Don't tell me that kiss was fake. It was more real than anything I've ever experienced short of that night in the truck bed, Daisy thought.

Emmett sat down in his rocker and slapped his thigh. "Now that's what I like to see. You made up. I knew you would. You two go on up and have your afternoon nap now," he said with a broad wink at Jarod. "I'm glad you're home, Daisy."

"Dear God," Daisy whispered.

"Amen! He's sweet as sugar when he gets his way and mean as a cougar when he doesn't. I don't know if I can take it, and I can't leave," Jarod whispered back.

Emmett tilted his chin up in a knowing gesture. "Just like I told you, sweet nothin's in her ear will work every time. Woman likes that more than anything. Glad to see you are finally listenin' to me."

Jarod let go of Daisy and opened the door for her. "So are you ready for a nap?"

She glared at Jarod, angry at him and Chigger and Jim Bob all three for putting her in such a pickle. If Chigger hadn't needed an alibi for her momma none of it would have started to begin with. So the majority of the blame and anger went towards her. A nap might be just the thing to clear her mind. At the very least it would keep her from strangling Jarod and then going after Chigger with her shotgun.

Once they were in the house he threw up both hands to ward off the evil looks. "Hey, don't shoot daggers at me. I didn't create this mess."

"And I did?" she smarted off.

"I did not say that."

"Which room is mine?" she snapped.

He pointed up the stairs. "Mine is the one with the computer in it. You can have the one right beside it. It's pink," he said.

She stomped across the hardwood floor and up the stairs. The door to the first one on the left was open and she peeked in. The faint smell of his cologne was still in the room and a computer sitting on a card table in the corner said the room belonged to him. She went on to the next door to the pink room. Just before she slammed the door, she thought about Emmett. If he heard the crack of a door he'd think they were fighting again and Jarod would have to kiss her to prove they weren't. Easing the door shut was the most difficult thing she'd done all day. She kicked off her boots and removed the snowy white chenille bedspread. No use in getting it all dusty just because she was angry. It hadn't created the mess she was in.

The bed was an antique cherry four-poster with a matching vanity that had a round mirror and a little bench with a pink velvet cushion top. A rocking chair with the same color velvet pads sat in the corner of the room. Every flat surface had a crocheted doily covered with knickknacks. Chigger should be the one playing at being the new bride. She'd love all the folderol sitting on every spare inch of space. It gave Daisy an acute case of claustrophobia.

She stared at the ceiling for a long time before she made her up mind to go along with the charade. She could easily kill the two proverbial birds with one big rock. Let Emmett die happy and put the crazy thing she had for Jarod behind her all at the same time. Jarod was probably a real son-of-a-bitch, just like Emmett, when he didn't get his way. She planned to provoke him often so that she could see him at his worst and then presto, the fascination with him would vanish.

She snapped her fingers in the air to show herself how fast it could be done and went to sleep with a smile on her face.

When she awoke she had a plan that she could live with so she bounded out of bed, picked up her boots, and bounced down to the living room. "Hey, I thought we were having steaks. I'm starving. Am I going to have to grill them myself? And after supper I think you should take me for ice cream."

Jarod dropped the book he'd been reading and his jaw at the same time. The book hit the floor with a bang. His jaw came close to unhinging.

"Okay?" he said slowly.

Emmett smiled. "I love ice cream."

"Car is air conditioned. You could come along if you want," she offered.

"Naw, y'all go on and have a good time. Me and Mavis used to go get ice cream on Sundays some of the time. I like it that you're goin'. But first, Jarod, get up off your lazy ass and get those steaks going. Didn't you hear the woman say she's hungry?"

"I'll even help," she offered.

Emmett began to hum. The expression on his face was happy and peaceful.

She shucked six ears of corn and put them in boiling water, popped a dozen brown-and-serve rolls into the oven with the foil-wrapped potatoes already baking, and set the table while Jarod grilled steaks.

Emmett was sitting at the table when Jarod brought in the steaks. "I been waitin' for half an hour. It's a wonder I ain't dead. You tryin' to kill me by starvin' me to death so you can have this ranch faster. If I don't eat I can't take my medicine and it's twenty minutes past time for me to have it. Y'all are the slowest cooks I ever did see."

Daisy put the potatoes and corn on the table. "It's here now so eat and stop your whinin'."

"If I die it'll be on your conscience because you didn't get my food to me so I could take my medicine." He picked up a long pill case with the days of the week lettered on the compartments. "See here, I ain't had my evenin' pills because I got to take them with food."

"Then eat," she said shortly.

"Don't you sass me."

"Don't be a pain in my ass."

Jarod chuckled under his breath.

They both shot him a dirty look.

"What?" He threw up his hands.

"Don't laugh at me."

Emmett settled down immediately. "No more fightin'. Let's eat these steaks. Don't they look good, Daisy?"

She cut a chunk off the corner and popped it into her mouth, chewed slowly, and tamed her anger. "How anyone could ever be a vegetarian is a mystery to me."

"Fools is what they are. God made the Angus for us to eat," Emmett agreed.

"Then why in the devil do you have a bunch of white faced cattle out there? Angus don't get pinkeye like they do and Angus grows off faster and bigger," Daisy said.

"Them white faces was cheaper on the day I bought them than Angus," Emmett said.

"Get rid of them and use the money to buy Angus," Daisy told him.

"You hear the woman. Get rid of them sorry white faces this week, Jarod. Take 'em to the sale barn," Emmett said.

"Last week you said we weren't sellin' off a single head of cattle."

"That was last week. This is today. Sell the sumbitches. If Daisy wants Angus steaks then we'll have Angus steaks. Maybe then I won't have to burn down that sumbitch Honky Tonk."

Daisy pointed her fork at him. "Hey, wait a minute."

"Angus or the Honky Tonk. Your decision," Emmett declared.

She shoved a piece of steak in her mouth to keep from smarting off. All the Angus cattle in the state of Texas could die of mad cow disease before she'd give up her beer joint.

"You going to answer me?" Emmett asked after a few seconds.

"I'm thinkin' about it," she said.

"Well, that's the way it is. You got until sale time to make up your mind. You ain't back here where you belong, I'll sell all the Angus and keep the white faces and you can deal with pinkeye forever."

Jarod coughed.

She huffed.

He grinned.

She bit her tongue to keep from lashing out with a string of cuss words long enough to scorch the hair out of Lucifer's ears.

After supper they shared the cleanup with Emmett rushing them to hurry so the ice cream parlor wouldn't be closed before they arrived.

"You two is the slowest critters on the earth. A possum ain't got a thing on you for lazy. You'd think you didn't even want any ice cream," he said.

"I've got to shake the tablecloth and then we'll go. Why do you want us to leave anyway? You got a hot date with some filly?" Daisy teased.

"Hell no, I ain't got no date with a woman. Mavis would claw her eyes out if I did. Get on out of here and let me watch my television in peace and quiet and don't you dare wake me up if I'm sleeping when you get home," he fussed.

Jarod was amazed when she tossed him the keys as they were leaving.

"You trust me to drive your precious car?" he whispered.

"You are driving because men drive when they go with their wives for ice cream and Emmett will have a fit if I do. We're going to the Honky Tonk so I can pack a few things. If I'm staying over until tomorrow evening, I'll need some clothes and my personal stuff. Can't have the old goat having a stroke out of anger, can we? But it's got to be our secret. Far as anyone knows I'm just coming out here to see you and Emmett. We aren't even dating. We are barely friends. That's the condition," she said softly so Emmett wouldn't hear.

Jarod started up the engine and backed the small car out of the driveway. It had been years since he'd driven anything but a truck and he felt cramped. "You got it."

She leaned her head back and shut her eyes. She could come to the ranch on Sunday morning and stay over until Monday; maybe make a couple of appearances through the week with the excuse she had to leave by seven to get back to the Honky Tonk. It would make Emmett happy.

When he stopped the car she opened her eyes and blinked several times. Surely that wasn't who she thought it was sitting on her back porch. It was simply a trick of the light and the fact that she'd just talked to

Cathy the week before. It had to be Chigger stopping by for one more beer or a glass of tea because she didn't want to go home. She squinted and narrowed her eyes.

"Very nice lookin' company," Jarod said.

"My cousin," Daisy mumbled.

Cathy opened the passenger's door for Daisy. "You said I could come anytime. I hope you meant it. I quit my job."

How in the devil am I going to explain Jarod and Emmett to Cathy? She'll have to know at least the part about Emmett being a dying man.

Daisy said, "Of course I meant it. This is Jarod McElroy. I was just coming by to pick up a few things. I'll be gone until tomorrow night. Think you can just hang out and make yourself at home without me?"

Cathy took a step back. "Nice to meet you, Jarod. How'd you talk her into driving her baby?"

"It's a mystery." He smiled.

Cathy was taller than Daisy. She had long, flowing blond hair and the same steely blue eyes as Daisy. Her waist was small and her hips rounded. A bright blue T-shirt was tucked into the waistband of tight jeans and stretched over her skin like blue paint. Not an extra ounce of fat or cellulite bubbled up under the shirt. If a man didn't take a second look he was either blind or stupid.

Jarod was neither. But she wasn't as pretty as Daisy. Even though her eyes were close to the same color, they didn't sparkle like Daisy's did when she was angry or tickled. She was so tall that if he ever held her in his arms she wouldn't fit there perfectly like Daisy did. And she didn't have the pizzazz that Daisy had when she walked, either. Pretty lady, and most men would already be drooling, but she didn't light up his desire button like Daisy did.

Cathy touched the car and peeled her eyes away from Jarod back to Daisy. "So since he got to drive it, are you goin' to let me drive it?"

"Hell, no. Last time you drove my car it wound up in the junkyard."

"It was a piece of junk anyway," Cathy said.

Daisy turned and looked at Jarod. "You comin' in?"

"No, ma'am. I'm waiting right here. Figure you two got some talkin' to do that'll be easier if I'm waitin' under the shade tree." He shut off the engine and rolled down the windows. The night breeze was still scalding hot but not as much as his thoughts. He'd started measuring women by Daisy and how she made him feel. Were all women going to come up on the short end of the stick when he looked at them?

Yes, they are, he thought with a groan. *What happened to "I'm not going to fall for a bartender?" So what if she's a vet tech too. She's in Texas and has stated more than once that she loves her bar and won't leave it. I'm going home to Oklahoma when this business with Emmett is over. What in the hell am I going to do?*

Daisy looped her arm through Cathy's. "It might have been a piece of junk but it was mine and it was all I had to get back and forth to work. So no, you cannot drive my car."

Cathy followed her to the back door of the Honky Tonk where several suitcases were stacked up. "Okay, I won't ask again if you'll give me a job."

Daisy looked around the parking lot and back at Cathy. "How in the hell did you get here? You damn sure didn't walk with all that baggage."

"It's a long story."

Daisy hadn't believed in coincidence or fate, not one bit, until the day her car played out and she met Ruby. Now here was Cathy parked on her doorstep needing a job the same day she'd made up her mind to go along with the lie about being married to Jarod. It had to be an omen that she was doing the right thing.

"Tell me the short version."

"Brad and I were saving money for a big wedding. We bought a car together and used both of our old ones for trade-ins. When he left he took the car so I rode a bus from Mena to Mineral Wells and caught a taxi from there to here."

"Good lord. The taxi fare would have bought a good secondhand car."

"I can afford it. I just didn't want to buy a vehicle until I found out whether I was staying here or not. Couch is new since I was here. Does this one make out into a bed?" Cathy asked.

"Yes, it does and yes, you can claim it. I haven't got time to explain the whole thing but I'm glad you are here. I need someone to close up for me at night. You've got experience in that. We'll both work until ten and then you can keep it going until two all by yourself. I'll be home tomorrow evening and tell you the whole story. You okay with that?"

"I'd be fine if you handed me a toothbrush and told me to scrub the toilet with it. I need a change of scenery that bad."

Daisy pointed. "Make yourself at home. There's food in the 'fridge and beer in the Honky Tonk. I'll be home after supper tomorrow. Got to grab a few things."

"Get on with it. Like I said, I'm sleepy. The ride down here was hell on wheels. Didn't know how much I loved to fly until I had to take a damned bus. Why couldn't you live in Dallas?"

"Want me to stay so you can talk?" Daisy asked.

"Nope. I want to sleep all day and all night and then we'll talk. Besides, if that hot sexy hunk out there in the car was waiting for me, I wouldn't have taken as much time as you already have."

Chapter 8

DAISY THREW HER SUITCASE IN THE BACKSEAT AND GOT into the car. Jarod had turned off the engine and rolled down the windows on both sides. Hot wind blew across the front seat.

"Why didn't you just leave it running?" she asked.

"Didn't know how long you were going to take. You've been hot before and it didn't kill you."

"Don't be a smart aleck, and if I remember right you were as hot as I was," she said.

"I wasn't talking about that. Is there air conditioning in the corrals when you work cattle?"

Daisy looked out the side window until her face stopped burning.

"I do want to thank you one more time for doing this," Jarod said.

"I'm not doing it for you. I'm doing it for Emmett," she said.

"Why? Would you do it for Billy Bob's dad?" Jarod said.

"He isn't dyin' and he doesn't have Alzheimer's," she said.

"If he was and Billy Bob asked you?"

"But he ain't and Billy Bob didn't. Why does it matter anyway? It's just a pretend job until the old goat is dead. Are you going to start the engine and turn on the air conditioning or are we going to sit here and bake like a couple of hams in the oven?"

Jarod turned the key and wound up his window. "Why do you call him an old goat?"

Daisy wound up the window on her side of the car. "When he and Mavis used to come into the Honky Tonk all the time, she called him an old goat. 'Give me a beer for the old goat before he gets thirsty and mean.' Or she'd say, 'The old goat is grumpy tonight. I must love him to live with him.' I barely knew his real name the first two years I bartended. He was the old goat and she was the sweetheart. It's not disrespectful. It's an endearment. Don't go south, go north. We'll drive the back way into Gordon. There's a convenience store and we'll have an ice cream sandwich or an Eskimo pie. We were going for ice cream, remember?"

Jarod made a right-hand turn out of the parking lot. "So they were like an uncle and aunt to you?"

"Maybe."

"Were you at Aunt Mavis' funeral?" He tried to picture her even in the shadows and couldn't.

"Of course I was. Ruby came with me. I don't remember seeing you."

"I was there," he said defensively.

"Hey, I'm not doubting that you were, but the church was packed. We sat in folding chairs all the way against the back wall."

Then she remembered. He'd been the tall man who'd walked beside Emmett when the family entered the church. She hadn't seen anything but his back at the funeral, which had been a good thing. A funeral sure wasn't the place for the thoughts she'd had about him ever since she'd seen him the first time.

"Did you go to the dinner?"

"No, that was for family."

Jarod gripped the steering wheel. Why hadn't he met her at the funeral? Why hadn't he known from the beginning that she was so much more than a bartender? Why did everything have to be so blasted complicated?

He hadn't answered a single question when he parked in front of the convenience store out beside the highway in Gordon. "What do you want?" he asked.

"One of those big ice cream sandwiches with Neapolitan ice cream in the middle. I'll wait in the car."

He reached to turn the key and she slapped his hand. "Don't you dare. It's just now getting cool."

Sparks ricocheted around the inside of the car like a bullet in an empty metal building. Ice cream might cool her tongue but it wouldn't do a blessed thing to stop the slow burn in her heart and soul.

Jarod went inside and picked up two sandwiches from inside the freezer. The brush of her hand against his had sent desire shooting through his veins. Had she felt the same thing?

"Have to eat them fast, hot as it is," the sales clerk said as he rang up the purchase.

"You got that right," Jarod said.

"Reckon we'll ever see a rain cloud again?"

"I'd be willin' to do a stomp dance if it would bring one around," Jarod teased.

"You got any notion that it'll work, I'll round up the FFA club over in Gordon and we'll help you. Here's your change, sir. Y'all have a nice day."

"You too," Jarod said as he left.

"They didn't have Neapolitan," he said as he tossed one in her lap. No way was he tempting fate again. A slight touch had him creating erotic mental images. Anything more and he'd be claiming his rights as a "pretend" husband, only the rights would be very real.

"This is fine." She peeled back the wrapper and bit into the cold ice cream. It didn't do jack shit to cool down anything but her mouth, but it did give her something to hold in her hands to keep them from straying over to his thigh—or higher.

Emmett was on the porch again when Jarod drove up. He yelled, "Take Daisy's car around to the garage and move my old truck out. It don't matter if that old truck gets wet if a rainstorm comes up but that car is too pretty to set out in the weather."

"I'll be damned."

"Now what's the matter with you? Did you drip ice cream on your shirt?" Daisy asked.

"He wouldn't let me park my truck in the garage."

"He loves you but he likes me. Bring in my suitcase and my vet bag, please."

"Yes, ma'am. Anything else the princess and the king desire from the measly peon hired help?"

"Only that you put your cranky mood in the garage with the car. I got you a donkey, maybe two, so be nice."

She got out and sat down on the top porch step. Jarod revved up the engine, popped the clutch, and backed up with enough force to create a dust storm.

Daisy yelled at him, "That's the last time you'll ever drive my car."

"Is he showin' out or has he got another burr in his ass? You wasn't gone long enough to go to Mineral Wells for ice cream," Emmett said.

"Did you ever show out for Mavis after you went for ice cream?"

A wide grin split his wrinkled face. "You're damn right I did. One time I spun out of her driveway, that's back before we was married, and I was drivin' an old 1945 model Ford, and scared the chickens so bad that her daddy said I couldn't come back unless I rode up in a buggy with horses pullin' it."

"Did you?" Daisy asked.

"Nope. But I was a sight more careful after that. How come you didn't go to Mineral Wells?"

Jarod opened the screen door and sat down so close to Daisy that their thighs touched. "We had to go to the Honky Tonk. Daisy forgot some things that she'll need to stay all night. We drove over there and got ice cream at that little store in Gordon."

"That ain't as romantic as going to the ice cream parlor, but I'm glad Daisy is moving in here at the ranch. We need to talk about our donkeys. I been sittin' here nigh on to an hour and ain't one of them critters showed its face yet. How they goin' to protect my cattle if they ain't around?"

"They're probably out in the pasture taking care of mean coyotes," Daisy said. She hoped her voice didn't sound as loud and squeaky to them as it did in her ears. "I kept a lookout and didn't see a single coyote on our way back from our drive."

She swallowed a sharp gasp when Jarod slung his arm around her shoulder. A million dollars couldn't pay for the effects his touch had on her; hell's bells, enough to buy her a ranch complete with cattle and dogs couldn't pay for it.

She told herself over and over that it was all acting. She'd seen her mother do it for years. Pretend to be happy in a situation from hell. Pretend to be unhappy when the hell producing man took off. Surely she had enough of her mother's genes to pull off a simple acting job.

Emmett's chair squeaked when he rocked. "I was watchin' a television show while y'all was gone. T. Boone Pickett was on it talkin' about these newfangled windmills that make electricity. Funny lookin' things stickin' up out of the ground, but T. Boone says they'll do the job. I visited with him one time at a cattle sale up in Kansas City. Seemed like a decent man. What do you think of him, Daisy?"

"Don't think he ever came into the Honky Tonk so I couldn't say," she answered.

"That beer joint isn't the only place on earth," Emmett snapped.

"Don't you get cranky with me. I never met the man so how can I give an opinion of him?" Daisy shot right back.

Emmett frowned. "Well, what do you think of the idea of them crazy lookin' windmills like they got growin' like a damn forest over by Abilene?"

"Hell, Emmett, I wouldn't know. I'd have to study on it."

"That's my girl. Don't be makin' no rash decisions. You study up on it and let me know in a few days what you think of the notion. I've been thinkin' if they're good enough for T. Boone that I might be gettin' me a couple of them. Bet that whirlin' blade thing would keep the coyotes out as good as the donkey which Jarod is hiding from me," he said.

Jarod stopped teasing her arm and his hand went tense. "I'm not hiding a damn donkey. Tomorrow mornin' I'll go round the critter up myself and bring it to sit with you on the porch. Hell, you can even tell it some of your stories if you want to."

Emmett slyly winked at Daisy.

If he had Alzheimer's she'd eat her dirty socks for breakfast. He was playing both of them and having a great time doing so. But then he hadn't remembered that he told her to come out on Sunday and work the cattle. However, he did remember that she was supposed to bring the cheesecake. Daisy's mind went in circles trying to decide whether or not he was playing them or was sincerely losing his ability to think.

What if he's not? What if he's just having a good evening and teasing? that niggling little voice of conscience asked.

Not knowing for sure is the thing that keeps me here.

Jarod wanted to take Daisy up to his bedroom and make passionate love to her until daybreak and forget all about a stupid jackass and windmills.

Emmett went on. "You go roust that jackass up and I'll tell him some stories all right. Another thing." He stopped long enough to inhale deeply so he could start again. "Why in the hell ain't you been to the sales yet? I told you last week to get rid of them damn white faces and use the money to buy some more Angus. Remember? If Daisy moved here and forgot that damned beer joint I said I'd buy more Angus. That was a week ago and I ain't seen a cattle truck leavin' here yet to go to the sale."

"That was today," Jarod said.

Emmett raised his voice. "Don't you tell me when it was. I ain't lost my mind."

Daisy bristled. "Don't you yell at us, Emmett McElroy. I didn't say you had lost your mind. We were waiting for the sale this week because I got news that the price of cattle was going up from last week to this one. I told you that yesterday. We'll be taking the white faced ones off on Tuesday."

"The sale in Abilene is on Wednesday, not Tuesday. You'll need to round them up on Tuesday, put them in the corral, and get up early on Wednesday to load them. Get to the sale late and you'll lose money," Emmett said.

"We'll be there when the doors open and we'll get a good price for the cattle. We aren't going to cheat you out of one red dime. Now I'm going to get my book and read while Jarod does the evening chores," Daisy said.

"You're going to play hell. You are a farm wife now. You'll help him," Emmett said.

"I don't have much to do this evening. Daisy can help me tomorrow," Jarod said. He would love to have her beside him while he took care of feeding the livestock but he'd already pressed his luck in getting her to stay the night.

"Okay, then Daisy can make breakfast in the morning. I'll have a slab of fried ham, some scrambled eggs, fried potatoes with onions in them, and maybe a pan of real biscuits. None of that canned shit like Jarod cooks."

"You aren't supposed to have any of that. You're on a salt-free, low-fat diet for your heart and—" Jarod protested.

"Let me eat what I want and die when I'm supposed to. I'm not stupid just because I'm old. I know my time is short, but I won't be treated like a panty waste. I'm a man and I'll die a man with a fork in my hand and bacon in my mouth," Emmett said.

"If you'd have told Dad earlier, I would have come down here and kept things going before now," Jarod said.

"Didn't want you to know. I'm dyin' and I don't give a damn. Quicker I go the quicker I can see Mavis. I miss her and I'm tired of livin' without her, so death ain't no big thing. I'm just glad you come down here and met Daisy when you did. Mavis told me she'd love to see you hooked up with a woman just like Daisy. Why, I bet she's sittin' up there on them clouds happy as a lark that you found Daisy. I ain't talkin' no more about this death shit so that's it."

Daisy swallowed the lump in her throat. "Okay, it's a deal. I get to read my book tonight and I'll make breakfast. Everything you just said. We got to keep your strength up if you are going to the sale on Wednesday."

"Hell, I ain't goin'. You are. With Jarod. And I expect those cattle to be in top shape so they'll bring the best price. You get them shot and treated for everything in the world and take the papers to show it."

"Yes, sir," Daisy saluted.

—⁂—

The sun was half of a big orange ball slowly lowering on the horizon by the time Jarod finished the evening chores at the ranch. Daisy rubbed Duck's ear. Her book was laid to one side and she was barefoot.

Jarod jumped the fence and sat down beside her.

"Why'd he name a dog Duck?" she asked.

"Same reason he named the other one Guinea. Says they make a racket when anyone drives up," Jarod answered.

"Not anymore."

Jarod scratched Guinea's ear. "I guess they're about worn out."

Emmett threw open the door. "Your purse is playin' music and I can't hear the television for it. Who in the hell are you anyway? Jarod, I told you not to bring women in here. She better be gone 'fore Mavis comes home with the groceries or she'll throw you off this ranch on your ass."

Daisy brushed past him on her way inside the house. "Jarod didn't invite me here. You did. Don't you remember? I'm Jarod's wife and Mavis passed on a while back."

"Ah, hell, I forgot. Sometimes I do that but you got to tell your purse to stop playin' music."

"I'll go turn it off right now."

She found her purse sitting on her suitcase at the foot of the staircase. Caller ID showed that the call had been from the Honky Tonk.

She poked in the numbers and waited.

Cathy picked up on the first ring. "Thank God you called back. There's a big fellow named Tinker who's trying to throw me out."

"Put him on the phone," Daisy said.

"Miss Daisy?" Tinker said.

"Tinker, that's Cathy. She's my cousin and she'll be moving in with me and helping at the Honky Tonk. What are you doing in town on Sunday?"

"Out riding my cycle and saw her sitting on the front porch. Told her the Honky Tonk ain't open on Sunday.

She swore she was here because y'all was kinfolks. I'll be on my way now. See you tomorrow night. Good-bye, Miz Daisy," Tinker said bluntly.

Daisy held the phone out and sure enough the connection was broken. Before she could hit the buttons to call Cathy back, it rang again.

"Hello."

"Daisy, that is one big, scary man," she said.

"He's my bouncer."

"Why didn't I ever meet him?"

"Because you've only been to Mingus one time and that was on Sunday. Everything else all right?"

"I was watching the sunset. It's gorgeous from here. I may never leave. This Honky Tonk may be my new love."

"I've heard that story before, girl. Only it was named Darrin or Bob or Blake or Jimmy. Six weeks and you'll be ready for a high-powered business suit type job."

"We'll see. There's peace here, Daisy. No wonder you squatted and never came back to Mena. See you tomorrow. I'm dyin' to hear what's goin' on with you and that handsome hunk you let drive your car."

"I'll tell you tomorrow. Good night," Daisy said.

"Good night and thanks for everything," Cathy said.

She hung up before Daisy could even tell her that she was welcome.

When she turned around Jarod was only inches from her face. She gasped, threw up an arm, and took a step back. "You scared me," she said.

"Who hit you?" he asked. The look on her face said it all and enraged Jarod to the point that he wanted to beat half to death whoever had laid a malicious hand on her. Hell, he might even beat him all the way to the cold stage. Daisy was too precious to be anyone's punching bag.

She was still stunned and answered before she thought, "His name was Chris and it was a long time ago. You startled me."

"Tell me about it."

She shook her head. "Nothing to tell. It's in the past. That was Cathy. Tinker stopped by and was fixing to throw her out in the street. Had to clear it up with him. Never thought about him coming into town on Sunday but he was out riding his cycle."

Jarod sat down on the steps. "Why don't you want to talk about Chris hitting you?"

"Dragging it up won't make it different, and besides, it's not a damn bit of your business," Daisy said.

"You are my wife," he said.

"Then I'll tell you a pretend story since I'm a pretend wife. You want the poor pitiful Cinderella story or the one where Daisy O'Dell pumped up her shotgun and made a believer out of a sorry bastard?"

"I wouldn't believe either one and it would take a saint to be married to you in real life," Jarod said.

"I don't see any halos or wings on you," Daisy smarted off.

"Why do I have to pull every damn thing out of you? Why didn't you tell me you were a vet?" Jarod asked.

"I'm not. I'm a vet tech. What I work at doesn't make me who I am, so what the hell difference does it make? You can either like me for who I am or forget it. What I am isn't only a paycheck."

"You are a hard woman, Daisy."

"Yes, I am."

"We've got a couple of hours before bedtime. What do we talk about if you are so picky about your ex?"

Two hours? Daisy looked at the hideous black plastic cat clock hanging on the wall in the foyer. Its eyes blinked and its tail wagged with each second that ticked off. It was only eight o'clock and Jarod expected her to go to bed at ten o'clock?

"Your old girlfriends," she suggested, hoping it would take him until two in the morning to tell about them all.

"Which story do you want?" he asked.

She propped her chin on her hands on the banister, the rails between them like a fence. "The true one," she said.

He shook his head. "You don't show me yours then I don't have to show you mine. You ready to tell all?"

"Not me. I'm going up for a long soaking bath in that claw-foot tub in the bathroom and then I'm going to read a romance book I've brought along. Do I really have to be up and cooking at six?"

"Long before that. He'll be sitting at the table at six cussin' a blue streak if it's not in front of him. Schedule keeps him as sane as possible and at that it barely keeps him livable. After that you just keep him happy. If you don't want to cook, I'll roust something up when I get home."

"I'll have supper ready. Dutiful little wife should cook or else Uncle Emmett might trade me in for Chigger."

Jarod shivered. "Jim Bob can have her. She's loud and crass and—" He stopped when Daisy held up her palm toward him.

"And she's my friend so don't talk about her if you

don't want a fight on your hands. Good night, Jarod. Tell Emmett I'll see him at breakfast."

"Good night, Daisy." He moved to one side so she could get past him and wished to the devil she hadn't left him with a visual of her naked in a tub big enough for two.

Chapter 9

DAISY PARKED EMMETT'S TRUCK AT THE SIDE OF THE Morgan Mill store. It was a combination gas, grocery, hay, and feed store as well as a café. By the time she made it around the tail end, he had the door open and was reaching for his walker. She followed him to the front and opened the door for him.

Inside, the usual convenience store items were stacked on shelves to the left. The checkout counter was to the right, and a couple of tables were in the middle of the store. Four elderly gentlemen looked up from one of the tables.

"Good morning. Coffee any good this mornin'?" Emmett called out.

"Naw, it ain't nothin' but murdered water. These younguns don't know how to make good strong coffee. It'll have to do until we can get home and make up something where you can't see the bottom of the cup if you look down through it. Bring Emmett a cup, darlin', and put it on my tab. Sorry old codger ain't been here in so long I figured he'd done died. We'll celebrate him still kickin'," one fellow said.

The lady that brought the cup of coffee couldn't be classified as a youngun in anyone's language. She was middle-aged, graying, and wore a wedding band on her left hand. She set the coffee in front of Emmett when he sat down and asked, "Where you been keepin' yourself? I ain't seen you in two months."

"Been busy. This is Daisy. She used to own the Honky Tonk up near Mingus until she married my nephew, Jarod, that's come to help me out this summer. She's been my vet for years. Takes care of my dogs and my cattle."

One of the men pulled out a chair and motioned to Daisy. "Well, don't just stand there, sweetheart. Come on over here and sit a spell and visit with us old fellers. What're you drinkin'?"

"Coffee is fine," Daisy said.

"Emmett, you might tell who these good lookin' men are," she said.

He glared at her with narrowed eyes and went on as if she hadn't spoken. "So what's the news?"

The man with the gray rim of hair around his bald head said, "I'm Bob. That'd be Gordon with the mustache. Tillman over there with the bald head and Martin next to him. Emmett's got so old and mean he probably don't even remember our names."

"I know every one of you fools and ain't a one of you good lookin'. Woman who just got married oughtn't to talk like that." Emmett narrowed his eyes again.

"Bullshit," Daisy said.

Emmett shook his finger at her. "Don't you sass me."

"Don't you ignore me. It's nice to meet you, Bob, Gordon, Tillman, and Martin," she said.

"I wasn't ignoring you. If I'd have wanted you to know these old farts' names I woulda told you at first," Emmett argued.

"We going to fight all morning or you going to drink that coffee before it gets cold?" Daisy asked.

He picked up the coffee and turned his shoulder away from her. "Anyone died?" he asked.

"Dick Tompson did," Bob said.

"Damn, he ain't nothin' but a kid." Emmett shook his head slowly.

"Wasn't but sixty-six," Tillman told him.

"That's too bad. What got him?"

"Had a ridin' accident. Horse fell on him and crushed his chest. They say he went in a flash," Martin said.

"That's the way to go. Better'n dyin' an inch at a time," Emmett said.

"Been hot enough for you?" Tillman asked.

"Oh, hell, it gets any hotter and the damned old horny toads is going to start off for the north in search of water," Emmett said.

"Leave them to their cussin' and discussin' and come on over here and talk to me," the lady whispered when she'd refilled the coffee cups.

Daisy nodded and followed her to the other table. "I'm Daisy. You run this place?"

"I'm Nita. My family owns and runs this place. When did you and Jarod get married?"

"Week ago Sunday."

"Y'all known each other long?"

"Just a few weeks." The hole was getting deeper and Daisy didn't know how to stop digging.

"One Wing in the Fire" by Trent Tomlinson began playing on the radio sitting beside the cash register. Tomlinson sang about his father being an angel with no halo and one wing in the fire.

The waitress looked at Emmett. "That singer had to have known old Emmett. He's a good man but a rough one."

Daisy was so glad to have the subject changed she would have discussed the price of a bag of cow manure.

"Well, he hasn't got a halo and if he's got wings one is definitely in the fire."

"That's the gospel truth. Don't know how Mavis put up with him. She was the saint, I'm tellin' you, and it's a good thing she went before him so she could talk God into lettin' him inside the pearly gates. Without her up there beggin' and pleadin', Emmett wouldn't have a fart's chance in a class five tornado of gettin' past the pearly gates. Heard he only had a few weeks to live. That right?"

Daisy nodded. "Kidney failure, old age, and Alzheimer's."

"Don't let him fool you. He hasn't got Alzheimer's. He's got pure old mean and cantankerous. There's a difference."

Daisy smiled.

"Y'all women through jawin' about us men?" Emmett called across the room.

"We got better things to talk about than an old goat like you," Daisy yelled back.

Tillman slapped Emmett on the shoulder. "She's like Mavis, ain't she? No wonder you're glad she's married Jarod. Be like havin' Mavis back in the house."

"Naw, she's sassier than Mavis. She had to be to run the Honky Tonk, and let me tell you something, ain't nobody gets rowdy in that place. She'd throw them out on their asses so quick they'd wonder if they'd sprouted wings and were flyin'. She keeps a shotgun hid by the door and it's loaded and I reckon she's fired it before."

"You braggin' on her?" Bob asked.

"Damn right. I'm proud to have her in the family. She'll keep my nephew on the straight and narrow."

Emmett motioned for her. "Now if you're done tellin'
stories on me and Jarod we'll be gettin' on home. It's
my nap time."

Daisy didn't move. "And if I'm not?"

"Then I'll leave your pretty little hind end settin'
right there and you can wash dishes for your dinner and
supper and hitch a ride back to the Honky Tonk tonight
to work."

She got up slowly. "Guess I'd better drive you home
then."

Maybe Nita had been right. He sure seemed lucid
enough in that moment.

She helped him into the truck as much as he'd let her
and drove north from the Morgan Mill store. She made
a left-hand turn on Farm Road 1188 and in less than ten
minutes turned back to the left again onto the Double
M ranch.

Jarod came out of the house to the truck to help
Emmett when Daisy parked. "Where'd you two go
this morning?"

Emmett slapped Jarod's hands away when he offered
him his arm for support. "I can get out by myself. I don't
need your help. We been over to Morgan Mill. Had to
introduce the new member of the family to the boys,
didn't I? Wouldn't want anyone to think I was ashamed
of her just because she used to run a beer joint."

Daisy's temper jacked up into high gear. "Why should
you be ashamed of me because of my job? I do an honest
night's work for an honest dollar."

"That sounds like you are a hooker. You ain't been
doin' more work after hours in the back room, have you?
Good God, Jarod, I told you to make sure you wanted a

woman like this before you married her, but oh, no, you had to run off to Oklahoma. Didn't even ask me and your momma if we'd like to be there when you married and you're Frankie's baby son. God Almighty, but she's goin' to be mad as hell when she finds out. I might just tell her tonight when she calls. And where's that jackass that I'm supposed to tell stories to all afternoon? Tell me that, would you, instead of tryin' to help me around like I'm an old man." He fumed and fussed all the way into the house.

Jarod slapped the leg of his overalls. "What in the hell did I say that set him off that time?"

"It wasn't you. It was me. And I'd bet dollars to doughnuts he's not got an ounce of Alzheimer's. When he doesn't want to answer something or he gets caught between a rock and a hard place he goes off the deep end and accuses everyone around of anything he can think of. He's sharp as a razor and knows exactly what he's doing."

"Then let's march in there and tell him we aren't married."

"Not me," Daisy said. "He's already outted me. I'm married to you for better or worse and in sickness and health until death do us part and that means death of one Emmett McElroy."

"Why are you staying if you think he's pulling the wool over our eyes?"

She shrugged. "Guess I'm afraid of the possibility I'm wrong."

"Maybe it won't go any further than Morgan Mill and they'll all think he's crazy and talkin' out of his head about us being married."

"I hope so," she sighed.

Daisy pushed knickknacks to one side of the dresser to set her makeup kit down. She looked around the room at all the clutter and shivered. What if all those little beady black eyes looking at her from ceramic animal faces came to life at night like in that movie she'd seen as a child? If she was going to stay in the room for weeks it had to go. Emmett never came upstairs anymore. She'd bring empty liquor boxes from the Honky Tonk and pack it all up in boxes and shove them under the bed. She was putting eye shadow on when Jarod poked his head in the door.

"Yes?" She looked up at him in the mirror.

"You will come back?"

"Yes, I'll be back. He'd have a hissy if I didn't. I'll be up at six for breakfast and then whatever I need to do to make him happy."

Jarod sat down on the bed and the springs squeaked. He pulled the bedspread up to find the old metal springs under the mattress. He bounced and they screeched again. He flipped back and started a steady rhythm by bouncing his butt up and down.

"Stop that," she hissed. "It's annoying as hell."

"What does it sound like?"

"It sounds like we're... isn't the living room right below this room?"

"Yep, it is and if he wants to play the marriage game, we can too. Want to give me a couple of good loud moans and some loud panting?"

"I do not! I'm going to slip out the front door so I don't have to look at him when I leave. This is embarrassing!" she whispered.

Jarod speeded up and then stopped it suddenly. "How was that? Was it as good for you as it was for me?"

"God, Jarod," she exclaimed forgetting to whisper.

"Ah, Daisy, you were wonderful," he said loudly.

Her cheeks were flame red. "I will get even."

Jarod eased off the bed with a loud moan. He bent and kissed the back of her neck. "That was wonderful, darlin'," he said in the same loud voice.

She inhaled the mixture of the soap he'd used to shower after working all day, the last dregs of that morning's aftershave and lemon from the iced tea he'd had at supper. The combination was so heady that she seriously wanted to throw him down on the bed for a second round, and it would be without clothing and last a hell of a lot longer than his rehearsal.

He raised his voice even louder as he left the room. "You just sleep in, darlin', tomorrow morning. I'll make breakfast. I'm sure you'll be worn out after workin' until two and that little session we just had. It won't be long until the new owners of the Honky Tonk will be comfortable without you."

She shook her fist at him and picked up a Japanese fan from the edge of the vanity and rapidly tried to cool her face. She hurriedly put on her makeup and rushed through the foyer, kitchen, and utility room into the garage. She pushed the button on the inside of the door. By the time the garage doors were up she was backing the Maverick out into the yard.

"Something needs to help me make it through the night," she said aloud as she listened to Sammi Smith singing "Help Me Make It Through the Night" on the classic country radio station. When that song ended,

Mel McDaniel began singing "Stand Up." In the song he asked if you'd ever had a hot date and ended up in the backseat? He said to stand up and testify. Daisy kept time with her fingers on the steering wheel as she drove.

"Does the bed of a pickup truck count?" she asked aloud.

When she pulled into the parking lot of the Honky Tonk, Willie Nelson was singing "Always on My Mind." She was humming it when she went in the back door to find Cathy sitting on the sofa, dressed in jeans and a tank top almost the same shade of blue as Daisy's.

"Who's always on your mind? That hunky cowboy? Is he coming into the Tonk tonight?"

Daisy shook her head. "Not tonight. I'll tell you about the jam I've gotten into while we get things ready to open the doors."

Cathy listened to the whole story beginning with the night Daisy and Jarod wound up in a tangle of arms and legs on the dance floor up through the squeaky bedsprings minutes before Daisy left the ranch. The only thing she left out was the episode in the back of the pickup truck.

"And you haven't taken him to bed? Have you lost your touch, girl?" Cathy asked.

"It's just that…"

"All or nothing. We are getting to that age." Cathy finished the sentence for her.

"I don't want to admit that so I'm not answering."

Tinker arrived, went to the old jukebox, and put in some coins. "Right or Wrong" by Wanda Jackson filled the Honky Tonk.

"That's an old one," Cathy said.

"Monday night is oldies night. Tradition."

"Well, it's an omen. Listen to the words."

Daisy threw up her hands. "I'm tired of listening to words. Every damn song I hear has a message for me. The damn thing is talking to me."

Cathy batted her eyes and sang along with Wanda. When the song ended they looked up to see Tinker smiling.

"You think that's funny, Tinker?" Daisy asked.

"Little bit." He sat down and folded his hands over his chest.

The next song was "Country Bumpkin" by Cal Smith and Daisy plugged her ears with her fingers. He talked about a tall cowboy coming into a bar and a barmaid looking him up and down.

Cathy patted her shoulder. "You got a bad dose, ain't you, honey?"

Daisy removed her fingers and nodded. "That's what I want. I want life to be something; not just a ho-hum stream of days."

"Well, he's the cowboy and you're the barmaid. Who knows? Maybe Cal Smith knows what he's talking about."

The rattle of semis pulling into the parking lot preceded the arrival of a dozen or more truckers. Daisy got busy introducing Cathy and filling Mason jars with beer and stopped listening to the lyrics of every song. Merle came in and dragged Mac away from the bar and to the pool table. A Jones fan, she plugged coins into the jukebox and George entertained the customers for three songs.

Thank goodness the lyrics aren't talking to me, so bless you, Merle, Daisy thought as she mixed up a martini for a middle-aged businessman. She had just served the man when she turned around to find Chigger and Jim Bob grinning at her.

"What?" she said.

"I'm pregnant," Chigger blurted out.

"And it's mine," Jim Bob said.

Daisy was speechless.

"She's goin' to marry me. Friday at the courthouse over in Palo Pinto. We're goin' to tell her momma that we sneaked off and got married six months ago and kept it secret. We're goin' to fly to Cancun for four days and call her from there," Jim Bob said.

Daisy still couldn't find words.

"And you're goin' to stand up with me," Chigger said. "I was mad today when Glorietta come in the shop and told me you and Jarod done beat us to the altar and you didn't even ask me to go along after we'd taken the both of you fishin', but I'm forgivin' you so you have to stand up with me."

"Dear God," Daisy mumbled.

"Are you pregnant too?" Chigger asked.

"I am not pregnant," Daisy sputtered and hoped to hell she was telling the truth.

"Well, you could be if you did. You can't tell me that you... who is that woman over there servin' beer?" Chigger noticed Cathy for the first time.

"My cousin, Cathy. She needs a job. I need help," Daisy said.

Billy Bob and Joe Bob each claimed a bar stool. Billy Bob threw a hand over his heart. "I'm hurt. We were engaged and you threw me over for that Okie."

"We were never engaged, Billy Bob."

Billy Bob pointed at Cathy. "Who is that?"

"That'd be her cousin who's helping now that she and Jarod are married," Chigger explained. "Are you thunderstruck?"

"Hell, no. I'll never marry. My heart is broken. I'm going to dance until there ain't no leather on my boots just to keep my old heart from bleedin' to death right here in the Honky Tonk. Can I dance with your cousin, Daisy?"

"Not while she's workin'. What she does after hours is up to her. What's the bunch of you doing in here on Monday, anyway?" Daisy asked.

"We come to celebrate the next generation of Walkers. Jim Bob done jumped out there ahead of me and Joe Bob. He'll be Momma's favorite if Chigger has a girl. If it's another rotten old boy, then me and Joe Bob is still in the runnin' for first place," Billy Bob said. "Give me a beer and would you look at that? A whole bunch of pretty women just got here to help me get through the night."

"Well, praise the lord," Daisy said.

"If he ain't good to you, you call me and I'll break his neck. I wouldn't mind bein' your second husband," Billy Bob whispered across the bar as he picked up his beer.

"He ain't good to me, I'll break his neck. Now go pick out a pretty girl and wear some leather off them boots. Looks to me like Jim Bob and Chigger are ahead of you on that matter too." Daisy pointed toward the engaged couple all wrapped up in each other's arms.

"What's that all about?" Cathy asked.

"The Walker triplets and Chigger. I'll explain later," Daisy said.

"The Chigger who you told me about?"

"The very one and that'd be Jim Bob two-stepping

with her. She just told me she's pregnant and they're getting married on Friday," Daisy said.

"I'm glad you told me they were triplets. For a minute I thought I had a brain tumor and was seeing triple," Cathy said.

At ten o'clock Cathy pointed to the clock. "Get out of here. Tinker and I can run this place. It's not all that busy and besides, you've got your second job to go to. Acting ain't easy."

"It's my third job. Did you forget I'm an underpaid vet tech too? Don't make out the sofa anymore. Sleep on my bed. It's a lot more comfortable. The only rule is that no men are allowed in the apartment. You want sex you make them take you to the nearest hay barn or motel. And watch Billy Bob, he'll propose six times tonight," Daisy said.

"He can propose a thousand times and the answer would be no. How in the hell would I know I was in bed with the right one? Besides, after Brad I don't want another man for a long time."

"Never known you to go without a man for more than thirty days," Daisy said.

"Get out of here." Cathy shoved her.

———⁓———

Daisy figured she'd sneak into a dark house and read a few hours since she wasn't used to going to bed before three in the morning. The garage door sounded like a tractor with a bad engine when it opened, so she opted to park the car in the driveway. She was tiptoeing up the porch steps when Jarod spoke from the shadows.

"Evenin'," he said in a deep drawl.

"Hell's bells, you scared the hell out of me."

"Sorry. Didn't mean to startle you."

He'd been leaning against a porch post and stepped out of the shadows into the moonlight not three feet from her. He wore orange cotton pajama bottoms with two-inch OSU letters written in black all over them and a white muscle shirt. Droplets of water from a very recent shower sparkled in his dark hair. Soap, shaving lotion, and a hot summer night all blended to send delicious shivers dancing up her spine.

"I thought you'd be asleep," she said.

"Not this early. Uncle Emmett turns in by nine thirty. I was listening to some music and trying to relax. That cluttered house sets my nerves on edge."

"I'm not a stuff person either. I meant to bring boxes from the Honky Tonk to pack up some of that stuff in my room. It drives me crazy."

He motioned toward the rocking chairs. "Sit with me."

She eased down into a chair and he turned a knob on a portable radio. Country music floated out across the yard. Bright stars hung in the sky. Fireflies lit up the yard in brief flashes of light and a coyote howled in the distance.

"Did you buy a donkey?"

"Did that howling coyote make you think of the donkey? I bought two donkeys. One is in the pasture right behind the house. Bought them from Billy Bob this morning. He opened the gate between this property and his and turned them loose for me. I went out and herded the spotted one up to the pasture so Uncle Emmett can talk to it tomorrow. It's the gentlest of the two. The other one is wild and mean."

She leaned her head back and shut her eyes, wishing he'd keep talking. She didn't care about what or who as long as she could listen to the deep timbre of his voice.

When she opened her eyes he was inches from her with his hand outstretched. "Dance with me?"

"Are you serious?"

"I am," he said.

He led her out into the yard, drew her next to his body, and began a slow waltz.

She pushed back and said, "Wait a minute."

"What?"

She sat down on the bottom porch step, jerked off her boots and socks, and tossed them toward the porch. "I want to feel the cool grass under my feet."

The angles of his face softened with a smile. She walked back into his embrace and he moved her around the yard through two slow country songs.

A faster song started and keeping her hands in his they did something between a polka and a square dance. She threw back her head and laughed when he spun her around. The stars were a blur and her heart raced.

The next song was another slow ballad and she could feel his heart beat against her cheek when she laid it on his chest. Midway through the song he tilted her chin back with his fist and brushed a soft sensual kiss across her lips.

She rolled up on her tiptoes, tangled her fingers in his damp hair, and pulled his face toward hers in a long, passionate, lingering series of kisses, during the course of which he picked her up off the ground like a bride and carried her toward the house. She knew the magic word was stop, but she couldn't say it any more that night than she could have when he kissed her the first time.

She reached out and opened the screen door. He didn't bump her head or her toes one time as he took the steps slowly. And his lips never left hers. Her eyes stayed shut until he took her into the bathroom instead of the bedroom.

"What are we doing in here?" she asked.

"Shhh. Tonight I'm making love to you, not having sex with you. Be still and enjoy," he whispered seductively.

He eased her down on a vanity stool and ever so slowly pulled her T-shirt out of her jeans. As the shirt went up so did the steamy hot kisses, each one making her gasp.

"Let's just go to bed," she said.

He stopped to taste the smoky skin at the nape of her neck when he tossed the T-shirt to one side. "You deserve more. Have I told you that you are the sexiest woman alive?"

"Not with words. I did see something like that in your eyes," she said.

"You are, Daisy. I can't get you out of my mind for more than five minutes at a time." He turned on the water in the old claw-foot tub. His eyes never left hers as he fiddled with the knobs to get the water temperature exactly right. He poured in bath oil that bubbled and she watched it, mesmerized as he sat down in front of her on the floor and started at her toes, kissing each one before moving on to the tender arch of her foot. Each touch was like pouring gasoline on the burning desire deep inside her body. Then he stood her up and unbuttoned and unzipped her jeans, tugging them down and pitching them into the corner with her shirt and socks.

"Please," she begged. "Jarod, I want you so bad. We can take a long bath together afterwards."

"We are making love, darlin'. Not havin' sex."

By the time he'd unhooked her bra and added her bikini underwear to the pile in the corner she believed in human combustion.

He picked her naked body up, turned around, and very gently put her into the warm water. He filled a Mason jar just like she used at the Honky Tonk and slowly poured it through her long dark hair. When he applied shampoo and began working the lather into her scalp, the only thing on her mind was that she'd never had love made to her before. He took his time and poured dozens of jars of water through her hair to get all the soap out, his lips kissing every part of her neck, face, and eyelids as he did.

"Enough. Take me to bed or get in this tub with me. I can't take anymore. Your kisses on my body are pure blazes," she whispered.

He picked up bar of sweet smelling soap and lathered up his hands. "We are just beginning, honey. Washcloths and sponges are cheaters," he said as he began to give her a bath with his soapy hands.

Her skin sizzled every place his hands slipped and slid and she vowed she would get even with him one day. When he finished he wrapped a towel around her hair and one around her body and carried her into the bedroom where he set her on a straight back chair. When he'd rubbed her hair almost dry he picked up the hair brush. Stringing kisses down her back with every brush stroke, he loved every shiver that his touch caused.

"Stretch out on the bed on your stomach," he whispered as he picked up a bottle of lotion from the bedside table.

"After?"

"Before and after, too, if you want. But definitely before. Daisy, let me love you my way tonight. Let me give you all a woman like you deserves."

She stretched out on her stomach and he started at her neck, massaging and kissing alternately from shoulders to toes. By the time he rolled her over to her back her eyes were glistening and she was amazed that she hadn't burned a hole in the bedsheets.

"I think I've died and gone to heaven," she said weakly.

He removed his clothing in a blur. He stretched out on top of her and she nipped him on the neck. He was right. Making love was different than having sex, she thought when she shut her eyes and let go of every thought except fulfilling every gnawing, demanding need.

She called his name twice before he said hers and collapsed on top of her. He could have stayed there all night with his dark chest hair tickling her nose and she wouldn't have uttered a single complaint. The glow in the room was far greater than the one she'd experienced in the back of the truck.

So there are even degrees of afterglow. Is there one bigger than this?

He rolled to one side, keeping her in his arms and burying his face in her hair, inhaling the sweet smell of the shampoo.

She didn't open her eyes for fear that it would all be a dream. She vowed that she'd never settle for sex when she could have love like she'd just experienced. There was a difference and if she never had it again, at least she'd experienced it once in a lifetime.

She fell asleep in his arms.

Chapter 10

DAISY AWOKE, SAT STRAIGHT UP IN A STRANGE BED, AND jerked her head with such force that her neck popped when someone threw a leg over hers.

"Jarod?" she whispered. Then she remembered dancing with him and being carried up the stairs. A glimmering flush covered her as the rest of the night flooded over her like the moonlight slipping through the lace curtains. She carefully untangled his leg, curled up with her face against his chest, and went right back to sleep. When she awoke the next time, sunrays filtered through sheer curtains into the room and she was alone.

It wasn't the first time she and Jarod had had sex, so it wasn't the first morning after, but it was still awkward. She fell back on the bed with a groan. The morning after making love was even more uncomfortable than the morning after sex. She'd have to face Emmett and Jarod that morning together!

She couldn't gather up her things and sneak out. Emmett would be devastated if she and Jarod suddenly "divorced." She took five minutes longer than normal to brush her hair. With slow steps she made her way to the table where Emmett sipped coffee and read the morning paper alone.

She peeked around the archway from the dining room into the kitchen to find it empty and went on inside to pour a cup of coffee. She carried it back to the dining room table and sat down.

The house was a perfect square and two stories up. The small foyer had a staircase up to the top floor. An archway to the left led into a dining room with a smaller arch into the kitchen. To the right was another arch that went into the living room and behind that was a den and office combination. Emmett spent most of his time at the dining room table or else in the living room.

"Good mornin'," she said.

He looked up over the top of his paper, grunted something that made no sense, and went back to reading.

She sipped her coffee and shut her eyes to the endless knickknacks sitting everywhere. If collecting clutter was genetic then Mavis and Chigger definitely shared a limb of the same family tree. Looking back at the way Mavis took charge of everything and nothing riled her, Daisy wondered if she'd secretly given birth to Chigger in her middle-aged years and given her away for adoption.

Emmett snapped his paper shut, folded it, and laid it aside. "It's about time you come crawlin' out of bed this mornin'. Sun's been up an hour already. I told you runnin' that Honky Tonk was going to be too much for you once you were a married woman. Runnin' a joint ain't no job for a married woman. Kids will be comin' along before long. Don't look at me like that. I heard them bedsprings yesterday afternoon and you don't want your kids goin' to school and havin' to say their momma is a barkeep."

"Why not?" She glanced upstairs. Maybe Jarod was in the bathroom.

"You know why not and he's not here this mornin' so stop huntin' him. He's got a cow havin' trouble calvin'. You ought to be out there with him and you would be if you hadn't slept so late because you were off at that beer joint last night. He's a damn good rancher but you are a vet."

She glanced at the clock on the wall behind Emmett's head. It was only seven thirty. She didn't think that should be a sin beyond forgiveness since she normally didn't open her eyes until noon or after.

She glared at Emmett. "Don't you lecture me. I'm twenty-eight years old. I've been making my own way in this world since I was a kid and I don't need your sass. If I want to take my kids to the Honky Tonk with me and put them in the back room while I serve beer and drinks to the customers, that's my business."

Emmett tucked his hands inside the bibbed part of his overalls. "You'll do no such thing with my grandchildren. I won't rest up there with Mavis if you take my blood kin to a honky tonk when they ain't nothing but babies. What's your business right now is to quit. I want you here full time before I die. I want to know there's a good woman behind Jarod, takin' care of him."

"They aren't your grandchildren, Emmett. They'd be your great-great nieces and or nephews. And Jarod's a big boy. He could run this ranch with one hand tied behind his back and cross-eyed, all by his lonesome little self. And I can help run this ranch and take care of my beer joint too." Her blue eyes flashed.

"You'll see I'm right one of these days, Daisy McElroy, and when you do I'll laugh at you," Emmett said.

Daisy McElroy! The name sounded strange in her ears.

"And I won't care if you do," she countered.

He laughed until his breath caught in his chest. "I knowed you were the woman for Jarod from the first

time he come home from that beer joint. It reminded
me of the first time I saw Mavis. Why, that next day he
wouldn't hardly even argue with me. I shoulda brought
him down here a long time ago. Let's go talk to the
boys at Morgan Mill again this mornin'. You can visit
with…" he stumbled on the name.

"Tillman?"

He shook his head.

"Bob?"

Another shake.

"Gordon?"

"Hell no. Not the guys. That woman. I remember
when she was born and when she got married and how
many kids she's got but I can't remember her name. I
even know her momma and daddy and her grandparents," he said.

"Nita is her name. I'm not hungry. I'll just grab a
doughnut at the café." Taking him to the café would buy
a little more time before she had to face Jarod.

"That's right. Nita. I'll put on my boots and you go
bring the truck around to the front door," he ordered.

She went out into the garage and picked out the right
keys from the hooks inside the door, fired up his truck, and
drove it around to the front yard. She waited a minute but
he didn't come out so she left the truck running and went
into the house to hear Jarod's frantic voice. Thinking he
was talking to her she rushed into the living room to find
Emmett sitting in his favorite old worn leather recliner
with one boot on and the other on his lap. His face was the
color of cold ashes and he was mumbling incoherently.

"Yes, ma'am. Ten minutes." Jarod kept his eyes on
Emmett.

"Day…" Emmett's eyes went to Daisy.

She sat down beside and him and held his hand. "I'm right here."

"Make him really marry you," his whisper was raspy.

"You old goat!" she said.

Emmett squeezed her hand with all the energy he had left.

"Promise?" he said before he shut his eyes. He had a smile on his face and Daisy's hand in his as he crossed the threshold to reach out for Mavis.

Tears streamed down Daisy's cheeks as she laid her face on his knee and wept. "He's gone."

The paramedics arrived with whining sirens ten minutes later and found them, Daisy on one side and Jarod on the other, their hands entwined together over his right one that still held Daisy's.

"I'm not getting a heartbeat or a pulse. They'll pronounce a time of death when we get to the hospital with him," a small dark-haired lady said. "Y'all can follow us but…" she left the sentence hanging.

Daisy pulled both her hands free. "We will go with him."

I didn't promise, she thought as she followed the paramedics out to the ambulance with Emmett's body. Fifteen minutes before she'd been arguing with him and now he was gone and she hadn't promised so he could go on into eternity without worrying about leaving unfinished business behind. Guilt flowed over her like baptismal water.

Jarod gripped the steering wheel in his truck so tightly that his knuckles turned white. He hadn't expected Emmett to go like that. He'd thought he'd have several sick spells, maybe spend time in the hospital, and finally go in a morphine-induced stupor. He sure hadn't expected the last words he'd hear from Emmett's mouth would be, "Daisy is your Mavis."

Daisy touched his hand.

He relaxed.

"We had an argument at the breakfast table. He wanted me to come to the ranch permanently. I'm glad he went like this, sitting in his chair surrounded by all his things, and after a rousting good fight with me. He laughed until he almost cried at the end of the argument. He lived until the last minute of his life and died with dignity," she said.

"About last night," Jarod said.

"I can't talk about that right now, Jarod. Let's just get today finished and I'll go home," she said.

"You could stay until after the funeral," he said.

"Your family will need the room and you'll be busy with the arrangements."

Jarod started the engine and followed the ambulance. "Emmett took care of everything. It's all written down. The overalls and shirt are hanging in a special place in his closet. They are the last things Mavis ironed before she died that morning. His boots are shined and ready. They are the last pair he wore when he danced with her at the Honky Tonk. His gray hair is to be parted and combed back like it was when he dated her and there's a picture of them on their wedding day that is to be put in his hands."

Daisy scooted across the truck seat and buried her face in Jarod's shoulder. "That's the kind of love I want."

Jarod swallowed hard but the lump in his throat didn't budge. He drove with one hand and drew her close with the other. Was Daisy truly his soul mate like Emmett kept fussing about and would she ever leave the Honky Tonk? She had the excitement of all those things that Toby sang about: bikers, truckers, hookers, lookers, loud music, even Tinker, and now her cousin, Cathy. He'd thought he'd have six weeks to decide what to do about the way he felt. That had just been snatched from him and it hurt as bad as losing Emmett.

He parked the truck behind the ambulance. He and Daisy walked beside Emmett's sheet-covered body into the emergency room. The doctors pronounced Emmett dead on arrival at the hospital with cause of death listed as an acute cardiac arrest. Jarod kept an arm around Daisy as they watched the doctors cover Emmett with a white sheet and the nurse make the phone call for the funeral home to come and take the body away.

It was only a few minutes before Jarod led her back out to his truck. He started up the engine, turned up the air conditioning, took his cell phone out of his pocket, and made a phone call.

Daisy looked out the side window to try to give him some privacy.

"Mother, Uncle Emmett had a heart attack this morning. He didn't survive it. He was gone in minutes. We are at the hospital and we're on our way back to the ranch. The hearse is here to get him now. Is there anything else I need to do before you all get here?"

He listened for a moment.

"I'm fine. Daisy is here with me. His final words were to Daisy." He held the cell phone to his chest and touched Daisy's shoulder. "What did he say?"

She swallowed hard and lied. "I couldn't understand it all. He was muttering. I think he wanted to see Mavis."

Daisy looked at the hearse backing up to the hospital doors. "You don't need to go talk to the funeral home people?"

"No, he did all that when Mavis died. He paid for his funeral at the same time he paid for hers. He'll be at the same funeral home she was and the services will be Thursday at ten o'clock," Jarod said.

"How do you already know that?"

"The first conversation we had when I came to the Double M concerned his going home to be with Mavis. He will be buried two days after he dies because the devil will come hunting him on the third day. And he'll already be 'up there' with Mavis so the devil will be shit-out-of-luck. His words exactly, not mine. He's already paid the funeral home extra to do whatever they have to do to make sure it's two days after his death and at ten o'clock in the morning because that's when Mavis had her services and they're to be held at the little country church they attended. After that he'll be buried at the Liberty Cemetery beside Mavis and we are all to go home to the ranch and have dinner under the shade trees like we did when Mavis died."

"I see," she said.

It was all so different from when her grandmother and mother died. Granny died in the middle of the night and they flew her body back to Cherokee, North Carolina, to be buried beside her husband. By the time Daisy and her mother drove from Arkansas to North Carolina, Granny's sisters had the arrangements under control. It was an Indian funeral and Daisy didn't understand a thing that went on for the most part. She and her mother stayed long enough to eat dinner with the relatives and then they drove straight back to Arkansas without stopping for anything but food and potty breaks. Her mother was exhausted by the time they got back and slept for two whole days before she went back to work at the bar.

When her mother died, she used what insurance money there was and buried her in the cemetery at Mena beside her first husband, Daisy's father. The latest boyfriend didn't even attend the graveside service. There were a dozen folks she'd worked with over the years who arrived to listen to one hymn and the preacher pray over her body. Cathy attended and stood beside Daisy. She hugged Cathy and they cried together, then she got into the old Maverick and drove back to southern Oklahoma.

Emmett had passion in his life. He argued with passion and he'd loved Mavis with passion. He'd lived, not merely existed.

"What are you thinking about?" she asked when Jarod pulled up in front of the ranch house.

"The donkey. He never even got to see the thing he fought so hard against and gave in to you so easily when you mentioned it. Damn it, anyway."

"I think he'd rather see Mavis than a donkey," Daisy said.

"I suppose so. What about you? What were you thinking about? I'm putting off going into the house. As bad as I hate all the fighting, it will be empty without him."

"Passion," she answered with one word.

"Last night."

"Not really. Passion as in zest for living and loving. I don't want to exist. I want to live like Emmett did."

"So last night? Was it not passion?"

"Last night was mind boggling and it was damn fine. But I want it all, not an hour a night of feeling like I'm the queen of the whole world. I want the arguing. I want the slow kisses after breakfast and the struggling to see if we can afford to buy something we really want. I want to look at what I've done with my life with pride when I get to the end and it all flashes in front of me. And I mean all of it. Not just the part everyone else thinks is good."

"Daisy, you deserve all of it. Any man should love you enough to make sure you have it all. When you reach the end and it flashes in front of you, you shouldn't have a single regret. You should never have to settle for second best. You deserve even better than the very best."

Tears stung her eyes but she didn't let them fall. She changed the subject. "What time will your folks be here?"

"In about an hour," he said.

"Good lord, are they flying?"

He nodded. "Mom and Dad will fly. They own a small plane that they get around in when they are in a hurry. Both of them are licensed. The rest of the family will be here before suppertime."

―◌◌◌―

Cathy was sitting at the dining room table with a cup of coffee in front of her. Her yellow oversized T-shirt had a hole in the sleeve. Her hair was mussed from sleeping too hard after a long night's work, and yesterday's makeup was smudged.

"What are you doing home? Trouble in paradise so early in the marriage?" she asked when Daisy carried in her suitcase.

"Moving back in. Emmett died this morning. You look like hell."

"Well, your eyes are all red and you are pale so that don't leave room for you to be passin' judgment on me. Sit down and I'll pour you a cup of coffee. Tell me what happened. Start at the beginning and tell it all. Then I'll take a shower. I feel like sin on Sunday morning. I'd forgotten how much work closing up a joint is."

Cathy moved gracefully around the kitchen. She poured coffee and dug around in a box for a couple of packages of toaster pastries. She put one package in front of Daisy and said, "Dip 'em in the coffee and you don't have to heat them up."

Daisy began the story without telling anything about the bedroom scene from the night before. That was too fresh and too personal to share even with Cathy. She'd finished her second cup of coffee by the time she finished.

"And you left him there alone?" Cathy asked.

"I did but his parents were in the air and were going to land in ten minutes."

"Where?"

"In the pasture and he was going to drive the truck out to get them."

"Scared to meet them, weren't you? Afraid they'd look down on you because you own the Tonk and they have an airplane and fly around the country. That makes them rich in your eyes and you poor in theirs," Cathy said.

Daisy had her mouth open to deny it but she couldn't.

"That means you give a shit and that means you like him and that means you're wadin' in deep shit, which means you could get hurt again. Be careful. I'm taking a shower now. You got anything black to wear to a funeral or do we need to shop today?"

"I've got a basic black dress that Ruby made me buy for things like funerals and weddings. Which by the way, we're going to a wedding on Friday," Daisy said.

Cathy finished the last bite of pastry and headed toward the bedroom. "For someone who said she'd never get all wound up in a small town, you are sure doing a good job of it again."

Daisy was still sitting at the table when Cathy came out with an oversized towel wrapped around her body and another one around her hair. She sat down and removed the towel from her hair, shaking out long wet blond strands.

"I really did run from getting involved. I lasted seven years. That damn Chigger is the culprit," Daisy said.

"We are bartenders. That's what we were destined to be, girl. Jarod is pretty and he'd make your heart hurt with want but…"

Daisy looked up. "Does there always have to be a but?"

"I'm 'fraid so, honey. Buts are as big a part of life as they are a part of our anatomy."

Daisy smiled weakly. "You sound like Ruby."

"I wish I had met her," Cathy said.

"Ruby was a hellcat in her day. I should've insisted you come down here and stay more than one day."

"She didn't have many buts in her life," Cathy said.

"She lived like Emmett did. With passion. She loved her motorcycle and tight blue jeans and beating Merle at pool. She liked the truckers and the bikers and she loved this old bar."

Cathy chuckled. "Like Toby sings about."

"Sometimes I think the song was written special for her."

"But it's not enough for you, is it?"

Daisy thought about that for a minute. "It will be if I can't have what I want with no buts."

"Well said. Now let's go clean up the joint. It'll take your mind off that funeral and the wedding. Both are depressing as hell but I'll go with you."

Cathy put money in the new jukebox. She poked the buttons and the empty joint filled with upbeat music. She picked up a broom and began sweeping up from the night before. Daisy filled a mop bucket and started cleaning behind her.

Jeff Bates sang about "Long Slow Kisses," and Daisy shook her head to erase the memories. Damn Emmett's sorry old hide, anyway, dying like that when she could have had six more weeks of long slow kisses every night in Jarod's arms. But... there was that word again... it was difficult enough leaving after one night. After six weeks it might have been impossible, so maybe Emmett's death was fate stepping in to save her after all.

———ᴍ———

Daisy awoke the next morning to someone pounding hard on the door to her apartment. She picked up her vet bag and staggered through the living room where Cathy was sitting straight up on the sofa bed, rubbing sleep from her eyes.

Daisy opened the door to find Jarod leaning against the jamb. He wore faded jeans, a blue chambray shirt with the top two buttons undone, and scuffed boots. His black hair was combed back and his eyes roamed over her body, clad in a white cotton sleeveless gown that reached the floor.

"You ready?" he asked. She'd only thought she was sexy wearing nothing at all. The look of her in that cotton gown and her dark hair going every which way shot desire through him.

"What in the hell for?" She dropped her bag.

"This is Tuesday. The sun is already up and it's going to be a hot day. We've got cattle to get into the corral and get ready for the sale. You promised Uncle Emmett, remember, and I need a vet? Evidently you remembered something about it, you picked up your bag on the way to the door."

"Good God, Jarod. He's lyin' in his coffin. We shouldn't be working. We should be down at the funeral home greeting guests or at least you should be," she said.

"He told me not to sling snot over him when he was dead. To get on with life. You going to help me or do I need to call another vet?"

"Give me two minutes to get dressed. I'll drive my own car."

"I'll take you and bring you back," he said.

"Wait for me outside. Cathy is a bear when she wakes up."

"You won't go back to sleep?" he asked.

"I'll be there in five minutes or less. I've got to get my supplies out of the garage. Pull around there," she said.

He handed her a biscuit stuffed with scrambled eggs, cheese, and bacon when she was in the truck. "Thought you might be hungry so I brought leftovers."

"Your momma already got up and made breakfast at this ungodly hour?"

"Yep, she did. Coffee is in the thermos right there at your feet. My brothers are already in the pasture rounding up every white face they can find and corralling them. We figured we'd rather be working as sitting around on our butts all day doing nothing. Besides, there's a lot of decisions that will have to be made and getting the white face cattle to the sale will help," he said as he drove south.

She bit into the biscuit and chewed slowly. "So when are you going back to Oklahoma?"

"It'll be a few weeks. We've got a lot to do to get the place ready. I'll stay until it is."

Her heart did one of those little half jumps. "Like what do you have to do? Sell the ranch?"

"Cleaning it out before my nephew moves down here. That'll take forever."

"How old is your nephew?" she asked.

"Twenty-three. He graduated from college and has been helping his dad on the ranch already. He's achin' for his own place. Got a girlfriend and it looks serious."

She poured coffee into the lid of the thermos and sipped it. "Is he helping corral cattle?"

"No, he and the rest of that generation will be here tomorrow. Someone has to run the business up there. They'll drive down tomorrow though and be at the funeral on Thursday."

She'd finished every drop of the coffee and the biscuit by the time Jarod parked the truck at the corral.

Cattle were milling around, bawling at being penned up. Two men rode up on horses and tethered them to the railing. They met Jarod and Daisy halfway from the truck to the corral.

"Daisy, this is my brother Stephen. And this is my brother Mitch."

"Pleased to meet you. I understand you're the vet?" Stephen said.

"My pleasure," Daisy said. "I'm a vet tech but I can make sure they're all ready for the sale. I brought the records with me."

"Well, hot damn. We couldn't find anything to tell us when they'd been vaccinated," Mitch said.

"I've been doing it for a few years and I keep records. Jarod, you can read and I'll get out the supplies," she said.

"We'll run them into the chute." Stephen nodded.

They were both good looking men, older than Jarod, and not as striking as he was, but then few men were. She dug into her kit and handed Jarod the paperwork. He studied the top chart and pointed out the white face that went with it.

"That one," he pointed.

His brothers herded that particular cow into a narrow chute. Daisy loaded up the needle and reached through the rails. The cow didn't even flinch when she shoved it into her flank.

"That'll fix that old girl. Who's next?"

It went like that all morning until they reached the last piece of paper in the stack.

"You havin' dinner with us?" Stephen asked.

Daisy shook her head. She was dirty, sweaty, and in no shape to meet the McElroy women. Besides, Jarod wasn't the one who'd invited her.

"No thanks. Jarod is taking me back home."

"You'd be welcome," Mitch said.

"Thanks, but I'll take a rain check," she said.

Jarod didn't press. "Okay then, vet. Let's take you home and figure up the bill. I'll need a receipt." He'd love to introduce her to his family, but he wasn't stupid. Even though she looked wonderful to him in her stained jeans and work boots, she wouldn't want to meet his parents for the first time looking like that.

"Yes, you will," she said.

"What's that supposed to mean?" he asked.

"That you will need a receipt. What I did doesn't come cheap and it's tax deductible."

"You sounded pretty curt."

"So did you."

"Are we fighting?"

She shrugged her shoulders as she organized her equipment and put the bag in the backseat. She figured the bill as he drove and handed it to him when he parked half an hour later in the Honky Tonk lot.

He pulled a checkbook from the glove compartment. "That's reasonable enough. Did you figure in your time or just the supplies?"

"I don't work for free, cowboy."

He wrote the check and handed it to her. "Can I see you tonight? Would you come out to the ranch for supper with the family?" He felt as if he'd done something wrong but couldn't think of a single thing.

"No thank you. I'm going to sleep until time to open the doors of the Honky Tonk. Don't bother getting out."

"Remember my badge of honor." He opened the truck door at the same time she did.

She was halfway to the Honky Tonk before he caught up to her. He grabbed her hand and held it all the way to the porch where he spun her around, wrapped his arms around her, and kissed her hard.

"God, you feel good in my arms. I wish you could be there all the time. Sleep tight, darlin'," he said and whistled all the way back to the truck.

"After that, I doubt it," she muttered as she watched him pull away from the parking lot.

She slept until six that evening and was amazed that her cell phone hadn't woke her with an animal emergency before that. Cathy tried to shoo her out of the Honky Tonk at midnight, but she stayed until Tinker told everyone that the doors were closing in five minutes. Then she and Cathy sat down, propped their feet up, and had a beer.

"I'm sleeping until noon tomorrow no matter what. We have to get up early on Thursday," Daisy said.

"Anyone comes knockin' on the door, I'll shoot them for you," Cathy said.

"I'm holding you to that promise," Daisy said.

Jarod pounded on the door at seven o'clock the next morning and Cathy didn't move a muscle. Daisy opened the door with a frown on her face. Some watchdog Cathy was. Her snores sounded worse than Jim Bob's fishing wagon.

"What are you doing here?"

"It's time to get on the road." He motioned toward a huge cattle trailer pulled by a semi truck.

Daisy wondered how in the hell Cathy was still sleeping with all those cows bawling in the back of the trailer.

"Are you crazy?"

"Last time the therapist checked he said I was in remission."

"I'm not going to a sale today." She wore a pink sleep shirt that barely reached her knees and she rubbed the sleep from her eyes with her knuckles like a little girl.

"Why not? You did promise him that you'd help me get rid of these sorry white face cattle. Didn't you tell him Angus made better steaks?" Jarod asked.

Promise? She remembered his last word. The one she hadn't answered.

"I'll be ready in ten minutes. Come on in. Sit at the table."

He sat down and looked around. Her apartment was tiny but furnished with nice pieces. No clutter and clean, simple lines. If an apartment described a woman, then Daisy was a no-nonsense lady. The sofa took up most of the living room when it was pulled out into a bed. The flat screen television rested on a plain black case surrounded with books. He looked at the titles. Mostly romance with a few Evanovich and Grafton thrown in among them.

The kitchen was a small galley, room for one in the aisle between the cabinets. Refrigerator and stove on one side surrounded by white cabinets. Sink with a window overlooking the woods behind the joint with the same white cabinets around it on the other side. No dishwasher or trash compactor. He made his way to the sink and looked out the window to see two deer and a fawn grazing at the edge of the trees. A cottontail wasn't far away and a 'possum lumbered across the yard in that direction.

—〰〰—

"Sorry, Ruby," she whispered as she jumped into a pair of jeans and pulled her boots on. "I let a man into the apartment but… hell, there's the word again… it's only for a few minutes and I'm not taking him to bed."

She pulled her hair up into a ponytail, grabbed her purse, and went into the kitchen to write a note to Cathy explaining that she'd be back in time to help open that evening. Jarod motioned for her to look out the window at a deer grazing between the treeline and the Honky Tonk. She wanted to lace her fingers in his as they shared the wonder but picked up a pencil instead and wrote a quick note.

When she finished she started for the door with Jarod right behind her.

"Think Cathy wants to go?" he asked.

"I wouldn't wake Cathy up unless her bed was on fire," Daisy said.

"Then I'm sure not," he whispered. He slung his arm around her shoulders, pulling her close to his side as they walked toward the truck. Before he opened the door he kissed her firmly and hugged her tightly.

The noise of the bawling bovines was wiped out by the roar of the truck's engine. The air conditioning worked, but the inside of the cab looked like it had survived a tornado. The seats were so ripped and torn and had been covered up with one of Mavis' worn quilts to keep the springs from poking. The vinyl dash had cracked and dust had settled into the crevices. The shocks were so worn that every time the wheels turned she bounced halfway to the ceiling.

"Rough ridin' sumbitch, ain't it?" Jarod laughed.

"If you can hang on, I can," she said.

They were out on the interstate before he asked, "You hungry?"

"Starving. Do they serve breakfast at the sale?"

"Yes, but if you're hungry we'll get something before that. Eastland has a Dairy Queen. We could get you a sausage biscuit there," he said.

"I'd like that and a tall iced tea. We can take it to go and I'll eat on the way," she said.

"Ever notice that just about every Texas town has a Dairy Queen?" he asked.

"Ruby said that in order to be classified as a town, a place had to build a beer joint and a church. Then they had to get a post office and put in a Dairy Queen. Population didn't make a damn. If it had fifty thousand people and was minus any one of those four things, it didn't qualify. But if it had five people and all of the above, it was a town."

Jarod laughed and it felt good. "She was every bit as opinionated as Emmett. How'd you live with her all those years, then?"

"Easy. I stayed out of her way and she did the same. Mostly we agreed on things, especially about the Honky Tonk. Only thing I ever had to fight her for was that new jukebox. Until I came into the picture she'd refused to update at all. She had the one with the old 45 records still on it and a stash of the same records in the storage room. When one wore completely out on the jukebox she'd have the mainte-nance man change it out. The clientele loved the old honky tonk, beer drinking, crying in your drink songs, but I thought they needed something more. The fits Emmett threw were mild compared to what Ruby pitched over that notion. We finally compromised. I got a new one. She kept the old one. Only one could be plugged in at a time and Monday nights were for the old one, exclusively, because that was the major trucker night."

"Why?" Jarod asked.

"Because even that much was a chore to get done."

"No, I mean why are there more truckers on Monday?" Jarod asked.

"Have no idea. It's the night when a lot of the regulars stop by and they like the old music so that's what they get."

"And besides, Ruby had to win part of the fight, didn't she?"

Daisy nodded slowly. "She and Emmett didn't give up power easily. How about you, Jarod? Do you give up easily?"

"Hell, no," he said.

She had no idea that he was answering his own question about if he wanted to convince her to leave the Honky Tonk and live with him. But he did and he made up his mind to pursue her until he won.

Daisy was everything he wanted in a woman. She was so pretty that he compared every other woman to her. She was smart enough to be a full-fledged vet and did the work of one. She was hardworking. Lord, she ran the Honky Tonk and kept up with at least two counties' worth of animals. She was funny and witty and she kept him on his toes every minute he was with her. He enjoyed being with her so much that when she wasn't around he kept wishing she was. Yes, surprising enough after his first impression of her being nothing but a barmaid, he was flat out in love with the woman.

Chapter 11

THERE WASN'T A WHITE CLOUD IN THE EXPANSE OF BLUE sky and the breeze was so slight it barely shook the tree leaves. Daisy wore her basic sleeveless black dress with a knee-length hemline and a scoop neckline and plain black pumps. Her dark hair was twisted up the back and held with a clamp with a few curls flipping back down to her neckline. She chose a simple herringbone gold chain necklace and small loop earrings. Cathy wore a dark blue sundress and matching sandals accented with silver and turquoise jewelry. When they crossed the church lawn several men stopped to stare, including Billy Bob and Joe Bob Walker.

They were about to go into the church when Chigger whistled. The shrill dog calling noise caused them to turn and look and she waved. There was no missing her. She wore a flamboyant red sundress printed with enormous white flowers, a floppy white hat, and white spike heels.

"I thought I was pushing the line with a sundress at a funeral," Cathy whispered.

"Chigger's brain works different," Daisy said.

Chigger hugged Daisy but was careful not to smudge makeup on either of them. "I hate funerals. Why aren't you waiting with the family?"

"Long story," Daisy said.

Chigger was about to insist on hearing a portion of it when Jarod appeared from the end of the church. He zeroed in on Daisy, went straight to her, and grabbed her hand. "Daisy, we were waiting on you. Jim Bob, could Cathy sit with you and Chigger?"

Daisy raised an eyebrow. "Why?"

"Because you are sitting with the family."

Jim Bob clapped a hand on his shoulder. "We'll take care of Cathy. She can sit with us. Momma and Dad are already in there holding a pew for us."

Cathy gave Daisy a little push. "Go on. Give 'em hell," she whispered.

Jarod led her around the church to the back door and down a short hallway to a small Sunday school room filled with family. Daisy could hear the noise of conversations as they neared the room, but when Jarod opened the door it was so quiet a pigeon feather floating down from the ceiling would have sounded like the wind from a tornado.

"This is Daisy O'Dell. Daisy, this is my family. You've met my brothers, Mitch and Stephen. This is my dad, Liam McElroy. My mother, Frankie. Mitch's wife, Maria. Stephen's wife, Jewel. The rest are grandchildren and a couple of great-grandkids. I'd tell you all their names but you'd forget them by the time the day was out. You'll get to know them later. We kind of took that business about going forth and multiplying seriously as you can see."

Jarod was nervous. His voice was an octave higher and he talked faster than normal. Daisy squeezed his hand and looked out over the dark-haired clan staring at her like she'd just left a flat saucer spaceship and had a long spiked tongue. She had the sudden urge to stick it out and show them it was a plain old normal tongue that didn't shoot poison.

"Hello, Jarod's family. I'm very glad to meet you all," she said. Maybe if they understood that she spoke English instead of a remote Martian dialect they'd start talking again and the awkward silence would be put to rest.

Liam, an older version of Jarod, held out a hand. His hair had been black at one time but it was almost silver. His shake was firm and his hands calloused from hard work.

"Pleased to meet you, Daisy," he said.

Frankie stepped forward. She was tall and slim, gray just beginning to salt her jet-black hair. She had dark brown eyes and high cheekbones.

"Jarod has told us how Emmett got it into his head you were married and that you played along with it. We're grateful to you. It probably made his last days a lot happier."

"Thank you," Daisy said.

"You a rancher too?" Jewel asked.

"No, ma'am, I own and operate a beer joint up near Mingus. It's called the Honky Tonk," Daisy said.

The room went even quieter. It was as if the pigeon feather hit the wood floor with enough noise that Homeland Security thought it was a bomb and raised the terrorist alert to orange. Frankie's body language changed and her smile faded. Her back stiffened and she quickly scanned Daisy from toes to hairdo.

"Honky Tonk?" a dark-haired man said from the far side of the room. "I saw a sign for that when we were driving here. It's over there by that Smokestack place where we ate, isn't it?"

"Just on up the road a little bit," Daisy said.

"You really own the place?" Frankie asked coolly.

Daisy nodded and tried to tug her hand free from Jarod's but he held on tightly. "I own the place and tend bar every night from eight to two in the morning with the help of Tinker, my bouncer. Last week I hired my cousin to help out so I could pretend to be Jarod's wife."

The dark-haired fellow crossed the room. "I'm Garrett McElroy. You got pool tables?"

Daisy nodded.

"I'll be moving down here to manage the Double M when everything is settled. Maybe I'll stop by your Honky Tonk."

"I'll throw in the first Mason jar of beer for free. After you show Tinker your ID," she said.

"I'm twenty-three," he said.

"Good, then Tinker won't have a problem."

Jarod squeezed her hand.

She didn't know if he appreciated her offer to give his nephew a free beer or if he wanted her to be quiet. He had a choice. He could say thank you for the free beer or whistle "Dixie" out his fanny if he wanted her to be quiet because it wasn't happening.

"Daisy is also a vet tech—" he started. Before he could say anything more, the preacher stuck his head inside and said, "When the music starts I'll ask the congregation to stand and you'll come in from the side door to sit in the reserved pews. If you'll line up, it would make things easier."

"I'm going to strangle you," Daisy whispered.

"Naked?" he whispered back.

Her neck got hot and her cheeks started to flush but she got control of it. By damn, she was tired of Jarod

McElroy making her blush. She'd vowed she'd get even with him and he would not like it.

Liam took Frankie's hand and they led the way when the pianist began to play a slow version of "Amazing Grace." Matt and Maria followed with Stephen and Jewel coming in next. Jarod and Daisy went into the sanctuary after them and the grandchildren and great-grandchildren filed in after that.

The preacher said a short prayer before he read the eulogy. "Emmett Mitchell McElroy was born on June 6, 1921. He married Mavis, the love of his life, on July 3, 1943. They were ranchers and made their home between Morgan Mill and Huckabay their whole married life. They had no children but leave behind…"

Daisy's mind wandered to ways she could make Jarod pay while the preacher listed the survivors and went on to tell stories about Emmett before he got down to the preaching part of the sermon. The things came to mind should have never been thought about in a church house. She checked the windows periodically to make sure lightning wasn't striking in spite of the sunny day. Everyone else had begun to sob quietly into tissues when the preacher talked about Emmett being in heaven with Mavis. Daisy looked around without turning her head. Jarod was as stiff as—what came to her mind should have caused instant death—and she stifled a giggle by pretending it was a sob. He squeezed her hand to comfort her and she almost whispered that it would take more than that, but she kept her mouth shut and wiped her eyes with the tissue he handed her.

After the service, Jarod put on his sunglasses and led her out to his truck, which was already in line for the procession to the cemetery.

"Why are you doing this?" Daisy asked.

"You are my wife," he said.

"I am not your wife. I was for a week and a day in a pretend world."

"You were in the biblical sense twice in a not-pretend world," he countered. "Why'd you tell them about the Honky Tonk right out of the chute? And why didn't you tell them you were a vet tech?" he asked.

"I was being honest and I'm not ashamed of what I do. Remember? Are you ashamed of what I do or who I am?"

"Hell no. I don't care if you are a bartender and it damn sure won't work."

"What won't work?"

"Runnin' me off. I will see you again," he declared. He might not have six weeks but he did have a few days.

"Again? We've never been on a date."

"We went fishin' and to the cattle sale. Those are dates in my world. What makes a date in your world?"

"Dinner. Movies. Walk me to the door. Kiss me."

"Miss Daisy O'Dell, would you go to dinner and a movie with me on Friday night?" he asked.

"Can't. Got to work. Only night I've got free for dating is Sunday."

"Then Miz Daisy, can I pick you up on Sunday morning for a cowboy date?"

"What in the hell is a cowboy date?"

"You'll never know if you don't say yes," he said.

She thought about it as they drove slowly behind the hearse toward Liberty Cemetery. "How does one dress for a cowboy date?"

"That fancy little dress you wore to the fish fry at Jim Bob's place to start with and your fanciest pair of boots. Bring a bag with shorts and a T-shirt for the afternoon and maybe some jeans and something to go to dinner in that evening if we decide to go out and your makeup in case you decide to spend the night," he said.

"In your dreams. It's our first date. You'll do well to get to first base on the first date," she said.

Jarod's heart skipped a beat.

Daisy held her hands tightly in her lap. She felt like a sexual arsonist. Playing with fire; couldn't stop; about to be burned.

They reached the cemetery and again he held her hand from the truck to the gravesite. Frankie's stony face said she didn't like what she was seeing. If just that little affectionate gesture caused such a sour expression, Daisy would have hated to see what kind of puckered up face she would make if she found out what went on in Jarod's bedroom a few nights before. Give 'em, hell, nothing. She didn't have to do anything but be Daisy O'Dell. They made their own hell.

The sun was almost straight up and scorching hot. Sweat trickled down inside Daisy's bra as she listened to the preacher read Psalm 23. She wished she'd been wise enough to wear a big floppy hat like Chigger to keep the sun from beating down on her head.

The preacher held up his hand to get everyone's attention and then said, "And now we'll close with a country song that Emmett requested after which there will be a few words and the service will be over. He was very explicit about the order of his funeral so here it is and then the service will be over."

Using her free hand, Daisy swiped at the sweat beads under her nose. The black dress drew the external heat as bad as Jarod did the internal.

Brad Paisley's voice came from a portable CD player behind the casket as he sang, "When I Get Where I'm Going."

Daisy laid her head on Jarod's shoulder and wet the front of his white shirt with her tears. She didn't care if Frankie McElroy popped a cranial fuse. He pulled her close and held his head high as tears dripped off his strong jawbone. At the end of the song, Emmett's voice came through the speakers.

Daisy jumped and looked at the flower covered casket. Surely to God that cantankerous old goat hadn't risen up out of that coffin and come back to life. If he had after she'd shed so many tears for him, he was in for one royal cussin'.

"It's not him. It's from the recorder," Jarod whispered.

Emmett's gravelly old voice continued, "Now it's all over and I'm where I want to be. Mavis and I are together again so dry up any tears you've shed and get on with life. Don't waste a minute of your precious time mournin' for this old cowboy. Love. Laugh. Fight and make up. Go on back to the ranch and have some dinner and remember me every so often with a smile. Good-bye, all my family and friends. Be happy that I've finished my race and I'm where I want to be."

Daisy cried harder.

Jarod handed her a snowy white handkerchief from his hip pocket. "By damn, he got the last word in, didn't he?"

Daisy looked up at him. "The mark of a true fighter. You think he'd go without having the very last word? It wouldn't be Emmett if he did."

Several people stopped to shake Jarod's hand and say a few words about Emmett. Daisy tried to slip away with Cathy and Chigger, but Jarod kept her squeezed up to his side. They were the last truck to leave the cemetery, and by the time they reached the ranch, dinner was already spread out on tables under the shade trees in the backyard. Two eight-foot folding tables were laden with casseroles of every kind and description along with fried chicken and ham, chocolate cakes, pecan pies, peach cobblers, and gallons of sweet tea.

Folding chairs surrounded ten other tables covered with every color plastic tablecloth imaginable. Salt and pepper shakers, paper napkins in holders, and plastic cutlery were scattered down the middle of each table. Chigger, Cathy, and the Walker triplets were already eating by the time Jarod and Daisy made it through the buffet line.

"Hey, y'all, we saved places for you two," Chigger raised her voice.

Daisy took off in that direction and left Jarod to either follow or find another table. She was seated when he pulled out a chair beside her.

"I heard that y'all ain't legally married after all," Chigger said.

Daisy looked across the table at Cathy.

She giggled and shrugged. "I ratted you out."

"Then I've still got a chance?" Billy Bob asked.

"Honey, you never had a chance so there ain't no still to it," Daisy said.

"Daisy O'Dell, you are a coldhearted woman. Watch her, Jarod. She'll leave you with nothing but the shattered pieces of a broken heart," Billy Bob said.

"Oh, eat your chicken and hush," Daisy said.

Chigger changed the subject abruptly. "What I want to know is what kind of name is Liam?"

"It's Irish," Jarod said.

"Well, I like it. I might want to name this baby that if it's a boy. Of course, it's not, but I need to have a name ready just in case, I guess."

Liam sat down beside his son. "I'm full-blooded Irish and I'd be honored if you gave your baby my name. My grandfather came over here from the old country and spoke with a heavy accent until he died. I'm supposed to have a temper to go with the name but…"

Frankie put her plate on the table, sat down beside him, and said, "…but he's mild tempered compared to me. I'm half Cherokee, the other half mixed mongrel. Momma was the Indian. Daddy was a plain old white man who didn't have a clue to his background. He must have had a temper gene somewhere because Momma was the most laid back, calmest woman you'd ever met. But me, I got a white hot temper that flares up like a forest fire especially if someone messes with my family. How about you, Daisy? You got a temper? With a name like O'Dell I'd guess you've got some Irish?"

Daisy took a long drink of her tea before she answered. "O'Dell is from my father who I never met. He was killed before I was born. My momma was Cherokee Indian too, a quarter. Her mother was half and brought up in Cherokee, North Carolina, on the reservation. And yes, ma'am, I have a temper. Don't surface real often but when it does it takes a lot of water to put it out. I pick my battles but I don't back down from anything."

Frankie nodded seriously. The lines were drawn. She'd laid out her cards and Daisy had put hers on the table. It didn't matter who had the full house or aces; Momma Frankie intended to win the jackpot because her son deserved better than a barmaid.

"You got that much water, Jarod?" Cathy asked.

"Jarod's got a pretty healthy dose of temper himself. Mitch is more laid back like me. Stephen got some of his momma's disposition, but Jarod got a big chunk of it," Liam said.

"Did I hear my name?" Stephen pulled out a chair beside his mother.

"We were talkin' about Irish tempers," Daisy said.

"Jarod got that. I got the good looks. Mitch got left out," Stephen said.

"Sounds like me," Billy Bob said. "I got the good looks. Joe Bob got the smarts and poor old Jim Bob got—"

"Me!" Chigger said and leaned over to kiss Jim Bob on the cheek. "You two are going to be left out here in seven months when I have a pretty little girl for his momma."

Jim Bob beamed and the conversation went to naming the baby. Daisy wouldn't have cared if they'd discussed dead bodies over the dinner table as long as they left her alone. That was another reason a serious relationship would never work between her and Jarod. Not even a romp in the bedroom could calm two equally scorching tempers. Like she'd said, it would take a lot of water to put out her temper. She couldn't imagine what it would take to extinguish both when she and Jarod both flared up at the same time. Texas didn't have that much water.

Jarod squeezed her thigh under the table and she jumped. Chigger winked from across the table and Cathy giggled.

"You want to walk home?" she asked Cathy.

"Ah, I was hopin' you'd let me drive the car home and Jarod could haul you home," Cathy said.

Daisy shook her head. "Not in this lifetime, cousin."

"Why can't she drive your car?" Joe Bob asked.

"Ask her," Daisy said.

"She carries a grudge forever, too. We were both sixteen and she had a waitress job so she bought this old junker of a car to get her back and forth. I had a crush on the quarterback of the football team so she let me take the car to the football game. I wrecked it and she won't let me drive her cars," Cathy said.

"Fender bender?" Joe Bob asked.

"Totaled it," Daisy said.

"Y'all kinfolks?" Frankie asked.

"On the O'Dell side. My daddy and hers were brothers. We're both only children and we're all that's left of that side of the family," Cathy said.

"And what do you do for a living? Are you a rancher?" Jewel asked.

"No, ma'am. I'm a bartender. Work at the Tonk for Daisy. It's a good beer joint. Got a big old burly bouncer named Tinker and he keeps things on the up-and-up. The folks around Mingus know Daisy don't put up with no shit. Pardon my language if it offends anyone's delicate ears. Me and Daisy, we just call 'em the way we see 'em. I've worked in worse places, let me tell you. So has Daisy," she said.

"I see," Frankie said coldly.

Daisy reached under the table and squeezed Jarod's leg. He gave a little start and smiled at her.

"Something I can do for you?" he whispered.

"You're in big trouble," she said out of the corner of her mouth.

"Probably, but it's worth it," he said.

Jewel leaned around Stephen and said, "Hey, Daisy, did he tell you that he's already bought three engagement rings so you could have had a choice if Uncle Emmett would have ever noticed you weren't wearing rings."

Jewel had red hair cut in a short bob, green eyes, and enough freckles to give her makeup hell. She might have weighed a hundred and ten but that was with rocks in her pockets.

"I heard he'd been engaged three times." Daisy's tone was one of icy dismissal before she looked across the table. "Cathy, did you tell Tinker we'd be back in plenty of time to open up tonight?"

Jarod's face was a study in anger.

"Just thought you'd like to know he's a three-time loser," Jewel said.

Daisy leaned forward and smiled at Jewel. "Diamonds don't mean squat to me, darlin'. I want a man's heart, not his damned old ring." She couldn't believe she was taking up for Jarod. She'd told Emmett that he could take care of himself and the first rattle out of the bucket she was fighting his battles. Maybe Emmett had been right when he said every man needed a good woman.

"Touché, Daisy. Well said. You ought to know that he's spoiled though. You ever hear that song by Blake Shelton, 'The Baby'?" Maria asked.

"It's on my new jukebox," she said.

"That's Jarod. He came along when the other two McElroy boys were half grown. Momma Frankie was tired so she spoiled him rotten and protects him like a mountain lion with a cub," Jewel said.

"Rest assured, Jewel. Jarod and I are not planning a wedding," Daisy said bluntly.

"Everyone he introduces to the family, he ends up engaged to. I just thought I'd give you the lowdown and save you some time," Jewel said.

Daisy frowned at Jewel that time. Honey didn't work. Maybe vinegar would shut the woman up. "It's my time and whether I waste it or not is my business."

"I'm just warnin' you. Everything goes pretty good until he puts the ring on your hand then it all goes in the toilet. We never have figured out why," Jewel kept on.

"Well, the toilet won't get clogged with my big diamond because I don't want one from any man. I'm not interested in marriage, engagements, or relationships. I'm very content in my Honky Tonk beer joint, and honey, when I leave it'll be after a night of drawing beer and listenin' to good country music. They'll take me out with my boots on and my hand wrapped around a longneck bottle of cold Coors. Now I'm going for a walk around the property one more time before I go home. I've had all this sweet company I can stand for one day." She pushed her chair back.

Jarod did the same.

"Where are you going?" she asked.

"With you," he said.

"I didn't ask you."

"I didn't ask you either, but I'm going."

They locked gazes and the rest of the world disappeared. He intended to pursue her until she was his. She intended to run as fast as she could so that she didn't have to face her own feelings for him.

She shrugged and started walking but her high heels sank in the ground with every step. After a few feet, she stopped, took them off, and tossed them toward the back porch, and walked out of the fenced yard in her bare feet. Jarod caught up to her, swooped her up in his arms, and carried her like a new bride to the nearest barn.

Her first impulse was to kick and scream until he put her down. But that would have made Jewel happy. Daisy would have endured walking through hell in her bare feet before she let Jewel win the catfight. The minute they were in the barn she wiggled and squirmed until he lost his grip and put her down.

She gritted her teeth. "Why'd you do that?"

"Goat heads," he said.

"Are you crazy? What has goat heads got to do with anything?"

"Pasture is full of them."

He tilted back her chin and claimed her lips with a burning kiss. She clung to him as the bones in her legs dissolved. She wanted more and was angry at herself for the lack of control. She didn't believe in love at first sight. It was something that happened in fairy tales, not real life.

He broke the kiss but kept her hugged up to his chest tight enough to hear her racing heart keeping time with his. "Tell me again about how you don't want relationships?"

She rolled up on her tiptoes, wrapped her hand around his neck, and pulled his face down for another searing kiss. "No commitments. Just long slow kisses and what they lead to."

"What's that?"

"In this barn with all those people seeing through the wide open doors, it will lead to nothing, especially right after a funeral. Some things are sacred. Carry me back to your truck and take me to my car. I'm ready to go home."

"Can I come into the apartment for a cup of coffee?"

"Hell, no. Men aren't allowed in the apartment," she said.

"I was in it yesterday," he argued.

"It won't happen again."

"Then walk," he said.

"You son-of-a-bitch," she said.

"Dad might get riled if you call his wife that. See you later, Daisy. Don't forget we got a cowboy date on Sunday." He left her standing there and whistled a tune by Lonestar all the way back to the yard.

She sat down on a hay bale and drew her bare feet up when she saw a mouse skitter across the barn floor. It's a good thing she didn't have her shotgun or Jarod would be having a close up and personal visit with Uncle Emmett.

He stopped at the table and said a few words to Cathy, then stopped to speak to some people at another table before he disappeared around the back corner of the house. Daisy bit at her lower lip. Walking across a pasture of burrs would be pure torture and it would be impossible to get her boots on for work that night. Sitting where she was all afternoon in the sweltering heat of the barn would cause dehydration. It was a lose-lose situation.

Cathy waved toward the barn. Chigger and Jim Bob did the same as they made their way to Jim Bob's truck and Daisy motioned for them to come and rescue her. Jim Bob backed the truck out of the parking place and drove away in the opposite direction from the barn. Daisy couldn't take her eyes from the tailgate of the big dual-tired truck as she watched her rescue disappear. Cathy was going to be calling a taxi to take her back to Dallas to catch a bus to Mena when Daisy got home that evening.

Another movement caught her attention and a white truck appeared out of the dust coming toward the barn.

"My knight-in-shining-damn-armor. Billy Bob, you never looked so good. Maybe I'll marry you after all," she said.

Billy Bob did not step out of the truck when it pulled into the big double doors of the barn. Jarod did with a big smile on his face. Without a word, he scooped her up into his arms for the second time and carried her to the driver's side where he gently set her down. "Scoot over, but not too far. I'd like to feel you next to me."

"You are a rat," she declared.

"Had you guessing, didn't I?"

"Hell, no! I was about to yell for Billy Bob. He wouldn't let me walk across a field of stickers," she said.

"That's alfalfa in that pasture, Daisy. There's not a sticker or goat head in it. Are you sure you are a vet tech?" he said.

"I'm a vet tech, all right, but I'm not a rancher. I don't know alfalfa from green beans."

"Want to learn?" He cocked his head to one side.

More than you'll ever know, she thought.

Chapter 12

CHIGGER'S WEDDING DRESS WAS A DEMURE WHITE spaghetti strap cotton sundress that flowed from an empire waist to the top of her new pink cowboy boots. A wreath of white roses with ribbons flowing down back circled her upswept blond hair and she carried a bouquet of pink and white roses. Jim Bob was dressed in black Wranglers, white shirt, and polished, black eel dress boots.

Daisy stood on Chigger's left in a pink and white checked sundress and white sandals. She wished she had a bouquet to hold to keep her hands from shaking. She'd expected Joe Bob and Billy Bob and maybe even the Walker parents to be present and they were. She had not expected to see Jarod there also. Yet there he was on the other side of Jim Bob, standing right beside Billy Bob and Joe Bob.

Jarod couldn't keep his eyes off Daisy or his mind on the ceremony. She was beautiful. She was smart. She was funny. She was so many things that he couldn't begin to list them all. And he wanted to be a part of every single bit of her life from that day forward, until death parted them. And not Emmett's death, either.

Daisy looked around Chigger and locked gazes with him. One eyelid slowly dropped and a slow smile curved his mouth upward.

Her heart quickened and her pulse raced.

She calmed both by making a mental list of what liquors were getting low at the Honky Tonk; how many bags of peanuts and pretzels were in the storage room; whether or not the old record of George Jones singing "I Always Get Lucky" should be replaced on the jukebox this week.

Now why in devil did I think of that song right now? I should be listening to vows, not playing a song about getting lucky. What is wrong with me?

She tried. She really did but Jones's song about getting lucky kept running through her mind. Would she get lucky with Jarod? Or would she never hear from him again when he moved back to Oklahoma? Did she even want to hear from him or would a clean break be the best thing?

She jumped like she'd stuck her finger in the light socket when the judge pronounced Jim Bob and Chigger man and wife. She watched Jim Bob wrap Chigger protectively up into his arms for the wedding kiss. She stepped back and waited to embrace Chigger until the Walkers and Jarod had their turn.

"Be happy," Daisy said when she finally hugged Chigger.

"I am happy. You could be too. Jarod has had your panties on fire for weeks. Do something about it before he's gone forever," she whispered.

"Chigger!" Daisy exclaimed.

Chigger giggled. "Truth is truth. Wrap it in chocolate or cow shit, it's still the truth."

Jim Bob claimed her again with another kiss. "I can't believe it but she's really my wife."

"You take care of her," Daisy said.

"You got my word on that, but we got to get going if we're going to make it to the airport on time," he said.

"Everyone come on outside," Thelma Walker said. "Y'all wait right here for a couple of minutes and then come on out. There might not be many of us but we can give you a sendoff."

They trooped out and down the courthouse steps, across the lawn to the curb where Jim Bob had parked his truck. Thelma handed each of them a handful of bird seed and a white balloon with JUST MARRIED written in pink letters and pink streamers.

"Throw the seed and we'll let the balloons go soon as they are in the truck," she said.

Jim Bob stopped on the steps and removed a blue garter from Chigger's leg. Billy Bob shouted from a few feet away to throw it toward him, but Chigger wrapped it around the stem of the bouquet.

"That's not tradition," Billy Bob said. "And I need that thing or else Daisy ain't never goin' to marry me."

"That garter won't make a bit of difference," Daisy said.

Instead of throwing the bouquet she dropped it in Daisy's hands as she passed her and said, "You give that garter to the cowboy you want to have it. The bouquet is yours and you are next."

Jim Bob picked Chigger up as if she were a piece of fine China and set her inside the cab of the truck and Daisy tried to shove the bouquet back at her through the window. Chigger just laughed and refused to take it.

"Give it to me." Jarod picked it out of Daisy's hand. He unwrapped the garter and slipped it on his left arm and handed the roses back to Daisy.

"But what if I wanted Joe Bob to have it?" she asked.

He popped the elastic out with the forefinger on his right hand. "You want one of the remaining Walker triplets to have it, then take it off and give it to him."

"Hell, Daisy, I don't want that thing. You can't play pool good enough to beat me. If Billy Bob wants it, give it to him," Joe Bob said.

Billy Bob kicked at the dirt in mock embarrassment. "Ahhh, shucks, I don't need that thing to woo Miss Daisy. I can steal her heart with my good looks and pretty eyes. You go ahead and keep it, Jarod, so the playing field will be even."

"Thank you both," Jarod beamed.

"Y'all be careful now and call us the minute you get settled in," Thelma said.

"Momma, them kids ain't going to be interested in talking to you when they get there. Y'all call us if you need anything. We'll see you in a few days," Harlin Walker said.

Jim Bob honked the truck horn as he backed out of the parking lot. The crew on the courthouse steps waved at them until they turned the corner and disappeared.

"That was nice." Thelma Walker wiped at her eyes.

Joe Bob patted her shoulder. "Ah, Momma, don't cry. Me and Billy Bob will stay with you forever."

Harlin grinned. "That's why she's cryin', son."

"I want you two to be as happy as Jim Bob," Thelma said.

Harlin slipped an arm around her waist. "Come on, honey. Let's go on home."

The Walkers had driven to Palo Pinto in one truck so they left together. Daisy looked from the roses to the garter on Jarod's arm and back again. Cathy should have been there to catch the bouquet. Hell, Merle would have been a better candidate than Daisy. Was it bad luck for Chigger if Daisy wasn't the next bride? If it was then Chigger was in for a world of hurt because Daisy was most definitely not going to get married.

"Go to dinner with me over in Mineral Wells?" Jarod asked.

"Too early for dinner, isn't it?"

"What time did you eat breakfast?" he asked.

"Didn't. I was in a rush to get dressed and make it here on time."

"Then it's not too early. By the time we get there it will be past eleven, anyway. Most of the restaurants start serving lunch at that time."

"My car?"

"Will be fine sitting right where it is. Might have some drool marks on it by the time I bring you back, but it should be all right. Or we can take your car and leave my truck."

She dug around in her purse and found the keys and tossed them at him.

"You are letting me drive your baby again?"

"Don't put a scratch on her or you'll never sit in that seat again."

"Yes, ma'am."

They listened to country music from Palo Pinto to Mineral Wells. Garth Brooks, Alan Jackson, and Sara Evans sang and Daisy felt the words sink into her being like she'd never known before. She'd grown up on country music, cut her teeth on Alabama, Marty Stuart, and Travis Tritt. Her grandmother listened to the likes of George Jones, Patsy Cline, Don Williams, and Loretta Lynn.

Daisy started to say something but Jarod's expression said that he was deep in thought and she didn't want to interrupt. What could he be thinking about anyway? Was all that about the garter just a show? Did he really wish she'd given the damn thing to Billy Bob?

Jarod didn't hear the words to the songs. His mother had called the night before. According to Frankie, he didn't need to take up with a bartender even if she did own her own beer joint and was a vet tech.

He'd reminded her that he was thirty-five years old and would take care of his own love life. She'd gone silent and hung up on him.

Mitch had called five minutes later and told Jarod that being on the Double M had turned him into an opinionated old fool like Uncle Emmett. Jarod thanked him for the compliment and hung up on him.

Ten minutes after that, Stephen's call had come in. "Hear you done pissed off the family powwow."

"Guess I did but the feeling is mutual."

"I can't believe that you argued with Momma."

"No arguing. She stated her opinion. I gave her mine. It's her problem if they don't agree," Jarod had said.

"Congratulations, Jarod."

"For what?"

"You think about it." Stephen had hung up.

He slapped the steering wheel and Daisy jerked her head around. "You don't like this song, change the station. I don't care what we listen to. This remind you of something painful? You look like you've been suckin' on a lemon."

"Song is fine. I was thinking about something else, not the song."

"What?"

"Something Stephen said," he answered.

"Oh?"

"He thinks I'm finally growing up because I stood up to my family."

"I think he's crazy," Daisy said.

"Why's that?"

"Just because you were the last child doesn't make you a baby. What's the matter with your family? My granny had more faith in my judgment when I was nine. And *I* was givin' Momma advice when I was fifteen. I'm sure you've been working at something since you were big enough to do a job. They're all too damn possessive," she said.

When he didn't say anything she continued, "Don't go all quiet and mad at me. Like Cathy said, we call 'em like we see 'em. You don't have to prove anything to anyone. You are a big boy."

More quietness.

"Okay, then let's change the subject," she said.

"Keep on talking. My ego is getting so big it won't fit in this car."

"You are rotten," she huffed.

"You just said I was smart," he protested.

"Attitude has nothing to do with ability," she said.

"What does that mean?"

"That you can be a smart rotten…" She stopped short of a bad word.

He waggled a finger at her. "Be careful."

She playfully slapped it away. "Keep both hands on the wheel or I'm driving. Where are we going for lunch?"

"You just changed the subject. You like Mexican?"

"Yes, I changed the subject. But it don't make you any more smart or any less rotten. And I love Mexican food," she said.

"This all right?" He pulled into the Chili's parking lot.

She unbuckled the seat belt, opened the door, and threw her long legs out in one fluid motion. "Mushroom jack fajitas and since you are driving, a margarita."

"Thought you were a Coors girl," he said. He wished he'd been fast enough to see the sight of those legs when they came out of the car.

"Most of the time I am. One a night after work to cool off is my limit. I damn sure don't have time to go to those AA meetings," she teased.

A hostess greeted them inside the restaurant from a small podium. "Two?" she asked.

"That's right," Jarod said.

She led them to a booth and laid two menus on the table. "Your waitress will be right with you. Y'all must've been to a wedding."

The lady had spiked burgundy hair and a Tweety bird tattoo peeking out from between her breasts. If she'd fastened one more button it wouldn't have shown, but then where was the fun in that?

Jarod touched the garter. "Yes, we were. Friends of ours got married this morning."

"So you are the next groom, are you? You got a bride picked out?"

"Never know," Jarod sidestepped the question. Of course he had a bride picked out, but she was as skittish as an unbroken pony and he had to go slowly. Slow when time was short wasn't an easy thing, either.

"Who caught the bouquet?"

"I did," Daisy said.

The hostess nodded. "Day late and a dollar short. That's me. Enjoy your meal."

"Thank you," Daisy said.

The waitress appeared before the hostess took two steps. "Appetizers or drinks while you think about what you want?"

"Iced tea for me. A Grand Patron Margarita for the lady. Endless chips and salsa while we study the menu, please," Jarod said.

"It'll be right out," she said. "So you caught the garter?"

"More like I stole it," he said.

"Does the magic work if you steal it?" she said.

"Long as it's on my arm it's magic," Jarod said.

"I'd think anything on you would be magic," the waitress said with a giggle before she carried their orders back to the kitchen.

Daisy suddenly understood the real reason three women had given back their engagement rings. Dealing with women on a regular basis with Jarod for a boyfriend or a fiancé would certainly be taxing on the psyche. She'd have to remember that when she was pining for him after he went back to Oklahoma.

"I want mushroom jack fajitas, beef and chicken mixed, with a side order of beans," she said to Jarod.

The waitress set their drinks on paper coasters in front of them. "Y'all ready or do you want a few more minutes?"

Jarod gave her Daisy's choice and then ordered a flame grilled rib-eye steak with mashed potatoes and corn on the cob for himself.

Daisy took a sip of the margarita. It was almost as good as one of Cathy's. "Does everyone flirt with you? She checked your hand for a wedding ring."

"I didn't notice. Did I tell you that you look lovely in that pink dress? Wear it on Sunday for the first part of our date."

"Why? Where are we going?"

"It's a surprise," he said.

The waitress brought the appetizer and set it in the middle of the table. "Y'all enjoy."

"I'm sure we will," Jarod said.

Daisy dipped a chip into her bowl of salsa and popped it into her mouth.

Jarod ate several chips loaded with salsa. "Ever been to Mexico and eaten the real Mexican food?"

"No. I've been to Oklahoma, Texas, Louisiana, Arkansas, and a trip when I was about nine to Cherokee, North Carolina."

She ate more chips and had another gulp of the margarita. "Granny wanted to go to a family reunion so we drove. Momma was workin' and on number umpteen boyfriend so she couldn't get away. Granny drove that Ford Maverick, only it had no air conditioning. When I had it rebuilt, I had air put in it. It was in the middle of June so it wasn't too hot, at least not to a nine-year-old."

"What was it like? The reunion?"

"Lots of Indian folks. We ate in a park along the side of a river and I played with all the cousins in the water that day. The women sat around the tables and talked about who died and who had babies and who left the reservation. The men fished downstream from where we were splashing around. We stayed a few days. Slept at a different house every night then we came home."

"No stomp dances?"

"That's for the tourists. You ever been on a reservation?"

"Every year we went up to Ralston for the Blackwolf family reunion. It was about the same thing you just said. We played with cousins when we were boys. The women talk. The men fish or drink beer and laugh about stunts they've pulled. When we got old enough to drive we ran around the small towns in that area and talked about cars and girls. Before long the youngsters were marrying off and there was a brand new crop of little Indian babies at the reunions. Haven't been to one in a few years so I don't know whether they're still as big as they used to be or not."

The waitress brought their lunch, refilled Jarod's tea, and glanced toward Daisy's margarita.

"She didn't flirt," Jarod whispered.

Daisy leaned forward and whispered back, "You lost your chance when you didn't flirt back with her the first time. Now she's got a tattooed fellow in a corner booth who's probably going to get lucky later this afternoon."

Jarod cut into his steak. "Win some. Lose some. Am I going to get lucky this afternoon?"

"I don't think so, cowboy," Daisy said. "Not unless you play up to the hostess who seated us. You might get to see all of that Tweety bird if you wink at her."

"You wouldn't be jealous?" he asked.

"Of course I'd be jealous. I'm supposed to be the next bride."

"For real, Daisy. Would you be jealous of me with another woman?"

She thought about it. Hell yes, she would, but what good would it do her? Finally she nodded, honestly.

He grinned. "Me too."

"I don't intend to make a play for another woman," she said.

"You know exactly what I'm talking about," he said.

"Dessert?" the waitress asked.

"I'd have to put it in my pocket. Daisy, you want something? I can vouch for their cheesecake," Jarod said.

She shook her head.

"Then I'll leave this and you can take care of it when you are ready." She placed a small folder with the bill inside on the edge of the table.

"What's my half?" Daisy asked.

"My treat." Jarod quickly shoved several bills into the folder.

"Does that make this a date?"

"Only if I get a kiss at the end of it."

"Then it's not a date," she said. She'd just eaten a plate of grilled onions and couldn't imagine anyone wanting to kiss her with that breath.

Halfway back to Palo Pinto she asked, "So have you been to Mexico?"

He nodded.

"Where's the prettiest place you've ever been?"

"Home in Oklahoma and right behind that is Montana. I went up there to a big cattle sale last fall. Bought a bull. It's Angus."

She smiled. "Who went with you?"

"No one. Daisy, it's been three years since the last woman I was involved with broke our engagement. It's not like I was engaged three times in six months. The first time I was twenty-two and right out of college. The second time I was twenty-seven. The third time I was thirty-two. She was employed by the university in Stillwater and got a job opportunity in New York. She wanted me to give up ranching and move there. Can't you just see that?"

With his looks and Texas drawl he could charm the hair off a frog's ass anywhere in the world. Those cute little business types in high heels and cute little suits wouldn't have a snowball's chance in hell against his sex appeal. But he would have been miserable outside ranch life.

"So your family trusted you with the bank account to buy a bull but they don't trust you in matters of the heart?"

"It wasn't their bank account. It was mine and the bull is mine but I did buy a few head of stock for them while I was there," he said.

"And?"

He nosed her car in beside his truck across the street from the courthouse. The distance from Palo Pinto to Mineral Wells was more than twenty miles but the time had gone by so fast he wanted to turn around and go back so he and Daisy could talk some more. "And it doesn't matter what they think when it comes to matters of the heart. Here we are. Margarita settled enough you can drive home, or do I need to follow you?"

"Honey, I might have some Indian blood that don't hold liquor worth a damn, but the other half is Irish and

I could drink you under the table any day of the week if push came to shove," she said.

They got out and started around the front of the Maverick. He headed toward his pickup and she was on the way to the driver's side. When they passed, he grabbed her around the waist and twirled her around to face him. His gaze locked with hers and he shut his eyes as he leaned in for the kiss.

She rolled up on her toes to make it easier.

He tasted onions and the after-effects of tequila mixed together and the combination was as heady as the kiss. He ran his tongue over her lower lip to get one more sample before he moved his mouth around to her neck and inhaled the sweet aroma of her hair.

"I guess it is a date since I got a kiss. See you later." He sped off before she could collect her bearings enough to get into her car.

When her vision cleared and she could see something other than his sexy face and gray eyes, she noticed two elderly ladies were sitting on a bench in front of the bank not five feet from her.

"You lettin' that get away?" one asked.

"Not for long," Daisy answered.

"I wouldn't have let him go for a minute if I was your age, especially with times being like they are today. In my time, a woman couldn't kiss a man like that on Main Street less they was loose-legged. I was always kinda jealous of them loose-legged ones, wasn't you, Ruth?"

Ruth had lilac hair that kinked all over her head and wrinkles upon wrinkles, but her blue eyes sparkled when she said, "God, yes, I was jealous. We were both born fifty years too soon, Arabelle. We'da been hellcats even more than we was. Why, you remember that time when—"

"Bye now," Daisy said and left them to reminisce about the time when they'd been a little naughty. She drove back to the Honky Tonk wishing she could be a hell of a lot more naughty without a guilty conscience afterwards.

The beer joint was busy that night, but without Chigger and Jim Bob things were unusually calm. A few truckers stopped by and Merle came in to beat Joe Bob at pool. Around nine thirty a party of six preppies came in, wearing their pleated slacks and sports jackets. They sat at a table and ordered two pitchers of margaritas.

"Patron?" Daisy asked.

"José is fine," one said. "What's your name? You available for some after-hour fun?" one asked.

"See that big old boy sittin' back there in the shadows beside the door?" Daisy pointed.

The cockiest of the group asked, "What's he got to do with anything?"

"You ask me anything like that again and he will throw your ass out the door."

"Hey, lady, we just saw the sign on the highway and stopped for a drink. We didn't come in here lookin' for trouble. We just want a few drinks, maybe a dance or two with the ladies, and we'll be on our way. Apologize to the lady, Shawn," one of the others said.

"Sorry, ma'am. I was out of line." Shawn blushed.

"Apology accepted. Enjoy your evening," she said.

"What was that all about?" Cathy asked when she made it back to the bar.

"Newcomers. Thought I was a hooker," Daisy said.

"Set 'em straight?"

"Yes, I did. You want to make a few extra dollars tonight?" Daisy teased.

"Not me. I'm sworn off men forever. I'm going to be like Ruby and go out in a blaze of glory. Then all the men I've known can come and weep over my dead body," Cathy said.

"I'll weep over either of you," Billy Bob said from the end of the bar.

"Good. We got our first mourner, but darlin', you're going to be so old when the time comes for weeping that you won't remember how to cry," Cathy said.

Merle came through the door and Joe Bob signaled Daisy for two draft Coors and carried them to the nearest pool table. Merle opened her fancy cue stick case and chalked it, took a long pull off the beer, and told Joe Bob he'd best get ready to lose.

Billy Bob nodded toward the middle of the floor. "Here comes the competition."

Jarod chose a stool in the middle of the bar so he could be close enough to talk to Daisy no matter where she was working. "Evenin', Daisy."

"Jarod."

"Beer, please," he said. Daisy was a classy woman even in jeans and a sweater. She'd never let on in public that they'd been wrapped up together naked more than once. More and more she was showing him all her sides and he liked every one. A classy wife in public. A hellcat in the bedroom. A fine cook in the kitchen.

Wife? The word stopped him in his thought process.

"Comin' right up."

"Hey, could we get a couple more pitchers of marga-ritas?" Shawn asked from the stool next to Jarod's.

"Cathy, you want to make them? José Quervo."

"Aww, shucks. You boys ain't had a decent one until you try Patron," Cathy said.

"Can't afford that high-dollar stuff," Shawn said. "What's your name?"

"I'm Cathy and the one who you offended earlier is Daisy. And honey, if you think Patron is high-dollar, you could never afford either of us."

Shawn smiled. "I ain't sayin' a word."

"You're a quick learner." Cathy mixed up two more pitchers of margaritas, took his money, and made change.

"Who offended you?" Jarod asked.

Daisy quickly said, "It was nothing. Boys hadn't been here before. Thought they could roust up some after-hours entertainment. We straightened it out real fast. Didn't even have to involve Tinker."

"You don't belong in a bar," Jarod said.

She set a jar of beer in front of him. "Oh, I don't? Then where do I belong?"

He held out a hand. "Want to dance?"

"I'm working, Jarod. I don't dance with the customers."

Billy Bob slid into the space Shawn had vacated. "Ain't no use in beggin' her. I been doin' that ever since the first night she went to work for Ruby. She don't dance with customers and men folks do not ever go behind that door back there into her house. Must be something awful damn important."

"You got that right," Cathy whispered. "What's back there isn't for male eyeballs to look upon. If you ever saw it, you'd go stone cold blind."

"Aw, come on," Billy Bob said.

Cathy crossed her heart with her hand. "Truth. Swear it."

"She tellin' the truth, Daisy?" Jarod asked.

"What do you think?"

"I was only in the living room and kitchen. Is the blinding stuff in the bedroom?" Jarod asked.

Billy Bob narrowed his eyes and glared at Jarod. "You rat. You got to go in there after less than a month and I been tryin' to sneak in all these years."

"Did you offer to take her to a cattle sale?" Jarod asked.

"That ain't the way to sweet-talk a woman! Cattle sale! I offered to take her on an Alaskan cruise or anywhere in the whole world for a week." Billy Bob pouted.

Daisy swiped at the bar in front of them. "Drink your beer and stop talking about me. I'm not going anywhere with either of you."

Jarod lowered his chin and looked up at her.

"Don't look at me like that. I'm not!"

Billy Bob poked him on the shoulder. "See, we're both wastin' our time. Cathy, darlin', would you invite me back into the apartment?"

"You want to go blind?" she asked.

"Maybe just in one eye," he said.

Cathy laughed and kept working. She wouldn't risk losing what she had for all the Billy Bobs in the world. Now, if Jarod was up for grabs she might reconsider that risk. However, that man had eyes for only one woman in the Tonk and that was Daisy. Matter of fact, it was pretty damn plain that he had eyes for only one woman in the state of Texas and that was Daisy too. The way he'd picked her up and carried her to the barn out on the ranch was so sweet and romantic it brought a tear to Cathy's eye.

Cathy's man would come along someday, like Jarod had. He'd appear on a bar stool in the Tonk and she'd feel that special feeling down deep in her gut. Only difference was that when Cathy got her lightning bolt she intended to chase it to the ends of the earth rather than refusing to admit how she felt.

"Hey Cathy, get that customer on the far end," Daisy said.

"Sure thing." Cathy came back to the real world with a jolt.

Jarod sipped his beer, making it last as long as possible, listened to country music blaring from the new jukebox, and watched Joe Bob lose three games to Merle and win one finally. At ten thirty a bunch of women came in, ordered a pitcher of hurricanes, and sat at the table next to the preppie guys. Before midnight the tight fitting jeans ladies had the preppies on the dance floor teaching them to line dance to Garth Brooks songs.

Daisy made her way to his barstool and asked, "So you ready for another beer?"

"No, I'm on a one beer limit. My friend taught me that trick today," he said.

"So your friend got a name?" she asked.

"Name is Daisy. Pretty woman. Wears her dark hair kinda long and has amazing eyes and legs that go from earth to heaven. I'll have to introduce you to her some-time. I'm taking her on a date Sunday," he flirted.

Billy Bob slapped the bar. "Well, I'll be damned. You got to go in the apartment and you got a real date with her too."

"Kind of looks that way," Jarod said.

"Life is a bitch. I might just go on up to the Boar's Nest tomorrow night."

"Suit yourself. See if they'll sell it to you," she said.

"I don't want to buy either of those places. I want this one and the pretty bartender that goes with it," Billy Bob said.

"Keep dreamin'. Ain't nobody in the world that lucky," she told him, but she looked at Jarod.

A wide grin split his handsome face. She could say what she wanted. Hell, she could even believe it that night, but he'd have her on his ranch if it took him five years to talk her into it.

He was a patient man.

Chapter 13

RAIN—OR THE LACK OF IT—DIDN'T USUALLY AFFECT THE Honky Tonk, especially on Saturday night, but the tornado warning that came with it that Saturday night kept people glued to their weather radios and television sets. A couple of truckers stopped by for a quick beer. Merle didn't wander out that night and Joe Bob stayed home so the pool tables were quiet. Daisy fed the jukebox coins a few times but she and Cathy had no dancers or drinkers. Finally, at eleven thirty, she closed the beer joint.

Tinker picked up his black leather jacket and slipped his arms into it. "See you Monday night," he yelled across the floor.

"Don't go, Tinker. You can stay here. We'll make you a pallet on the floor or I'll give you my couch and I'll sleep on the floor," Cathy said.

"Girl, I'm so fast on that motorcycle I can drive between the raindrops," he teased.

Daisy and Cathy followed him and reached the porch just as the cycle roared out of the parking lot. A streak of lightning lit him up and thunder rolled behind him. The smell of rain was sweet in the night air. Daisy leaned against a porch post and inhaled deeply.

"Sometimes I miss the mountains. Rain always reminds me of home and the smell of the rain as it came through the mountains," she said.

"Will he be safe?" Cathy asked.

"Who?" Daisy asked.

"Tinker. Will he be safe? I don't like to think of runnin' this place without him."

"I wouldn't mess with Tinker. Not even if I was lightning. I bet he could pick a lightning streak out of the sky and pitch it out into the bar ditch without getting burned," Daisy said.

Cathy sat down in one of the rocking chairs. "Rain does smell good, don't it?"

Dark clouds shifted from one part of the sky to the other and lightning lit up the sky down to the southwest.

"Smells good, but the storm makes for a bummer of a night. Wonder if the other two places are doing any better than we are?" she asked.

"Probably not. If the Tonk is empty you can bet they are too. Let's go watch an old movie and make popcorn. Can't neither one of us sleep until after two, anyway," Cathy said.

"What've you got in mind?"

"I brought my favorites with me."

A smile turned up the corners of Daisy's mouth. "Are you still carrying around *Lucky Seven*?"

Cathy nodded. "Every time I watch it I think that my lucky seven is coming someday."

Daisy yawned. "I might fall asleep. And I have to get up early. Remember tomorrow is my cowboy date."

"If you snore I'll pinch you," Cathy said.

Cathy stood up and Daisy turned around, but they both stopped when a black Cadillac pulled into the parking lot.

"What do we tell them?" Cathy said.

"That we are closed. No use in opening back up for one or two people."

"Well la-tee-dah," Cathy mumbled.

The driver got out of the car and opened the back door. A man wearing a three-piece suit crawled out under the umbrella the driver popped up. They walked across the parking lot together: Mr. Chauffeur getting hit by a few drops of rain; Mr. Important staying dry. "We're closed," Daisy called out.

"That's fine. I'm not here for a good time. I'm here on business," the man beneath the umbrella said.

When they reached the steps the driver lowered the umbrella and shut it before joining his boss under the protection of the porch roof.

A clap of thunder made the boss man jump several inches. "I hate storms. I'm Hayes Radner. Is the owner inside?"

"I'm Daisy O'Dell. I'm the owner. What's on your mind?" Daisy said.

He smiled showing off a mouthful of gorgeous white teeth. He had dark hair and eyes and a deep voice. "I'm here to buy your beer joint."

"It's not for sale," she said.

"Why do you want it anyway?" Cathy asked. "You don't strike me as the type to want to own or run a beer joint."

Hayes smiled again. "I'm buying all the property in Mingus. I'm going to turn this area into a Six Flags–type amusement park."

"The Tonk isn't part of Mingus. We are actually closer to Thurber," Daisy said.

"My park entrance will be right here where your beer joint is. I'm willing to give you a very fair price and throw in some park stock with the deal."

"How many other folks have you got a contract with?" Daisy asked.

"Not any but this is my first day to throw out my bids. I'm just giving you fair warning that this place will be bought and it will be razed to the ground," Hayes said.

"Over my dead body," Daisy told him.

"It's just a matter of time. Two years max. My goal is to have the resort up and running in five years. Be thinkin' about it. You can make a decent profit," Hayes said.

Lightning danced around in the sky, jumping from one place to the other like sugared up six-year-olds after a birthday party. Thunder sounded like bombs falling from the dark clouds. Rain began to fall in drops as big as silver dollars.

Hayes motioned for the driver to take him back to the car. "It's your decision. Come on, Wayne. Let's get back to the car before we both get wet. Here's my card. Call me when you've had time to figure out a price."

"Don't that beat all," Daisy said as they watched the Cadillac disappear into the night.

Cathy popped her hands on her hips. "Some folks in Mingus might sell out but those who've lived there forever won't. Can't you just see Tinker selling Ruby's house or his land, wherever it is, so a big amusement park could go in? Mr. Hayes Radner's been drinkin' too much high-dollar whiskey. That'll rot your brain quick as the cheap stuff. Let's go watch our movie and wish someone wanted to be our lucky seven."

"How many more have you got to go before you reach seven?" Daisy slipped his card into the pocket of her jeans.

Cathy looped her arm through Daisy's. "Next one up is lucky number seven. How about you?"

"I don't have a lucky number. I'm going to run this beer joint forever and men like Hayes Radner can drop dead if they think I'll ever give it up," Daisy said.

Daisy awoke to the sound of gravel hitting her bedroom window and Jarod's voice calling her name. At first she thought she'd been dreaming and slapped the pillow over her head and shut her eyes. But it didn't stop so she crawled out of bed and peeked out the window.

Jarod waved and dropped the handful of gravel he had in his hand. He pointed toward the truck. She looked at the clock just as the numbers rolled to seven a.m. She padded to the door and opened it to find him leaning on the porch post. He wore dark Wranglers, shined boots, and a starched yellow button-up shirt.

"Up and at 'em. We've got miles to burn and a full day ahead of us."

She yawned. "This early?"

"Cowboy date day. I'm not wasting one moment of it. How long before you can be ready to ride?"

"Bulls, horses, or in a truck?"

"Truck. Wear that pink thing you wore to the wedding and bring your best cowboy boots and—"

"I know how to dress, Jarod," she said grumpily.

"Then get with it. We should be on the road," he said.

She stalled. "Want to tell me about the day?"

"No, I want to start the day. Want me to come inside and help you out of that nightshirt?"

Daisy put up her hands. "You wait right there. I'll be out in ten minutes."

She shoved her feet into a pair of pink round-toed boots and jerked the nightshirt over her head before putting on the pink and white checked dress. She hurriedly brushed her hair and applied makeup. When she looked at the ticking clock she'd used up all ten minutes and was glad she'd packed the night before. Shorts and a T-shirt for the afternoon. Jeans and a shirt for the evening. Another pair of boots and a pair of sandals.

When she set her bags out on the porch he raised an eyebrow. "Ten minutes and thirty seconds. You are a little late but you look so beautiful, you are forgiven."

"I can always go back to bed if I'm too late to go with you," she said.

"Only if I can go with you. That would be better than anything I've got planned."

"Oh, hush and tell me, where we are going?"

He threw her bags into the backseat and helped her inside. "Not yet. I want it to be a surprise. I will tell you it'll take five hours to get there."

"Five hours? Is that a cowboy date?"

"Sure is. For five hours I've got you in the cab of this truck with me and you can't get away so I get to look at you all I want and talk to you all I want. Life don't get no better than that."

"So is this a big old circle and in five hours I'll be back at the Honky Tonk?"

"No, ma'am. You will not," he said.

"Then it'll be five more hours to get home?"

"That's the way I figure it."

She moaned. "Ten hours of riding? Take me back to the Honky Tonk."

"Can't do that. Truck don't go backwards today. Only forward."

"Stop and I'll walk back," she said.

Jarod shook his head slowly. "Can't do that, either. Truck don't stop 'til we get to Weatherford, which is where we'll be eating breakfast."

"You are a—"

He finished the sentence for her, "—a very lucky cowboy today because he's got the prettiest girl in either Erath or Palo Pinto counties in the truck with him and she don't get to go home until tomorrow."

"Tomorrow?" She moaned again.

"I'll have you back in time to open the Tonk tomorrow evening. That's a McElroy promise and we stand by our word."

"But I didn't bring things for that long."

"Lots of stores along the way. Anything you need, we'll stop and buy," he said.

"I'm not sleeping with you tonight," she said bluntly.

He reached for the radio knob. "I'm very sure you won't be sleeping with me tonight. Music?"

"No, thank you, and what does that mean about not sleeping with you?"

"You'll see later. I figured you'd listen to country music all the time but you probably like the quiet after all that noise," he said.

"Actually, it's not quiet but the fresh air that I appreciate most."

"You don't like all the smoke smell either?"

"Never have, but it goes with a beer joint. Cigarettes, drinks, and country music. The three things that make up a good old country honky tonk. Throw out anyone of the three and you'll fold in six weeks. Ruby's words, not mine."

"That's about right. How was business last night? Storm bring them in or keep them out?"

"We shut the doors before midnight for the first time since I've been there. You ever heard of Hayes Radner?"

"Rich entrepreneur. Lives in Dallas. Featured in money-making type magazines."

"Right after we closed a Caddy drove up into the parking lot. His driver even held an umbrella over his head so he wouldn't get his hair or fancy suit wet. He wanted to buy the Honky Tonk. Says he's buying out the whole town of Mingus and putting in a resort like Six Flags."

"You sellin'?"

"Hell, no! I don't care if every boarded-up business in Mingus gives him their property for a dollar, he's not getting the Tonk. It's mine and I'm keeping it. Besides," she laughed, "just think of all the business I'll get if I'm sittin' right outside the gates of a big amusement park."

She waited for him to express an opinion.

He didn't.

She waited a few more minutes and still he didn't say anything. "Well?" she finally huffed.

"Well, what?"

"What have you got to say about that?"

"I think you said it all, Daisy. Hayes might have met his match. When's all this going to happen anyway?"

"He says in five years."

"Sounds like it's an idea right now and he's out scouting for a place. He might find more opposition in a little town like Mingus than he realizes. Folks stay there because it's home and they'll fight for that quicker than if it was just a house."

"Thank you," she said.

"For what?"

"For agreeing with me."

Her cell phone rang and she fished it out of her purse. "Hello," she said.

"It's me, Edith. George won't eat his chocolate pie this morning. It can't be bad. I made it last night and it's been in the refrigerator. I put a slice on a saucer and he turned up his nose. He's dyin'. I know he's dyin'," Edith yelled.

"How's he actin'?" Daisy screamed into the phone.

Jarod jumped and practically lost control of the truck. He quickly got it back and jerked his head around to look at Daisy who shook her head.

"He's just sittin' in front of the refrigerator like he wants something else. Well, hot damn, I believe I figured it out. He's wantin' the last of his beer that he didn't drink last night. Poor old boy left half of it in his bowl, so I put it in the refrigerator to keep it cool. Do you reckon he'd rather have a fresh one? This one has gone flat," Edith shouted.

"That one is fine," Daisy said. "It won't bloat him as bad."

"Oh, he does better on Coors. Miller gives him the dog farts terrible," Edith said. "You go on back to sleep, darlin'. George is happy now."

Jarod was laughing when she put the phone away.

"George is a nightmare."

"You love it," he said.

"I do. I really do."

"Next exit is breakfast," he said.

"Good, I'm starving."

The Iron Skillet restaurant was the first step of the cowboy date. Everything on the buffet looked good and Daisy piled a platter with eggs, bacon, sausage, biscuits, and gravy and filled a bowl with fresh fruit.

"Little hungry there, are you?" Jarod asked. *Add healthy appetite to the things I like about the woman,* he thought.

"Yep, I am. I never pass up a good breakfast. You sayin' I eat too much?"

"I am not saying anything like that. I'm glad to see a woman sit up to the table and enjoy her food."

She put a forkful of the scrambled eggs into her mouth. "Where are we going?"

He shook his head. "You tried to trick me, Daisy O'Dell, but it didn't work. It's a surprise. Enjoy each step of the way."

"Okay, what's the next step?"

"Riding and listening to good music. Maybe you can take a nap and I can watch you sleep. Or you can talk to me and tell me all about your life. Whatever you want to do in a truck for another four hours."

"I could tell you everything about my life from birth to present in five minutes. What'll we do with the other three hours and fifty-five minutes? Step one is very good, by the way. This is a great breakfast."

"I'm glad you like it," he said.

"I don't just like it. I love it. Only time I ever had a big breakfast when I was growing up was when Granny was alive. Momma slept in the mornings because she always was on the close-up crew at the bar so she didn't get to bed until after three most nights. Pop-Tarts and milk was my usual fare before I went to school. And that's about one minute of my life story, so you only get four more on the trip."

"I bet there's more than four minutes. But since I got you up so early, you can take a nap before you tell me the whole story," he offered.

She took him up on it and fell asleep five minutes after they left the restaurant. He looked at her all he wanted, just like he'd said. Dark eyelashes fanned out across her high cheekbones and her eyes did that rapid movement thing causing him to wonder what she was dreaming about. Was it him? Or was it that old boyfriend she'd mentioned? Or was she fighting with Hayes Radner about selling the Honky Tonk?

Part of him wanted to know exactly how Daisy felt about him. Was the difference in him and Billy Bob Walker simply that he'd had sex with Daisy and Billy Bob hadn't? Or did she truly have feelings for him? Could she learn to care?

The other part feared knowing because he didn't want to lose her.

A third part reminded him that he couldn't lose what he probably never had.

Jarod argued with every annoying little voice.

"Emmett knew what he was talkin' about when he told me you were my Mavis. Those were his last words," he mumbled under his breath.

Daisy was dreaming about her grandmother. They were in the kitchen making cookies and she heard a deep voice in the distance say something about Mavis. One second she was in the dream, the next she was wide awake.

"What time is it?"

"Good morning to you too." Surely she hadn't heard him talking out loud. If she knew what Emmett had said, she'd bolt like a jackrabbit being chased by a whole pack of hungry coyotes.

"I could use a cup of coffee and a bathroom. Where are we?"

"On I-35 headed north," he said.

She looked puzzled. "Are we still in Texas?"

"Crossed the Red River about an hour ago. We're between Ardmore and Pauls Valley right now. There's a service station up ahead on Exit 55 with an A&W inside it. We'll get coffee there. You slept a long time. Feel better?"

"Better than what?"

"Cathy's not the only grumpy one in the family when she first wakes up, is she?"

"It's an O'Dell trait. Get me some coffee and I'll turn into a human."

He nosed the truck into a space right in front of the service station. She stretched when she was outside, putting her hands above her head and wiggling the kinks out of her neck.

"Hey, look, Jarod. There's one of those Indian casinos across the street. Treasure Valley, the sign says. Let's go drop twenty dollars into the slots and win a million."

"Can't today. Have to make it to the next step on time. But I promise if you want to gamble we'll stop on the way back tomorrow."

She touched up her makeup and hair in the bathroom mirror. Jarod waited outside the door with two cups of coffee and they were back on the road in minutes. She sipped coffee and watched the scenery speed past at seventy-five miles an hour. They passed the Pauls Valley exit and kept going north. Her mind began to run in circles. Where on earth could they be going?

The sign for Exit 91 said that they were passing Purcell on the west side. In a few minutes they went through Norman, home of Oklahoma University and the OU Sooners. Mercy, were they going all the way to Kansas?

The busy hubbub of city traffic faded behind them when they left Oklahoma City. In Guthrie he took Highway 33 east toward Stillwater and she began to get very nervous. They went through Langston and Perkins and the next sign she saw said Cushing was ten miles ahead. Nervousness turned to panic.

He pulled off on a gravel section line road and drove a couple of miles before he turned back to the left down a lane. At the end was a long low slung ranch house with dozens of trucks and cars parked in the pasture to the north. It reminded her of the vehicles parked at the Double M when Emmett died. Surely Liam or Frankie hadn't died or he'd have been a hell of a lot sadder.

"What is going on here and where are we?" she asked.

"Today is my parents' fiftieth wedding anniversary. In fifteen minutes they are renewing their vows in the backyard."

"You. Are. A. Dead. Man," she said slowly.

"Do I get to choose the method of death?"

She crossed her arms. "Go on. I'll be right here when it's over and you can take me to the nearest motel."

"You can either get out or I'll carry you over my shoulder with your cute little underpants shining."

She shot him a mean look and got out of the truck. "You're going to pay."

"Probably, but I wanted you beside me today." He threw an arm around her bare shoulders. When everyone turned around in their seats to see who was arriving he waved. He took his place beside Stephen and Mitch on the front row of folding chairs with Daisy at his side.

The back door of the house opened and the preacher motioned for everyone to stand as Liam led Frankie down the center aisle between the rows of chairs to the archway set up under the shade trees.

Frankie was dressed in a gorgeous gold silk dress with thin straps. No one would have ever guessed she'd been married fifty years. That meant she was somewhere close to seventy years old and she didn't have enough wrinkles to make her look guilty of being fifty.

Liam wore the cowboy trademark dark jeans and a white shirt, but he had topped it with a Western cut short tux jacket. No wonder his mother loved Jarod so much. He was the younger version of his father. Stephen looked more like Frankie with the high cheekbones and dark eyes. Mitch was a healthy mixture of the two, but Jarod was Liam forty years before.

The preacher cleared his throat, motioned for everyone to sit down again, and began, "Dearly beloved, we are gathered here today to hear Liam Stephen and Fransell Raine Blackwolf McElroy exchange their wedding vows again in honor of their fiftieth wedding anniversary. In today's world that is a wonderful testimony and example. In 1958, Liam met Frankie. They were married the next year. At this time we will hear them repeat their original vows and say some new ones. So Liam, do you take Frankie as your lawfully wedded wife for another fifty years to love, honor, cherish?"

Two weddings in less than a week; Daisy couldn't remember going to two weddings in her life before that time. Her mother had brought her second husband home with the news that they'd been to the courthouse that day and Daisy had a new stepfather. With the third one she had gone to Las Vegas and Granny kept Daisy. But by the time the newlyweds arrived back in Mena a week later, the bloom was already off the honeymoon. After the divorce her mother said she'd never marry again and she didn't. But that didn't mean there were no more men in her life.

Listening to Frankie say her vows wasn't easy with Jarod holding her hand. The way his thumb kept making lazy circles on the tender skin between her thumb and forefinger was about to drive her insane. Would Jewel pull a pistol from her cute little handbag and shoot her if she dragged Jarod out to that barn in the distance? It was either that or else die from blistering desire and Daisy was too damn young to die. Besides, what would they put on her tombstone? *Here lies Daisy O'Dell who died of a sexual heat stroke.* She smiled at the visual of those words engraved under her name on a chunk of granite.

"And now I pronounce you man and wife for another fifty years," the preacher said and Liam kissed Frankie. Not a little "old people peck on the check" kiss either. Sparks lit up the whole area like they did when Jarod kissed her. She blinked to get rid of that thought, but it didn't do a whole hell of a lot of good.

Everyone clapped as Liam led Frankie back to the house.

"Liam and Frankie have asked me to thank each of you for sharing in their special day to invite you to a reception set up out in the barn. The one you can see out just beyond the yard fence with the caterers' vans parked to one side. There will be food and wedding cake and you can all congratulate the couple there," the preacher said.

A white carriage pulled by six white horses appeared with Liam and Frankie inside. The horses stepped high and pranced as they carried them back to the barn. Daisy couldn't take her eyes off the sight. It was so very romantic, like something from one of her castle romance books.

"What now?" Daisy asked.

"Still ready to make me a dead man?" Jarod whispered.

"Depends on what kind of food there is out there and if I get to eat because I've been a good girl," she teased.

Stephen slapped him on the shoulder. "You old rascal. We'd given up on you makin' it on time. Pleased to see you again, Daisy. Welcome to our shindig. Hey, there's old Marty Flannery. I've got to go see him. Catch you in the barn, Jewel." He nodded toward his wife and crossed the lawn in long strides.

Jewel's expression wasn't one of welcome when she looked at Daisy.

Jewel touched Jarod's arm. "You need to stick around after you eat. There will be pictures so don't run off to the nearest beer joint with your..." she shot Daisy a long, hateful look, "*whatever* she is. Just don't go too far. Momma Frankie wants pictures of *her* family," she told Jarod and walked away without even saying hello to Daisy.

"Sorry about that," Jarod said.

"You don't ever have to apologize for someone else's actions. And she didn't hurt my feelings. I'm a bartender, remember? If she wants a catfight I can deliver one but not until after I eat. I'm hungry and I just offered to be good," Daisy said.

Jarod bent down and brushed a kiss across her lips. "Want to skip the food and go do something more fun?"

"I wouldn't have the energy. I'm hungry enough to eat a cow. Horns, hooves, and all, so Jewel better make sure she's in line before me or she can starve to death."

Jarod was stopped by so many people on the way to the barn that Daisy feared there wouldn't even be a chicken wing left for her. She'd been introduced to half the state of Oklahoma in the short distance between the house and the barn. They were all a blur, so remembering names was next to impossible.

"Sorry that—" Jarod started when it finally looked as though they were going to make it to the barn without someone wanting to visit.

"I told you not to apologize. I might not be hungry after all with that many bodies crammed into a hot barn," Daisy said.

"Honey, we do things right up here. That's the sale barn. It's air conditioned."

"You are shittin' me."

"No, ma'am. Our cattle sale is in September. We wouldn't hold a high-dollar buyer very long if they had to sit in a hot barn."

Cool air and the smell of barbecue met her when Jarod opened the door. White linen covered tables were set up around a dance floor. Waiters in black slacks, white tux shirts, and black bow ties took orders and carried food and drinks back and forth. The whole scene was one out of a fancy restaurant.

They got into the buffet line behind Jewel and Stephen. Jewel turned around and flicked imaginary lint from Jarod's shirt. "Did I tell you that Mallory is divorced again? She moved back to Cushing. Called me last week. I invited her to come to the party but she said she didn't think it would be appropriate unless you didn't have a date. I don't think she's ever gotten over you."

Daisy looked up at him with a question on her face.

"Mallory is number two. Sasha is number one, and Emily, number three," he explained.

"I'm sorry, darlin'. You did mention them but I keep the past where it belongs. In the past. Are those ribs? I love smoked ribs," Daisy said.

Jewel pursed her thin lips. "Emily is back in Stillwater too. She says that New York wasn't for her and the biggest mistake she ever made was leaving you."

"I could care less, Jewel," Jarod said. "Yes, Daisy, those are ribs and smoked chicken and pork loin. Which one looks best?"

"All of it. Jewel, darlin', you and Stephen best load up your plates really good. There might not be anything left when I get through fixin' my plate."

"Thank you but I'm sure I'll only be able to eat a few bites. I never eat more than a saucer will hold," Jewel said coolly.

"Not me. I can eat a platter full and still go back for seconds. Especially when the food smells this good," Daisy said.

"Momma ought to love you. She's always fussin' at Jewel to eat more," Stephen said.

Jewel shot all of them a dirty look.

After they loaded their plates, Jarod led the way to the head table where Frankie and Liam were already seated. Mitch sat on Frankie's right with Maria was beside him. Daisy could see name plates for Jewel and Stephen on the other side of them. On Liam's left a place card engraved with Jarod's name waited. The one beside that simply said "Date."

"It's nice to know that I now have a new middle name. I'm Daisy Date O'Dell. It does have a nice ring to it though, doesn't it? Maybe I'll drop the one Jewel gave me. Daisy Date Whatever O'Dell is just too much, isn't it?" Daisy set her plate down. A waiter appeared instantly to ask them what they wanted to drink.

"You got a longneck Coors?" Daisy asked.

"Yes, ma'am."

"Make that two," Jarod said.

"You drinkin' it because you want it or to keep me from lookin' like a hick?" Daisy smarted off.

Jarod leaned over and kissed her on the cheek. "In that getup, you look like a Texas model, not a hick. Next week every woman in the place will be dressed like you and drinkin' Coors. I'm buying stock in the company tomorrow mornin'."

She couldn't suppress the giggle. "You are rotten."

"It's been said many times."

"Eat your dinner and be nice."

"I'm sorry about the name thing. I didn't tell them who I was bringing but to leave a space. That was six weeks ago when this was all in the planning stages. Better to have a seat for my date than for her to have to sit in my lap." He grinned wickedly. "But then maybe not?"

His mother leaned forward and waved at Jarod. She was smiling so maybe that meant Daisy had time to devour the smoked ribs and baked potato before the woman threw her off the ranch. If she could eat she might have enough energy to make it to the highway where she could thumb a ride back south.

The waiter returned with two bottles of beer and two glasses on a tray. Daisy picked up a bottle and took a long swallow from it. "I don't need the glass. Take it back," she said.

Jarod rose to his feet and tapped his water glass. The barn went silent.

"I'd like to thank everyone in the barn for coming today to celebrate with us. I'd like to propose a toast to my mother and father. I'm Jarod, the youngest McElroy son, and I'd like to thank my parents for their love and support. Like one country song says, they were there to fix my bike and my heart when both were broken. They've been wonderful parents and I for one am glad to have been their son. To fifty more years, Mom and Dad."

He picked up his beer bottle and tapped it to their wine glasses. Afterwards he gave them each a hug while everyone yelled, "To fifty more!"

When he sat back down he leaned over and kissed Daisy on the cheek again. "Momma wants to know if you would please serve the groom's cake after we have eaten."

Chapter 14

A PHOTO SHOOT HAD BEEN SET UP AT THE END OF THE BARN. An archway had been arranged with yellow roses and twining ivy with two velvet chairs for Liam and Frankie centered under it. The photographer arranged groups and Daisy watched from a table back in a far corner. The further she could stay from Jewel, the better. She was studying Jarod, thinking that he definitely was the best looking one of the McElroy sons, when someone touched her bare arm. It startled her so badly that she jumped and came close to falling backwards, chair and all.

"Didn't mean to scare you. You must have had your mind somewhere else," Frankie said.

"I thought I was the only one in this corner."

If you knew what I was thinking about doing to your son, you'd be the one startled out of your mind.

Frankie touched her arm. "I snuck up on your blind side. I haven't had formal pictures of my boys in years."

"Good looking bunch of men. I'm sure you are very proud of them," Daisy said. *And that youngest one can sure make my body sing a country song about getting lucky.*

"I wanted a minute with you alone. I'm glad Jarod brought you to the party today. I owe you an apology," Frankie said.

Daisy was glad she didn't have beer in her mouth. She would have spewed it all over the woman.

Frankie went on. "I judged you by those other three and it wasn't fair."

"Apology accepted, then."

The floodgates were opened and Frankie couldn't stop talking. "Jarod came along after I thought I was all through with having babies. Mitch and Stephen were born a year apart right after we married and fifteen years later I had Jarod. I spoiled the hell out of him. When he brought Sasha home I thought she was the one who'd complete his life. That fell through and we helped Jarod pick up the pieces. A few years later he brought Mallory to meet us and she and I became friends. I wanted to string her up with a worn out rope when she left him. Then there was Emily wanting a rancher to move to New York City. Three times I was nice and three times he got burned. It's not easy to be nice again," Frankie said.

"You don't have to be nice. I was dead serious when I told the whole bunch of you that I love my bar. I like my job. I like the people. I like the hours. It's my life and I have no desire to change it," Daisy said.

"We'll see." Frankie smiled.

Liam crossed the room and held his hand out to Frankie. "May I have this dance, pretty lady?"

She smiled brightly up at him, put her hand in his, and walked beside him to the middle of the dance floor. The band struck up the first chords to an old Faron Young song, "Slowly."

Jarod sat down beside Daisy and draped an arm loosely around the back of her chair. "I'm glad that's over. I've smiled enough for six years. Do you have that song on your old jukebox? It's the first song they ever danced to. Daddy used to bring out Faron's album and play it on the record player on their anniversary and they'd dance around the living room floor."

It wasn't hard to believe they'd danced more than fifty years together. They were as smooth as Ginger Rogers and Fred Astaire.

"That is so sweet," Daisy said.

"Takes a lot of practice to get that good. Think we'll ever match them?"

"Only if we spent the next few weeks dancing every minute of the day," she laughed.

During the instrumental in the middle of the song, the singer spoke into the microphone. "Liam says this is the song that was playing the first time he asked Frankie to dance with him. Now they're inviting their three sons to join them in the dance."

Mitch and Maria were on the floor first.

Then Jewel and Stephen.

Jarod held out his hand to Daisy.

She looked across the floor at Frankie who slyly winked.

Daisy put both her arms around Jarod's neck. He looped his around her waist, pulled her close, and sang the words to the rest of the song softly in her ear as they moved gracefully around the floor.

The song ended and the singer said, "And now the golden couple have asked that their grandchildren come on out to the dance floor for the next one. After we finish this song, everyone is invited to dance. A light supper buffet will be served at six and Miz Frankie says the party will be over at seven thirty. So grandkids, come on and honor your grandparents as we sing 'Rockin' Years.'"

Jarod wrapped his arms around Daisy's waist again. She fit like she had been molded especially for him.

"We aren't grandchildren," she said.

"It's a whole family dance and today you are part of it," he said.

Today. That word stuck in her head. Today she was part of the family. Today she could win the catfight with the abominable Jewel. Today she could serve groom's cake with the real daughters-in-law. Today she could pretend to be Jarod's woman. That part wasn't so difficult; she'd already been his wife.

Tomorrow she'd be the bartender. Tomorrow she'd take care of Rack's hairballs and check on Tommy's goat, Runt. Tomorrow she'd be plain old Daisy O'Dell.

Today was fantasy. Tomorrow was reality.

After the final notes of the song, the McElroy sons led their women to the cake table. Jewel cut the white bride's cake topped with the same bride and groom figurine that had been used on Frankie and Liam's original wedding cake. Maria poured punch from a brass punch bowl into crystal cups. Daisy took her place behind the three-tiered chocolate cake topped with fresh dipped strawberries.

"I'm surprised Momma Frankie asked you to do that job," Jewel said.

"I promised her I wouldn't lick my fingers or pick my nose between bites," Daisy said.

Maria giggled. "Jewel, be nice. She's not Emily or Mallory or even Sasha. You aren't going to intimidate her."

"What's your problem with me anyway, Jewel?" Daisy asked.

"You are a gold digger. You know he's rich and you're nothing but a bartender," Jewel said.

"I didn't know he was rich and it wouldn't matter to me if he had nothing or owned Fort Knox. But I do know that you are a bitch," Daisy said.

"How can you say something like that?" Jewel snapped sharply.

"I know as much about you as you do me and you made a judgment on me without knowing me so I can make one about you," Daisy said.

"Touché, Daisy," Maria said.

"Whose side are you on anyway?" Jewel asked.

"I'm not on either side, Jewel McElroy. You know me better than that after twenty-five years of marriage for both of us. But you are doing the same thing Momma Frankie did. You're judging her by those other three and it's not fair. We didn't judge you by Stephen's former lovers and we damn sure didn't judge you for yours, did we?" Maria said.

Jewel's mouth gaped like a fish out of water for a couple of seconds. "That was all in the past."

"So are Jarod's former relationships. Don't be so narrow-minded," Maria said.

An elderly lady with blue hair stopped and picked up a piece of groom's cake. "How did you and Jarod meet? Don't remember ever seein' you around these parts. You a Texan?"

"Arkansas is my home state, but I've been in Texas eight years. We met in a beer joint," Daisy answered.

She gasped and hurried back to her table of friends so fast that Daisy feared she'd fall forward and land with her face in the chocolate cake. She hoped the strawberry didn't poke her in the eye. She delivered the news in whispers behind her veined and diamond ring-decorated hand.

She'd barely finished talking when another of the gossip squad decided she needed groom's cake also.

"So are you a rancher like Jarod or maybe into the oil business like the McElroys?" she asked when Daisy handed her the cake.

"No, ma'am, I'm the owner and bartender at the Honky Tonk beer joint in Mingus, Texas," she said.

"I see. Well. Okay, then. I—" She rushed back to the table.

When the third one headed in her direction, Daisy sighed.

"I'm Inez Perkins. Don't believe I've seen you around before."

"Pleased to meet you, ma'am. I'm Daisy O'Dell from Mingus, Texas. I knew Jarod's Uncle Emmett and Aunt Mavis," she said.

"Oh, that side of the family. So what is it you do, darlin'? Got to give it to you, you got a good sense of humor. When you told Wanda you were a bartender she about stroked out. That can't be true. You're just jerking them around, aren't you?"

"Yes, ma'am, it surely is true. I own a beer joint called the Honky Tonk. I'm a bartender most of the time. If you are ever down in my area, stop by and I'll make you a margarita that'll knock your socks off," Daisy said.

Inez barely took the time to nod and hurried back to the table where eight women put their heads together.

"What'd you do that for?" Jewel asked.

"It's the truth. Cover it with cow shit or chocolate and it's still the same underneath," Daisy repeated Chigger's saying.

"It's a wonder Inez didn't have a heart attack and ruin the party. You could have said you were a business woman or even a vet tech," Jewel said.

"I could have but I didn't. I'm not ashamed of the Honky Tonk or being a bartender. It's good honest work. The rest of the cake is cut and ready. See you two around," Daisy said.

She made a beeline for the door. No one had better get in her way or ask a million and two questions either. She'd had all she could stand of Jewel and nosy neighbors. Luckily she made it to the pickup truck where she crawled inside the steaming hot vehicle, left the passenger door open, and leaned the seat as far back as it would go. She'd rather have a root canal with no Novocaine than go on another cowboy date. She shut her eyes against the hot sunlight and hoped that when she opened them it would all be a crazy nightmare.

When Jarod touched her arm, her eyes flew open. She sat straight up. Damn it! She was still in the pickup. She was still in northern Oklahoma and it damn sure wasn't a dream.

"Jarod!" Jewel screamed not two feet from the truck. "It's Butler and the vet is out of town in Albuquerque on a convention. He sent his regrets, but what are we going to do?"

"What in the hell are you talking about?" Jarod asked. Leave it to Jewel to interrupt a private moment.

"Look," she pointed. "I was coming to the house to get Frankie some aspirin for a headache."

An old dog with a white muzzle was trying to get under the fence, dragging a hind leg that was bleeding profusely.

Daisy was out of the truck before anyone could say another word. She opened the back door, grabbed her black bag, and started to run toward the dog.

Jarod hadn't even realized one of the bags he'd loaded had been her vet bag. He'd just figured they were all luggage. He reached the fence at the same time Daisy did and sat down in the grass beside Daisy. He had the bag open when Jewel arrived, out of breath and still crying. Daisy took out a hypodermic and shot the wound full of deadening medicine to start with, then set about cleaning the tear.

"Looks like he's been in a terrible fight. Has he had his rabies shots?" she asked.

"Probably coyotes and yes, he's had his shots," Jewel said.

"How old is he?"

"Ten this last spring. He don't know he's old and he'll go after a coyote with blood in his eye. Never came home like this," Jewel said.

Daisy gave him a shot of antibiotic, sewed him up, and carried him to the porch where she laid him in the shade. "You'll be fine, Butler, but you've got to stop chasin' coyotes. Let the younger boys have that job and you supervise."

Jarod followed every step she took. Admiration and pride filled his heart and soul. This was his woman, and after today by damn Jewel should stop giving her a hard time.

"I was so scared. Thank you so much," Jewel stammered.

"I'm a vet tech, not a vet. I did the best I could but you might want to take him in for his normal doctor to take a look at him," Daisy said.

"You did fine and he likes you," Jewel said. "And I'm sorry."

"Me too. I can't stand to see an animal hurting."

"I mean I'm sorry I gave you a hard time. Forgive me?" she asked.

Daisy looked at Jarod and back at Jewel. "Of course."

"I'll stay with him. You two go on and do whatever you want." She sat down beside Butler and rubbed his head.

He whined and licked her hands.

"Take a ride with me," Jarod whispered in Daisy's ear.

"You can't just run out on a party," she said as she allowed him to carry her bag and lead her around the house.

"Oh, yes I can. I've smiled enough for a year. I'm glad these things aren't every week. I'll bring in your bags. You'll want to change into something else. We'll be taking a four wheeler out for a ride over the property. I'd like to check on my cattle. The sale is in a few days and I want to double-check what I've got down to sell this year. We'll get our bags out of the truck and change our clothes."

"How in the devil do you decide which ones to sell and which ones to keep? If I ever had a ranch that would be the hardest part."

"Depends on a lot of things. How much money I need to make for the year. How productive each head of cattle is. You should know all that. You are a vet tech. You've probably helped lots of ranchers make those decisions," he said.

"Nope, not once. I've vaccinated. I've given medicine for hairballs, set broken hips when cats and dogs got run over by cars, put them down when they couldn't be saved, lots of things. But no one ever asked me to help decide which cow to save and which one to grind up into hamburger," she said.

He wasn't sure that he'd make the right decisions with Daisy at his side. Ever since she stepped out of the Honky Tonk that morning wearing that cute little dress that stopped at her knees and those pink boots, he'd had tunnel vision and the light at the end did not have an Angus cow blocking the view.

He unloaded her bags into a bedroom at the end of the hall. "This is where you'll be sleeping unless you want to go home tonight. I'll be across the hallway. There's a bathroom through that door."

When he left she threw herself across the queen-sized bed. The room was spacious with the bed taking up only a small portion of the room. The walls were painted a soft summer sky blue and the view looked out over a pasture full of black cattle. Sheer white curtains fluttered at the windows when the air conditioner clicked on.

After five minutes she hopped off the high bed and went to the bathroom. The mirror said she'd sweated off every bit of her makeup but she didn't apply more. Not when they were about to ride four wheelers out into the pastures. She opened her bag, removed ponytail holders, and quickly braided her hair into two ropes. She peeled the sundress off her body and replaced it with a bra, plaid shorts, and a hot pink knit tank top. She changed into old worn mustard colored work boots. Pasture grasses could be tough on bare legs and chiggers, in the real sense, were miserable creatures.

Thinking about the red bugs, she remembered that Chigger and Jim Bob were still on their honeymoon. She wished she had a phone number so she could call Chigger and tell her all about the day. Jewel, in particular.

"I probably shouldn't tell Chigger a damn thing. She'll read more into it than really happened. She's already got me and Jarod halfway down the aisle toward the preacher. And if she knew about bitchy Jewel, she'd be buying a couple of brand new shovels and driving up here to help me dig a six foot hole to put her in."

Jarod peeked inside. "Who are you talking to?"

"Myself. I'm a hermit. I talk to myself," she said.

He opened the door wider. Jesus, but those long legs were sexy as hell going from the hems of those short shorts all the way down to the pink boots. "Nice outfit," he said huskily.

He wore a white gauzy undershirt that hugged his muscular stomach and hung outside a pair of jean shorts with a cargo pocket on the side. He'd changed his dress boots for hiking boots that laced up to his ankles where the rim of white socks showed. His calves and his arms looked like they belonged on a professional boxer or wrestler, but then ranching was hard business and not for sissies. Even the Walker triplets with their tall lanky frames had strong arms.

"Get thee behind me, Satan." She smiled.

"So you think I'm the devil?"

"Yes, I do. Only the devil could make me think things that are this sinful. Let's go before I not only think but do sinful things," she said.

Jarod blinked several times. "Did I hear you right?"

"You did. I never said you weren't one hell of a sexy man. I never said there's not a sizzle between us and that every time you touch me I feel like I've been hit with a hot branding iron. What I did say is that I do not intend to do anything about it because I love my life as it is. I can get over this infatuation if I work at it." She shimmied past him.

He leaned against the wall and folded his arms across his chest. Life would never be dull with Daisy. Uncle Emmett had been so right when he said that she was his Mavis. Now he just had to convince her to leave the Honky Tonk and go home with him permanently. He couldn't sneak up on her blind side and he couldn't use persuasion. The only way it would ever work was for her to believe it was her idea.

They went out the kitchen door, across the yard to a multi-vehicle garage beyond the yard fence. He pushed a button at the edge of one door and it rose with a loud creaking noise. Several four wheeled machines were lined up and Jarod rifled through keys hung in a long line inside the garage door and settled on one that had a red fishing bobble hanging from the chain along with the keys.

"Why this one?" Daisy asked as she crawled on the back of the ATV and wrapped her arms around his waist.

"Because it's mine," he said.

He drove out of the garage, through the pasture, and down a dirt road to the back of the property. The hot wind whipping her braids and rushing across her face was exhilarating but not as much as hugging up to

Jarod's broad muscular back. When he stopped under a tree to look at a herd of cattle, she unwrapped her arms and threw one leg over the seat like it was a saddle. She slid off and checked the area around a pecan tree for poison ivy before she sat down. She tucked an errant strand of hair behind her ear and sat down at the base of the pecan tree, her back against the rough bark.

"So do you run all Angus?" she asked when he removed a notepad from his pocket and started flipping through the pages.

"Mostly. I've got a small herd of Lowline."

"Really? Can I see them? I've read a lot about them but I've never seen anything but pictures. No one down around Mingus is even interested in them. But then Texans wouldn't want a small steak. If it doesn't cover up a good sized platter, it's not a real steak."

"Sure. I keep them back behind the house in a separate pasture."

"Is it true they live totally on the pasture and that saves money, plus the calves are ready for market sooner than Angus?"

"This is my first year to have them but it's lookin' pretty good," he said.

He sat down and wrapped a strong arm around her, drawing her close to his side. She looked up to find his eyes locked on her mouth. He bent forward and kissed her eyelids shut then moved down to the sensitive skin under her ear. By the time he reached her mouth it was slightly open in anticipation. His tongue made love to hers until they were both breathless.

"I've wanted to do that all day and couldn't."

"But you said—" she started.

He shut her up with a lingering kiss. When he broke away he said, "I was thinking about in my parents' house with their bedroom right down the hall. I didn't say we wouldn't have it under a shade tree in a pasture."

She pushed out of his arms. "Jarod, I can't do this."

"Why?"

"Because one more minute and I couldn't stop."

"Why would you want to stop?"

"Sex blinds me," she said.

He grinned and made a lunge at her, toppling her over into the green grass. "Then we'll just do it until you can't see in one eye. It's good enough to give up sight in one eye, isn't it?"

She laughed. "That line is old and worn out."

He stretched out on the grass beside her after a quick chaste kiss on the lips. "I've never felt like this before."

"And that line is older than you and me both."

"I'm being honest, Daisy. How about you?"

"You've been engaged three times, Jarod. Don't tell me you've never felt like this."

He crossed his heart with his finger. "Cross my heart. Not even with the girl I took to the senior prom and I was head over heels in love with her."

In love?

Those two words sent cold chills up Daisy's back-bone. She wrapped her arms around her bent legs, resting her chin on her knees.

Love?

Chris threw that word around. Then he cheated on her and hit her. She'd heard her mother's husbands and boyfriends use the word like it was magic. Tell her that they loved her and she'd do anything, including ironing their shirts, supporting drinking habits, and paying the rent while they sat in a recliner all day and watched reruns on television.

"You've gone quiet all of a sudden. One minute I'm Satan I look so sexy and the next you aren't even talking."

"Right then I was thinking about what you said. Love is a powerful word."

"Yes, it is and it's a powerful emotion or it wouldn't endure fifty years of marriage or wanting to leave this life to go on to the next to be with your wife like Uncle Emmett did."

Daisy inhaled deeply and asked the question that was on her mind. "Did you ever use it when you didn't mean it?"

"No, I don't think I did. This is a pretty heady conversation for a four wheeler ride to steal a few kisses."

"Then we'll change the subject. Where did you live when you were here? Surely at thirty-five you weren't still in the house with your parents."

He sat up beside her and leaned against the tree. "My house is back across the pasture. If you are going there by car you go out to the road, go one mile north, and catch that section line road back east for two miles and turn back to the south. From here its about fifteen minutes on a four wheeler to my backyard."

"Can I see it?" Daisy asked.

"You sure you want to see it?

"Yes, I do. Is there something there you need to cover up before you let a woman into the house?"

"Hell, no, it's just a house," he said coldly.

"Then why are you getting an attitude with me?"

"Because you said you'd never leave the Honky Tonk, and you can't kiss me because it might lead to something. You sure you want to see my bedroom? You sure you can trust me?"

"Hell no, I'm not sure about anything right now." Exasperation filled her voice.

"Are we fighting?" he asked.

"If we are, I'm winning."

"Well hot damn. Uncle Emmett said that the best part of the day was when he and Aunt Mavis fought and they could make up. So come on over here, sweetheart, and make up with me," he teased.

She flipped around and threw one leg over both of his, sat square in the middle of his lap, and wrapped her arms around his neck. The kiss she planted on his lips shut him up and had him panting in record time. She'd teach him to light a fire and then not put it out.

Jarod groaned. "Be gentle," he teased with another age old line when she slid her hands up under his shirt.

"Not in the grass, cowboy. I don't want a dose of chiggers. I'm only testing the water to see how deep it is." She kissed him again, just as hard, just as lingering, just as passionate.

"One more kiss like that and we'll both drown," he said.

"Then we'd better stop making out, hadn't we?" She rolled to one side and put some distance between them.

"If you say so. Get back on the four wheeler and I'll take you to see where I live. It's not a mansion but I like it," he said.

Twenty minutes later she was staring at a sprawling brick home with a wide front porch. Half a dozen cats lounged in the porch rockers. That many hounds claimed the steps and yard. They all came running when Jarod called to them. Cats around his ankles. Dogs jumping up on him.

Finally, Jarod pushed them away and led her into the house. The door opened into a great room. Living room, dining room, kitchen all in one huge area divided by floor types. Hardwood in the dining room. Neutral colored beige tile in the kitchen and plush light brown carpet in the living area. Leather furniture flanked a natural stone fireplace. Beams supported the wide expansive ceiling. Clean lines with one room flowing into the other. Daisy was instantly in love with the place.

"Bedrooms are down that hall. Four of them and two bathrooms. One in the hall and one in the master bedroom. Utility room is through that door and opens out into the backyard. There's a sink and shower in there so I can clean up before I ever come in the house."

"It's beautiful. I can see where Emmett's house would have suffocated you, though. You aren't a 'stuff' person."

"Takes one to know one," he said. "I've been gone for weeks but there's probably a few Cokes in the refrigerator. Want one?"

She nodded.

He took two out, popped the top on one, and handed it to her. She took a long drink and set it on the cabinet. When she looked up he was right in front of her, his eyes hungrily looking into hers. He bent. She tiptoed.

Ten minutes later they were naked in his big king-sized bed, their clothing strung from the kitchen cabinets and down the hallway.

"Please," she whispered. "Don't make me wait today. I want you now."

"Yes, ma'am," he whispered, his breath cold against her hot body.

He began a long slow rhythm under the cool sheets watching her face and eyes the whole time. He could get lost in those blue eyes and live behind them forever and ever.

"Jarod, I want pure old sex, not love," she whispered seductively in his ear.

"Sure?"

"I'm positive."

"It won't last as long. You deserve the best, sweetheart, not a five-minute romp."

"Please!"

They reached the apex together in less than two minutes.

"I—" he said softly.

She put a finger over his mouth. "Not now. Don't say it now, Jarod. They're just words. I want more than words."

He rolled to one side and drew her close to his side. "You should have more than words, Daisy. You really should have all of it. Promise not to leave me tonight. Let me wake up with you beside me."

"My things are at the other house," she mumbled sleepily.

"I'll call after a while and have Garrett bring them back here."

"But they'll know we are... and Jewel will bring a gun... I swear to God she's more protective than Frankie," she said.

"Who gives a damn? I'm thirty-five and I believe you said something about being twenty-eight. And besides, you just saved her dog and she apologized for being so hateful. Darlin', I believe you've got my whole family in your pocket."

"Okay," she agreed and shut her eyes. Her last thought before she went to sleep was that if she truly was not going to fall in love with Jarod, this had to be the last time she was alone with him.

Every time they were alone they wound up having sex. She couldn't keep that up and watch him leave Texas in a few weeks. It was going to tear her heart out already. And she couldn't go with him... or could she?

Chapter 15

DAISY AND CATHY OPENED THE DOORS AT EIGHT O'CLOCK on Monday night just an hour after Jarod dropped Daisy off at the Honky Tonk. Daisy was ready for a few nights of solid dull routine; anything to slow down the speeding emotional train that she'd been riding the past few weeks.

"So tell me what happened. You look tired but happy. Did you like what you saw up there?" Cathy asked as they lined up sterile jars for beer.

Daisy bit back a giggle because the visual she got about liking what she saw involved bedsheets tangled around Jarod's legs the previous afternoon. And yes, ma'am, she most certainly did like it.

"It's a ranch. They're all about the same," she said.

"Yeah, right. You got laid. It's written all over your face."

"Cathy!"

"Well, you did and you are happy and that scares the shit out of me. What will I do if you go runnin' off to be a rancher's wife? God, girl, you've drooled over ranches and animals your whole life. Now throw something sexy as Jarod into the mix and I'm liable to be out in the cold."

"I doubt that. What's your portfolio worth these days?" Cathy smiled.

"And you can always find a job."

Cathy whined, "But I love what I'm doing now."

"Well, you don't have to worry about anything. Jarod's nephew is coming to run the ranch and Jarod is going home to his own place. This was never a permanent thing for him. I'll probably never see him again."

"And how does that make you feel?" Cathy asked.

"Sad as hell. He is sexy!" Daisy attempted a laugh but it was weak.

Merle was waiting on the porch when Daisy turned on the flashing neon Honky Tonk lights and opened the doors. She marched into the joint, laid her fancy cue stick case on top of the bar, hopped up on a stool, and ordered a shot of Jack Daniels, neat with a Coke chaser. Her black hair had been freshly done and her nails were blood red. She wore a solid red shirt with turquoise roses on the back yoke that matched the pearl snaps. Her jeans were creased and her turquoise boots shined. She threw back the whiskey with the finesse of an old barmaid in a spaghetti Western movie. She didn't even blink when she took a sip of the icy Coke.

"It's damn quiet in here," she grumbled.

"What's on your mind, Merle? Something upsetting you?" Daisy asked.

"We need music. Hell's bells, we can get quiet in a funeral home. We come in here for noise. Can't expect me to keep the boys drinkin' beer if you don't provide the music so I can hustle them for a game of pool. When they lose they drink. It's a circle that all comes back to the music," Merle said shortly.

Daisy handed Cathy a fistful of coins. "Go make Merle happy," she said and turned back to Merle. "You got anything in mind? Jones, Strait, Shelton, or Trett?"

"Not the old stuff. Put that new one on even if it is Monday," Merle said. "And pour me one more shot. I need it."

"Did someone die?" Daisy asked.

"Be easier if they did," she said.

Joe Bob and Billy Bob lumbered through the door, their boots sounding like firecrackers on the wooden floor in the quietness.

"What's it going to be?" Cathy hollered from the jukebox.

"Anything to pep me up. Joe Bob, you ready to lose?" Merle asked.

"Not tonight. I ain't touchin' a cue stick tonight. I came in here to dance," he said.

Merle threw back the second shot and frowned. "If it wasn't for bad luck, I'd have no luck at all."

The music started with Mary Chapin Carpenter singing "Passionate Kisses."

Merle sipped at the Coke and said, "I love this old bar. I loved Ruby and I even love you, Daisy. I love Joe Bob even if he isn't coordinated enough to shoot decent pool. I love Mac even though he's married and thirty years younger than me."

Daisy picked up Merle's case and moved it to the end of the bar. "Okay, talk to me. Cathy can mind the bar."

Merle carried her Coke to the end stool. "I've got this niece who just got a degree in petroleum geology. I put a word in with Amos for her and be damned if he didn't hire her."

"That's good, isn't it?"

"Sure, but I didn't figure on what would be coming next. She's movin' in with me," Merle said with a long face.

"That a problem? I bet she could find a house to rent if you don't want her to live with you."

"Hell yes and hell no. It's a problem because I've lived by myself since me and Ruby came here back in the sixties. I don't know what to do with a twenty-three-year-old girl. And hell no she can't rent a house because it's a waste of money, and besides, my house is huge and there's plenty of room. On top of all that she's the one who's always thought I hung the moon. I've enjoyed living on her pedestal but hell, I never thought I'd be expected to live with her."

"What's the real problem here, Merle?" Daisy asked. "Spit it out."

"Promise you won't laugh at me," Merle said.

"Promise."

"She's better than I am at pool."

"Oh, my!" Daisy exclaimed.

"Now you see. I've been the queen here at the Honky Tonk for more than forty years and I'm not ready to give up my crown. You know damn well she's going to come in here because this is where the pool tables are. She'll get tired of playing me in the game room at my house so there it is," Merle said.

"When she moving in?"

"Christmas. Starts to work for Amos the day after New Year's."

"What's her job?"

"He's settin' up an office in Mingus for the new wells he's drilling up north of town. She's some kind of wizard when it comes to telling folks where to drill. She'll be runnin' the field for him. It ain't easy gettin' old, Daisy," Merle said.

"You're tough as nails. I bet you get through it all."

"Enough spillin' my guts. Here comes Mac. I'll talk him into a game or two since Joe Bob ain't up to par with his brother off on a honeymoon."

Daisy shook her head. "Merle, maybe you just *think* she's better than you. Could be that if you play someone other than Joe Bob, you'll hone up on your skills and still keep your crown."

Merle finally grinned. "You are a good friend, but honey, Angel is a natural. She can outshoot me with a pirate's patch on one eye and half a fifth of Jack in her gullet."

"Angel?"

"Yep, that's her real name. Angel Merlene Avery. And if you've got any notion that you want to put a brand on Jarod, you'd best get it done before she gets here. She's pretty and smart as well as the best shooter this side of the Mississippi," Merle said. "Hey, Mac, bring that beer on over to the tables. We'll play for jukebox music tonight so these kids can have something to dance to."

"You're on," Mac said.

Daisy started back down the bar to help Cathy with a group of twenty or more who'd just come inside, all talking at once about the nice dance floor and ordering beers for everyone to be taken to the table, along with two pitchers of piña coladas.

"Hey, I'm Joanie. How long has this place been here, anyway?" a middle-aged lady asked.

"Little over forty years," Daisy said.

"Well, I'll be damned. Been going up to Sulphur, Oklahoma, for years almost that long and comin' within a half a mile of this place. We go up there and camp out with our square dancing gang and we never noticed it until tonight. Got any live music?"

"No, just those two jukeboxes. One antique with music to match. One new one with the hot new tunes," Daisy answered.

"Hell, honey, music is music whether it comes from a live bunch or straight off the jukebox. We've been ridin' a long time and we don't care what we dance to long as we get to dance," Joanie said. "Hey, guys, it's jukebox only. Thank God it's not karaoke or we'd have to listen to Clayton try to sing Hank Williams. Wet your whistles and let's do some dancing."

A slow song started and everyone grabbed a drink of beer then paired off for a two-step to Toby Keith's "Who's Your Daddy." Joe Bob danced with a woman with long legs and dyed blond hair. They glided around the floor so gracefully that it took Daisy a while to realize the woman was actually leading and Joe Bob was following.

From the corner of her eye she saw Tinker get up slowly and make his way toward the back pool table where two truckers were engaged in a pushing contest. He stepped between the men and leaned forward to say something to the biggest one. The smaller of the two picked up a cue stick and drew back as if to hit Tinker in the back of the head. He'd barely started the swing when Tinker turned quickly, grabbed the cue stick, and twisted the man's arm behind his back. Whatever he whispered in the man's ear turned his face ashy gray and when Tinker let go, he gently laid the cue stick on the table and walked out. Tinker nodded toward the door to the other man who threw up his hands in defeat and made his way to the door.

"What's he sayin' to them?" Cathy asked.

"Have no idea. I saw him do that the first time when I'd been here about a week. Same situation. Two big old burly men arguing over a pool shot. I asked Ruby what he said to them. She told me that was his job and his business. Mine was to take care of the bar and see to it everyone paid for their drinks. Whatever it is, it works," Daisy said.

"He's worth his weight in gold and that's a lot of gold," Cathy giggled.

"Yes, he is and I've tried to give him a raise but he won't have any of it. Says he's got more than he needs already and doesn't want any more money."

"Oh my God!" Cathy exclaimed.

"Hey, it's not really that big of a deal. I'd pay him twice the amount he's getting if he'd take it," Daisy told her.

"I'm not talking about Tinker. Look who just walked in the door." Cathy pointed, quickly poured a shot of Wild Turkey, and tossed it back.

Daisy turned and frowned. The man wore pleated black slacks with black wingtipped shoes and a blue plaid tie that matched his shirt perfectly. His brown hair was feathered back. He had his eyes trained on Cathy and nothing or no one else existed.

"Hello, Cathy. What in the hell are you doing here?" He hiked a hip onto a bar stool.

Tinker got up and lumbered slowly across the floor. He sat down beside the man and said, "Coffee with two teaspoons of sugar, please."

Cathy looked at him as if she were seeing two ghosts. Tinker had never ordered anything at the bar. He kept a small cooler under his chair and each evening he put six Dr. Peppers in it. By the time they closed the bar all six were gone and he put the empty cans in the trash before he went home.

"What's your name, cowboy?" Tinker asked. "Haven't ever seen you at the Honky Tonk before."

He eyed Tinker up and down and asked, "Who are you?"

"I'm the bouncer and the ID checker. Don't need to check your license. You're definitely over twenty-one," Tinker said.

"What are you doing here?" Cathy asked.

"Looking for you. This is atrocious."

"What?" Cathy asked.

"You working behind a two-bit dive of a bar. I've come to take you home."

"I'm not going anywhere with you, Brad. The first time you hit me ended the whole thing. I'm happy here and I'm not leaving."

Tinker leaned over and whispered in Brad's ear.

He held up a finger. "One minute."

"I think it's time for you to leave. Cathy has spoken her mind and it's over between you two," Daisy said.

Billy Bob sat down on the bar stool next to Brad and chuckled. "Beer, please, darlin'."

"What's so funny?" Brad looked at him in the mirror rather than turning his head.

"I'm going to explain something to you. What you do with it determines whether I whip your ass tonight or shake your hand," Billy Bob said.

Cathy and Daisy were both speechless.

Billy Bob winked at Cathy and went on, "It's all right, darlin'. He don't know but he's fixin' to find out. You'd be Cathy's old boyfriend. Well, I'm Cathy's new husband, Billy Bob. That makes me Daisy's cousin. Me and Cathy got married last Friday over at the Palo Pinto courthouse. Now that you know how things are, I reckon you'd better get on out of here."

Brad spun the stool around and looked Billy Bob up and down. From his red hair and freckled face to his scuffed up boots, then he turned to glare at Cathy. "You married this? God, I thought you'd do better as smart as you are."

Billy Bob squared his shoulders and grinned. "Kind of amazin', ain't it? I don't even care if she married me for my money. I'm the one who gets to go to bed with her and she's the one who cooks my bacon for breakfast, so I'm the luckiest sumbitch in the world, way I see it."

Brad slapped the bar with both hands, causing Billy Bob's beer to slosh out over the top of the jar.

"I'm leaving. Damn, I thought you'd do better than a redneck farmer." He threw up his hands and stomped across the dance floor between two songs.

Cathy opened the cooler and took out a quart of milk, poured a glass, and downed it without coming up for air.

"Ulcer?" Tinker asked.

She nodded.

"Tinker, how did you know?" Daisy asked again.

"Saw her throw back a shot. Y'all never drink when you are working. Had to be something bad."

"Well, thank you very much for noticing."

"Give the man a raise. Double his salary," Cathy whispered.

Tinker shook his head hard. "Don't want a raise. Don't need more money. And Miss Daisy, that man comes around again, you call me. I know places where they'll never find his body."

"I got a feeling he ain't comin' back," Billy Bob laughed. "I think I plumb put his nose out of joint."

Cathy opened the cash register and handed Billy Bob a fistful of change. "You decide what music we're listening to and the drinks are on the house tonight for you."

"Well, gosh dang, I didn't know there were benefits beyond sleeping with you and having my breakfast cooked," Billy Bob said in mock bashfulness.

"How'd you know who he was?" she asked Billy Bob.

"I heard him say he was taking you home. Figured you wasn't married to him or he'd of said something about you bein' his wife."

"Well thank you," Cathy said.

"And now I will go and play some music for my sexy wife," Billy Bob teased.

Chigger popped an elbow on the bar. "You been sleeping with Cathy? Dr. Pepper, Cathy. Can't drink but I can sure enjoy the company around here. Gawd, but I missed everyone even if it was the most fantastic honeymoon in the world. Now what in the hell are you talking about, sleeping with Billy Bob? Are you going to be my sister?"

Cathy shook her head at Chigger. "No, but I'd almost sleep with him after the favor he just did." She pointed at Billy Bob. "Go play something fast and upbeat."

Chigger took his stool when he left and looked at Daisy and Cathy who were both still jittery, their eyes never leaving the door for more than a few minutes. "Talk," she said.

Cathy filled her in on the Brad events and Daisy told her about Jarod kidnapping her for two days. Chigger finished one soft drink and ordered another. "I missed all the fun."

"I'd think that you had more fun than we did," Daisy said.

Chigger giggled. "Did I really have more fun than you? Surely you didn't get kidnapped and hauled off to a party and didn't even get laid?"

"Seems like I did," Daisy said honestly.

"What? Kidnapped or laid?" Chigger asked.

"I'm not tellin'," Daisy said.

"How the hell you goin' to know if you two are any good in bed if you don't go there? Surely, you ain't plannin' on marryin' him without testin' the waters first. Might be they're too damn shallow and you can't even swim in them," Chigger fussed.

Daisy's laughter came out high pitched, a release of built up tension, but it felt wonderful. Everything was in the right place again. Brad was gone. Chigger was home. Jim Bob was at a table with his brothers and...

She narrowed her eyes. When had Jarod arrived?

Chigger sighed. "Lord, I'd love a longneck bottle of Coors or a pitcher of margaritas. Just knowin' I can't drink for seven more months makes me want it even more. And Jim Bob made me stop smoking, too. I'd go stark ravin' mad if the doctor said I couldn't have sex for seven months too."

A whole crowd pushed through the doors. Tinker looked up but it was evident none of them needed to produce identification. Not with those bald heads, gray hair, and wrinkles.

Joanie yelled at Daisy, "Hi, darlin', we're on our way back to San Antone. Decided to bring the whole bunch of us in for some dancin'. We got to braggin' about our good time on Monday and everyone wanted to come see the place. Make us thirty beers and four pitchers of piña coladas for the ones who don't drink beer."

Jarod stood up and crossed the floor in a dozen long strides, walked through the swinging door back behind the bar, and started filling Mason jars.

"What are you doing?" Daisy asked.

"Helping. You make piña coladas. Chigger and Cathy can carry them to the table. It's going to be a profitable night," he said.

Chigger winked. "And what's your payment?"

"I'll discuss that later with Daisy." Jarod grinned.

He filled jars and lined up six to a tray. Cathy carried them and Chigger took care of the pitchers and glasses for piña coladas. By the time the second song was finished drinks were sitting on four tables that had been pushed together. Billy Bob and Joe Bob were both dancing with the new customers. Merle had one of them cornered at a pool table and by the smile on her face she was wearing the crown that night.

The jukebox was belting out one tune after the other and they were either doing a long line dance or else a fast two-step. Jarod kept the handles down on the beer taps, filling two jars at a time. Cathy ran her legs off going back and forth to the tables and Chigger continued to help with the mixed drinks until one o'clock in the morning, when Jim Bob insisted they go home.

The square dancers shut down the place at two, getting into their RVs and pulling out of the lot going south down Highway 281 to San Antonio. They declared they were already planning a trip back to Sulphur, Oklahoma, and they'd be back the next year at the end of August so to make sure there was plenty of beer.

"And tell that woman who stole all my money at the pool tables I'm practicing up and I'll get it back next year," a fellow yelled as he got into his RV.

"Her name is Merle and you better practice everyday," Cathy yelled back and waved.

Tinker must have decided that Jarod could be trusted because he took his empty soda cans to the back and told Daisy he'd see her the next night. She heard the rumble of his cycle as he rode north at a few minutes past two.

Cathy took one look at the empty jars on the tables and threw up both hands. "My feet hurt. I'm going to take a shower and go to sleep. Good night, you two."

"Night, Cathy," Jarod said.

"Save me some hot water," Daisy said as she popped the tops on two longneck Coors and handed one to Jarod. "Set down and rest your feet before you go."

She pulled out a chair and propped her aching feet on a table. She sucked down a fourth of the beer and burped when she came up for air. "Pardon me," she said.

"You are excused," he said. Working in the hay field all day hadn't worn him out like the previous four hours. "Time to discuss my payment."

"Beer ain't enough?" she asked.

"Not on your life, honey."

"What have you got in mind?"

He wiggled his eyebrows.

"Forget it, cowboy. I'm too tired."

He took a draw on the beer. "Wednesday is payback."

"What's happening Wednesday?"

"A whole convoy of trucks is coming from Cushing. Cattle. Furniture. Tractors and equipment."

"What's that got to do with me?"

He wanted to say, *Just everything since I'm going to convince you to live with me someday*. But instead he said, "Garrett is moving in. There'll be thirty or forty hungry men. I'll order chicken and pizza but I need help getting it out to the ranch. Plus I need your help with the cattle. We need a vet on hand."

"Don't feed them sorry old takeout food. I'll get Chigger and Cathy to help and we can put up those eight-foot tables out under the shade trees and serve them out there. What time will they arrive?"

"They'll start pulling in midmorning. Furniture will arrive first, then the cattle and finally the equipment. Some of it's so big that it has to have lead cars to bring it down the highway."

"Lead cars?" she asked.

"You know, those cars that announce there's an extra wide load behind them so the drivers can be aware," he explained.

"Where are you putting furniture?" A visual of Emmett's house with all the clutter in every single corner flitted through her mind.

"In a barn until Garrett and I can clean out the house. It'll take a few weeks," he said. "And thanks, Daisy. They'll appreciate a home cooked meal.

Whatever you need, just keep the tickets and I'll pay for it."

"Any preferences?"

"You cook. We'll eat. Lots and lots of sweet tea. They'll be thirsty. I can order food but I do need a vet."

She made plans even though she was exhausted. "I'll come on out on Tuesday night."

He found enough energy to wiggle one eyebrow.

"Go home before you fall asleep," she said.

"I'd sleep better if you were beside me."

It was tempting but it was so much closer to her bed and there was the rule about no men in the apartment. It had been a nerve-racking night and she needed to digest it all, from Brad to Billy Bob to Jarod, anyway.

"I'm almost too tired to walk across the floor to my apartment. You going to be all right driving home?"

"Don't know if I can make it to the ranch without runnin' off the road," he said as he cleaned off the three square tables and pushed them up together. Then he stretched out on top of them on his back. He handed her the empty Coors bottle and shut his eyes. "Let me take a thirty-minute nap and I'll be fine. Crawl up here with me."

"You can't sleep here," she said.

"Why not?"

The table was closer than her bed. She pushed him and he shifted over slightly. When she crawled up on the table he wrapped her up in his arms and drew her close to his side.

"This is crazy when there's a bed," she said.

"I could sleep on a rock with you in my arms."

"That's sweet but we are two adults and we're not sleeping on hard tables. Come on." She slid off the table.

She led him through the door into the dark apartment. The water was running in the shower and a sliver of light showed under the bathroom door. Daisy didn't even slow down. She went straight to her bedroom, pulled Jarod down on the bed beside her, and curled back up in his arms when he stretched out.

"Ah, this is definitely better," he sighed.

"Softness and pillows beat tables and no pillows every time. Good night, Jarod." She brushed a kiss across his lips and tasted beer.

"Good night, darlin'."

She shut her eyes but couldn't sleep. Not even when Jarod's breathing told her that he was sound asleep. She wiggled and he drew her closer as if even in his sleep he knew she was about to leave him. She inhaled and let it out slowly. Lying in his arms felt so right, even without sex before or glow afterwards.

Chapter 16

Jarod eased off the bed and slipped his pillow into Daisy's arms. Sunrays filtered through slats on the mini-blinds, making stripes across her face. Heritage from her mother's Indian blood showed in dark lashes fanning out on high delicate cheekbones. Her full mouth begged to be kissed even in sleep. He could have stood there for hours and watched her but another five minutes and he would have crawled back into the bed and spent the whole day making love to her. He tiptoed out of the bedroom and made his way around the sofa where Cathy slept.

He tried to convince himself as he drove south back to the ranch that Daisy was right. If they got married—there, he'd actually thought the M word without shuddering—the heat between them might be like a flash in a pan. Quick. Hot. Out in a minute. They'd both wake up one day and realized they'd based a lifetime commitment on the bedroom fire.

He could have driven all the way to Houston and talked the whole way and it wouldn't have worked. He loved the woman and the person he had to convince was Daisy. Not to leave him, either, but to move to Oklahoma with him. He'd have to take it slow. Maybe ask her to come spend the weekends with him, then build it up to a holiday for a whole week. Make her love the place, the ranch, and the area. Then hope and pray that she fell in love with him as hard as he'd fallen for her.

———

Daisy snuggled up to the pillow in her arms and threw a leg over Jarod's. Only to open her eyes to find that the pillow wasn't Jarod and she'd thrown her leg over nothing but a tangled mass of quilt. In a fit of anger she threw the pillow across the room.

Cathy poked her head into the bedroom. "Jarod left right after the sun came up. He bumped the sofa bed and woke me but I pretended to be asleep so he wouldn't be embarrassed. Looks like all y'all did was sleep. You're still wearing clothes."

Daisy made a noise somewhere between a grunt and a growl.

Cathy handed her a cup of coffee. "Don't get mad at me because you were too tired to do anything other than sleep. Take this to the shower with you. I'll meet you in the kitchen when you are done. I'm making pancakes."

Daisy carried the coffee to the bathroom, turned the water on, and set the coffee on the back of the toilet. By the time the water was the right temperature she'd dropped her smoky smelling clothing on the floor. She let the warm water flow over her for a full two minutes, then lathered up her hair and reached out from behind the shower curtain for the coffee. She turned around and let the warm water massage her shoulders as she sipped the coffee. It wasn't nearly as good as a Jarod massage, but it and the caffeine woke her up. She finished the coffee, quickly rinsed her hair, and finished showering.

"It's alive," Cathy said when Daisy stumbled back into the kitchen. She still wore knit short pajamas and was barefoot.

Daisy set her empty cup on the table. She'd dressed in a red T-shirt and khaki knee-length shorts. Her feet were bare and her dark hair hung in damp strings down her back.

"Barely alive," she said.

"So?" Cathy asked.

"So what?"

"Did you pay for his help?"

"Haven't yet but I'm going to and you and Chigger are helping me." Daisy went on to tell her the plans as Cathy made pancakes.

"I love a party. We could make the desserts today and maybe even get some of the other things ready. There might be a feller with my name written on his forehead," Cathy said.

"This is not a party. It's a bunch of sweaty, hungry men. No black formals or diamonds," Daisy said.

"If there's food and men, it's a party. I'll leave the formal and the diamonds in my suitcases. You can even stay all night if you'll trust me to drive back or if Chigger will bring me. That way you won't be dead tired in the morning. Well, you won't be unless…" Cathy let the sentence dangle.

Daisy cut her off, saying, "No, you cannot drive my car back. I've got another idea."

Cathy set a stack of pancakes in the middle of the table. "I won't wreck the car. I'll drive twenty-five miles an hour the whole way back. Dig in," she said.

Daisy slid three of the oversized pancakes onto her plate. "Why in the devil did you and Brad trade in your cars for one?"

"I had a three-year-old Mustang and Brad was driving a Taurus. We traded for an Escalade two months before he got mean and hateful. His name is on the title. Hell, we were getting married and after the wedding I was getting one of those new little smart cars to run around town and go to work in. It seemed like the thing to do at the time. I have to go shopping for a car or maybe a truck if you're going to let me stay around."

"Let you! Damn, girl. I was thinking about giving you a raise," Daisy said around a mouthful of syrupy pancakes.

"Well, thank God for that. I love it here," Cathy said.

"Sorry bastard. Treating you like that."

"Sorry bastard, Chris. Doing the same to you."

They both giggled.

"Thank goodness for Billy Bob. He's a good man to marry me the way he did when his heart was really set on marrying the owner of a beer joint, not just the hired help," Cathy said.

"Too bad you didn't marry him too," Daisy said as she finished the last bite. "I'll do the dishes. You get ready. Wear something old. If your feller with your name tattooed on his forehead is really there, he'll have to meet you in work clothes. We'll go to the ranch first and take stock of what's already there and then drive into Stephenville if we need anything else."

Daisy had just put the last plate in the dish rack when Cathy appeared back in the kitchen. She'd chosen denim shorts and a bright blue knit top and had sandals on her feet. "So do I get to drive out to the ranch just to show you that I can drive your little car without putting a scratch on it?" she asked.

"I told you, nobody drives my car."

"Jarod did."

"I'm not even discussing it with you. You are not driving my Maverick." Daisy led the way out the door and across the backyard to the garage. She pressed a button on the remote and the garage door creaked upwards.

Cathy sucked air when she saw the big Harley sitting in the corner. "Oh, my! Can I ride it? Please, Daisy. I'll be careful."

"No, you cannot ride that thing. Ruby was killed on it. I'd be scared to death to let you ride it," Daisy said.

"But I'm not Ruby and I'd be very careful. You know how much I love motorcycles." Cathy was almost to the drooling stage.

Daisy pointed toward the nine-year-old candy apple red Cadillac still in mint condition. "Answer is no but you can drive that thing."

"That's a pretty nice second choice." Cathy grinned.

Daisy handed her the keys. "Take care of it."

"You mean I get to drive it more than just today?"

"It's yours."

"Thank you! Coming to Texas has been the best thing that ever happened to me."

"My car breaking down was the best thing that ever happened to me," Daisy said.

Cathy slid behind the wheel of the Caddy. "I think the best thing that ever happened to you was Jarod McElroy."

Daisy buckled her seat belt. "You've got stars in your eyes. All the cowboys in the area better stay away from the Honky Tonk. Every time I see you look like that you call and tell me you've got another boyfriend."

"One cowboy puts stars in your eyes," Cathy shot right back at her.

"What if…"

"Don't judge Jarod by Chris' measly half bushel."

"And that's supposed to mean what?"

"One person might have only a half bushel of common sense and dignity while another could have a whole bushel and there you'd be with the wrong ideas."

"You are right, but…"

"No buts. I am right. Leave it at that."

—⁓—

Jarod was standing in the front yard when they arrived. His overalls were dusty and had stains on the knees. The sleeveless T-shirt underneath didn't have a dry thread on it. They both got out at the same time and he waved.

"You are early," he said. "Nice car. Did you just buy it, Cathy?"

"It's my bonus for not killing a man last night," Cathy said.

"Who'd you almost kill?" Jarod asked but his eyes never strayed from Daisy.

"Old boyfriend showed up at the Tonk. Billy Bob put him going though," Cathy said. "I'm going to pet the dogs. Daisy can explain."

Jarod took two steps and stopped a foot from Daisy. "I want to hug you but I'm too dusty and dirty. Been out countin' cattle on a four wheeler."

"Who gives a damn? If I get dirty maybe this cowboy I know will give me a bath." She stepped into his arms and rolled up on her toes for a kiss.

He inhaled the fresh scent of clean hair and perfume. He could never drive away in the sunset toward northern Oklahoma without her. He couldn't live without Daisy.

Cathy rounded the end of the house, two old dogs plodding along behind her. "Hey, hey, if that don't stop I'll have to cook the whole dinner by myself."

Jarod broke away with a grin. "I'm going back to work. I'll be in around suppertime. Reckon you'll still be here then?"

The rumble of a vehicle kicking up dust coming down the lane caused them to break the heated visual of massages, baths, and passionate lovemaking.

The truck came to a halt and Chigger stepped out. "Hi, y'all. I came to help. I can't cook worth a damn but I'll keep y'all company while you do and I'm a crackerjack dishwasher."

"Thanks, Chigger," Jarod said and whistled as he went to the backyard.

"Looks like you two are making love today and not fighting. That's a step in the right direction," Chigger said.

"He's a hopeless romantic. A romp in the hay can't lead to a permanent relationship," Daisy said.

"And you aren't a romantic?" Cathy asked.

"Not anymore. It's just one nightmare after another. Makes me wish for the boring old days back before Jarod found the Honky Tonk."

"Ah, you wouldn't trade all this excitement for anything. Now let's go cook. I hope he's got cocoa and plenty of eggs. I'm making a chocolate sheet cake. What are you making for the dinner party?" Cathy said.

Daisy threw up her hands in bewilderment. "Peach cobblers, and it's not a party, it's a dinner for a bunch of ranchers. You are a hopeless optimist. I'm a realist."

"Sure you are," Chigger said.

The first thing Jarod noticed was the red Caddy was gone. That meant he was coming home to an empty house. The upside was that Daisy had promised to be there after hours at the Honky Tonk that night. As tired as he was, he'd be sound asleep when she arrived. The next day would be so hectic he wouldn't have time to blink. So a hell of a lot of good it did him to think that was an upside to anything. What he wanted was for her to be there to tell him about her day and for him to share his with her.

He went straight up to the bathroom and took a long, hot shower. He dressed in soft knit gray pajama bottoms and a white knit tank top and padded back to the kitchen, hoping to at least find enough ham to make a sandwich. Forget cooking even a microwaveable TV dinner; he was too tired. Besides, the house smelled like fresh yeast bread and onions from when the women had been cooking all day. A TV dinner would taste like sawdust after that aroma.

The kitchen table caused him to stop dead in his tracks and blink several times to make sure it wasn't a mirage. It was set for two. The centerpiece was a roast surrounded with baby carrots and potatoes. Side dishes included asparagus with hollandaise sauce, a crisp garden salad, and a basket of hot rolls.

"I've died and gone to heaven," he whispered.

Daisy came out of the utility room. "I hope not. There's a lot of work to be done here tomorrow. Sit down and let's eat. There's nothing more yucky than cold asparagus."

He pulled out a chair for her. "You are eating with me, aren't you?"

She sat down. "I'm not going hungry."

"I will sign on to work at the Honky Tonk every night if you'd cook like this for me." He popped the first of a buttered hot roll into his mouth. "You making these for the hired help tomorrow?"

"No, Cathy is. She's the bread maker. I made cobblers."

"Will you please wear one of Mavis' old housecoats and put some lard in your hair in the morning?"

"Why?"

"Because you're already so damn pretty it hurts to look at you. When the fellows find out you can cook pies too, well, let's just say, if you looked real ugly, it might help a little bit."

"You sure are charming when you are hungry and you've got such a romantic way with words," she laughed.

Her laughter was like tinkling bells. Had he not been so hungry, he would have picked her up and carried her to bed right then.

She saw the look in his eyes and changed the subject. "So how is Garrett going to turn this ranch around by himself?"

"Our family has a rule. The ranch produces what it uses. That means the ranch grows its own hay for the cattle and food for the people. Keeps the wolf away from the door. It means that if you go borrowing money and have a bad year, you owe the bank. Couple of bad years and the bank owns you. Lots of small ranches go belly up when the owners buy into the big-or-bust idea."

"Which is?"

"More cattle than the land can support so you have to buy hay and grain. More equipment than they need to keep up appearances. Taking money out of the ranch for things they don't need like big vacations and condos in Florida or Paris."

Daisy slathered butter onto a hot roll. "Ruby basically said the same thing about the Honky Tonk. Mingus was the perfect place for a beer joint and the reason so many had failed was because the owners got the idea they were in Dallas or Nashville. They had to have live entertainment; they were only open on Friday and Saturday nights; they spent megabucks on advertisement. And presto, a year later they were declaring bankruptcy. Ruby took a salary from the profits at the Honky Tonk. She paid Tinker and me and what was left after bills went into a savings account. When she died she split the savings account between me and Tinker. I'm not rich but if we had a couple of bad years at the Honky Tonk I wouldn't go under."

"Same general idea. Is this what y'all are serving tomorrow?" he asked.

"No, I found two whole hams in the freezer. They're thawing out. Also found another stove out in the utility room. I'd seen it there when I was here before but I had no idea it was hooked up," she answered.

"Mavis fixed it that way so she could cook out there in the hot summer and it wouldn't heat up the house. Are you cooking one in each oven?"

She nodded. "Menu tomorrow is ham, baked beans, potato salad, and hot rolls. Cathy made a couple of her famous chocolate cakes and I put together three peach cobblers for dessert. We found everything we needed right here so we didn't have to go to the store. You still didn't answer my question about Garrett running this place alone."

Jarod buttered a second hot roll. "He's bringing a crew. Uncle Emmett was like your Ruby. He left a savings account and we felt like the wise thing to do was let Garrett have it to run the ranch. He'll have a foreman, three full-time hired hands, and a cook and housecleaner. The foreman and housekeeper are married. They'll live in the house for a couple of weeks. Garrett has bought two trailers. One will be for Ben and Livvy, the other for the hired hands. They'll live in them a couple of years but eventually the foreman and his wife will have a house and there'll be a bunkhouse for the hired help."

"Sounds like Garrett is going to have his work cut out even with help. The ranch has sure gone down the past few years." Daisy eyed Jarod. "Whatever is making that frown on your face? Cold asparagus? I told you it wasn't as good when it got cold. Save room for peach cobbler. I made a small one for supper."

He looked across the table and she read his mind.

"For an Indian you sure don't have a flint face expression," she said.

"Oh? What was I thinking?"

"Let's just say you were not thinking about peach cobbler," she answered.

"No, actually I wasn't. I was thinking about peach cobbler with ice cream. What were you thinking about?"

"That romp in the sheets at your house in Cushing."

He almost choked on a bite of potato. Daisy spoke her mind and did not stutter. Life with her would never be a guessing game.

She smiled sweetly. "I was lying. I was really thinking about how I'd like a repeat performance up in your bedroom right here."

"Before or after cobbler?" He laid his napkin to one side and held out a hand. She put hers in it and followed him upstairs to the bedroom. He left the door open and sat down on the edge of the bed, pulling her down beside him.

"I want you. I've thought about you all day and was disappointed when I thought you weren't here when I came in for the day. Every waking thought centers around you, Daisy. I want to make love to you until neither of us can see straight."

"I see a but in your face and it's not part of anyone's anatomy."

"There is a but. I want more. I want a relationship with you. I don't want a quick tumble in the sheets. I want to date you. I want to introduce you as my girlfriend even though that seems young and silly. I want to be able to say the words."

"Can we talk about this after we make love?"

"No, I'm not making love to you right now even though I want to so bad it aches. I want an exclusive relationship and I don't want sex without it," he said.

"What if all I want is a friendship with benefits?"

"Then you'll have to find it somewhere else. I can be your acquaintance but I can't be only your friend with benefits."

"Kiss me," she said.

"Is it friendship with benefits?"

She let go of his hand and stood up.

You've blown it, he thought.

She threw one leg over both his and sat in his lap, facing him. Grabbing a fist full of hair she pulled his lips down to hers and ran her tongue around his lips.

He broke away and leaned back. "Why did you do that?"

"Testing the water, darlin' man," she said.

He frowned.

"I was afraid that if I said I'd commit to you that it would change things. It didn't. Kissing you made me just as hot ever. Have I ever told you that touching your hand puts my mind in the gutter and I want to haul you to bed every time you look at me?"

"And?"

"I'll be your girlfriend, Jarod. I'll be your exclusive, committed relationship, but don't pressure me for anything more for a very long time," she said.

"It's a deal, sweetheart." He hugged her tightly. "Will you sleep with me tonight? I'm so tired I'm not sure I can do anything more than that, but I want to cuddle with you like we did last night. I want to wake up with you beside me like I did at my house in Cushing. I want to hold you and feel your sweet breath on my chest all night."

"I promise I'll sleep with you but peach cobbler with ice cream is waiting, honey," she whispered in his ear.

"Lie down here with me for five minutes. Let me feel your body next to mine. I'd rather feel you than taste peach cobbler and it's my favorite dessert," he said.

"I'm flattered," she giggled softly.

"You should be. Darlin', I have never given up peach cobbler for another woman," he laughed with her.

They snuggled for half an hour, whispering as if the house was full of relatives who might overhear their sweet talk.

"I could sleep until morning just like this," he said.

"Me too."

They didn't sleep or make love but lay in each other's arms for another thirty minutes. He made lazy circles on her back and upper arms and she breathed softly on his chest.

"Want to go watch the sunset with me?" Jarod finally asked.

"I'd love to," she said.

They hurriedly cleaned up the kitchen and dipped cobbler and ice cream into one bowl with two spoons to take to the porch to watch the sunset. They sat side by side on the porch steps and shared cobbler as the sun slowly sunk below the horizon.

The clock struck nine times in the dining room. That was the first time Daisy had thought of the Honky Tonk all evening. Guilt flowed over her; she loved that place. How could she forget it even for an evening?

Easy. You found something that you love even more, that pestering voice inside her heart said.

Oh, no, she argued. *I'm in a committed relationship now. I love the sex. I love the attention. I love the afterglow and even this peach cobbler, but I will not admit that I've fallen in love with Jarod. Not tonight. I can't do that much in one day and keep my sanity.*

"Peach cobbler and a sunset are almost as beautiful as my girlfriend. It don't get no better than this," Jarod said.

"You are sure using that word a lot," she said.

"Yes, and you'll be hearing it even more tomorrow when I introduce you to everyone who drives a truck onto this property, or when we go to the Honky Tonk and I tell Billy Bob and everyone who'll stand still and listen to me crow that you are a marked woman now," he said.

She tried to find a smart aleck remark to snap back at him but her mind went blank. She sighed. She hadn't thought of the teasing Chigger and Cathy would give her.

Chapter 17

CHIGGER TOOK ONE LOOK AT DAISY AND WINKED. "YOU got laid."

"Did you?" Cathy's big blue eyes widened.

"I don't kiss and tell but the answer is no. I have agreed to a committed relationship. I did not agree to anything past that," Daisy said.

"If you are thinking of anything past that you'd better get on the ball or else wait until after Valentine's Day because I'm going to be in the wedding and I refuse to look like I've got a watermelon under my fancy dress when I am," Chigger said.

Daisy looked at Cathy. "What about you?"

Cathy put both palms up. "I've got a new car and a job. I don't care if you take fifty years to do anything past that."

"Good, guess that's settled. I can use it. Hams are cooking. You can make the yeast rolls. The cattle trucks won't be here until lunch or after so I can help in the house until then," Daisy said.

"You are a woman of many talents," Chigger said. "I can't cook and barely know a cow from a bull."

"But what you do in the bedroom makes up for that, don't it?" Daisy teased.

Chigger headed for the kitchen. "You are damned right! But I can help with this dinner in other ways that cookin'. I've helped Momma do hundreds of funeral dinners at the church and this ain't much different than that. I'll get the table arranged. We'll start 'em on this end by the door. They can pick up a tray, fill it up, and go find a place to sit. Where's the paper plates? Bet they're in the pantry out here with the extra stove." She pulled a stack of divided Styrofoam plates from the shelf, along with plastic cutlery and glasses.

"I'll get busy on hot rolls." Cathy started searching through the pantry for the flour, yeast, sugar, and oil. "So did you?" she asked Daisy.

Daisy stirred up the dressing for the potato salad. "Did I what?"

"Get laid," Cathy asked.

"You two are obsessed with sex. And I understand. I really do. Chigger just got married and had it on the brain even before she said 'I do.' Cathy, you've always liked a man in your life. I swear you'll be leaving the Honky Tonk in another week and searching for a new boyfriend. But I'm content with a committed relationship for a very long time."

"Bite your tongue!" Cathy said.

"Did you get laid?" Chigger asked.

"I'm not answering that question. Which reminds me, you never did tell me what your momma had to say about your marriage," Daisy said.

Chigger stopped working and poured a cup of coffee. "She cried and then she got mad that I didn't have it at the church so she could buy a new dress. Can you just imagine all the frills and ruffles she would have picked out? I would have looked like Little Bo Peep. All I would have needed was a shepherd's hook and a parasol. Hell, she might have made me carry a parasol too. After the tears she was happy because she didn't have to pay for a big shindig and she was excited that she was going to have a new grandbaby. She couldn't wait to get to church on Sunday and tell everyone that we got married six months ago and was keeping it a secret. Said it sounded so romantic. All I could think was, 'Hot damn, I got off that one easy.'"

"What cock-and-bull story did you tell her about *why* you got married secretly?" Daisy asked.

"She hadn't asked yet. You got any ideas?"

Daisy peeled cooled boiled potatoes and diced them. "It's your lie. Concoct it anyway you want."

Cathy poured two cups of hot water into a bowl and added yeast and sugar. "You two sure do fight a lot to be best friends."

Chigger put a plastic cloth on the table. "Best friends don't always see eye-to-eye. We respect each other's opinions. Wait until you meet Momma. You'll understand."

"Am I going to meet Momma soon?" Cathy asked.

Chigger smiled brightly. "Oh, yes. She's coming to Sunday dinner, not this weekend but the next and both of you are going to be there and so is Jarod and he's going to have to be married to Daisy that day so you'd best get him ready for the part."

"Oh, no, not again," Daisy moaned.

"You will do it, won't you?" Chigger asked.

"Of course I'll do it," Daisy said.

"And Cathy, you are Joe Bob's girlfriend that day," Chigger giggled.

"Dear God," Cathy muttered.

"What about poor old Billy Bob?" Daisy asked.

"Oh, he'll be there all right but he made me mad this week so he doesn't have a girlfriend. Know what that means?"

Cathy shook her head.

Daisy shivered.

Chigger nodded seriously, "You get the prize, Daisy, 'cause you figured it out right away. He isn't going to have a girlfriend and Momma will fix him up with someone from her church. He'll learn to be nice to me and Jim Bob. Momma's matchmaking skills are even worse than voodoo. And while we're at it, you'd better tell Cathy the cover story."

Daisy filled her in.

"Monopoly?" Cathy frowned.

"That's right. Cards are sinful and will lead you straight to hell so we don't play cards on Saturday night."

"And I'm a Sunday school teacher and I live with Daisy and I do *what*?" Cathy could hardly believe the lie.

"Bookkeeping. It's not a lie. You do work for Daisy and you do take money and count the till so that makes you a bookkeeper. Say it often enough and it don't sound so far-fetched. Momma's a pain in the ass but she's my momma and she's the only one I'll ever get. I wouldn't hurt her for the world and she's got a bad heart so it's not really lies but heart protection," Chigger said.

"Did Daisy tell you about my other job? Is that why you said I was a bookkeeper?" Cathy stopped stirring the yeast mixture. "Do you read tea leaves or practice voodoo?"

Chigger glanced up from her job. "Are you a real bookkeeper?"

Daisy answered the question. "She's an accountant. She's got a college degree and she worked at an oil company along with a son-of-a-bitch who slapped her around. She gave a notice and came to Mingus to get away from him and the area."

"Well I'll be damned."

Jarod slipped into the kitchen through the back door and asked, "What will you be damned about?"

"Daisy will tell you later but save a week from Sunday for dinner at my house. Momma is coming to visit," Chigger said.

"Strength in numbers?" Jarod draped an arm around Daisy's shoulder. "Have you two met my girlfriend?"

"We have and we know," Cathy said.

Jarod brushed a kiss across her forehead. "Just came after a glass of tea and to tell you the first load of cattle will be here right before noon. We've got most of Emmett's herd rounded up and in the corral. If you'll bring the paperwork down right after lunch we'll go through them and decide what to turn out and what to send back with the trucks. Jim Bob, Joe Bob, and Billy Bob are here helping us too."

"Maybe I should've made three hams." Daisy shrugged his arm away and went to straighten the wrinkle-free table cloth.

Jarod filled a plastic glass with tea and carried it out the back door. "See you in at noon."

"Whew! What was that all about?" Chigger asked when he left.

"What?" Daisy asked.

Chigger pulled out a dining room chair and sat down. "Okay, let's get this thing talked through before the fellers come in for dinner. Another ice storm like that and Jarod will be introducing you as his ex-girlfriend.

You know what I'm talking about, Daisy, so don't give me that blank stare. I could feel the chill. Right here in the middle of the summer, it felt like an icy winter wind filled the house. Don't you think he could feel it too? Last time I gave Jim Bob the cold shoulder like that was a year ago when this woman at the Honky Tonk backed him up in a corner and had his belt buckle in her hands when I caught them."

Daisy sighed. "I don't know what it was. Last night I really wanted to enter into a committed relationship. Today, when he said that girlfriend thing, it made me mad and I have no idea why."

"Better figure it out right soon," Cathy said.

"I'm not sure it's even Jarod. I think it might be all this stuff around me. I feel like I'm being smothered to death just trying to fix a meal in this house with all the clutter around me and then he's smothering me by being so damn possessive. I couldn't breath when he put his arm around me. I felt like all these damned fake animals were giving me the evil glare. His sister-in-law, Jewel, looks at me like that and…" Daisy stopped talking and threw up her hands in bewilderment.

"Physical things are affecting the emotions. I can understand that," Chigger said. "Everything chose that moment to close in on you and make you crazy."

"You should be a psychiatrist," Daisy said.

"Hairdresser. Rancher's wife. Psychiatrist. One and the same. Got to get to the bottom of a problem, then unravel the damn thing no matter what you are. Here's the deal. Momma's church owns an old house that they keep things like this in, along with clothing and used eyeglasses to give to the needy. If Jarod is willing we'll get rid of it."

"I'll ask him," Daisy said.

"Hey, you know what this house reminds me of? My grandmother's. She loved all this folderol," Cathy said.

"So do I," Chigger said. "Like I said, it's cozy to me, but to each his own, and if this drives Daisy crazy enough to produce icicles when Jarod touches her, it's time for the damn stuff to go."

As he worked that morning Jarod kept thinking about the way Daisy shrugged off his touch. She'd offered to make the lunch; he hadn't asked. He'd given her a chance to back out of the relationship and she'd agreed to it—quite wholeheartedly. So what in the devil did he do wrong from the time he walked out the door that morning and she'd kissed him passionately until the time he ran inside for a glass of tea?

She was behaving like most of the women he'd had in his life and that didn't set well with him. Get him committed and then play little mind games that kept him confused. If he'd judged her wrong then he could and would get out of the relationship. He was too old and had been through too many women with issues to play the game again.

He hadn't figured out a single thing when he and the Walker triplets trooped into the house for dinner. Jarod spoke to several of the men already in the backyard with plates piled high in front of them as he made his way across the yard. He wasn't in a hurry to face Daisy again even though his stomach was growling and he was as thirsty as if he had just crossed the Sahara.

Once inside the house, the dinner line was still long. Daisy, Chigger, and Cathy were busy behind the table and the noise level was even higher than when Uncle Emmett had the television and the CD player running at the same time. Daisy looked up and smiled at him. What should have sent his spirits soaring plunged them to the pits of depression. Too hot to touch. Cold enough to freeze him. Now warm. Those abrupt changes in temperature could ruin a relationship and squelch love.

Jarod picked up a plate at the dinner buffet only to have Daisy move around and get in front of him. "You won't mind if your girlfriend cuts in line, will you?"

"Not at all," he said flatly.

A band appeared around Daisy's heart and began to tighten. Had she just destroyed the best thing that had ever happened to her?

"Did you get the cattle all penned up for me?" she asked as they loaded their plates.

"We did. Just a few more stragglers to herd in and they're all ready."

She could feel the frost coating his words.

He started out the back door and she touched his arm. "In the living room. Alone. Please."

He followed without saying another word.

She set her plate on the coffee table and sat down cross-legged in front of it. "I'd like to explain about this morning, but you're going to think I'm crazy."

He sat across from her. "Explain away."

Daisy took a deep breath. "This is going to sound like I'm trying to justify a bad mood and I'm not really sure how to put it. But I hate all this clutter. I feel like

I'm being smothered to death and I didn't even realize it until Chigger pointed it out."

"Chigger always going to have to point it out when you are bitchy?"

She cut her blue eyes around at him. "I admit it. I'm so sorry for the way I behaved. It was mean and bitchy and just plain ugly. I felt like all the junk in this house was closing in on me. And then there you were all happy because I'm your girlfriend, as you put it, with your arm around me and it felt like you were closing in on me too. Everything in the place was sucking the life out of me. The evil eyes of those animals damned me. You were all possessive. You want to end our committed relationship because I was bitchy one time, then evidently I was wrong about you anyway."

"I don't want to end it. I want to work through it. You never acted like that before," Jarod said, the ice crystals melting from the words.

Daisy went on. "And I will never act that way again because I've worried all morning that you would take it just the way you did and it wasn't a good feeling. I would have hated for you to have treated me like that in front of your friends and family. I'm truly sorry. Please, please forgive me," she said as she locked gazes with him across the table.

He touched her hand. "Forgiven." Daisy was different. When she was wrong she apologized. She hadn't let it fester for days but had cornered him as soon as he was back in the house, and he had a very good feeling that she'd never bring it up again. Yes, sir, his Daisy was honest and he believed her when she said it wouldn't happen again.

"Just like that?" she asked.

"Just like that. Forgiven and forgotten."

"You are a good man, Jarod." *I love you. I really do but I can't say the words. Please don't give up on me. I'll be able to say them someday.*

"You keep right on thinking that. I've got a confession. All this junk drives me crazy, too. I hate to be in the house with it. Garrett says the night he spent here when Emmett died was like a horror movie. He said their eyes watched him every time he moved. He's planning on making a bonfire out of it all."

"Chigger says we can box it all up and take it to her mother's church. They give away stuff to folks who need it."

"Bless her heart. Garrett will pay you all to take care of it."

"No payment necessary. Can we make up now?" Her eyes twinkled.

He leaned across the table and brushed a quick kiss across her lips. "Don't do that again. I'll meet you halfway. Hell, I'll even meet you three quarters. But I can't read your mind. Makeup will have to wait. Remember Garrett, Livvy, and Ben are all moving in today. Garrett is taking your old room. Livvy and Ben will take the other one until their trailer is hooked up. We will have to put makeup on the back burner but I guarantee it will be worth it when we get around to it."

She moved around the table to sit close enough that their hips and shoulders touched. "Why didn't you tell me that last night?"

Joe Bob eased open the door and peeked in. "Mind if I join you? Tables are full in the backyard and besides,

I want to talk to Jarod about this Sunday thing. Lord, can you just see me acting all lovey-dovey with Cathy? She's liable to slap my face."

"What Sunday thing?" Jarod asked.

Joe Bob frowned. "You didn't tell him, Daisy? I'll eat on the front porch. I just figured you could give me some advice since you played like you were married to Daisy." He left without shutting the door.

"Explain please," Jarod said.

"It's like this. Chigger figured out that I had hot flashes the first time I laid eyes on you. Don't look at me with that grin. It's hard enough for me to admit all this but I'll be damned if I ever keep a single thing from you again," she said and went on to tell him the whole story.

It started as a mild chuckle and wound up a loud guffaw that had him reaching in the pocket of his bibbed overalls for a red bandanna to wipe at his eyes. "So we get to be married again on Sunday?"

"Married twice. They say the third is the charm. We'll have to be very careful," she giggled.

The laughter stopped when he tipped back her face and his gray eyes locked with her dark blue ones. He bent and she stretched. Their lips met in a long drawn out kiss that left them both aching.

"I'm going to get hot flashes thinking about you," she said.

He kissed her forehead. "Good. I hope you have to take a cold shower just like I will. I'm going now before I carry you off to a hay loft and put a 'do not disturb' sign on the door. Give us thirty minutes and then come on out to the corral. Keys to my truck are on the top of the refrigerator. Bring it. That rutted path out there will rattle your cute little car to death."

"Thanks for the truck but I'd rather go to the hay loft," she said.

He laughed softly. "Me too, darlin'."

Cathy poked her head into the living room after Jarod left. "I see what you mean about stuff. It's everywhere. The longer I'm here the more I see. How on earth did anyone collect so much in just one lifetime? Looks to me like it would take three lifetimes to get this much gathered up."

Daisy motioned her on into the room. "It could have taken three lifetimes. There's probably stuff here from Mavis' parents and maybe even from Emmett's. But Jarod said Garrett would be very thankful to have it out of here."

Cathy plopped down on the sofa and leaned her head back. "It's been a morning and I'm tired but Chigger and I will get started once we put the leftovers away. I don't have to be home until six. It'll take you that long to get your outside jobs done anyway. Y'all get that tiff straightened out? We heard a lot of giggling going on in here. I don't suppose you did anything hinky though. Never known a man to like a woman to giggle while he's putting the make on her."

"Yes, we did get it straightened out. Now about this mess we've got to clean up. Got any ideas?" Daisy was getting damn good at changing the subject away from her and Jarod.

Cathy shrugged. "Don't worry about it. Me and Chigger can take care of it today while you are outside. I can't believe I'm supposed to be hankering after Joe Bob Walker on Sunday. He's been avoiding me like the plague. How are we supposed to convince Momma Jones that we are an item if he's afraid to be in the same room with me?"

"We convinced her that Jim Bob was as shy as Willa Mae," Daisy said.

"Who in the hell is Willa Mae? Oh, that's Chigger. Well, neither she nor Jim Bob have a shy bone. I'll never keep all the secrets and family ties straight."

"I still have a hard time of it too," Daisy said.

"But you've had seven years to get used to it. I wish I'd have come down here when you first went to work at the Honky Tonk. I thought you were crazy for working in a beer joint in some podunk place even smaller than Mena, Arkansas."

"I loved it from day one. What am I going to do about Jarod?"

"That's your decision. He's in love with you."

"Don't say that. I don't want to hear it right now."

"Not saying it doesn't make it go away. Enough talk. Time to get on with the packing. When we finish this horrible job we're driving to Abilene in my Caddy and I'm going shopping for new jeans. Chigger is going too, and she says she hopes maternity jeans don't make her look like a clown."

"Do you think Victoria's Secret makes sexy maternity clothes? I can't see Chigger in plain old plaid shirts and jeans. Keep that in mind while I go help Jarod take care of the cattle," Daisy said.

She found him at the corral where they had the rest of Emmett's herd penned up and waiting for her to pass judgment.

"Hey, sweetheart, I thought I was going to have to come back to the house and wrestle you away from Chigger and Cathy." Jarod met her halfway between the car and the corral and slung an arm around her shoulder.

"Those two broads couldn't keep me away from you," she teased.

A smile turned the corners of his mouth up. Life was good.

"Run the first one in the chute," she said.

"All business and no love," he asked.

She stopped dead in her tracks and wrapped her arms around his neck, grabbing a fist full of dark hair and dragging his mouth down to hers for a hard kiss right there in front of the hired hands, his nephew, and even God.

"You decide which one," she whispered seductively in his ear when the kiss ended and he still held on to her in a tight hug.

He laughed in amongst the whistles and shouts of all the men around them. "Guess it'd better be business with an audience like this."

His Daisy would show them that she was a smart vet as well as his woman. His heart swelled with pride as he carried her black bag to the corral. How on earth he could have ever thought it was a tackle box was a mystery.

"This heifer is good stock but God only knows what she's bred to. Emmett had everything from Limousin to Angus on the ranch. There at the end he wasn't culling anything. I'd sell her at the sale if you want to keep pure Angus on the Double M," she said.

"Put her in the trailer to take back to Oklahoma for the sale," Garrett told the men.

"That bull calf has a lot of potential, don't you think, Jarod?" she asked when they ran the next animal into the chute.

"I do. He's a big old boy for his age. I vote we keep him," Jarod answered.

The third one was a yearling, definitely mixed blood even if it was a healthy calf.

"To the sale barn," Jarod said.

"I agree," Daisy told him.

"Hey, you two, we got a problem down by those trees. There's a heifer down having a hell of a time delivering. She's one of the Angus that we brought down from Oklahoma. If we'd known she was this close to calvin' we'd have left her up there," Rudy said.

"Let's go," Daisy picked up her bag.

Jarod grabbed her hand and they jogged to the spot where the cow was lying on her side and heaving with every contraction. Daisy dropped to her knees, opened her bag, and pulled out a stethoscope. She laid it on the cow in several different places before she looked up at Jarod.

"Calf has a strong heartbeat so it's still alive. Let's see if it's too big or breach or what the problem is. Here, you keep a monitor on the heartbeat and I'll check out the calf. Tell me if the heartbeat gets faster or slows down." She moved to the back end of the heifer, rolled up her sleeves, and shoved her arm up into the cow's uterus halfway from elbow to armpit. Jarod listened to the calf and watched Daisy.

"Good lookin' stock Garrett has," she said. "This heifer is in great shape. This is just her first baby and she doesn't know what to do."

"I'd have thought nature would take care of that," he said.

"Not always. Sometimes they get scared. It's not breach but it's got one big head. Tell me when the next contraction is and I'll pull," she said.

"Right now," he said. He'd pulled dozens of calves himself but sitting there with Daisy helping him felt so right and so perfect.

She pulled hard and felt the calf move several inches.

"Again," she said.

He waited a minute and said, "Now."

She pulled again and two hooves popped out. She was able to get a better hold at that time and waited until the cow contracted again before she gave a hard tug. The black calf came out in a whoosh, spurting fluids all over Daisy. She jerked her overshirt off and wiped the calf's nose.

"Breathe, you lazy boy. Your momma didn't work all day for you to die now," Daisy said.

Jarod bit back a chuckle. She didn't care that she was covered in gunk—she didn't even know it. All she saw was a newborn calf. In that moment Jarod loved her more than ever before.

The calf sucked up air and let out a whimper.

She shouted, "Look, darlin', he's alive! He's a fine bull calf."

The heifer slowly got to her feet and began to lick the new baby while Jarod and Daisy stood to one side and watched. His arm was tightly around her shoulders. Her fingers were hooked in one of his back belt loops.

"We did good," she said.

"We sure did," he agreed.

It took every bit of ten days but on the Sunday of Chigger's family dinner and wedding reception combination the house was cleaned out. The old furniture took on a new look without all the stuff shoved in every spare square inch. The walls were a mess with all the nail holes. The carpet was a sight with dark places where the extra tables had kept the light from fading the color. But the next week a crew was scheduled to patch and paint one day. On the next day the carpet layers would arrive.

Jarod awoke on Sunday morning knowing that his job was finished. It was time to go home. An empty hole was in the middle of his heart and the only one who could fill it was Daisy. He had less than a week to convince her that her place was with him permanently.

He pulled a pair of creased jeans from the closet and laid them across the chair in his empty bedroom. Today he would be Daisy's husband. Their children, two little girls, had gone for a play day with their church Sunday school class or they would have brought them along. That was the story line or was it the story lie?

He grinned.

What would it be like to share two little girls with Daisy? Would they have his black hair and her dark blue eyes? Would they be as sassy as she was or as bullheaded as him? It didn't matter to Jarod as long as Daisy was their mother.

Daisy found Cathy already up and at the breakfast table with a cup of coffee in front of her.

"Good morning, Joe Bob's girlfriend. What did you teach in Sunday school this morning?" She poured herself a cup and grabbed a package of toaster pastries out of the box.

"I taught your two little girls, Janene and Julianna, the story of Jonah and the whale. It's kind of like the story of you and Jarod. Jonah is symbolic of the love you share, only it's been swallowed up by this big whale called fear who refuses to spit it out until you own up to the fact that you really are in love."

"That's enough!" Daisy pointed at Cathy.

"Okay, okay. Then I'll tell you about your sweet little girls. It is so cute the way you gave them J names like their father," Cathy smarted off.

Daisy's eyes twinkled. "Janene and Julianna. I'll tell Jarod so we can pass it on to Momma Jones. But if you ever think I'll name my daughters such names you are crazy."

"You won't have girls. You'll have a whole yard full of mean boys. Chigger's going to have girls," Cathy said.

"That written in stone or is there some wiggle room?"

It was Cathy's turn to laugh. "I'm just jealous. You get to have a handsome hunk husband all day and all I get is a red-haired boyfriend."

"What's the matter with Joe Bob?"

"Two things. I've never been attracted to red-haired men. Not after Bubba McMann spit chocolate on my shirt and told me it was tobacco when I was in the first grade."

"What's the second thing?"

"I'm not so good at pool. He'd never stay with a woman who couldn't challenge him on the tables."

"Guess that's enough to keep a relationship from working. You'd best get to primping though. Oh, did I tell you that Chigger invited her brothers and their wives to the shindig too?"

Cathy groaned.

Chapter 18

JAROD ARRIVED IN HIS SATURDAY NIGHT HONKY TONK clothes: creased jeans, boots, and a plaid Western shirt. "Is my wife and Joe Bob's girlfriend ready for the party?" he asked when Cathy answered the door.

"Daisy, your husband is here," Cathy yelled over her shoulder.

Jarod met her in the middle of the living room floor, tipped her chin up with his fist, and kissed her hard.

"I missed you so much," he said.

"Me too," she whispered.

"Ahem!" Cathy cleared her throat.

"I wouldn't care if God was standing where you are, Cathy," Jarod said.

"But you have seen each other every day. Most of the time you've spent every minute together," Cathy said.

"We saw each other and we haven't had a spare minute to be alone." Jarod held the door for them and then helped them into the truck.

"Aha, not only a husband but a gentleman and no one is even looking," Cathy said.

"A man has to be good to his wife and cousin-in-law or they'll leave him high and dry. Old Joe Bob has to be good or else his girlfriend won't give him a good night kiss. Me, I've got to worry about alimony and child support." He shut the doors and whistled as he rounded the truck and strapped himself into the seat.

"Alimony and child support are the least of your worries," Cathy said as he started the engine. "Little Janene and Julianna would be so upset if you two divorced."

"Who?"

"The two little girls you have."

Daisy whipped around in the seat and pointed. "That's enough."

"Actually, I was thinking more of Brand and Creed and they're boys not girls. Of course, Momma would be tickled to death to have girls. We're a little heavy on the male side at family reunions. Seems the McElroys throw boys more than girls."

Daisy jerked her head back around and pointed at Jarod. "Don't be talking about children before the marriage."

"And when is that happening?"

"In ten years, maybe, if you are nice."

———~~~———

At noon, more than thirty people gathered round the buffet set up on the deck at Jim Bob and Chigger's place. Mixed aromas of fried catfish, roast beef, and ham had the cats rubbing against legs and meowing.

"Momma, would you say grace for us?" Chigger asked.

Heads bowed. Jarod reached for Daisy's hand. Jim Bob wrapped his arm around Chigger. Joe Bob shoved his thumbs in the hip pockets of his jeans. Cathy laced her fingers together behind her back.

"Dear Lord," Momma Jones began. "Accept our thanks for this bountiful dinner spread before us. Help us to keep your commandments even when it's not easy and to tell the truth even when it hurts. Amen."

It took a moment for everyone to realize the prayer was over so quickly and heads rose slowly making sure that Momma hadn't just paused for more air and had truly said, "Amen."

"To those who don't know me as Momma or Gran, I'm Aleda Jones, Willa Mae's momma, and while everything is still quiet in this room I have something to say. I'm glad to be here for a late wedding reception for these two. I'm glad my daughter slowed down enough that Jim Bob could catch her. I just now prayed that the Lord would help us follow his commandments even when it ain't easy. So I've got a confession to make."

"Momma, this is a Sunday dinner and there's not a priest in sight so you don't have to go to confession," Chigger giggled nervously.

Aleda patted her on the shoulder. "I confess to God, not a priest. But today it's laid upon my heart to put an end to the charades and clear the air before we eat this good food. So I'm going to do it or else I'm sure that fish will make me sick. Fish is my favorite food and I do not intend to be sick on it and never be able to enjoy it again."

"Well, then I expect you'd best 'fess up," Jim Bob said.

She nodded seriously. "Okay, here goes. Daisy, you and Jarod are not married and you own and run the Honky Tonk, a beer joint over south of Mingus. I hope someday you two get married because you belong together. Joe Bob and Cathy are not dating and they shouldn't. They don't fit together at all and I shall find both him and Billy Bob a good woman from my church."

She nodded her head seriously and scared the bejesus out of them.

"Now to you, Chigger," she said.

High color flushed Chigger's cheeks. Daisy thought even her blond hair would turn burgundy on the spot.

"Who?" she gasped.

"Don't play innocent with me. I know where you've been and what you've been up to all these years. Only thing I don't know is why you chose a name like Chigger for a nickname. You ain't little and you don't have red hair which is the only two reasons I'd think would be right, but that don't matter." She paused.

Chigger was struck mute.

"Truth is I didn't really care. I knew you were as wild as your Granny Jones was when she was young, and honey, that's goin' some. Rumor had it that she marched on the White House for women's rights at one time. Actually, I was proud because you lived your life the way you wanted and loved me enough to keep it hid from me. I know you and Jim Bob got married at the courthouse and I was mad as hell that I wasn't there but Jim Bob is a good man and I'm glad you found him. The last thing on my confession is that I was tickled to death for you to go away on weekends all these years because every Friday and Saturday night I've been playing bingo. I like the people and the fun and it might be gambling but God didn't strike me dead so evidently it's not too big of a sin. I've been very lucky and I tithed on my winnings which bought the church a new piano this past year. That was ten percent. Fifty percent I put in a fund for your wedding. Twenty percent I plowed right back into the game. That left twenty percent to take to the bank and next week me and some of my senior citizen bingo buddies are going on a month long cruise around the world and back. The fifty percent for your wedding is in this envelope for your wedding gift. It's yours to use anyway you want since you didn't want the big white dress and wedding cake." She pulled an envelope from her pocket and laid it on the cabinet.

Chigger couldn't even blink.

"So there it is. Confession is good for the soul and my stomach is growling. You are the bride and Jim Bob is the groom so you get to eat first but I'm right behind you."

"Well, I'll be hung with a new rope from a tall oak tree," Jim Bob said.

"Please don't. That baby needs a father," Aleda said.

"Thank you, Momma," Chigger said.

"For the money or for outing you?"

"Both," Chigger answered. "Would someone start talking before I cry?"

Jarod spoke up. "And here I was hoping to play the dutiful husband all day. Now all I get to be is the boyfriend."

Joe Bob exhaled loudly. "Thank goodness you confessed. I wasn't looking forward to being Cathy's boyfriend. She scares the liver out of me. But I can find my own wife so you don't have to worry about it."

"Ain't no worryin' on my part, Joe Bob. I'll go to work on finding you a sweet little Christian woman next week. And honey, there no use in runnin' because once I set my mind, it's a done deal. By this time next year you'll both be married."

Joe Bob looked like a cottontail trying to escape a hungry bobcat.

Aleda patted him on the arm. "Good lookin' as you boys are, why it won't take but a few words."

"I'm already datin' a woman," Billy Bob piped up.

"Too bad," Aleda said. "If I can't help Willa Mae choose, then I get to play matchmaker with you two. And after that I'm working on you, Cathy."

"Good luck. I've sworn off men forever," Cathy said.

"You could be the smartest one in the room then, darlin', but it won't work. I'm going to find someone to make you a happy woman."

Everyone started talking at once, laughing at Aleda's confession, congratulating Chigger and Jim Bob, filling plates, and carrying them to the tables on the deck.

"So you're free and I'm still single," Daisy teased Cathy as they made their way down the buffet line.

"Thank God for both. I'm not so sure I could manage a boyfriend and a bar," Cathy said.

"I manage both," Daisy said.

"Yeah, but you are special." Jarod kissed her on the cheek.

Cathy shivered. "And you don't have Aleda breathing down your neck. Only good thing is that the men she'll choose won't be those who'd step foot in a beer joint anyway. That might be Joe Bob and Billy Bob's salvation. They can always hide out in the Honky Tonk because a good Christian woman wouldn't chase them inside there. What would you do, Daisy, if you had to choose between the boyfriend and the Honky Tonk?"

Jarod held his breath and waited.

Daisy didn't miss a single bite of fish. "That's an unfair question. It's like asking which of your children you love the most."

He exhaled slowly.

Even though she found the right words to answer the question, it brought Daisy up short. How could she ever choose between the Honky Tonk and Jarod? She loved the bar and she loved Jarod. Couldn't a woman have both?

Love Jarod!

It was the first time she'd ever allowed herself to think the word and it had snuck up on her just as she sat down to eat. The revelation should have come with afterglow on her body, not with catfish in her mouth. But there it was in living Technicolor in the front of her brain lobe yelling in a faintly southern voice that she loved Jarod McElroy.

Just when did all this happen? her inner voice asked.

It happened so slowly that I can't put my finger on an exact date and time, she answered. *But now that I've admitted it, what do I do with it?*

Cathy chanted as she waved a napkin in front of Daisy's face. "Earth to Daisy, where are you zoning out to?"

Daisy blinked a couple of times.

"Well?" Cathy asked.

"What was the question?"

"Where were you? We were talking about boyfriends and the Honky Tonk and you went all still like you were about to faint."

"Oh. I was off somewhere in la-la land I suppose."

Damn it all, what if I just figured out that I really do love this man and he's going to Oklahoma in a week or two at the most? Timing is everything and our clocks might not be synchronized.

"Well, you both looked like you were somewhere other than here," Cathy said.

Daisy looked over at Jarod. "Where's *your* mind?"

"This is going to sound very unromantic but I was thinking about carpet. I need to put new carpet in my house in Oklahoma," he said.

Daisy laughed nervously. "You are right. That isn't very romantic but then we aren't the newlyweds. Jim Bob and Chigger are so it's all right."

"Don't pick out purple carpet," Cathy giggled.

"Why?"

"Because she hates purple," Cathy said. "Her mother painted their living room purple once and had a red couch. She was so embarrassed she wouldn't let anyone come over except me. I thought it was way too cool."

"The many sides of Daisy," Jarod said softly. "You're like an onion. Just one layer after another."

"And they all stink," Daisy said.

"Depends on whether you like onions. I love them," Jarod said.

Jim Bob's father, Harlin, stood up and tapped his beer bottle with a fork to get everyone's attention. "For those who don't know me, I'm Harlin Walker, father to these red-haired triplets. After three rough and rowdy boys I never could talk my wife into trying for a girl. She'd just shiver and ask me if I wanted to raise six boys all alone because if she had another set of triplets they could just take her on to the funny farm. So we had to wait a long time for Chigger to come into our family. I'd like to propose a toast to my new daughter, Chigger. I know her real name but she will always be Chigger to us." He held his beer bottle up high. "To Chigger Walker, the daughter we love as much as our son Jim Bob does. May your marriage last as long as the love you share and may that last forever."

He touched his glass to Chigger's and she wiped away a tear.

Jarod pushed back his chair. "It's traditional for the best man to give a toast. I've known these three fellows since we were all barefoot boys fishing in Uncle Emmett's pond. Couldn't tell them apart then and still have trouble now. I do know Jim Bob is the one with the pretty lady beside him so that'll make it easier. I hear that the reason Jim Bob married Chigger is because she can tell them apart."

He paused while everyone laughed. "Here's an old Irish wedding blessing on the couple. 'May God be with you and bless you. May you see your children's children. May you be poor in misfortune, rich in blessings. May you know nothing but happiness from this day forward.' To Chigger and Jim Bob." He raised his beer bottle.

The whole crowd repeated, "To Chigger and Jim Bob."

"That was beautiful," Daisy said. When she looked up Chigger was wiping a tear from her eyes and nodding.

"Me?" Daisy mouthed.

Chigger nodded again.

Daisy rose to her feet slowly. "I was the maid of honor and I don't have anything prepared so I'll tell a story. The first time I saw Chigger I thought she was a hooker."

Everyone including Aleda laughed loud and long.

Daisy blushed. "Well, I did. I got to admit the Honky Tonk wouldn't be the same without her and the Walker triplets. It's only this summer that she and I've gotten to be friends and I was honored to stand up with her at the wedding. But I'm more honored to say that she's my good friend and she's been there for me through thick and thin these past weeks. So here's to Chigger and Jim Bob. Since

I'm Irish, too, I'll give them my blessing. 'May you both live to be a hundred years old — with one extra to repent!'"

That brought on more laughter and Chigger stood up next. "This one is to my family and friends. I love you all but not as much as I love Jim Bob. And Jarod, I really can tell the difference in him and his brothers, and he's the best of the lot."

"Thank you, darlin'." Jim Bob grinned.

Jarod slung an arm around Daisy and said, "Pretty good blessing. Don't know that I've heard that one."

"It was our grandmother's," Cathy said.

"She said it at all Christmas dinners," Daisy said.

"Is that where you two got your fiery tempers?" Jarod asked.

"Hell, no. Gran was as mild tempered as they make 'em. She never got mad about anything. She wasn't the Irish. Grandpa was and he had the temper to go with it," Daisy answered.

Two Irish people in love? Would that much temper and fire burn out too quickly to last for the long haul? she wondered as she sipped sweet tea.

"How much longer do we have to stay?" Jarod whispered in her ear.

"Why?"

"I was thinking about doing something this afternoon that we'd have to repent for that last year we're alive. How about a motel and room service?"

She smiled brightly. "How about one more hour?"

"I can last that long if you can but think about a Jacuzzi big enough for two people?"

"Thirty minutes. Billy Bob can take Cathy home."

Chapter 19

THE HONKY TONK WAS BOOMING ON SATURDAY NIGHT. Cathy and Daisy had trouble keeping orders filled so Jarod was behind the counter filling draft beers while they made mixed drinks. Tinker put out one pair of feuding pool players at midnight and fifteen minutes later a couple got into a heated argument on the dance floor. Tinker had barely started toward them when the girl drew back and decked the fellow with a hard right hook, knocking the man to his knees.

"That's enough. Take your fighting outside," Tinker said.

The woman turned on him, fists flailing and curses lighting up the Honky Tonk like a fireworks display. "Don't you tell me what to do, old man. This sumbitch ain't goin' to talk to me like that and I'll damn well fight with him wherever the hell I want to and there ain't nothin' you can do to stop me."

Cathy came out from behind the bar, grabbed the woman's arm, and twisted it up behind her back. "Yes, he can stop you, lady, and so can I. You want to fight, you take it outside like Tinker said."

"Hey, now, don't get all het up. I'll leave but that bastard better not get to stay."

The man rubbed his swollen jaw. "I'm going too. You'll find your stuff on the front lawn when you get home. I'm sick to death of you and your whining."

Tinker put them out the door and then cornered Cathy. "I didn't need your help."

"Probably not but I needed these people to see that I'm not taking shit either, so let me have my victory."

Tinker nodded.

"Got that settled?" Daisy asked.

"Yes, I did," Cathy answered.

"You ever done any bouncing?" Jarod asked during a brief lull.

Cathy checked the pretzels and peanut bowls and refilled both. "No, but I could, and no one is going to tear up this joint."

At five minutes until two Daisy unplugged the jukebox in the middle of Toby Keith singing about loving the bar.

Tinker put his cooler on the bar and said, "And Cathy, you done good."

"Thanks, Tinker." She turned and asked Daisy, "Do I get the bed tonight?"

"Not tonight," Daisy answered.

Jarod groaned.

Daisy pushed him toward the door. "I'll be out there at the ranch by noon."

"Promise?" He hugged her close to him. "We could drive to the motel and sleep together tonight."

"We are both too damn tired to do anything but sleep. I'll be there by noon to help you get everything packed."

"Sit with me a minute or two before I go. I've got something to say." He sat down in a chair and pulled her down to sit in his lap. "Let's say hypothetically that one sexy, sassy bartender had fallen for an old Oklahoma cowboy. Let's say that his roots were in

Oklahoma and she loved her bar, but that if she would go to Oklahoma with him, he'd be more than willing to buy her another beer joint close to the town where he lives. I forgot to mention that this barmaid is also a vet tech, but she's smart enough to be a full-fledged vet. That cowboy's so all-fired proud of her, he'd be even more happy to see her working for a vet or just taking care of the cattle on his ranch. Hell, he'd even be proud of she just worked a few nights a week in a bar if that's what she wanted. So what would that bartender think, hypothetically, of course?"

She kissed him long and hard. "That bartender would think she'd just fallen into a gold mine. Now go home and get some sleep and we'll talk about the hypothetical barmaid and cowboy when we aren't both about to drop."

He gave her another good-night kiss. "Oh yeah, I almost forgot. Momma and Dad are flying down for dinner tomorrow. They want to see how the house has shaped up."

"They'll be surprised." She locked the door behind him.

He left with an extra spring in his step. There was hope.

Daisy was so tired when she slipped between the sheets in her bed and shut her eyes that she figured she'd be snoring like Cathy in five minutes. But she tossed and turned for an hour, checking the clock so often that she wondered if it was ever going to change the minutes.

Jarod had just given her the best of three worlds. He'd said he wouldn't be ashamed of her working in a beer joint or even owning one. That he'd be honored to have her as the vet for his ranch. But he hadn't proposed. Was he asking her to move to Oklahoma? To live with him? Or to marry him?

His parents were flying down to see the house? What would they think of Jarod's offer? Or did it even matter what they thought?

She checked the clock. Ten minutes past four. She didn't want to be in the bed alone. She wanted to be snuggled up against Jarod's side, his arm around her, her leg thrown over his body.

"I love Jarod," she whispered. "I want to spend the rest of my life with him and I want to be there when he comes in for dinner and for supper every night. I want to wake up with him and spend all my time on the ranch with him. Dear Lord, what am I going to do? I've said time and time again that I'm not ever leaving the Honky Tonk. I wouldn't even let him say the words. What if he's changed his mind?" She fell back on the bed with such force that she bounced.

Go tell him, her heart said.

"It's the middle of the night," she moaned.

Time doesn't mean a thing to me, her heart reminded her.

She pulled a kimono-style, red silk robe over her sleep shirt that had Betty Boop on the front, shoved her feet into fluffy orange slippers, and picked up her purse. She couldn't sleep and if she waited until daylight, she'd lose her courage.

Doubts and fears made her turn around in the Smokestack parking lot. But after a two-minute lecture she drove on toward the ranch.

"I've got to do it," she whispered.

When she turned left off Highway 108, she pulled off to the side of the road and bit her nails. Finally she drove on, still arguing back and forth with herself. Should she go back to the Honky Tonk and wait for him to finally to ask her to go to Oklahoma with him, or go full speed ahead and tell him exactly how she felt?

She drove up into the yard and he met her on the porch.

"Daisy? What's wrong? I had the window open for the fresh night air and heard the car door. Is Cathy all right? Did Chigger lose the baby? Did Tinker die?"

"None of the above. I just figured out that I love you and I had to tell you before I could sleep," she said.

He stopped in his tracks and shook his head as if trying to dislodge water from his ears. "What did you say?"

She took a deep breath. "After you left I took a shower and I went to bed and I couldn't sleep. I thought it was because your parents were coming and I was dreading facing them, but then I realized I couldn't sleep because—" She ran out of air and sucked up another lung full. "Because I didn't want to be sleeping alone. I wanted to be with you and not just for one night. I want to spend the rest of my life with you. I want to wake up with you and help take care of the ranch. I want to be a vet tech and your wife and I want to go home with you. Right now I don't care about owning a beer joint because I think it'll take all my time to be your wife and your vet for the ranch, but if I want to later, then I'm glad you wouldn't be ashamed of me. Now it's your turn to tell me that I'm a bartender for God's sake and I'm crazy for being out here in the yard dressed like this and talking too fast. All I know is that I love you, Jarod, and

I'm scared to death that you have changed your mind because I wouldn't let you say the words, and please say them now."

Silence prevailed.

"Well?" she asked.

"You finished?" he asked.

She nodded.

He dropped down on one knee, took her hand in his, and looked up, "I have been waiting for this moment since I first realized I was desperately in love with you. I love you when we are making love, having sex, or just cuddling. I love you when we are dancing in the grass together. I love you when we have just pulled a calf together. I love you when I'm filling Mason jars with beer and you are by my side. Daisy O'Dell, will you marry me?"

She didn't hesitate a minute but fell to her knees and wrapped her arms around him.

"Yes, I will," she said.

—⁓—

Two weeks later, they were married on a Sunday afternoon at the Honky Tonk. In spite of the fact that Chigger's momma wanted to dress her in frills and ruffles, Daisy stuck to her guns and chose an ivory brocade sheath with a hem that touched the top of her new off-white boots. Instead of a veil she wore a white Stetson hat with a puffy bow attached to a bit of illusion at the back. She carried a bouquet of white daisies with a very special set of keys tucked into the flowers.

Amos walked her out of the apartment and across the hardwood floor to the place in front of the bar where

Jarod waited. He moved toward her when he saw her and took her hand from Amos' to lead her the rest of the way to the ivy covered arch where Cathy and Chigger waited on one side and Mitch and Stephen on the other.

"You look like an angel straight from heaven," he whispered.

She gave him a once-over and said, "You look like sex on a stick."

He swallowed the laughter.

"Dearly beloved, we are gathered here today to unite Jarod and Daisy in holy matrimony," the preacher said.

Daisy said the vows she'd written.

Jarod said his.

There wasn't a dry eye in the place.

They exchanged plain gold wedding bands and the preacher told Jarod he could kiss his bride.

He hugged her close to him before he claimed with a kiss that sent shivers all the way to the ends of her toenails.

The reception was held right there in the beer joint with Jewel and Maria serving the cakes and Chigger pouring punch.

"I'm surprised Daisy let you cut the groom's cake," Chigger said to Jewel.

"Not any more than I am," Jewel said.

"Way I see it is you got a choice, lady. I'll be talking to Daisy right regular and visiting her every few months. You give her any trouble and you will answer to me."

Jewel looked up at Chigger. "You trying to scare me? I apologized and she forgave me."

"I'm statin' facts. You'd have to be blind not to see that I'd make two of you and I'm tellin' you just so you know that I'm meaner than a constipated rattlesnake. I'll whip your tiny little ass all over Oklahoma if you are ugly to my friend. Do we have an understandin'? And one other thing, Daisy forgave you. I didn't."

"I think we have an understanding, all right. But you didn't have to take up for her. I think she could do a fine job of takin' care of herself. She sure did when she came to the reception," Jewel said.

"Then you be nice," Chigger whispered as Daisy and Jarod got in line to be served first.

"I think I can manage that," Jewel said.

Tinker plugged in the old jukebox and pushed the buttons to "Amazed" by Lonestar after the cake cutting ceremony. Jarod removed his black Western cut tux jacket and laid it over a chair. He picked Daisy up and carried her to the middle of the dance floor.

"You don't work here anymore so I can dance with you, Mrs. McElroy. I love you, lady."

"And I love you," she said.

"Don't they look cute? I knew this day was coming the first time I saw the two of them all tangled up together on the bar room floor. I think they both thought for a minute with all those sparks flyin' around them that they'd just had sex," Chigger said.

"What?" Frankie's brown eyes popped out.

"It's a story they can tell you later," Chigger said.

"It couldn't be any better. She's got Jarod and she gave me the Honky Tonk," Cathy said.

"Gave it to you. I thought you bought it," Chigger said. "Don't tell Billy Bob. He offered her a ton of money for it."

Cathy shook her head. "She says it was good to her and now it can be good to me."

When the song ended, Tinker raised a crystal punch cup. "A toast to Daisy and Jarod," he said loud enough that everyone stopped talking and listened. "They were meant for each other from the beginning. Here's to their happiness."

Daisy hugged him when everyone had tapped cups together and had a sip of punch which Billy Bob had spiked with a healthy dose of Patron. "Come up to Oklahoma and see us," she whispered.

"I don't think I'd better ride that far. I got to help Cathy keep this place in line. She's mean and she can take care of herself but there might be a time she'll need me," Tinker said.

Late that afternoon Jarod carried Daisy out to the white truck in a shower of rice. The younger crowd had done a fine job of decorating it with crepe paper, shoe polish, and a hundred feet of beer cans tied to the rear bumper.

"You ready?" he asked.

"In one minute," she said.

He raised a dark eyebrow.

"Hey, Cathy," she yelled above the din.

Cathy's head went up.

"Got something for you," she said.

Cathy looked up. Daisy had already handed over the keys to a Cadillac and the Honky Tonk. There was no way she was catching that damned bouquet if that's what Daisy was talking about.

"What?" she asked.

"I wanted to hug you one more time," Daisy said.

Cathy crossed the distance in a few long strides and the two cousins wrapped their arms around each other.

"Thanks for all you've done to make this possible," Daisy said.

Cathy's eyes welled up with tears. "I love you, Daisy. It's me who should be thanking you. Call me in a couple of days when you get bored in the bedroom."

"If you wait until then you'll never hear from me again," Daisy laughed.

Cathy couldn't say anything else without breaking down and sobbing so she headed back to the Honky Tonk to clean up the aftermath.

"Hey, Cathy?" Daisy yelled again.

When Cathy turned around it was to see the bouquet coming right at her. On reflex she reached out and caught it.

"You're next," Daisy yelled.

"You rat!" Cathy said. "I'm never getting married. And what is this?"

They were driving out of the lot when Cathy realized that she was holding a set of Harley Davidson motorcycle keys.

Daisy stuck her head out the window. "You want them?"

"Hell, yeah!" Cathy grinned from one ear to the other.

Jarod picked Daisy up outside the door and carried her inside the honeymoon suite at the Hyatt Regency in Dallas. The bed was covered in yellow rose petals and a bottle of champagne chilled in a crystal ice bucket. Two fluted glasses waited beside a crystal platter mounded high with fresh fruit and an assortment of fresh cheeses.

"It's beautiful," Daisy gasped.

"Not as much as you are," Jarod told her and punched a button on a CD player.

"Amazed" by Lonestar played as he laid her on the bed and very slowly began to undress her.

"I am amazed by you," he whispered.

"Not as much as I am by you. You made me love you more than anything in the world."

"And that is just the beginning. Wait until you see the finale," he teased.

"I don't want to see it until we are both a hundred years old and after we've had our year to repent; I hope we take our last breaths together," she said.

THE END

Dear Reader,

There are many, many people who helped make this book possible and I'm eternally grateful to each of them for their part in it. Thank you.

To my husband, Charles, for taking pictures and driving me through miles and miles of backwoods country while I took notes for the Honky Tonk series. There really is a Mingus, Texas, and a Thurber (population 5) where there is a Smokestack restaurant that serves wonderful chicken fried steak. There really is a Morgan Mill, Texas, with a combination feed store, café, and gathering place for the locals to drink coffee. If you're ever in that area visit both of them. You'll find good food, smiles, and lots of friendly down-home folks.

To every country music artist mentioned in the book. I cut my teeth on country music and Momma was a happy woman when her radio could pick up the Grand Ole Opry on Saturday night. Merle (a character in the book) says that country music tells the story of living and she got that right on the button. A really big thank you to a fellow Okie, Toby Keith: your song helped inspire the writing of this book!

To my editor, Deb Werksman, and the staff at Sourcebooks who continue to believe in me. And to my agent, Erin Niumata. You are all great people.

And to each of you readers who continue to read my books and spread the word to your family and friends… here's hoping you fall in love with Daisy and Jarod. Remember it's not over on the last page. There are three more in the Honky Tonk series on the way.

Thank you and bless your hearts, every one of you!

Carolyn Brown

About the Author

Carolyn Brown is an award-winning author who has more than forty books published and credits her eclectic family for her humor and writing ideas. She is the author of *Lucky in Love, One Lucky Cowboy,* and *Getting Lucky*. She was born in Texas but grew up in southern Oklahoma where she and her husband, Charles, a retired English teacher, make their home. They have three grown children and enough grandchildren to keep them young.

HELL, YEAH

"TEN, HELL YEAH!"

The women yelled with Gretchen Wilson as she sang "Redneck Woman" and asked the redneck girls to give her a big "hell yeah" as the New Year's countdown began.

"Nine, hell yeah."

"Eight, hell yeah."

Everyone held up their plastic flutes of champagne.

"Seven, hell yeah!"

The men in the Honky Tonk beer joint joined in with the women.

"Six, hell yeah!"

"Five, hell yeah!"

Cathy O'Dell was halfway across the dance floor headed for the bar when she stopped to look at everyone who'd be kissing someone in four more seconds. She remembered the previous year when she'd had someone to kiss. Even if he did turn out to be a first-rate son-of-a-bitch, she missed the excitement of bringing in a brand new year with a kiss.

"Four, hell yeah!"

She looked up to see a cowboy coming right at her.

She blinked several times. It wasn't possible. Her imagination was playing tricks like it had for twelve years.

"Three, hell yeah!"

Watching him cross the floor in those long strides made goose bumps the size of mountains rise up on her arms.

"Two, hell yeah!"

Was he deranged or just drunk? If he didn't stop soon he would plow right into her.

"One! Hell yeah!" The noise shook the rafters.

He stopped with the toes of his scuffed up boots barely an inch from her feet and wrapped his strong arms around her, tilted her chin with the flat part of his fist, and kissed her hard and passionately.

"Hell yeah!" the whole crowd roared when their kisses ended.

"Hell, no!" Cathy mumbled. She wiped the back of her hand across her mouth, but it didn't take the red-hot sting from her lips.

He was exactly what she liked in a man. Tight jeans, denim jacket over a knit shirt, blond hair, and dear lord, were those blue eyes? He looked so much like a grown-up version of her first love that, after the kiss and when time and noise at last stood still, she wondered why he didn't wear contact lenses. Eyes the color of a Texas summer sky stared down into hers from behind wire-rimmed glasses. A wide grin split his face, showing off perfectly even and white teeth. No one had teeth that perfect. No one except Bobby Cole, and that was water under a bridge that had been burned years and years ago. Evidently a million-dollar smile hadn't left much for haircuts, though, because blond curls touched his shirt collar.

"Happy New Year." He was surprised that he could speak a coherent sentence. He only meant to kiss the woman for New Year's. He didn't mean for it to glue his boots to the hardwood dance floor and put a shit-eating grin on his face. If he'd had to wipe the smile from his face or eat dirt, he'd have had to open up his mouth and shovel in a spoonful. Hot damn, but that woman had the softest, sexiest lips he'd ever kissed.

"Who the hell are you?" Cathy asked.

"I'm Travis Henry. I'm supposed to meet Merle and Angel Avery here. I am at the Honky Tonk, aren't I?"

Cathy pointed to the pool tables. His name was Travis Henry but he damn sure reminded her of Bobby Cole with those pretty blue eyes. On second look, Travis had darker blond hair and wore it a lot longer than Bobby's crew cut. After a third look she decided Travis Henry was a hell of a lot sexier.

"Angel, darlin'," Travis yelled and left Cathy standing there with a bar rag thrown over her shoulder, a tray in her hand, a burning mouth, and a gushy warm feeling down deep in her gut.

She got out a dozen Mason jars for the next rush to the bar for beer. Her crowd might toast with champagne, but it wouldn't be long until they'd be lined up wanting something to take that sweet taste out of their mouths. Besides, she needed something to focus on other than the tall cowboy who reminded her of the boy who'd set her hormones into overdrive when she was sixteen. He'd been so damn pretty and was the star of the football team. He'd been the one to kiss her the first time and then the next day he asked Alice James to the prom. He and Alice married right out of high school and he ran a service station in Mena, Arkansas. Alice worked as a teller at the bank and they had two kids in grade school.

"Who kissed you? You been holdin' out on me. That is one fine lookin' cowboy. If I was twenty years younger he'd be goin' to bed with me tonight. Give me a Miller, darlin'. Gawd Almighty, but that champagne shit is horrible," Jezzy said as she set her empty champagne flute on the bar and slid onto a stool.

"He just plowed through the door, came across the floor, and kissed me when the countdown hit one," Cathy said.

"Looks like he's big buds with Angel Avery. Guess he didn't kiss her because Garrett had a lip lock on her. Wonder if Garrett's kiss is powerful enough to throw her off her pool game. Handsome as that Garrett McElroy is, it would damn sure make me think about something other than racking up wooden balls if I was thirty years younger."

Cathy drew up a quart of Miller and set it in front of Jezzy. "Who were *you* kissin'?"

"See that big old biker back there with the Celtic cross tat on his arm?"

Cathy looked across the room at a middle-aged biker with a Mohawk haircut, a braided goatee, and a leather vest with enough chains to rope in a forty-acre farm. She quickly scanned the rest of the room and didn't see another tattooed cross.

She couldn't take her eyes from the biker. "Are you serious?"

"Not him. That cute little feller next to him in the red sweater. Couldn't you just take him home and eat him up for a midnight snack?" Jezzy fanned her face with her hands.

Cathy sized up the man. Tall, lanky, middle-aged with a few wrinkles. Definitely not sexy and absolutely not Jezzy's type.

Jezzy laughed so hard that she lost her breath. When she finally got control, she wiped her eyes with a paper napkin then held up her finger and thumb like a gun. "Bang. You've been had. I really did have you goin', didn't I? I kissed the biker, Cathy. That man next to him is married. His wife is in the bathroom. Can't you see the cottontail expression on his face?"

"I'll get even," Cathy said. "And what is a cottontail expression?"

"Little wifey is in the bathroom. He's imagining that all the cute little things with perky boobs and barely enough on top to cover them are honing in their sights on him. He's gettin' ready to run faster than a cottontail with a coyote hot after his cute little white tail."

"Why?"

"Because if the wife comes out of the bathroom she'll think he encouraged the women to make a play for him and he won't get anything but a cold shoulder tonight. And he only gets *laid* once a year on New Year's when she's about half plastered," Jezzy explained.

"You should write a book," Cathy said.

"Not me. I'm no writer. I'm a plain old beer-drinkin', good-timin' woman who's going to learn the difference in bull balls and cow udders if it kills me. Don't be over-sleepin' tomorrow mornin'. Dinner is at noon. Come late and you might find yourself goin' hungry." Jezzy picked up her beer, slid off the stool, and carried it over to the table where her friends, Leroy and his daughter, Sally, waited.

Cathy made her way down the bar, refilling pint and quart Mason jars of beer, making an occasional mixed drink, and wiping the spills. When she reached the end toward the pool tables, Travis waited with a bill in his hand.

"One of them big jars of Coors and not that damned light stuff either. And Angel wants a margarita," he said.

She reached for the bill and he dropped it. They both grabbed at the same time and their hands touched, sending sparks flashing around them like a meteorite shower. It didn't surprise him since he'd always been drawn to tall blond girls. Besides, she was downright hot. Cheap whiskey hitting an empty stomach wouldn't be a bit hotter than that kiss. He got a sudden visual of those long legs stretched out beside him on a bed with her hair spread out on a pillow right beside him. It put another idiot grin on his face.

"Patron or Jose?" she asked.

"Patron. Only the best for the Angel." He liked the bartender's voice. Just enough husky to go with that deep southern accent.

"You from Alabama or Georgia?" he asked.

"Neither. I'm from Arkansas." She filled the beer first and slid it toward him.

He reached out, stopped the motion, and brought it to his mouth for a long draw. He'd grown up in Fort Smith and he didn't have that much of a Southern accent. She must be from way down south toward Louisiana.

Anger rose from Cathy's boots all the way to the top of her blond hair. Travis had kissed her and minutes later ordered an expensive drink for another woman. Something damn sure wasn't right with that picture other than it was a hell of a way to start the New Year!

**Available August 2010 from
Sourcebooks Casablanca**

Lucky IN LOVE

BY CAROLYN BROWN

BEAU HASN'T GOT A LICK OF SENSE WHEN IT COMES TO WOME

Everything hunky rancher "Lucky" Beau Luckadeau touch
turns to gold—except relationships. Spitfire Milli Torres ca
mend a fence, pull a calf, or shoot a rattlesnake between t
eyes. When Milli shows up to help out at the Lazy Z ranc
she's horrified to find that Beau's her nearest neighbor—t
very man she'd hoped never to lay eyes on again. If Beau ev
figures out what really happened on that steamy Louisiai
night when they first met, there'll be the devil to pay...

Praise for Carolyn Brown:

*"Engaging characters, humorous situations, and a bump
romance... Carolyn Brown will keep you reading until
the very last page."* —Romantic Times

*"Carolyn Brown's rollicking sense of humor asserts itsel
on every page."* —Scribes World

978-1-4022-2435-5 • $6.99 U.S. / $8.99 CAN

ONE *Lucky* COWBOY

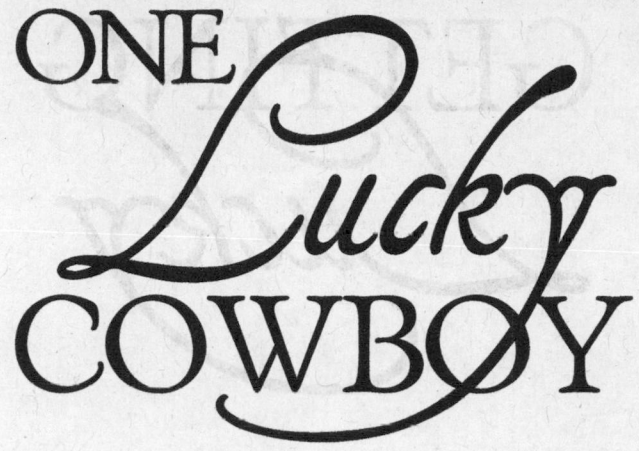

BY CAROLYN BROWN

No big blond cowboy is going to intimidate this spitfire!

If Slade Luckadeau thinks he can run Jane Day off his ranch, he's got cow chips for brains. She's winning every argument, and he's running out of fights to pick. But when trouble with a capital "T" threatens Jane *and* the Double L Ranch, suddenly it's Slade's heart that's in the most danger of all.

Praise for *Lucky in Love*:

"I enjoyed this book so much that I plan to rope myself some more of Carolyn Brown and her books. Lucky in Love *is a must read!"* —Cheryl's Book Nook

"This is one of those rare books where every person in it comes alive... as they share wit, wisdom, and love." —The Romance Studio

978-1-4022-2437-9• $6.99 U.S. / $8.99 CAN

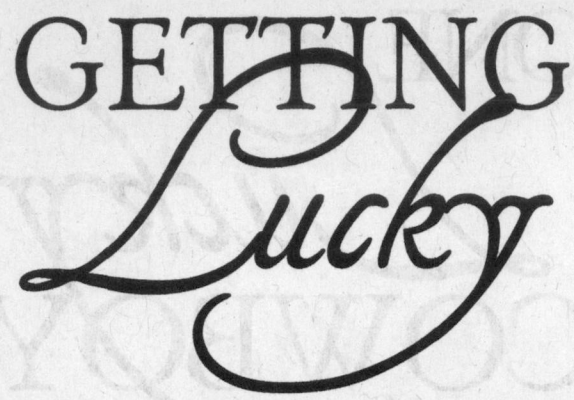

GETTING *Lucky*

BY CAROLYN BROWN

Griffin Luckadeau is one stubborn cowboy...

And Julie Donovan is one hotheaded schoolteacher who doesn't let anybody push her around. When Griffin thinks his new neighbor is scheming to steal his ranch out from under him, he's more than willing to cross horns. Their look-alike daughters may be best friends, but until these two Texas hotheads admit it's fate that brought them together, running from the inevitable is only going to bring them a double dose of miserable...

Praise for Carolyn Brown:

"A delight to read." —Booklist

"Engaging characters, humorous situations, and a bumpy romance... Carolyn Brown will keep you reading until the very last page." —Romantic Times

"Carolyn Brown's rollicking sense of humor asserts itself on every page." —Scribes World

978-1-4022-2436-2• $6.99 U.S. / $8.99 CAN